THE LADY VANISHES
&
THE SPIRAL STAIRCASE

The first of these two successful novels by Ethel Lina White was originally published in 1936 as *The Wheel Spins* but became famous as *The Lady Vanishes* when it was made into a film in 1938. Starring Margaret Lockwood and Michael Redgrave and memorably directed by the celebrated Alfred Hitchcock, the film has become a major movie classic. The story has been adapted for stage, radio and television, and once more for the screen in 1979, but it is the Hitchcock version that remains a landmark in cinema history.

The other novel presented here was published as *Some Must Watch* in 1933 but the title was changed to *The Spiral Staircase* when it was made into a film in 1946. Under the same title, the story was filmed again in 1975 and adapted for television in 2000.

THE LADY VANISHES

and

THE SPIRAL STAIRCASE

◆

Ethel Lina White

WORDSWORTH CLASSICS

For my husband
ANTHONY JOHN RANSON
with love from your wife, the publisher.
Eternally grateful for your unconditional love.

Readers who are interested in other titles from
Wordsworth Editions are invited to visit our website at
www.wordsworth-editions.com

For our latest list and a full mail-order service, contact
Bibliophile Books, 5 Datapoint, South Crescent, London E16 4TL
TEL: +44 (0)20 7474 2474   FAX: +44 (0)20 7474 8589
ORDERS: orders@bibliophilebooks.com
WEBSITE: www.bibliophilebooks.com

The Lady Vanishes, filmed in 1938 and again in 1979,
was first published as *The Wheel Spins* in 1936.
Some Must Watch was first published in 1933 and
later filmed as *The Spiral Staircase* in 1946.
This edition first published in 2015 by
Wordsworth Editions Limited
8B East Street, Ware, Hertfordshire SG12 9HJ

ISBN 978 1 84022 576 1

Text © Wordsworth Editions Limited 2015

Wordsworth® is a registered trade mark of
Wordsworth Editions Limited

Wordsworth Editions
is the company founded in 1987 by
MICHAEL TRAYLER

All rights reserved. This publication may not be
reproduced, stored in a retrieval system or
transmitted, in any form or by any means, electronic,
mechanical, photocopying, recording or otherwise,
without the prior permission of the publishers.

Typeset in Great Britain by Antony Gray
Printed and bound by Clays Ltd, St Ives plc

Contents

The Lady
Vanishes

1

Without Regrets

THE DAY BEFORE the disaster, Iris Carr had her first pre-monition of danger. She was used to the protection of a crowd, whom – with unconscious flattery – she called 'her friends'. An attractive orphan of independent means, she had been surrounded always with clumps of people. They thought for her – or rather, she accepted their opinions, and they shouted for her – since her voice was rather too low in register for mass social intercourse.

Their constant presence tended to create the illusion that she moved in a large circle, in spite of the fact that the same faces recurred with seasonal regularity. They also made her pleasantly aware of popularity. Her photograph appeared in the pictorial papers through the medium of a photographer's offer of publicity, after the press announcement of her engagement to one of the crowd.

This was Fame.

Then, shortly afterwards, her engagement was broken, by mutual consent – which was a lawful occasion for the reproduction of another portrait. More Fame. And her mother, who died at her birth, might have wept or smiled at these pitiful flickers of human vanity, arising, like bubbles of marsh-gas, on the darkness below.

When she experienced her first threat of insecurity, Iris was feeling especially well and happy after an unconventional health-holiday. With the triumph of near-pioneers, the crowd had swooped down on a beautiful village of picturesque squalor, tucked away in a remote corner of Europe, and taken possession of it by the act of scrawling their names in the visitors' book.

For nearly a month they had invaded the only hotel, to the delighted demoralisation of the innkeeper and his staff. They scrambled up mountains, swam in the lake and sunbathed on every available slope. When they were indoors, they filled the bar, shouted against the wireless and tipped for each trifling service. The proprietor beamed at them over his choked cash-register, and the smiling waiters gave them preferential treatment, to the legitimate annoyance of the other English guests.

To these six persons, Iris appeared just one of her crowd, and a typical semi-Society girl – vain, selfish and useless. Naturally, they had no knowledge of redeeming points – a generosity which made her accept the bill, as a matter of course, when she lunched with her 'friends', and a real compassion for such cases of hardship which were clamped down under her eyes.

But while she was only vaguely conscious of fugitive moments of discontent and self-contempt, she was aware of a fastidious streak, which kept her aloof from any tendency to saturnalia. On this holiday she heard Pan's pipes, but had no experience of the kick of his hairy hind quarters.

Soon the slack convention of the crowd had been relaxed. They grew brown, they drank and were merry, while matrimonial boundaries became pleasantly blurred. Surrounded by a mixed bag of vague married couples, it was a sharp shock to Iris when one of the women – Olga – suddenly developed a belated sense of property, and accused her of stealing a husband.

Besides the unpleasantness of the scene, her sense of justice was outraged. She had merely tolerated a neglected male, who seemed a spare part in the dislocated domestic machine. It was not her fault that he had lost his head.

To make matters worse, at this crisis, she failed to notice any signs of real loyalty among her friends, who had plainly enjoyed the excitement. Therefore, to ease the tension, she decided not to travel back to England with the party, but to stay on for two days longer, alone.

She was still feeling sore, on the following day, when she accompanied the crowd to the little primitive railway station. They had already reacted to the prospect of a return to civilisation. They wore fashionable clothes again, and were roughly sorted into legitimate couples, as a natural sequence to the identification of suitcases and reservations.

The train was going to Trieste, which was definitely on the map. It was packed with tourists, who were also going back to pavements and lamp-posts. Forgetful of hillside and starlight, the crowd responded to the general noise and bustle. It seemed to recapture its old loyalty as it clustered round Iris.

'Sure you won't be bored, darling?'

'Change your mind and hop on.'

'You've simply *got* to come.'

As the whistle was blown, they tried to pull her into their carriage – just as she was, in shorts and nailed boots, and with a brown glaze of sunburn on her unpowdered face. She fought like a boxing-kangaroo to break free, and only succeeded in jumping down as the platform was beginning to slide past the window.

Laughing and panting from the struggle, she stood and waved after the receding train, until it disappeared round the bend of the gorge.

She felt almost guilty as she realised her relief at parting from her friends. But, although the holiday had been a success, she had drawn her pleasure chiefly from primeval sources – sun, water and mountain-breeze. Steeped in nature, she had vaguely resented the human intrusion.

They had all been together too closely and too intimately. At times, she had been conscious of jarring notes – a woman's high thin laugh – the tubby outline of a man's body, poised to dive – a continual flippant appeal to 'My God'.

It was true that while she had grown critical of her friends she had floated with the current. Like the others, she had raved of marvellous scenery, while she accepted it as a matter of course. It was a natural sequence that, when one travelled off the map, the landscape improved automatically as the standard of sanitation lapsed.

At last was alone with the mountains and the silence. Below her lay a grass-green lake, sparkling with diamond reflections of the sun. The snowy peaks of distant ranges were silhouetted against a corn-flower-blue sky. On a hill rose the dark pile of an ancient castle, with its five turrets pointing upwards, like the outspread fingers of a sinister hand.

Everywhere was a riot of colour. The station garden foamed with exotic flowers – flame and yellow – rising from spiked foliage. Higher up the slope, the small wooden hotel was painted ochre and crimson lake. Against the green wall of the gorge rose the last coil of smoke, like floating white feathers.

When it had faded away, Iris felt that the last link had been severed between her and the crowd. Blowing a derisive kiss, she turned away and clattered down the steep stony path. When she reached the glacier-fed river, she lingered on the bridge to feel the iced air which arose from the greenish-white boil.

As she thought of yesterday's scene, she vowed that she never wanted to see the crowd again. They were connected with an episode which violated her idea of friendship. She had been a little fond of the woman, Olga, who had repaid her loyalty by a crude exhibition of jealousy.

She shrugged away the memory. Here, under the limitless blue, people seemed so small – their passions so paltry. They were merely incidental to the passage from the cradle to the grave. One met them and parted from them, without regrets.

Every minute the gap between her and them was widening. They were steaming away, out of her life. At the thought, she thrilled with a sense of new freedom, as though her spirit were liberated by the silence and solitude.

Yet, before many hours had passed, she would have bartered all the glories of nature to have called them back again.

2

The Threat

Some four hours later Iris lay spread-eagled on a slope of the mountain, high above the valley. Ever since she had left the chill twilight of the gorge, at a shrine which marked a union of paths, she had been climbing steadily upwards, by a steep zigzag track.

After she had emerged from the belt of shadow, the sun had beat fiercely through her, but she did not slacken her pace. The fury of her thoughts drove her on, for she could not dislodge Olga from her mind.

The name was like a burr on her brain. *Olga*. Olga had eaten her bread, in the form of toast – for the sake of her figure – and had refused her salt, owing to a dietetic fad. This had made trouble in the kitchen. Olga had used her telephone, and misused her car. Olga had borrowed her fur coat, and had lent her a superfluous husband.

At the memory of Olga's Oscar, Iris put on a sprint.

'As if I'd skid for a man who looks like Mickey Mouse,' she raged.

She was out of breath when, at last, she threw herself down on the turf and decided to call it a day. The mountain which had challenged her kept withdrawing as she advanced, so she had to give up her intention to reach the top.

As she lay with her eyes almost closed, listening to the ping of the breeze, her serenity returned. A clump of harebells, standing out against the skyline, seemed hardened and magnified to a metallic belfry, while she herself was dwarfed and melded into the earth – part of it, like the pebbles and the roots. In imagination she could almost hear the pumping of a giant heart underneath her head.

The moment passed, for she began to think of Olga again. This time, however, she viewed her from a different standpoint, for the altitude had produced the usual illusion of superiority. She reminded herself that the valley was four thousand feet above sea-level, while she had mounted about five thousand feet.

On the basis of this calculation she could afford to be generous, since she was nine thousand feet taller than her former friend – assuming, of course, that Olga was obliging enough to remain at sea-level.

She decided to wash out the memory as unworthy of further anger.

'But never again,' she said. 'After this, I'll never help anyone again.'

Her voice had the passionate fervour of one who dedicates herself to some service. With the virtuous feeling of having profited by a lesson, for which heavy fees had been paid, she smoked a cigarette before the return journey. The air was so clear that mountains she had never seen before quivered out of invisibility and floated in the sky in mauve transparencies. Far below she could see an arm of the lake – no longer green, but dimmed by distance to a misted blue.

Reluctantly she rose to her feet. It was time to go.

The descent proved not only monotonous, but painful, for the continual backward jolt of her weight threw a strain on unexercised muscles. Her calves began to ache and her toes were stubbed on the stony path.

Growing impatient, she decided to desert the zigzag in favour of a direct short-cut down the face of the mountain. With the lake as a guide to direction, she hurled herself down the slope.

It was a bold venture, but almost immediately she found that the gradient was too steep. As she was going too quickly to stop, her only course was to drop down to a sitting posture and glissade over the slippery turf – trusting to luck.

From that moment things happened quickly. Her pace increased every second, in spite of her efforts to brake with her feet. Patches of blue and green sped past her as the valley rushed up to meet her and smashed into the sky. Bumping over the rough ground, she steered towards a belt of trees at the bottom, in the hope that they might save her from a complete spill.

Unfortunately they proved to be rotten from age, and she crashed through them, to land with a bump in the middle of the stony pass.

Her fall had been partially broken, but she felt very sore and shaken as she scrambled to her feet. In spite of her injuries, she did not forget to give the forced laugh which had been drilled into her at school as the accompaniment to any games casualty.

'Rather amusing,' she murmured, picking splinters out of her legs.

But she was pleased to notice the shrine, a few yards farther up the track, for this was a definite tribute to her steering. As she was not far from the hotel, she clattered down the gully, thinking of the comforts which awaited her. A long cold drink, a hot bath, dinner in bed. When she caught sight of a gleam of water, at the bend of the gorge, in her eagerness she broke into a limping run.

She rounded the corner and then stopped, staring before her in utter bewilderment. All the familiar landmarks had disappeared, as though some interfering person had passed an india-rubber over the landscape. There were no little wooden houses, no railway station, no pier, no hotel.

With a pang of dismay she realised that she had steered by a faulty compass. This was not their familiar green lake, in which she and her friends had bathed daily. Instead of being deep and ovoid in shape, it was a winding pale-blue mere, with shallow rushy margins.

In the circumstances, there was but one thing to do – retrace her steps back to the shrine and follow the other gully.

It was definitely amusing and she achieved quite a creditable laugh before she began to plod slowly upwards again.

Her mood was too bleak for her to appreciate the savage grandeur of the scenery. It was a scene of stark desolation, riven by landslips and piled high with shattered rocks. There was no crop of vegetation amid the boulders – no chirp of bird. The only sounds were the rattle of loose stones, dislodged by her feet, and the splash of a shrunken torrent, which foamed over its half-dried course, like a tangled white thread.

Used to perpetual company, Iris began to long for faces and voices. In her loneliness, she was even reduced to the flabbiness of self-pity. She reminded herself that when she returned to England she would not go home, like others. She would merely go back.

At present she was living at a hotel, for she had sublet her small luxury flat. Although her mode of living was her own choice, at such a time and such a place she felt that she paid a high price for freedom.

Her mood did not last, for, at the top of the pass, she was faced with a call upon her fortitude. Casting about, to pick up her bearings, she made the discovery that the shrine was different from the original landmark where she had struck the mountain zigzag.

This time she did not laugh, for she felt that humour could be carried too far. Instead she was furious with herself. She believed that she knew these mountains, because she and the others had clattered up and down the gorges like a pack of wild goats.

But she had merely followed – while others led. Among the crowd was the inevitable leader – the youth with the map.

Thrown on her own resources, she had not the least idea of her direction. All she could do was to follow the gorge up to its next ramification and trust to luck.

'If I keep on walking, I must get somewhere,' she argued. 'Besides, no one can get lost who has a tongue.'

She had need of her stoicism, for she had grown desperately weary, in addition to being handicapped by a sore heel. When, at last, she reached a branch which gave her a choice of roads, she was too distrustful of her own judgement to experiment. Sitting down on a boulder, she waited on the chance of hailing some passer-by.

It was her zero-hour, when her independence appeared only the faculty to sign cheques drawn on money made by others – and her popularity, but a dividend of the same cheques.

'I've been carried all my life,' she thought. 'And even if someone comes, I'm the world's worst linguist.'

The description flattered her, for she had not the slightest claim to the title of linguist. Her ignorance of foreign languages was the result of being finished in Paris and Dresden. During the time she was at school, she mixed exclusively with other English girls, while the natives who taught her acquired excellent English accents.

This was her rendering of the line in the National Anthem – 'Send us victorious.'

Patriotism did not help her now, for she felt slightly doubtful when a thickset swarthy man, wearing leather shorts and dirty coloured braces, swung up the pass.

Among Iris's crowd was a youth who was clever at languages. From his knowledge of common roots, he had managed to use German as a kind of liaison language; but he had to draw on his imagination in order to interpret and be understood.

Iris had a vivid recollection of how the crowd used to hoot with derision at his failures when she called out to the man in English and asked him to direct her to the village.

He stared at her, shrugged, and shook his head.

Her second attempt – in a louder key – met with no better success. The peasant, who seemed in a hurry, was passing on, when Iris barred his way.

She was acutely aware of her own impotence, as though she were some maimed creature, whose tongue had been torn out. But she had to hold his attention, to compel him to understand. Feeling that she had lapsed from the dignity of a rational being, she was forced to make pantomimic gestures, pointing to the alternative routes in turn while she kept repeating the name of the village.

'He must get that, unless he's an idiot,' she thought.

The man seemed to grasp her drift, for he nodded several times. But, instead of indicating any direction, he broke into an unfamiliar jargon.

As Iris listened to the torrent of guttural sounds, her nerve snapped suddenly. She felt cut off from all human intercourse, as though a boundary-line had been wiped out, and – instead of being in Europe – she were stranded in a corner of Asia.

Without money and without a common language, she could wander indefinitely. At that moment she might be headed away from the village and into the wilds. The gorge had many tributary branches, like the windings of an inland sea.

As she grew afraid, the peasant's face began to waver, like the illusion of some bad dream. She noticed that his skin glistened and that he had a slight goitre; but she was definitely conscious of his steamy goatish smell, for he was sweating from his climb.

'I can't understand you,' she cried hysterically. 'I can't understand one word. Stop. Oh, *stop*. You'll drive me mad.'

In his turn the man heard only a string of gibberish. He saw a girl, dressed like a man, who was unattractively skinny – according to the local standard of beauty – with cut dirty knees. She was a foreigner, although he did not know her nationality. Further, she was worked up to a pitch of excitement, and was exceptionally stupid.

She did not seem to grasp that she was telling him less than half the name of the village, when three different hamlets had the same prefix. He had explained this to her, and asked for the full word.

Iris could not have supplied it even if she had understood the man. The name of the village was such a tongue-twister that she had never tried to disentangle it, but, like the rest, had called it by its first three syllables.

The position was stalemate. With a final grimace and shrug, the peasant went on his way, leaving Iris alone with the mountains.

They overhung her like a concrete threat. She had bought picture postcards of them and broadcast them with the stereotyped comment 'Marvellous scenery!' Once she had even scrawled 'This is my room,' and marked a peak with a derisive cross.

Now – the mountains were having their revenge. As she cowered under the projecting cliffs, she felt they had but to shake those towering brows to crush her to powder beneath an avalanche of boulders. They dwarfed her to insignificance. They blotted out her individuality. They extinguished her spirit.

The spell was broken by the sound of English voices. Round the bend of the pass came the honeymoon couple, from the hotel.

This pair of lovers was respected even by the crowd, for the completeness of their reserve and the splendour of their appearance. The man was tall, handsome and of commanding carriage. His voice was authoritative, and he held his head at an angle which suggested excessive pride. Waiters scampered at his nod, and the innkeeper – probably on the strength of his private sitting-room – called him 'Milord'.

His wife was almost as tall, with a perfect figure and a flawless face. She wore beautiful clothes which were entirely unsuitable for the wilds;

but it was obvious that she dressed thus as a matter of course, and to please only her husband.

They set their own standard and appeared unconscious of the other visitors, who accepted them as belonging to a higher social sphere. It was suspected that the name 'Todhunter', under which they had registered, was a fiction to preserve their anonymity.

They passed Iris almost without notice. The man raised his hat vaguely, but his glance held no recognition. His wife never removed her violet eyes from the stony track, for her heels were perilously high.

She was speaking in a low voice, which was vehement in spite of its muffled tone.

'No darling. Not another day. Not even for *you*. We've stayed too –'

Iris lost the rest of the sentence. She prepared to follow them at a discreet distance, for she had become acutely aware of her own wrecked appearance.

The arrival of the honeymoon pair had restored her sense of values. Their presence was proof that the hotel was not far away, for they never walked any distance. At the knowledge, the mountains shrank back to camera-subjects, while she was reconstructed, from a lost entity, to a London girl who was critical about the cut of her shorts.

Very soon she recognised the original shrine, whence she had deserted the pass. Limping painfully down the track, presently she caught the gleam of the darkening lake and the lights of the hotel, shining through the green gloom.

She began to think again of a hot bath and dinner as she remembered that she was both tired and hungry.

But although apparently only the physical traces of her adventure remained, actually, her sense of security had been assailed – as if the experience were a threat from the future, to reveal the horror of helplessness, far away from all that was familiar.

3

Conversation Piece

When the honeymoon pair returned to the hotel the four remaining guests were sitting outside on the gravelled square, before the veranda. They were enjoying the restful interlude 'between the lights'. It was too dark to write letters or read – too early to dress for dinner. Empty cups and cake crumbs on one of the tables showed that they had taken afternoon tea in the open and had not moved since.

It was typical of two of them, the Misses Flood-Porter, to settle. They were not the kind that flitted, being in the fifties and definitely set in their figures and their habits. Both had immaculately waved grey hair, which retained sufficient samples of the original tint to give them the courtesy-title of blondes. They had also, in common, excellent natural complexions and rather fierce expressions.

The delicate skin of the elder – Miss Evelyn – was slightly shrivelled, for she was nearly sixty, while Miss Rose was only just out of the forties. The younger sister was taller and stouter; her voice was louder, her colour deeper. In an otherwise excellent character was a streak of amiable bully, which made her inclined to scold her partner at contract.

During their visit, they had formed a quartette with the Reverend Kenneth Barnes and his wife. They had travelled out on the same train, and they planned to return to England together. The vicar and his wife had the gift of pleasant companionship, which the Misses Flood-Porter – who were without it – attributed to mutual tastes and prejudices.

The courtyard was furnished with iron chairs and tables, enamelled in brilliant colours, and was decorated with tubs of dusty evergreen shrubs. As Miss Flood-Porter looked round her, she thought of her own delightful home in a Cathedral city.

According to the papers, there had been rain in England, so the garden should look its best, with vivid green grass and lush borders of asters and dahlias.

'I'm looking forward to seeing my garden again,' she said.

'Ours,' corrected her sister, who was John Blunt.

'And I'm looking forward to a comfortable chair,' laughed the vicar. 'Ha. Here comes the bridal pair.'

In spite of a sympathetic interest in his fellows he did not call out a genial greeting. He had learned from his first – and final – rebuff that they had resented any intrusion on their privacy. So he leaned back, puffing at his pipe, while he watched them mount the steps of the veranda.

'Handsome pair,' he said in an approving voice.

'I wonder who they *really* are,' remarked Miss Flood-Porter. 'The man's face is familiar to me. I know I've seen him somewhere.'

'On the pictures, perhaps,' suggested her sister.

'Oh, do you go?' broke in Mrs Barnes eagerly, hoping to claim another taste in common, for she concealed a guilty passion for the cinema.

'Only to see George Arliss and Diana Wynyard,' explained Miss Flood-Porter.

'That settles it,' said the vicar. 'He's certainly not George Arliss, and neither is she Diana.'

'All the same, I feel certain there is some mystery about them,' persisted Miss Flood-Porter.

'So do I,' agreed Mrs Barnes. 'I – I wonder if they are really married.'

'Are *you*?' asked her husband quickly.

He laughed gently when his wife flushed to her eyes.

'Sorry to startle you, my dear,' he said, 'but isn't it simpler to believe that we are all of us what we seem to be? Even parsons and their wives.' He knocked the ashes out of his pipe, and rose from his chair. 'I think I'll stroll down to the village for a chat with my friends.'

'How can he talk to them when he doesn't know their language?' demanded Miss Rose bluntly, when the vicar had gone from the garden.

'Oh, he *makes* them understand,' explained his wife proudly. 'Sympathy, you know, and common humanity. He'd rub noses with a savage.'

'I'm afraid we drove him away by talking scandal,' said Miss Flood-Porter.

'It was my fault,' declared Mrs Barnes. 'I know people think I'm curious. But, really, I have to force myself to show an interest in my neighbour's affairs. It's my protest against our terrible national shyness.'

'But we're proud of that,' broke in Miss Rose. 'England does not need to advertise.'

'Of course not . . . But we only pass this way once. I have to remind myself that the stranger sitting beside me may be in some trouble and that I might be able to help.'

The sisters looked at her with approval. She was a slender woman in the mid-forties, with a pale oval face, dark hair and a sweet expression. Her large brown eyes were both kind and frank – her manner sincere.

It was impossible to connect her with anything but rigid honesty. They knew that she floundered into awkward explanations, rather than run the risk of giving a false impression.

In her turn, she liked the sisters. They were of solid worth and sound respectability. One felt that they would serve on juries with distinction, and do their duty to their God and their neighbour – while permitting no direction as to its nature.

They were also leisured people, with a charming house and garden, well-trained maids and frozen assets in the bank. Mrs Barnes knew this, so, being human, it gave her a feeling of superiority to reflect that the one man in their party was her husband.

She could appreciate the sense of ownership because, up to her fortieth birthday, she had gone on her yearly holiday in the company of a huddle of other spinsters. Since she had left school, she had earned her living by teaching, until the miracle happened which gave her not only a husband but a son.

Both she and her husband were so wrapped up in the child that the vicar sometimes feared that their devotion was tempting fate. The night before they set out on their holiday he proposed a pact.

'Yes,' he agreed, looking down at the sleeping boy in his cot. 'He is beautiful. But . . . It is my privilege to read the Commandments to others. Sometimes, I wonder – '

'I know what you mean,' interrupted his wife. 'Idolatry.'

He nodded.

'I am as guilty as you,' he admitted. 'So I mean to discipline myself. In our position, we have special opportunities to influence others. We must not grow lopsided, but develop every part of our nature. If this holiday is to do us real good, it *must* be a complete mental change . . . My dear, suppose we agree not to talk exclusively of Gabriel while we are away?'

Mrs Barnes agreed. But her promise did not prevent her from thinking of him continually. Although they had left him in the care of a competent grandmother, she was foolishly apprehensive about his health.

While she was counting the remaining hours before her return to her son, and Miss Flood-Porter smiled in anticipation of seeing her garden, Miss Rose was pursuing her original train of thought. She always ploughed a straight furrow, right to its end.

'I can't understand how anyone can tell a lie,' she declared. 'Unless, perhaps, some poor devil who's afraid of being sacked. But – people like *us*. We know a wealthy woman who boasts of making false declarations at the Customs. Sheer dishonesty.'

As she spoke, Iris appeared at the gate of the hotel garden. She did her best to skirt the group at the table, but she could not avoid hearing what was said.

'Perhaps I should not judge others,' remarked Mrs Barnes in the clear carrying voice of a form-mistress. 'I've never felt the slightest temptation to tell a lie.'

'Liar,' thought Iris automatically.

She was in a state of utter fatigue, which bordered on collapse. It was only by the exercise of every atom of willpower that she forced herself to reach the hotel. The ordeal had strained her nerves almost to breaking-point. Although she longed for the quiet of her room, she knew she could not mount the stairs without a short rest. Every muscle felt wrenched as she dropped down on an iron chair and closed her eyes.

'If anyone speaks to me, I'll scream,' she thought.

The Misses Flood-Porter exchanged glances and turned down the corners of their mouths. Even gentle Mrs Barnes's soft brown eyes held no welcome, for she had been a special victim of the crowd's bad manners and selfishness.

They behaved as though they had bought the hotel and the other guests were interlopers, exacting preferential treatment – and getting it – by bribery. This infringement of fair-dealing annoyed the other tourists, as they adhered to the terms of their payment to a travelling agency, which included service.

The crowd monopolised the billiard-table and secured the best chairs. They were always served first at meals; courses gave out, and bath-water ran lukewarm.

Even the vicar found that his charity was strained. He did his best to make allowance for the animal spirits of youth, although he was aware that several among the party could not be termed juvenile.

Unfortunately, Iris's so-called friends included two persons who were no testimonial for the English nation; and since it was difficult to distinguish one girl in a bathing-brief from another, Mrs Barnes was of the opinion that they were all doing the same thing – getting drunk and making love.

Her standard of decency was offended by the sunbathing – her nights disturbed by noise. Therefore she was specially grateful for the prospect of two peaceful days spent amid glorious scenery and in congenial company.

But, apparently, there was not a complete clearance of the crowd: there was a hang-over, in this girl – and there might be others. Mrs Barnes had vaguely remarked Iris, because she was pretty, and had been pursued by a bathing-gentleman with a matronly figure. As the man was married, his selection was not to her credit. But she seemed to be so exhausted that Mrs Barnes's kindly heart soon reproached her for lack of sympathy.

'Are you left all alone?' she called, in her brightest tones.

Iris shuddered at the unexpected overture. At that moment the last thing in the world she wanted was mature interest, which, in her experience, masked curiosity.

'Yes,' she replied.

'Oh, dear, what a shame. Aren't you lonely?'

'No.'

'But you're rather young to be travelling without friends. Couldn't any of your people come with you?'

'I have none.'

'No family at all?'

'No, and no relatives. Aren't I lucky?'

Iris was not near enough to hear the horrified gasp of the Misses Flood-Porter; but Mrs Barnes's silence told her that her snub had not miscarried. To avoid a further inquisition, she made a supreme effort to rise, for she was stiffening in every joint, and managed to drag herself into the hotel and upstairs to her room.

Mrs Barnes tried to carry off the incident with a laugh.

'I'm afraid I've blundered again,' she said. 'She plainly resented me. But it seemed hardly human for us to sit like dummies, and show no interest in her.'

'Is she interested in *you*?' demanded Miss Rose. 'Or in us? That sort of girl is utterly selfish. She wouldn't raise a finger, or go an inch out of her way, to help anyone.'

There was only one answer to the question, which Mrs Barnes was too kind to make. So she remained silent, since she could not tell a lie.

Neither she – nor anyone else – could foretell the course of the next twenty-four hours, when this girl – standing alone against a cloud of witnesses – would endure such anguish of spirit as threatened her sanity on behalf of a stranger for whom she had no personal feeling.

Or rather – if there was actually such a person as Miss Froy.

4

England Calling

Because she had a square on her palm, which, according to a fortune-teller, signified safety, Iris believed that she lived in a protected area. Although she laughed at the time, she was impressed secretly, because hers was a specially sheltered life.

At this crisis, the stars, as usual, seemed to be fighting for her. The mountains had sent out a preliminary warning. During the evening, too, she received overtures of companionship, which might have delivered her from mental isolation.

Yet she deliberately cut every strand which linked her with safety, out of mistaken loyalty to her friends.

She missed them directly she entered the lounge, which was silent and deserted. As she walked along the corridor, she passed empty bedrooms, with stripped beds and littered floors. Mattresses hung from every window and the small verandas were heaped with pillows.

It was not only company which was lacking, but moral support. The crowd never troubled to change for the evening, unless comfort suggested flannel trousers. On one occasion, it had achieved the triumph of a complaint, when a lady appeared at dinner dressed in her bathing-slip.

The plaintiffs had been the Misses Flood-Porter, who always wore expensive but sober dinner-gowns. Iris remembered the incident when she had finished her bath. Although slightly ashamed of her deference to public opinion, she fished from a suitcase an unpacked afternoon frock of crinkled crêpe.

The hot soak and rest had refreshed her, but she felt lonely as she leaned over the balustrade. Her pensive pose and the graceful lines of her dress arrested the attention of the bridegroom – Todhunter, according to the register – as he strolled out of his bedroom.

He had not the least knowledge of her identity, or that he had acted as a sort of guiding-star to her in the gorge. He and his wife took their meals in their private sitting-room and never mingled with the crowd. He concluded, therefore, that she was an odd guest whom he had missed in the general scramble.

Approving her with an experienced eye, he stopped.

'Quiet, tonight,' he remarked. 'Refreshing change after the din of that horrible rabble.'

To his surprise, the girl looked coldly at him.

'It is quiet,' she said. 'But I happen to miss my friends.'

As she walked downstairs she felt defiantly glad that she had made him realise his blunder. Championship of her friends mattered more than the absence of social sense. But, in spite of her triumph, the incident was vaguely unpleasant.

The crowd had gloried in its unpopularity, which seemed to it a sign of superiority. It frequently remarked in complacent voices, 'We're not popular with these people,' or, 'They don't really like us.' Under the influence of its mass-hypnotism, Iris wanted no other label. But now that she was alone, it was not quite so amusing to realise that the other guests, who were presumably decent and well bred, considered her an outsider.

Her mood was bleakly defiant when she entered the restaurant. It was a big bare room, hung with stiff deep-blue wallpaper, patterned with conventional gilt stars. The electric lights were set in clumsy wrought-iron chandeliers, which suggested a Hollywood set for a medieval castle. Scarcely any of the tables were laid, and only one waiter drooped at the door.

In a few days, the hotel would be shut up for the winter. With the departure of the big English party, most of the holiday staff had become superfluous and had already gone back to their homes in the district.

The remaining guests appeared to be unaffected by the air of neglect and desolation inseparable from the end of the season. The Misses Flood-Porter shared a table with the vicar and his wife. They were all in excellent spirits and gave the impression of having come into their own, as they capped each other's jokes, culled from *Punch*.

Iris pointedly chose a small table in a far corner. She smoked a cigarette while she waited to be served. The others were advanced in their meal and it was a novel sensation for one of the crowd to be in arrears.

Mrs Barnes, who was too generous to nurse resentment for her snub, looked at her with admiring eyes.

'How pretty that girl looks in a frock,' she said.

'*Afternoon frock*,' qualified Miss Flood-Porter. 'We always make a point of wearing evening dress for dinner, when we're on the Continent.'

'If we didn't dress, we should feel we were letting England down,' explained the younger sister.

Although Iris spun out her meal to its limit, she was driven back ultimately to the lounge. She was too tired to stroll and it was early for bed. As she looked round her, she could hardly believe that only the night before it had been a scene of Continental glitter and gaiety –

although the latter quality had been imported from England. Now that it was no longer filled with friends, she was shocked to notice its tawdry theatrical finery. The gilt cane chairs were tarnished, the crimson plush upholstery shabby.

A clutter of cigarette stubs and spent matches in the palm pots brought a lump to her throat. They were all that remained of the crowd.

As she sat apart, the vicar – pipe in mouth – watched her with a thoughtful frown. His clear-cut face was both strong and sensitive, an almost perfect blend of flesh and spirit. He played rough football with the youths of his parish, and, afterwards, took their souls by assault; but he had also a real understanding of the problems of his women parishioners.

When his wife told him of Iris's wish for solitude, he could enter into her feeling, because sometimes he yearned to escape from people and even from his wife. His own inclination was to leave her to the boredom of her own company; yet he was touched by the dark lines under her eyes and her mournful lips.

In the end, he resolved to ease his conscience at the cost of a rebuff. He knew it was coming, because as he crossed the lounge she looked up quickly, as though on guard.

'Another,' she thought.

From a distance she had admired the spirituality of his expression; but tonight he was numbered among her hostile critics.

'Horrible rabble.' The words floated into her memory, as he spoke to her.

'If you are travelling back to England alone, would you care to join our party?'

'When are you going?' she asked.

'Day after tomorrow, before they take off the last through train of the season.'

'But I'm going tomorrow. Thanks so much.'

'Then I'll wish you a pleasant journey.'

The vicar smiled faintly at her lightning decision as he crossed to a table and began to address luggage-labels.

His absence was his wife's opportunity. In her wish not to break her promise, she had gone to the other extreme and had not mentioned her baby to her new friends, save for one casual allusion to 'our little boy'. But, now that the holiday was nearly over, she could not resist the temptation of showing his photograph, which had won a prize in a local baby competition.

With a guilty glance at her husband's back she drew out of her bag a limp leather case.

'This is my large son,' she said, trying to hide her pride.

The Misses Flood-Porter were exclusive animal-lovers and not particularly fond of children. But they said all the correct things with such well-bred conviction that Mrs Barnes's heart swelled with triumph.

Miss Rose, however, switched off to another subject directly the vicar returned from the writing-table.

'Do you believe in warning dreams, Mr Barnes?' she asked. 'Because, last night, I dreamed of a railway smash.'

The question caught Iris's attention and she strained to hear the vicar's reply.

'I'll answer your question,' he said, 'if you'll first answer mine. What *is* a dream? Is it stifled apprehension – '

'I wonder,' said a bright voice in Iris's ear, 'I wonder if you would like to see the photograph of my little son, Gabriel?'

Iris realised dimly that Mrs Barnes – who was keeping up England in limp brown lace – had seated herself beside her and was showing her the photograph of a naked baby. She made a pretence of looking at it while she tried to listen to the vicar.

'Gabriel,' she repeated vaguely.

'Yes, after the Archangel. We named him after him.'

'How sweet. Did he send a mug?'

Mrs Barnes stared incredulously, while her sensitive face grew scarlet. She believed that the girl had been intentionally profane and had insulted her precious little son to avenge her boredom. Pressing her trembling lips together she rejoined her friends.

Iris was grateful when the humming in her ears ceased. She was unaware of her slip, because she had only caught a fragment of Mrs Barnes's explanation. Her interest was still held by the talk of presentiments.

'Say what you like,' declared Miss Rose, sweeping away the vicar's argument, 'I've common sense on my side. They usually try to pack too many passengers into the last good train of the season. I know I'll be precious glad when I'm safely back in England.'

A spirit of apprehension quivered in the air at her words.

'But you aren't really afraid of an accident?' cried Mrs Barnes, clutching Gabriel's photograph tightly.

'Of course not.' Miss Flood-Porter answered for her sister. 'Only, perhaps we feel we're rather off the beaten track here, and so very far from home. Our trouble is we don't know a word of the language.'

'She means,' cut in Miss Rose, 'we're all right over reservations and coupons, so long as we stick to hotels and trains. But if some accident happened to make us break our journey, or lose a connection, and we were stranded in some small place, we should feel *lost*. Besides it would be awkward about money. We didn't bring any travellers' cheques.'

The elder sister appealed to the vicar.

'Do you advise us to take my sister's dream as a warning and travel back tomorrow?'

'No, *don't*,' murmured Iris under her breath.

She waited for the vicar's answer with painful interest, for she was not eager to travel on the same train as these uncongenial people, who might feel it their duty to befriend her.

'You must follow your own inclinations,' said the vicar. 'But if you do leave prematurely, you will not only give a victory to superstition but you will deprive yourself of another day in these glorious surroundings.'

'And our reservations *are* for the day after tomorrow,' remarked Miss Rose. 'We'd better not risk any muddles . . . And now, I'm going up to pack for my journey back to dear old England.'

To the surprise of everyone her domineering voice suddenly blurred with emotion.

Miss Flood-Porter waited until she had gone out of the lounge before she explained. 'Nerves. We had a very trying experience just before we came away. The doctor ordered a complete change so we came here, instead of Switzerland.'

Then the innkeeper came in, and, as a compliment to his guests, fiddled with his radio until he managed to get London on the long wave. Amid a machine-gun rattle of atmospherics, a familiar mellow voice informed them, 'You have just been listening to . . . '

But they had heard nothing.

Miss Flood-Porter saw her garden, silvered by the harvest moon. She wondered whether the chrysanthemum buds, three to a pot, were swelling, and if the blue salvias had escaped the slugs.

Miss Rose, briskly stacking shoes in the bottom of a suitcase, quivered at a recollection. Again she saw a gaping hole in a garden-bed where overnight had stood a cherished clump of white delphiniums . . . It was not only the loss of their treasure, but the nerve-racking ignorance of where the enemy would strike next . . .

The vicar and his wife thought of their baby, asleep in his cot. They must decide whether they should merely peep at him, or risk waking him with a kiss.

Iris remembered her friends in the roaring express, and was suddenly smitten with a wave of home-sickness.

England was calling.

5

The Night Express

Iris was awakened that night, as usual, by the express screaming through the darkness. Jumping out of bed, she reached the window in time to see it outline the curve of the lake with a fiery wire. As it rattled below the hotel, the golden streak expanded to a string of lighted windows, which, when it passed, snapped together again like the links of a bracelet.

After it had disappeared round the gorge, she followed its course by its pall of quivering red smoke. In imagination, she saw it shooting through Europe, as though it were an explosive shuttle ripping through the scorched fabric of the map. It caught up cities and threaded them on a gleaming whistling string. Illuminated names flashed before her eyes and were gone – Bucharest, Zagreb, Trieste, Milan, Basle, Calais.

Once again she was flooded with home-hunger, even though her future address was a hotel. Mixed with it was a gust of foreboding – which was a legacy from the mountains.

'Suppose – something – happened, and I never came back.'

At that moment she felt that any evil could block the way to her return. A railway crash, illness or crime were possibilities which were actually scheduled in other lives. They were happening all round her and at any time a line might give way in the protective square in her palm.

As she lay and tossed, she consoled herself with the reminder that this was the last time she would lie under the lumpy feather bed. Throughout the next two nights she, too, would be rushing through the dark landscape, jerked out of every brief spell of sleep by the flash of lights whenever the express roared through a station.

The thought was with her when she woke, the next morning, to see the silhouette of mountain-peaks iced against the flush of sunrise.

'I'm going home today,' she told herself exultantly.

The air was raw when she looked out of her window. Mist was rising from the lake which gleamed greenly through yellowed fans of chestnut trees. But in spite of the blue and gold glory of autumn she felt indifferent to its beauty.

She was also detached from the drawbacks of her room, which usually offended her critical taste. Its wooden walls were stained a crude shade of raw sienna, and instead of running water there was a battered washstand which bore a tin can, covered with a thin towel.

In spirit, Iris had already left the hotel. Her journey was begun before she started. When she went down to the restaurant she was barely conscious of the other guests, who, only a few hours before, had inspired her with antipathy.

The Misses Flood-Porter, who were dressed for writing letters in the open, were breakfasting at a table by the window. They did not speak to her, although they would have bowed as a matter of courtesy had they caught her eye.

Iris did not notice the omission, because they had gone completely out of her life. She drank her coffee in a silence which was broken by occasional remarks from the sisters, who wondered whether the English weather were kind for a local military wedding.

Her luck held, for she was spared contact with the other guests, who were engrossed by their own affairs. As she passed the bureau, Mrs Barnes was calling a waiter's attention to a letter in one of the pigeon-holes. Her grey jersey-suit, as well as her packet of sandwiches, advertised an excursion.

The vicar, who was filling his pipe on the veranda, was also in unconventional kit – shorts, sweater, nailed boots and the local felt hat, adorned with a tiny blue feather, which he had bought as a souvenir of his holiday.

His smile was so happy that Iris thought he looked both festive and good, as though a saint had deserted his shrine, knocking his halo a trifle askew in the process, in order to put a coat of sunburn over his pallid plaster.

Her tolerance faded as she listened to a dialogue which was destined to affect her own future.

'Is that a letter from home?' called the vicar.

'Yes,' replied his wife, after a pause.

'I thought grandma told us to expect no more letters . . . What's she writing about?'

'She wants me to do a little shopping for her on our way through London. Some Margaret Rose silk. The little princess, you know.'

'But you'll be tired. It's not very considerate.'

'No.' Mrs Barnes's voice was exceptionally sharp. 'It's *not*. Why didn't she *think*?'

Iris condoned her own ungracious conduct of the preceding night as she left them to their discussion. She told herself that she was justified in protecting herself from the boredom of domestic trifles.

As she strolled past the front of the hotel, she had to draw back to avoid trespassing on the privacy of the honeymoon pair, whose sitting-room opened on to the veranda. They were breakfasting in the open air, off rolls and fruit. The man was resplendent in a Chinese dressing-gown, while his wife wore an elaborate wrapper over satin pyjamas.

The Todhunters annoyed Iris, because they affected her with vague discontent. She was conscious of the same unacknowledged blank when she watched a love-scene played by two film stars. Theirs was passion – perfectly dressed, discreetly censored and with the better profile presented to the camera.

She felt a responsive thrill when the man looked into his bride's eyes with intense personal interest.

'Has it been perfect?' he asked.

Mrs Todhunter knew exactly how long to pause before her reply. 'Yes.'

It was faultless timing for he understood what she did not say.

'Not perfect, then,' he remarked. 'But, darling, is anything – '

Iris passed out of earshot, while she was still slightly envious. Her own experience of love had been merely a succession of episodes which led up to the photographic farce of her engagement.

The morning seemed endless, but at length it wore away. She had little to pack, because – following tradition – her friends had taken the bulk of her luggage with them, to save her trouble. An hour or two were killed, or rather drowned, in the lake, but she was too impatient to lie in the sun.

After she had changed for her journey, she went down to the restaurant. The dish of the day was attractively jellied and garnished with sprigs of tarragon, chervil and chopped eggs; but she suspected that it was composed of poached eels. Turning away, with a shudder, she took possession of a small buttercup-painted table in the gravelled garden, where she lunched on potato soup and tiny grapes.

The sun flickered through the dense roof of chestnuts, but the iron chair was too hard and cold for comfort. Although the express was not due for more than an hour, she decided to wait for it at the railway station, where she could enjoy a view.

She had worked herself up to a fever, so that the act of leaving the hotel seemed to bring her a step nearer to her journey. It gave her acute pleasure to pay her bill and tip the stragglers of the staff. Although she saw none of her fellow-guests, she hurried through the garden like a truant from school, as though she feared she might be detained at the last minute.

It was strange to wear a sophisticated travelling-suit and high heels again, as she jolted down the rough path, followed by a porter with her baggage. The sensation was not too comfortable after weeks of liberty, but she welcomed it as part of her return to civilisation. When she was seated on the platform, her suitcase at her feet, and the shimmer of the lake below, she was conscious of having reached a peak of enjoyment.

The air was water-clear and held the sting of altitude. As the sun blazed down on her, she felt steeped in warmth and drenched in light. She took off her hat and gazed at the signal post, anticipating the thrill of its drop, followed by the first glimpse of a foreshortened engine at the end of the rails.

There were other people on the platform, for the arrival of the express was the main event of the day. It was too early for the genuine travellers, but groups of loiterers, both visitors and natives, hung round the fruit- and paper-stalls. They were a cheerful company and noisy in many languages. Iris heard no English until two men came down the road from the village.

They leaned over the palings behind her, to continue an argument. She did not feel sufficient interest, at first, to turn and see their faces, but their voices were so distinctive that, presently, she could visualise them.

The one whom she judged the younger had an eager untidy voice. She felt sure that he possessed an active brain, with a rush of ideas. He spoke too quickly and often stumbled for a word, probably not because his terms were limited, but because he had a choice of too many.

Gradually he won her sympathy, partly because his mind seemed in tune – or rather, in discord – with hers and partly because she disliked the other speaker instinctively. His accent was pedantic and consciously cultured. He spoke deliberately, with an irritating authority, which betrayed his inflexible mind. 'Oh, no, my dear Hare.' Iris felt it should have been "Watson". 'You're abysmally wrong. It has been proved conclusively that there can be no fairer or better system of justice than trial by jury.'

'Trial by fatheads,' spluttered the younger voice. 'You talk of ordinary citizens. No one is ordinary, but a bag of his special prejudices. One woman's got a spite against her sex – one man's cranky on morality. They all damn the prisoner on different issues. And they've all businesses or homes which they want to get back to. They watch the clock and grasp the obvious.'

'They are directed by the judge.'

'And how much of his direction do they remember? You know how your own mind slips when you're listening to a string of words. Besides, after he's dotted all the i's and crossed the t's for them, they stampede and bring him in the wrong verdict.'

'Why should you assume it is wrong? They have formed their own conclusion on the testimony of the witnesses.'

'*Witnesses.*' In his heat the young man thumped the railing. 'The witness is the most damnable part of the outfit. He may be so stupid as to be putty in the hands of some wily lawyer, or he may be smart and lie away some wretched man's life just to read about his own wonderful memory and powers of observation and see his photograph in the papers. They're all out for publicity.'

The elder man laughed in a superior manner which irritated his companion into striking a personal note.

'When I'm accused of bumping you off, professor, I'd rather be tried by a team of judges who'd bring trained legal minds and impartial justice to bear on the facts.'

'You're biased,' said the professor. ' . . . Let me try to convince you. The jury is intelligent in bulk, and can judge character. Certain witnesses are reliable, while others must be viewed with suspicion. For instance, how would you describe that dark woman with the artificial lashes?'

'Attractive.'

'Hum. *I* should call her meretricious and so would any average man of the world. Now, we'll assume that she and that English lady in the Burberry are giving contrary evidence. One of the two must be telling a lie.'

'I don't agree. It may depend on the point of view. The man in the street, with his own back garden, is ready to swear to lilac when he sees it; but when he goes to a botanical garden he finds it's labelled syringa.'

'The generic name – '

'I know, I know. But if one honest John Citizen swears syringa is white, while another swears it's mauve, you'll grant that there is an opportunity for confusion. Evidence may be like that.'

'Haven't you wandered from my point?' asked the conventional voice. 'Put those two women, separately, into the witness-box. Now *which* are you going to believe?'

In her turn, Iris compared the hypothetical witnesses. One was a characteristic type of county Englishwoman, with an athletic figure and a pleasant intelligent face. If she strode across the station as though she possessed the right of way, she used it merely as a short cut to her legitimate goal.

On the other hand, the pretty dark woman was an obvious loiterer. Her skin-tight skirt and embroidered peasant blouse might have been the holiday attire of any Continental lady; but, in spite of her attractive red lips and expressive eyes, Iris could not help thinking of a gypsy who had just stolen a chicken for the pot.

Against her will, she had to agree with the professor. Yet she felt almost vexed with the younger man when he ceased to argue, because she had backed the losing side.

'I see your point,' he said. 'The British waterproof wins every time. But Congo rubber was a bloody business and too wholesale a belief in rubber-proofing may lead to a bloody mix-up . . . Come and have a drink.'

'Thank you, if you will allow me to order it. I wish to avail myself of every opportunity of speaking the language.'

'Wish I could forget it. It's a disgusting one – all spitting and sneezing. You lecture on Modern Languages, don't you? Many girl students in your classes?'

'Yes . . . Unfortunately.'

Iris was sorry when they moved away, for she had been idly interested in their argument. The crowd on the platform had increased, although the express was not due for another twenty-five minutes, even if it ran to time. She had now to share her bench with others, while a child squatted on her suitcase.

Although spoiled by circumstances she did not resent the intrusion. The confusion could not touch her because she was held by the moment. The glow of sunshine, the green flicker of trees, the gleam of the lake, all combined to hypnotise her to a condition of stationary bliss.

There was nothing to warn her of the attack. When she least expected it, the blow fell.

Suddenly she felt a violent pain at the back of her neck. Almost before she realised it, the white-capped mountains rocked, the blue sky turned black and she dropped down into darkness.

6

The Waiting-Room

When Iris became conscious, her sight returned, at first, in patches. She saw sections of faces floating in the air. It seemed the same face – sallow-skinned, with black eyes and bad teeth.

Gradually she realised that she was lying on a bench in a dark kind of shed while a ring of women surrounded her. They were of peasant type, with a racial resemblance accentuated by intermarriage.

They stared down at her with indifferent apathy, as though she were some street spectacle – a dying animal or a man in a fit. There was no trace of compassion in their blank faces, no glint of curiosity in their dull gaze. In their complete detachment they seemed devoid of the instincts of common humanity.

'Where am I?' she asked wildly.

A woman in a black overall suddenly broke into guttural speech, which conveyed no iota of meaning to Iris. She listened with the same helpless panic which had shaken her yesterday in the gorge. Actually the woman's face was so close that she could see the pits in her skin and the hairs sprouting inside her nostrils; yet their fundamental cleavage was so complete that they might have been standing on different planets.

She wanted someone to lighten her darkness – to raise the veil which baffled her and blinded her. *Something* had happened to her of which she had no knowledge.

Her need was beyond the scope of crude pantomime. Only some lucid explanation could clear the confusion of her senses. In that moment she thought of the people at the hotel, from whom she had practically run away. Now she felt she would give years of her life to see the strong saintly face of the clergyman looking down at her, or meet the kind eyes of his wife.

In an effort to grip reality she looked round her. The place was vaguely familiar, with dark wooden walls and a sanded floor, which served as a communal spittoon. A bar of dusty sunlight, slanting through a narrow window, glinted on thick glasses stacked upon a shelf and on a sheaf of fluttering handbills.

She raised her head higher and felt a throb of dull pain, followed by a rush of dizziness. For a moment she thought she was going to be sick; but the next second nausea was overpowered by a shock of memory.

This was the waiting-room at the station. She had lingered here only yesterday, with the crowd, as it gulped down a final drink. Like jolting trucks banging through her brain her thoughts were linked together by the connecting sequence of the railway. She remembered sitting on the platform, in the sunshine, while she waited for a train.

Her heart began to knock violently. She was on her way back to England. Yet she had not the least idea as to what had happened after her blackout, or how long ago it had occurred. The express might have come – and gone, leaving her behind.

In her overwrought state the idea seemed the ultimate catastrophe. Her head swam again and she had to wait for the mist to clear from her eyes before she could read the figures on her tiny wristwatch.

To her joy she discovered that she had still enough time in which to pull herself together before her journey. 'What happened to me?' she wondered. 'What made me pass out? Was I attacked.'

Closing her eyes, she tried desperately to clear her brain. But her last conscious moment held only a memory of blue sky and grass-green lake, viewed as though through a crystal.

Suddenly she remembered her bag and groped to find it. To her dismay it was not beside her, nor could she see it anywhere on the bench. Her suitcase lay on the floor, and her hat had been placed on top of it, as though to prove the limit of her possessions.

'My bag,' she screamed, wild-eyed with panic. 'Where's my bag?'

It held not only her money and tickets, but her passport. Without it, it was impossible for her to continue her journey. Even if she boarded the train, penniless, she would be turned back at the first frontier.

The thought drove her frantic. She felt sure that this ring of women had combined to rob her when she was helpless and at their mercy. When she sprang from the bench they pulled her down again.

The blood rushed to her head and she resisted them fiercely. As she struggled she was conscious of a whirl of confusion – of throbbing pain, rising voices, and lights flashing before her eyes. There were breathless panting noises as an undercurrent to a strange rushing sound, as though an imprisoned fountain had suddenly burst through the ground.

In spite of her efforts, the woman in the black pinafore dragged her down again, while a fat girl, in a bursting bodice, held a glass to her lips. When she refused to swallow they treated her like a child, tilting her chin and pouring the spirit down her throat. It made her cough and gasp, until her head seemed to be swelling with pain. Terrified by this threat of another attack, she relaxed in helpless misery. Her instinct warned her that, if she grew excited, at any moment the walls might rock – like the snow-mountains – as a prelude to total extinction.

Next time she might not wake up. Besides, she dared not risk being ill in the village, alone, and so far away from her friends. If she returned to the hotel she could enlist the financial help of the English visitors, while, doubtless, another passport could be procured; but it meant delay.

In addition, these people were all strangers, whose holiday was nearly ended. In another day they would be gone, while she might be stranded there, indefinitely, exposed to indifference, and even neglect. The hotel, too, was closing down almost immediately.

'I mustn't be ill,' thought Iris. 'I must get away at once, while there is still time.'

She felt sure that if she could board the train, the mere knowledge that she was rolling, mile by mile, back to civilisation, would brace her to hold out until she reached some familiar place. She thought of Basle on the milky jade Rhine, with its excellent hotels where English was spoken and where she could be ill, intelligibly, and with dignity.

Everything hung upon the catching of this train. The issue at stake made her suddenly desperate to find her bag. She was struggling to rise again, when she became conscious that someone was trying to establish contact with her.

It was an old man in a dirty blouse, with a gnarled elfin face – brown and lined as the scar on a tree-trunk from which a branch had been lopped. He kept taking off his greasy hat and pointing, first upwards and then to her head. All at once she grasped his meaning. He was telling her that while she sat on the platform she had been attacked with sunstroke.

The explanation was a great relief, because she was both frightened and baffled by the mystery of her illness. She rarely ailed and had never fainted before. Besides, it had given her proof that, in spite of her own misgivings, the channels were not entirely blocked, provided the issues were not too involved.

Although she still felt sick with anxiety about her train, she managed to smile faintly at the porter. As though he had been waiting for some sign of encouragement, he thrust his hand into the neck of his dirty blouse and drew out her bag.

With a cry, she snatched it from him. Remembering the crowd on the platform, she had no hope of finding her money; but there was a faint chance that her passport had not been stolen.

She tore at the zip-fastener with shaking fingers, to find, to her utter amazement, that the contents were intact. Tickets, money, passport – even her receipted hotel-bill were still there.

She had grossly maligned the native honesty, and she hastened to make amends. Here, at last, was a situation she understood. As usual, someone had come to her rescue, true to the tradition of the protective square in her palm. Her part, which was merely to overpay for services rendered, was easy.

The women received their share of the windfall with stolid faces. Apparently they were too stunned with astonishment to show excitement or gratitude. The old porter, on the other hand, beamed triumphantly and gripped Iris's suitcase, to show that he, too, had grasped the situation.

In spite of her resistance to it, the raw spirit, together with her change of circumstances, had revived Iris considerably. She felt practically restored again and mistress of herself as she showed her ticket to the porter.

The effect on him was electric. He yammered with excitement, as he grabbed her arm and rushed with her to the door. Directly they had passed through it, Iris understood the origin of the curious pervading noise which had helped to complicate her nightmare.

It was the gush of steam escaping from an engine. While she had let the precious minutes slip by, the express had entered the station.

Now it was on the point of departure.

The platform was a scene of wild confusion. Doors were being slammed. People were shouting farewells and crowding before the carriages. An official waved a flag and the whistle shrilled.

They were one minute too late. Iris realised the fact that she was beaten, just as the porter metaphorically snatched at the psychological moment and was swung away with it on its flight. He took advantage of the brief interval between the first jerk of the engine and the revolution of the wheels to charge the crowd, like an aged tiger.

There was still strength and agility in his sinewy old frame to enable him to reach the nearest carriage and wrench open the door.

His entrance was disputed by a majestic lady in black. She was a personage from whom – as a peasant – his bones instinctively cringed. On the other hand, his patron had paid him a sum far in excess of what he earned in tips during the whole of a brief season.

Therefore, his patron must have her place. Ducking under the august lady's arm, he hurled Iris's suitcase into the compartment and dragged her inside after it.

The carriage was moving when he scrambled out, to fall in a heap on the platform. He was unhurt, however, for when she looked back to wave her thanks, he grinned at her like a toothless gnome.

Already he was yards behind. The station slid by, and the lake began to lap against the piles of the rough landing-stage. It rippled past the window in a sheet of emerald, ruffled by the breeze and burnished by the sun. As the train swung round the curve of the rails to the cutting in the rocks, Iris looked back for a last view of the village – a fantastic huddle of coloured toy-buildings, perched on the green shelf of the valley.

7

Passengers

As the train rattled out of the cliff tunnel and emerged in a green tree-choked gorge, Iris glanced at her watch. According to the evidence of its hands, the Trieste express was not yet due at the village station.

'It must have stopped when I crashed,' she decided. 'Sweet luck. It might have lost me my train.'

The reminder made her feel profoundly grateful to be actually on her way back to England. During the past twenty-four hours she had experienced more conflicting emotion than in a lifetime of easy circumstance and arrangement. She had known the terrifying helplessness of being friendless, sick and penniless – with every wire cut. And then, at the worst, her luck had turned, as it always did.

From force of contrast the everyday business of transport was turned into a temporary rapture. Railway travel was no longer an infliction, only to be endured by the aid of such palliatives as reservations, flowers, fruit, chocolates, light literature, and a group of friends to shriek encouragement.

As she sat, jammed in an uncomfortable carriage, in a train which was not too clean, with little prospect of securing a wagon-lit at Trieste, she felt the thrill of a first journey.

The scenery preserved its barbarous character in rugged magnificence. The train threaded its way past piled-up chunks of disrupted landscape, like a Doré steel-engraving of Dante's Inferno. Waterfalls slashed the walls of granite precipices with silver-veining. Sometimes they passed arid patches, where dark pools, fringed with black-feathered rushes, lay in desolate hollows.

Iris gazed at it through the screen of the window – glad of the protective pane of glass. This grandeur was the wreckage of a world shattered by elemental force, and it reminded her that she had just been bruised by her first contact with reality.

She still shrank from the memory of what had happened, even though the nightmare railway station was the thickness of the mountain away. Now that it was slipping farther behind the coils of the rails with every passing minute, she could dare to estimate the narrow margin by which she had escaped disaster.

Amid the crowd at the station there must have been a percentage of dishonest characters, ready to take advantage of the providential combination of an unconscious foreigner – who did not count – and an expensive handbag which promised rich pickings. Yet the little gnome-like porter chanced to be the man on the spot.

'Things always do turn out for me,' she thought. 'But – it must be appalling for some of the others.'

It was the first time she had realised the fate of those unfortunates who had no squares in their palms. If there were a railway accident, she knew that she would be in the unwrecked middle portion of the train, just as inevitably as certain other passengers were doomed to be in the telescoped coaches.

As she shuddered at the thought, she glanced idly at the woman who sat opposite to her. She was a negative type in every respect – middle-aged, with a huddle of small indefinite features, and vague colouring. Someone drew a face and then rubbed it nearly out again. Her curly hair was faded and her skin was bleached to oatmeal.

She was not sufficiently a caricature to suggest a stage spinster. Even her tweed suit and matching hat were not too dowdy, although lacking any distinctive note.

In ordinary circumstances, Iris would not have spared her a second glance or thought. Today, however, she gazed at her with compassion.

'If *she* were in a jam, no one would help her out,' she thought.

It was discomforting to reflect that the population of the globe must include a percentage of persons without friends, money or influence; nonentities who would never be missed, and who would sink without leaving a bubble.

To distract her thoughts, Iris tried to look at the scenery again. But the window was now blocked by passengers, who were unable to find seats, so stood in the corridor. For the first time, therefore, she made a deliberate survey of the other occupants of her compartment.

They were six in number – the proper quota – which she had increased to an illegal seven. Her side was occupied by a family party – two large parents and one small daughter of about twelve.

The father had a shaven head, a little waxed moustache, and several chins. His horn-rimmed glasses and comfortable air gave him the appearance of a prosperous citizen. His wife had an oiled straight black fringe, and bushy eyebrows which looked as though they had been corked. The child wore babyish socks, which did not match her adult expression. Her hair had apparently been set, after a permanent wave, for it was still secured with clips.

They all wore new and fashionable suits, which might have been inspired by a shorthand manual. The father wore stripes – the mother, spots – and the daughter, checks. Iris reflected idly that if they were broken up and reassembled, in the general scramble they might convey a message to the world in shorthand.

On the evidence, it would be a motto for the home, for they displayed a united spirit as they shared a newspaper. The mother scanned the fashions; the little girl read the children's page; and from the closely-printed columns Iris guessed that the head of the family studied finance.

She looked away from them to the opposite side of the carriage. Sitting beside the tweed spinster was a fair pretty girl, who appeared to have modelled herself from the photograph of any blonde film actress. There were the same sleek waves of hair, the large blue eyes – with supplemented lashes, and the butterfly brows. Her cheeks were tinted and her lips painted to geranium bows.

In spite of the delicacy of her features, her beauty was lifeless and standardised. She wore a tight white suit, with a high-necked black satin blouse, while her cap, gauntlet-gloves and bag were also black. She sat erect and motionless, holding a rigid pose, as though she were being photographed for a 'still'.

Although her figure was reduced almost to starvation-point, she encroached on the tweed spinster's corner in order to leave a respectful gap between herself and the personage who had opposed Iris's entrance.

There was no doubt that this majestic lady belonged to the ruling classes. Her bagged eyes were fierce with pride, and her nose was an arrogant beak. Dressed and semi-veiled in heavy black, her enormous bulk occupied nearly half the seat.

To Iris's astonishment, she was regarding her with a fixed stare of hostility. It made her feel both guilty and self-conscious.

'I know I crashed the carriage,' she thought. 'But *she's* got plenty of room. Wish I could explain, for my own satisfaction.'

Leaning forward, she spoke impulsively to the personage.

'Do you speak English?'

Apparently the question was an insult, for the lady closed heavy lids with studied insolence, as though she could not endure a plebeian spectacle.

Iris bit her lip as she glanced at the other passengers. The family party kept their eyes fixed on their paper – the tweed spinster smoothed her skirt, the blonde beauty stared into space. Somehow, Iris received an impression that this well-bred unconsciousness was a tribute of respect to the personage.

'Is she the local equivalent of the sacred black bull?' she wondered angrily. 'Can't anyone speak until she does? . . . Well, to *me*, she's nothing but a fat woman with horrible kid gloves.'

She tried to hold on to her critical attitude, but in vain. An over-powering atmosphere of authority seemed to filtrate from the towering black figure.

Now that her excitement was wearing off, she began to feel the after-effects of her slight sunstroke. Her head ached and the back of her neck felt as stiff as though it had been reinforced with an iron rod. The symptoms warned her to be careful. With the threat of illness still hanging over her, she knew she should store up every scrap of nervous force, and not waste her reserves in fanciful dislikes.

Her resolution did not save her from increasing discomfort. The carriage seemed not only stuffy, but oppressive with the black widow's personality. Iris felt positive that she was a clotted mass of prejudices –

an obstruction in the healthy life-stream of the community. Her type was always a clog on progress.

As her face grew damp, she looked towards the closed window of the compartment. The corridor-end, where she sat, was too crowded to admit any of the outer air, so she struggled to her feet and caught the window strap.

'Do you mind?' she asked with stressed courtesy, hoping, from her intonation, that the other passengers would grasp the fact that she was asking their permission before letting down the glass.

As she expected, the man of the family party rose and took the strap from her. Instead of finishing the job, however, he glanced respectfully at the personage, as though she were sacrosanct, and then frowned at Iris, shaking his head.

Feeling furious at the opposition, Iris returned to her corner.

'I've got to take it,' she thought. 'Take it on the chin. I'm the outsider here.'

It was another novel sensation – for the most popular member of the crowd to be in a minority. Besides having to endure the lack of ventilation, the inability to explain her actions, or express a wish, gave her the stunted sense of being deprived of two faculties – speech and hearing.

Presently the door was opened and a tall man squeezed into the carriage. Although she realised that her feelings had grown supersensitive, Iris thought she had never seen a more repulsive face. He was pallid as potter's clay, with dead dark eyes and a black spade beard.

He bowed to the personage and began to talk to her, standing the while. His story was evidently interesting, for Iris noticed that the other passengers, including the child, were all listening with close interest.

As he was speaking, his glasses flashed round the compartment, and finally rested on her. His glance was penetrating, yet impersonal, as though she were a specimen on a microscope-slide. Yet, somehow, she received the impression that she was not a welcome specimen, nor one that he had expected to see.

Stooping so that his lips were on a level with the personage's ear, he asked a low-toned question. She replied in a whisper, so that Iris was reminded of two blowflies buzzing in a bottle.

'Am I imagining things, or do these people really dislike me?' she wondered.

She knew that she was growing obsessed by this impression of a general and secret hostility. It was manifestly absurd, especially as the man with the black spade beard had not seen her before. She had

merely inconvenienced some strangers, from whom she was divided by
the barrier of language.

Shutting her eyes, she tried to forget the people in the carriage. Yet
the presence of the man continued to affect her with discomfort. His
white face seemed to break through her closed lids, and float in the air
before her.

It was a great relief when the buzzing ceased and she heard him go
out of the compartment. Directly he had left, she grew normal again,
and was chiefly conscious of a very bad headache. The most important
things in life were tea and cigarettes; yet she dared not smoke because
of the threat of sickness, while tea seemed a feature of a lost civilisation.
The train was now rushing through a deserted country of rock and
pine. The nearest reminder of habitation was an occasional castle of
great antiquity, and usually in ruins. As she was gazing out at the
fantastic scenery, an official poked his head in at the door and shouted
something which sounded like blasphemy.

The other passengers listened in apathy, but Iris began to open her
bag, in case tickets or passport were required. As she did so, she was
amazed to hear a crisp English voice.

The tweed spinster had risen from her seat and was asking her a
question.

'Are you coming to the restaurant-car to get tea?'

8

Tea Interval

Iris was too stunned with surprise to reply. She looked incredulously at
the sandy, piny stretches flowing past the window, as though expecting
to see them turn to Swiss chalets, or blue Italian lakes.

'Oh,' she gasped, 'you're English.'

'Of course. I thought I looked typical . . . Are you coming to tea?'

'Oh, yes.'

As Iris followed her guide out of the carriage, she was rather dis-
concerted to find that their compartment was at the end of the corridor.
It looked as though her protective square had not insured her against
railway smashes, after all.

'Are we next to the engine?' she asked.

'Oh, no,' the tweed lady assured her. 'There are ordinary coaches in
between. It's an extra long train, because of the end-of-the-season rush.
They had to pack them in with a shoehorn.'

Apparently she was the type that collected information, for she began to broadcast almost immediately.

'Just glance at the next carriage to ours as you go by – and I'll tell you something.'

Although Iris felt no curiosity, she obeyed. Afterwards she was sorry, because she could not forget what she saw.

A rigid figure, covered with rugs, lay stretched on the length of one seat. It was impossible to tell whether it were a man or a woman, for head and eyes were bandaged and the features concealed by a criss-cross of plaster strips. Apparently the face had been gashed to mutilation-point.

Iris recoiled in horror, which was increased when she realised that the pallid man with the spade beard was in charge of the invalid. Beside him was a nun, whose expression was so callous that it was difficult to connect her with any act of mercy.

While they chatted together, the patient feebly raised one hand. Although they saw the movement, they ignored it. They might have been porters, responsible for the transport of a bit of lumber rather than a suffering human being.

The fluttering fingers affected Iris with a rush of acute sympathy. She shrank from the thought that – had the cards fallen otherwise – she too might be lying helpless, neglected by some indifferent stranger.

'That nun looks like a criminal,' she whispered.

'She's not a nun,' the tweed lady informed her, 'she's a nursing-sister.'

'Then I pity her patient. Ghastly to be ill on a journey. And she's not a spectacle. Why can't they pull down the blind?'

'It would be dull for them.'

'Poor devil. I suppose it's a man?'

Iris was so foolishly anxious to break the parallel between the motion-less figure and herself that she was disappointed when her companion shook her head.

'No, a woman. They got in at our station, higher up. The doctor was telling the Baroness about it. She's just been terribly injured in a motor smash, and there's risk of serious brain injury. So the doctor's rushing her to Trieste, for a tricky operation. It's a desperate chance to save her reason and her life.'

'Is that man with the black beard a doctor?' asked Iris.

'Yes. Very clever, too.'

'Is he? I'd rather have a vet.'

The tweed lady, who was leading, did not hear her muttered protest. They had to force their way through the blocked corridors, and had covered about half the distance when the spinster collided with a tall dark lady in grey, who was standing at the door of a crowded carriage.

'Oh, I'm so sorry,' she apologised. 'I was just looking out to see if our tea was coming. I gave the order to an attendant.'

Iris recognised Mrs Barnes's voice, and shrank back, for she was not anxious to meet the vicar and his wife.

But her companion gave a cry of delight.

'Oh, you're English, too,' she said. 'This is my lucky day.'

As Mrs Barnes's soft brown eyes seemed to invite confidence, she added, 'I've been in exile for a year.'

'Are you on your way home?' asked Mrs Barnes, with ready sympathy.

'Yes, but I can't believe it. It's far too good to be true. Shall I send a waiter with your tea?'

'That would be really kind. My husband is such a wretched traveller. Like so many big strong men.'

Iris listened impatiently, for her temples were beginning to throb savagely. Now that Mrs Barnes had managed to introduce her husband's name into the conversation, she knew that her own tea might be held up indefinitely.

'Aren't we blocking the way?' she asked.

Mrs Barnes recognised her with a rather forced smile, for the Gabriel episode still rankled.

'Surprised to see us?' she asked. 'We decided, after all, not to wait for the last through train. And our friends – the Misses Flood-Porter, came with us. In fact, we're a full muster, for the honeymooners are here, too.'

When they had struggled a little farther down the surging corridor, the tweed lady spoke to Iris over her shoulder.

'What a sweet face your friend has. Like a suffering madonna.'

'Oh, no, she's very bright,' Iris assured her. 'And she's definitely not a friend.'

They crossed the last dangerously clanking connecting-way, and entered the restaurant-car, which seemed full already. The Misses Flood-Porter – both wearing well-cut white linen travelling-coats – had secured a table and were drinking tea.

Their formal bow, when Iris squeezed by them, was conditional recognition before the final fade-out.

'We'll speak to you during the journey,' it seemed to say, 'but at Victoria we become strangers.'

As Iris showed no inclination to join them, Miss Rose could not resist the temptation to manage a situation.

'Your friend is trying to attract your attention,' she called out.

Iris turned and saw that her companion had discovered the last spare corner – a table wedged against the wall – and was reserving her a place. When she joined her, the little lady was looking round with shining eyes.

'I ordered the tea for your nice friends,' she said. 'Oh, isn't all this *fun*?'

Her pleasure was so spontaneous and genuine that Iris could not condemn it as gush. She stared doubtfully at the faded old-gold plush window-curtains, the smutty tablecloth, the glass dish of cherry jam – and then she glanced at her companion.

She received a vague impression of a little puckered face; but there was a sparkle in the faded blue eyes, and an eager note in the voice, which suggested a girl.

Afterwards, when she was trying to collect evidence of what she believed must be an extraordinary conspiracy, it was this discrepancy between a youthful voice and a middle-aged spinster, which made her doubt her own senses. In any case, her recollection was far from clear, for she did not remember looking consciously at her companion again.

The sun was blazing in through the window, so that she shaded her eyes with one hand most of the time she was having tea. But as she listened to the flow of excited chatter, she had the feeling that she was being entertained by someone much younger than herself.

'Why do you like it?' she asked.

'Because it's travel. We're moving. Everything's moving.'

Iris also had the impression that the whole scene was flickering like an early motion-picture. The waiters swung down the rocking carriage, balancing trays. Scraps of country flew past the window. Smuts rained down on the flakes of butter and the sticky cakes. Dusty motes quivered in the rays of the sun, and the china shook with every jerk of the engine.

As she tried to drink some tea before it was all shaken over the rim of her cup, she learned that her companion was an English governess – Miss Winifred Froy – and was on her way home for a holiday. It came as a shock of surprise to know that this adult lady actually possessed living parents.

'Pater and Mater say they can talk of nothing else but my return,' declared Miss Froy. 'They're as excited as children. And so is Sock.'

'Sock?' repeated Iris.

'Yes, short for Socrates. The Pater's name for him. He is our dog. He's an Old English sheepdog – not pure – but so appealing. And he's really devoted to me. Mater says he understands that I'm coming home, but not *when*. So the old duffer meets every train. And then the darling comes back, with his tail down, the picture of depression. Pater and

Mater are looking forward to seeing his frantic joy the night I *do* come.'

'I'd love to see him,' murmured Iris.

The old parents' happiness left her unmoved, but she was specially fond of dogs. She got a clear picture of Sock – a shaggy mongrel, absurdly clownish and overgrown, with amber eyes beaming under his wisps, and gambolling like a puppy in the joy of reunion.

Suddenly, Miss Froy broke off, at a recollection.

'Before I forget I want to explain why I did not back you up about the window. No wonder you thought I could not be English. It was stuffy – but I didn't like to interfere, because of the Baroness.'

'D'you mean the appalling black person?'

'Yes, the Baroness. I'm under an obligation to her. There was a muddle about my place in the train. I'd booked second-class, but there wasn't a seat left. So the Baroness most kindly paid the difference, so that I could travel first-class, in her carriage.'

'Yet she doesn't look kind,' murmured Iris.

'Perhaps she is rather overwhelming. But she's a member of the family to which I had the honour of being governess . . . It's not wise to mention names in public, but I was governess to the very highest in the place. These remote districts are still feudal, and centuries behind us. You can have no idea of the *power* of the – of my late employer. What he says *goes*. And he hasn't got to speak. A nod is enough.'

'Degrading,' muttered Iris, who resented authority.

'It is,' agreed Miss Froy. 'But it's in the atmosphere, and after a time one absorbs it and one grows spineless. And that's not English . . . I feel so reinforced, now I've met you. We must stick together.'

Iris made no promise. Her fright had not changed her fundamentally, only weakened her nerve. She had the modern prejudice in favour of youth, and had no intention of being tied to a middle-aged spinster for the rest of the journey.

'Are you going back again?' she asked distantly.

'Yes, but not to the castle. It's rather awkward, but I wanted another twelve months to perfect my accent, so I engaged to teach the children of the – Well, we'll call him the leader of the opposition.' She lowered her voice to a whisper. 'The truth is, there is a small but growing Communist element, which is very opposed to my late employer. In fact, they've accused him of corruption and all sorts of horrors. I don't ask myself if it's true, for it's not my business. I only know he's a marvellous man, with wonderful charm and personality. Blood tells . . . Shall I confide something rather indiscreet?'

Iris nodded wearily. She was beginning to feel dazed by the heat and incessant clatter. Her tea had not refreshed her, for most of it had splashed into her saucer. The engine plunged and jolted over the metals with drunken jerks, belching out wreaths of acrid smoke which streamed past the windows.

Miss Froy continued her serial, while Iris listened in bored resignation.

'I was terribly anxious to say goodbye to the – to my employer, so that I could assure him that my going over to the enemy – so to speak – was not treachery. His valet and secretary both told me that he was away at his hunting-lodge. But somehow I felt that they were putting me off. Anyway, I lay awake until early morning, before it was light, when I heard water splashing in the bathroom . . . Only one, my dear, for the castle arrangements were primitive, although my bedroom was like a stage royal apartment, all gilding and peacock-blue velvet, with a huge circular mirror let into the ceiling . . . Well, I crept out, like a mouse, and met him in the corridor. There we were, plain man and woman – I in my dressing-gown, and he in his bathrobe, and with his hair all wet and rough . . . But he was charming. He actually shook my hand and thanked me for my services.'

Miss Froy stopped to butter the last scrap of roll. As she was wiping her sticky fingers, she heaved a sigh of happiness.

'I cannot tell you,' she said, 'what a relief it was to leave under such pleasant circumstances. I always try to be on good terms with everyone. Of course, I'm insignificant, but I can say truthfully that I have not got an enemy in the world.'

9

Compatriots

'And now,' said Miss Froy, 'I suppose we had better go back to our carriage, and make room for others.'

The waiter, who was both a judge of character and an opportunist, presented the bill to Iris. Unable to decipher the sprawling numerals, she laid down a note and rose from her seat.

'Aren't you waiting for your change?' asked Miss Froy.

When Iris explained that she was leaving it for a tip, she gasped.

'But it's absurd. Besides, they've already charged their percentage on the bill . . . As I'm more familiar with the currency, hadn't I better settle up for everything? I'll keep an account, and we can get straight at our journey's end.'

The incident was fresh evidence of the smooth working of the protective-square system. Although Iris was travelling alone, a competent courier had presented herself, to rid her of all responsibilities and worries.

'She's decent, although she's a crashing bore,' she decided, as she followed Miss Froy down the swaying restaurant-car.

She noticed that the Misses Flood-Porter, who had not finished their leisurely tea, took no notice of her, but looked exclusively at her companion.

Miss Froy returned Miss Rose's stare with frank interest.

'Those people are English,' she whispered to Iris, not knowing that they had met before. 'They're part of an England that is passing away. Well-bred privileged people, who live in big houses, and don't spend their income. I'm rather sorry they're dying out.'

'Why?' asked Iris.

'Because, although I'm a worker myself, I feel that nice leisured people stand for much that is good. Tradition, charity, national prestige. They may not think you're their equal, but their sense of justice sees that you get equal rights.'

Iris said nothing although she admitted to herself that while they were at the hotel the Misses Flood-Porter were more considerate of persons and property than her own friends.

When they made their long and shaky pilgrimage through the train, she was amazed by Miss Froy's youthful spirits.

Her laugh rang out whenever she was bumped against other passengers, or was forced, by a lurch of the engine, to clutch a rail.

After they had pushed their way to a clearer passage, she lingered to peep through the windows of the reserved compartments. One of these specially arrested her attention and she invited Iris to share her view.

'Do have a peek,' she urged. 'There's a glorious couple, just like film stars come to life.'

Iris was feeling too jaded to be interested in anything but a railway collision; but as she squeezed her way past Miss Froy, she glanced mechanically through the glass and recognised the bridal pair from the hotel.

Even within the limits of the narrow coupé, the Todhunters had managed to suggest their special atmosphere of opulence and exclusion. The bride wore the kind of elaborate travelling-costume which is worn only on journeys inside a film studio, and had assembled a drift of luxurious possessions.

'Fancy,' thrilled Miss Froy, 'they've got hot-house fruit with their tea. Grapes and nectarines . . . He's looking at her with his soul in his eyes, but I can only see her profile. It's just like a beautiful statue. Oh, please let her turn her head.'

Her wish was granted, for, at that comment, Mrs Todhunter chanced to glance towards the window. She frowned when she saw Miss Froy and spoke to her husband, who rose instantly and pulled down the blind.

Although she was not implicated, Iris felt ashamed of the incident; but Miss Froy only bubbled with amusement.

'He'll know me again,' she said. 'He looked at me as if he'd like to annihilate me. Quite natural. I was the world – and he wants to forget the world, because he's in paradise. It must be wonderful to be exclusively in love.'

'They may not be married,' remarked Iris. 'Anyone can buy a wedding-ring.'

'You mean – guilty love? Oh, no, they're too glorious. What name did they register under?'

'Todhunter.'

'Then they *are* married. I'm so glad. If it was an irregular affair, they would have signed "Brown" or "Smith". It's always done.'

As she listened to the gush of words behind her, Iris was again perplexed by the discrepancy between Miss Froy's personality and her appearance. It was as though a dryad were imprisoned within the tree-trunk of a withered spinster.

When they reached the end of the corridor, a morbid impulse made her glance towards the carriage which held the invalid. She caught a glimpse of a rigid form and a face hidden by its mass of adhesions before she looked quickly away, to avoid the eyes of the doctor. They frightened her because of their suggestion of baleful hypnotic force. She knew that they would be powerless to affect her in ordinary circumstances; but she was beginning to feel heady and unreal, as though she were in a dream, where every emotion is intensified.

In all probability this condition was a consequent symptom of her sunstroke, and was due, partly, to her struggle to hold out until she could collapse safely at her journey's end. She was directing her will-power towards one aim only, and therefore draining herself of energy.

As a result she was susceptible to imaginary antagonism. When she caught sight of a blur of faces inside the gloom of her carriage, she shrank back, unwilling to enter.

She received unexpected support from Miss Froy, who seemed to divine her reluctance.

'Don't let's sit mum like charity-children any longer,' she whispered. 'Even if I *am* under an obligation to the Baroness, I am going to remember that these people are only foreigners. They shan't impress me. We're English.'

Although the reminder reduced patriotism to crude Jingoism, it braced Iris to enter the compartment with a touch of her old abandon. Precaution forgotten, she lit a cigarette without a glance at the other passengers.

'Have you travelled much?' she asked Miss Froy.

'Only in Europe,' was the regretful reply. 'Mater doesn't really like me going so far from home, but she holds the theory that the younger generation must not be denied their freedom. Still, I've promised to stick to Europe, although, whenever I'm near a boundary, I just ache to hop over the line into Asia.'

'Is your mother very old?'

'No, she's eighty years young. A real sport, with the spirit of the modern girl. Pater is seventy-seven. He never let her know he was younger than she, but it leaked out when he had to retire at sixty-five. Poor Mater was terribly upset. She said, "You have made me feel a cradle-snatcher." . . . Oh, I can't believe I'm really going to see them again soon.'

As she listened, Iris watched the smoke curling up from her cigarette. Occasionally she saw a vague little puckered face swaying amid the haze, like an unsuccessful attempt at television. Out of gratitude for services rendered – and still to come – she tried to appreciate the old parents, but she grew very bored by the family saga.

She learned that Pater was tall and thin, and looked classical, while Mater was short and stout, but dignified. Apparently Pater had unquenchable ardour and energy, for at the age of seventy he began to learn Hebrew.

'He's made a detailed timetable for every month of his life up to ninety,' explained Miss Froy. 'That's what comes of being a school-master. Now, Mater is passionately fond of novels. Love ones, you know. She makes a long bus journey every week to change her library book. But she says she can't imagine them properly unless she makes *me* the heroine.'

'I'm sure you have a marvellous time,' said Iris.

Miss Froy resented the attempt to be tactful.

'Have, and had,' she declared. 'Pater was a parson before he kept a school, and his curates always proposed to me. I expect it is because I have fair curly hair . . . And I still have the excitement and hope of the eternal quest. I never forget that a little boy is born for every little girl. And even if we haven't met yet, we are both growing old together, and if we're fated to meet, we *shall*.'

Iris thought sceptically of the mature men who refuse to adhere to the calendar, as she listened with rising resentment. She wanted quiet –

but Miss Froy's voice went on and on, like the unreeling of an endless talking-picture.

Presently, however, Miss Froy recaptured her interest, for she began to talk of languages.

'I speak ten, including English,' she said. 'At first, when you're in a strange country, you can't understand one word, and you feel like a puppy thrown into a pond. You flounder and struggle, so unless you want to drown you've simply got to pick it up. By the end of a year you're as fluent as a native. But I always insist on staying a second year, for the sake of idiomatic polish.'

'*I* expect foreigners to speak English,' declared Iris.

'When you're off the map they may not, and then you might find yourself in a terrible fix. Shall I tell you a true story?'

Without waiting for encouragement, Miss Froy spun a yarn which was not calculated to cool Iris's inflamed nerves. It was all very vague and anonymous, but the actual horror was stark.

A certain woman had been certified as insane, but owing to a blunder the ambulance went to the wrong house and forcibly took away an Englishwoman, who did not understand a word of the language, or of her destination. In her indignation and horror at finding herself in a private asylum, she became so vehement and violent that she was kept, at first, under the influence of drugs.

When the mistake was found out, the doctor – who was a most unscrupulous character – was afraid to admit it. At the time he was in financial difficulties, and he feared it might ruin his reputation. So he planned to detain the Englishwoman until he could release her as officially cured.

'But she couldn't know she wasn't in for life,' explained Miss Froy, working up the agony. 'The horror of it would probably have driven her really insane, only a nurse exposed the doctor's plot, out of revenge. But can you imagine the awful position of that poor Englishwoman? Trapped, with no one to make enquiries about her, or even to know she had disappeared, for she was merely a friendless foreigner, staying a night here and a night there at some pension. She didn't understand a word – she couldn't explain – '

'Please *stop*,' broke in Iris. 'I can imagine it all. Vividly. But would you mind if we stopped talking?'

'Oh, certainly. Aren't you well? It's difficult to be sure, with your sunburn, but I thought you looked green, once or twice.'

'I'm very fit, thanks. But my head aches a bit. I've just had a touch of sunstroke.'

'Sunstroke? When?'

Knowing that Miss Froy's curiosity had to be appeased, Iris gave a brief account of her attack. As she did so, she glanced round the carriage. It was evident, from the blank faces, that – with one exception – the passengers did not understand English.

Iris could not be certain about the Baroness. She had the slightly stupid expression of an autocrat who has acquired power through birth and not enterprise; yet there was a gleam of intelligence in her eyes that betrayed secret interest in the story.

'Oh, you poor soul,' cried Miss Froy, who overflowed with sympathy. 'Why didn't you stop me chattering before? I'll give you some aspirin.'

Although she hated any fuss, it was a relief to Iris when she was able to sit back in her corner while Miss Froy hunted through the contents of her bag.

'I don't think you had better have dinner in the restaurant-car,' she decided. 'I'll bring you something here, later. Now, swallow these tablets, and then try to get a little nap.'

After Iris had closed her eyes, she could still hear Miss Froy fluttering about her, like a fussy little bird on guard.

It gave her a curious sense of protection, while the carriage was so warm that she soon became pleasantly drowsy.

As the drug began to take effect, her thoughts grew jumbled, while her head kept jerking forward. Presently she lost consciousness of place but felt herself moving onwards with the motion of the train, as though she were riding. Sometimes she took a fence, when the seat seemed to leap under her, leaving her suspended in the air.

Clankety-clankety-*clank*. On and on. She kept moving steadily upwards. Clankety-clankety-*clank*. Then the rhythm of the train changed, and she seemed to be sliding backwards down a long slope. Click-click-click-click. The wheels rattled over the rails, with a sound of castanets.

She was sinking deeper and deeper, while the carriage vibrated like the throbbing of an aeroplane. It was bearing her away – sweeping her outside the carriage – to the edge of a drop . . .

With a violent start she opened her eyes. Her heart was leaping, as though she had actually fallen from a height. At first she wondered where she was; then, as she gradually recognised her surroundings, she found that she was staring at the Baroness.

In slight confusion she looked away quickly to the opposite seat.

To her surprise, Miss Froy's place was empty.

10

The Vacant Seat

Iris was ungratefully glad of Miss Froy's absence. Her doze had confused rather than refreshed her, and she felt she could not endure another long instalment of family history She wanted peace; and while it was impossible to have quiet amid the roar and rush of the train, she considered herself entitled, at least, to personal privacy.

As regarded the other passengers, she was free from any risk of contact. Not one of them took the slightest notice of her. The Baroness slept in her corner – the others sat motionless and silent. Inside the carriage, the atmosphere was warm and airless as a conservatory.

It soothed Iris to a tranquil torpidity. She felt numbed to thought and feeling, as though she were in a semi-trance and incapable of raising a finger, or framing two consecutive words. Patches of green scenery fluttered past the window, like a flock of emerald birds. The Baroness's heavy breathing rose and fell with the regularity of a tide.

Iris vaguely dreaded Miss Froy's return, which must destroy the narcotic spell. At any moment, now, she might hear the brisk step in the corridor. Presumably Miss Froy had gone to wash, and had been obliged to wait her turn, owing to the crowd.

Hoping for the best, Iris closed her eyes again. At first she was apprehensive whenever anyone passed by the widow, but each false alarm increased her sense of security. Miss Froy ceased to be a menace and shrank to a mere name. The octogenarian parents went back to their rightful place inside some old photograph-album. Even Sock – that shaggy absurd mongrel, whom Iris had grown to like – was blurred to an appealing memory.

Clankety-clankety-*clank*. The sound of breathing swelled to the surge of a heavy sea, sucking at the rocks. Muted by the thunder of the train, it boomed in unison with the throb of the engine. Clankety-clankety-*clank*.

Suddenly the Baroness's snores rose to an elephantine trumpet which jerked Iris awake. She started up in her seat – tense with apprehension and with every faculty keyed up. The shock had vibrated some seventh sense which made her expectant of disaster, and she glanced swiftly at Miss Froy's place.

It was still empty.

She was surprised by her pang of disappointment. Not long ago she had been praying for Miss Froy's return to be delayed; but now she felt lonely and eager to welcome her.

'I expect I'll soon be cursing her again,' she admitted to herself. 'But, anyway, she is human.'

She glanced at the blonde beauty, who was beginning to remind her of a wax model in a shop window. Not a flat wave of her honey-gold hair was out of place. Even her eyes had the transparency of blue wax.

Chilled by the contrast to the vital little spinster, Iris looked at her watch. The late hour, which told her that she had slept longer than she had suspected, also made her feel rather worried about Miss Froy's prolonged absence.

'She's had enough time to take a bath,' she thought. 'I – I hope nothing's wrong.'

The idea was so disturbing that she exerted all her common sense to dislodge it.

'Absurd,' she told herself. 'What could happen to her? It's not night, when she might open the wrong door by mistake, and step out of the train in the dark. Besides, she's an experienced traveller – not a helpless fool like myself. And she knows about a hundred languages.'

A smile flickered over her lips as she remembered one of the little spinster's confidences.

'Languages give me a sense of power. If an international crisis arose in a railway carriage, and there were no interpreters, I could step into the breach and, perhaps, alter the destinies of the world.'

The recollection suggested an explanation for Miss Froy's untenanted seat. Probably she was indulging her social instincts by talking to congenial strangers. She was not divided from them by any barrier of language. Moreover, she was in holiday mood and wanted to tell every one that she was going home.

'I'll give her another half-hour,' decided Iris. 'She must be back by then.'

As she looked out of the window, the clouded sky of late afternoon filled her with melancholy. The train had been gradually descending from the heights, and was now steaming through a lush green valley. Mauve crocuses cropped up amid thick pastures, which were darkened by moisture. The scene was definitely autumnal and made her realise that summer was over.

The time slipped away too quickly, because she dreaded reaching the limit which she had appointed. If Miss Froy did not return she would have to make a decision, and she did not know what to do. Of course, as she reminded herself, it was not really her business at all; but her uneasiness grew with the passing of each five minutes of grace.

Presently there was a stir among the other passengers. The little girl began to whine fretfully, while the father appeared to reason with her. Iris guessed that she had complained of sleepiness, and had been persuaded to take a nap, but first had to endure the mother's preparations to keep her daughter's trim appearance intact.

After the black patent belt and the organdie collar had been removed, she drew out a net and arranged it carefully over the little girl's permanent wave. The blonde beauty showed her first signs of animation as she watched the process, but her interest died when the matron pulled off her child's buckled shoes and replaced them with a pair of shabby bedroom-slippers.

Finally she pointed to Miss Froy's vacant place.

Iris felt a rush of disproportionate resentment when she saw the little girl sitting in the spinster's seat. She wished she could protest by signs, but was too self-conscious to risk making an exhibition of herself.

'When she comes back, Miss Froy will soon turn her out,' she thought.

Upon reflection, however, she was not so sure of direct action. When she remembered the friendly spirit Miss Froy displayed towards every one, she felt certain that she had already established a pleasant understanding with her fellow passengers.

The little girl was so heavy with sleep that she closed her eyes directly she curled up in the corner. The parents looked at each other and smiled. They caught the blonde beauty's attention, and she, too, nodded with polite appreciation. Only Iris remained outside the circle.

She knew that she was unjustly prejudiced, since she was the real interloper, yet she hated this calm appropriation of Miss Froy's place. It was as though the other passengers were taking unfair advantage of her absence – since she could not turn out a sleeping child.

Or even as though they were acting on some secret intelligence.

They were behaving as though they *knew* she was not coming back. In a panic, Iris looked at her watch and found, to her dismay, that the half-hour had slipped away.

The lapse of time was registered outside the window. The overcast sky had grown darker and the first mists were beginning to collect in the corners of the green saturated fields. Instead of crocuses, she saw the pallid fungoid growths of toadstools or mushrooms.

As the sadness of twilight stole over her, Iris began to hunger for company. She wanted cheerful voices, lights, laughter; but although she thought wistfully of the crowd, she was even more anxious to see a little lined face and hear the high rushing voice.

Now that she was gone, she seemed indefinite as a dream. Iris could not reconstruct any clear picture of her, or understand why she should leave such a blank.

'What was she *like*?' she wondered.

At that moment she chanced to look up at the rack. To her surprise, Miss Froy's suitcase was no longer there.

In spite of logic, her nerves began to flutter at this new development. While she told herself that it was obvious that Miss Froy had moved to another compartment, the circumstances did not fit in. To begin with, the train was so overcrowded that it would be difficult to find an empty unreserved place.

On the other hand, Miss Froy had mentioned some muddle about her seat. It was barely possible that it had proved available, after all.

'No,' decided Iris, 'the Baroness had already paid the difference for her to travel first. And I'm sure she wouldn't leave me without a word of explanation. She talked of bringing me dinner. Besides, I owe her for my tea. I'm simply bound to find her.'

She looked at the other passengers, who might hold the key to the mystery. Too distracted now to care about appearances, she made an effort to communicate with them. Feeling that 'English' was the word which should have lightened their darkness, she started in German.

'Wo ist die Dame *English*?'

They shook their heads and shrugged, to show that they did not understand. So she made a second attempt.

'Où est la dame *English*?'

As no sign of intelligence dawned on their faces, she spoke to them in her own language.

'Where is the English lady?'

The effort was hopeless. She could not reach them, and they showed no wish to help her. As they stared at her, she was chilled by their indifference, as though she were outside the pale of civilised obligations.

Feeling suddenly desperate, she pointed to Miss Froy's seat, and then arched her brows in exaggerated enquiry. This time she succeeded in arousing an emotion, for the man and his wife exchange amused glances, while the blonde's lip curled with disdain. Then, as though she scented entertainment, the little girl opened her black eyes and broke into a snigger, which she suppressed instantly at a warning glance from her father.

Stung by their ridicule, Iris glared at them as she crossed to the Baroness and shook her arm.

'Wake up, please,' she entreated.

She heard a smothered gasp from the other passengers, as though she had committed some act of sacrilege. But she was too overwrought to remember to apologise when the Baroness raised her lids and stared at her with outraged majesty.

'Where is Miss Froy?' asked Iris.

'Miss Froy?' repeated the Baroness. 'I do not know anyone who has that name.'

Iris pointed to the seat which was occupied by the little girl.

'She sat *there*,' she said.

The Baroness shook her head.

'You make a mistake,' she declared. 'No English lady has sat there ever.'

Iris's head began to reel.

'But she *did*,' she insisted. 'I talked to her. And we went and had tea together. You must remember.'

'There is nothing to remember.' The Baroness spoke with slow emphasis. 'I do not understand what you mean at all. I tell you this . . . There has been no English lady, here, in this carriage, never, at any time, except you. You are the only English lady here.'

11

Needle in a Haystack

Iris opened her lips only to close them again. She had the helpless feeling of being shouted down by some terrific blast of sound. The Baroness had made a statement which was an outrage on the evidence of her senses; but it was backed up by the force of an overpowering authority.

As she held the girl's eye, challenging her denial, Iris looked at the leaden eyelids, the deep lines graven from nose to chin – the heavy obstinate chin. The lips were drawn down in a grimace which reminded her of a mask of the Muse of Tragedy.

She realised that further protest was useless. The Baroness would flatten any attempt at opposition with relentless pressure. The most she could do was to acknowledge defeat with a shrug which disdained further argument.

Her composure was only bluff for she felt utterly bewildered as she sank back in her seat. She was scarcely conscious of slides of twilight scenery streaming past the window, or of the other passengers. A village shot out of the shadows and vanished again in the dimness. She caught the flash of a huddle of dark roofs and the white streak of a little river, which boiled under a hooded bridge.

The next second the church tower and wooden houses were left behind as the express rocked on its way back to England. It lurched and shrieked as though in unison with the tangle of Iris's thoughts.

'No Miss Froy? Absurd. The woman must be mad. Does she take me for a fool? . . . But why does she say it? *Why*?'

It was this lack of motive which worried her most. Miss Froy was such a harmless little soul that there could be no reason for her suppression. She was on friendly terms with everyone.

Yet the fact remained that she had disappeared, for Iris was positive now that she would not come back to the carriage. In a sudden fit of nerves she sprang to her feet.

'She must be somewhere on the train,' she argued. 'I'll find her.'

She would not admit it, but her own confidence was flawed by the difficulty of finding a reason for Miss Froy's absence. She had taken Iris under her wing, so that it was entirely out of line with her character as a kindly little busybody for her to withdraw in such an abrupt and final manner.

'Does she think I might be sickening for some infectious disease?' she wondered. 'After all, she's so terribly keen to get back to her old parents and the dog, that she wouldn't dare run risks of being held up. Naturally she would sacrifice me.'

Her progress down the train was a most unpleasant experience. It had been difficult when Miss Froy acted the part of a fussy little tug and had cleared a passage for her. Now that more passengers had grown tired of sitting in cramped compartments and had emerged to stretch, or smoke, the corridor was as closely packed with tourists as a melon with seeds.

Iris did not know how to ask them to step aside and she did not like to push. Moreover, the fact that she was attractive did not escape the notice of some of the men. Each time a swerve of the express caused her to lurch against some susceptible stranger, he usually believed that she was making overtures.

Although she grew hot with annoyance her chief emotion was one of futility. She had no hope of finding Miss Froy in such confusion. Whenever she peered inside a fresh compartment, she always saw the same blur of faces.

Because she was beginning to run a temperature, these faces appeared as bleared and distorted as creations of a nightmare. It was a relief when, having worked her way down the train in an unavailing search, she saw the vicar and his wife in one of the crowded carriages.

They were sitting opposite each other. Mr Barnes had closed his eyes and his face was set. In spite of his sunburn it was plain that he was far from well and was exerting his willpower to subdue his symptoms.

His wife watched him with strained attention. She looked wan and miserable, as though – in imagination – she was sharing his every pang of train-sickness.

She did not smile when Iris struggled inside and spoke to her.

'Sorry to bother you but I'm looking for my friend.'

'Oh, yes?'

There was the familiar forced brightness in Mrs Barnes's voice but her eyes were tragic.

'You remember her?' prompted Iris. 'She sent the waiter with your tea.'

The vicar came to life.

'It was kind indeed,' he said. 'Will you give her my special thanks?'

'When I find her,' promised Iris. 'She went out of the carriage some time ago – and she hasn't come back.'

'I haven't noticed her pass the window,' said Mrs Barnes. 'Perhaps she went to wash. Anyway, she couldn't possibly be lost.'

Iris could see that she was concentrating on her husband and had no interest in some unknown woman.

'Can I find her for you?' offered the vicar manfully, struggling to his feet.

'Certainly *not*.' His wife's voice was sharp. 'Don't be absurd, Kenneth. You don't know what she looks like.'

'That's true. I should be more hindrance than help.'

The vicar sank back gratefully and looked up at Iris with a forced smile. 'Isn't it humiliating to be such a wretched traveller?' he asked

'Try not to talk,' advised his wife.

Iris took the hint and went out of the compartment. She, too, considered the vicar's weakness was a major misfortune. He was not only a man of high principle but she was sure that he possessed imagination and sympathy; yet she was unable to appeal to him for help because nature had laid him low.

Because she was beginning to fear that she faced failure she grew more frantic with determination to find Miss Froy. If she failed she was loaded with a heavy responsibility. Of all the people in the train she – alone – seemed conscious of the disappearance of a passenger.

She shrank from the prospect of trying to arouse these callous strangers from their apathy. As she clung to handrails and was buffeted by the impact of other tourists pushing their way past her, she hated them all. In her strung-up condition she could not realise that these people might experience her own sensations were they suddenly placed in a crowded London Tube or New York Subway and jostled by seemingly hostile and indifferent strangers.

When she reached the reserved portion of the train, the blind was still pulled down over the Todhunters' window, but she recognised the Misses Flood-Porter in one of the reserved coupés. They sat on different sides of the tiny compartment – each with her feet stretched out on the seat. The elder lady wore horn-rimmed glasses and was reading a Tauchnitz, while Miss Rose smoked a cigarette.

They looked very content with life and although kind-hearted, the sight of others standing in the corridors subtly enhanced their appreciation of their own comfort.

'Smug,' thought Iris bitterly.

They made her realise her own position. She reminded herself that her place, too, was in a reserved compartment, instead of fighting her way into the privacy of strange people.

'Why am I taking it?' she wondered as she met the unfriendly glance of the ladies. Miss Rose's was perceptibly more frigid as though she were practising gradations in preparation for the cut *direct* at Victoria Station.

At last she had combed the train with the exception of the restaurant-car. Now that tea was finished it was invaded by men who wanted to drink and smoke in comfort.

As she lingered at the entrance to make sure that Miss Froy was not inside seeking her soul-mate of whom she had spoken, a hopeful young man touched Iris's arm. He said something unintelligible, which she translated as an invitation to refreshment, and leered into her face.

Furious at the liberty, she shook him off and was on the point of turning away, when, amid the rumble of masculine voices, she distinguished the distinctive vowels of an Oxford accent.

She was trying to locate it when she caught sight of the spade-bearded doctor. His bald, domed head, seen through the murk of smoke, reminded her of a moon rising through the mist. His face was blanched and bony – his dead eyes were magnified by his thick glasses.

As they picked her out with an impersonal gaze, she felt as though she had been pinned down and classified as a type.

Suddenly – for no reason at all – she thought of the doctor in Miss Froy's tale of horror.

12

Witnesses

Although she was conscious of the interest she aroused, Iris was too overwrought to care. Raising her voice she made a general appeal.

'Please. Is there anyone English here?'

The spectacle of a pretty girl in distress made a young man leap to his feet. He was of rather untidy appearance with a pleasant ordinary face and audacious hazel eyes.

'Can I be of use?' he asked quickly.

The voice was familiar to Iris. She had heard it at the railway station, just before her sunstroke. This was the young man who had been opposed to trial by jury. He looked exactly as she had pictured him; he had even a rebellious tuft of hair, of the kind that lies down under treatment, as meekly as a trained hound, but which springs up again immediately the brush is put away.

In other circumstances she would have been attracted to him instinctively; but in this crisis he seemed to lack ballast. 'Gets fresh with barmaids and cheeks traffic-cops,' she reflected swiftly.

'Well?' prompted the young man.

To her dismay Iris found it difficult to control her voice or collect her thoughts when she tried to explain the situation.

'It's all rather complicated,' she said shakily. 'I'm in a jam. At least, it's nothing to do with me. But I'm sure there's some horrible mistake and I can't speak a word of this miserable language.'

'That's all right,' said the young man encouragingly. 'I speak the lingo. Just put me wise to the trouble.'

While Iris still hesitated, doubtful of her choice of champion, a tall, thin man rose reluctantly from his seat, as though chivalry were a painful duty. In this case his academic appearance was not misleading, for directly he spoke Iris recognised the characteristic voice of the professor of modern languages.

'May I offer my services as an interpreter?' he asked formally.

'He's no good,' broke in the young man. 'He only knows grammar. But I can swear in the vernacular and we may need a spot of profanity.'

Iris checked her laugh for she realised that she was on the verge of hysteria.

'An Englishwoman has disappeared from the train,' she told the professor. 'She's a *real* person, but the Baroness says – '

Her voice suddenly failed as she noticed that the doctor was looking at her with fixed attention.

The professor's glacial eye also reminded her that she was making an exhibition of herself. 'Could you pull yourself together to make a coherent statement?' he asked.

The chill in his voice was tonic for it braced her to compress the actual situation into a few words. This time she was careful to make no allusion to the Baroness but confined herself to Miss Froy's non-return to the carriage. To her relief the professor appeared to be impressed, for he rubbed his long chin gravely.

'You said – an *English* lady?' he asked.

'Yes,' replied Iris eagerly. 'Miss Froy. She's a governess.'

'Ah, yes . . . Now, are you absolutely certain that she is nowhere on the train?'

'Positive. I've looked everywhere.'

'H'm. She would not be likely to leave her reserved seat for an inadequate reason. At what time precisely did she leave the compartment?'

'I don't know. I was asleep. When I woke up she wasn't there.'

'Then the first step is to interview the other passengers. If the lady does not return during that time, I may consider calling the guard and asking for an official examination of the train.'

The young man winked at Iris, to direct her attention to the fact that the professor was in his element.

'Gaudy chance for you to rub up the lingo, professor,' he said.

The remark reminded Iris that while the professor's acquaintance with the language would be academic, the young man promised a more colloquial knowledge. This was important, since she was beginning to think that the confusion over Miss Froy sprang from the Baroness's imperfect command of English. Her accent was good, but if she could not understand all that was said she would never admit ignorance.

Determined to leave nothing to chance, Iris appealed to the frivolous youth. 'Will you come, too, and swear for us?' she asked.

'Like a bird,' he replied. 'A parrot, I mean, of course. Lead on, professor.'

Iris's spirits rose as they made their way back through the train. Although she was still worried about Miss Froy, her companion infused her with a sense of comradeship.

'My name's Hare,' he told her. 'Much too long for you to remember. Better call me Maximilian – or, if you prefer it, Max. What's yours?'

'Iris Carr.'

'Mrs?'

'Miss.'

'Good. I'm an engineer out here. I'm building a dam up in some mountains.'

'What fun. I'm nothing.'

Full of confidence in the support of her compatriots, Iris felt exultant as they neared her carriage. Tourists – seated on their suitcases – blocked the way and children chased each other, regardless of adult toes. As a pioneer Hare was better than Miss Froy. While she hooted to warn others of their approach, he rammed a clear passage, like an ice-plough.

The professor stood aside to allow Iris to enter the compartment first. She noticed immediately that the spade-bearded doctor was seated beside the Baroness and was talking to her in low rapid tones. He must have left the restaurant-car in a hurry.

The fact made her feel slightly uneasy.

'He's one jump ahead of me,' she thought.

The family party shared a bag of nectarines and took no notice of her, while the blonde was absorbed in rebuilding the curves of her geranium lips. The Baroness sat as unmoved as a huge black granite statue.

There was a glint in Iris's eyes when she made her announcement.

'Two English gentlemen have come to make some enquiries about Miss Froy.'

The Baroness reared up her head and glared at her, but made no comment. It was impossible to tell whether the announcement were a shock.

'Will you kindly allow me to enter?' asked the professor.

In order to make more room for the investigation, Iris went out into the corridor. From where she stood she could see the invalid's carriage and the nursing-sister who sat at the window. In spite of her pre-occupation, she noticed that the woman's face was not repulsive but merely stolid.

'Am I exaggerating everything?' she wondered nervously. 'Perhaps, after all, I'm not reliable.'

In spite of her pity for the wretched patient it was a real relief when the original nurse, with the callous expression, appeared at the door. The fog of mystery, together with the throb of her temples, combined to make her feel uncertain of herself.

She smiled when Hare spoke to her.

'I'm going to listen-in,' he told her. 'The professor's bound to be a don at theory, but he might slip up in practice, so I'll check up for you.'

Iris looked over his shoulder as she tried to follow the proceedings. The professor seemed to carry out his investigation with thoroughness, patience and personal dignity. Although he bowed to the Baroness with respect before he explained the situation, he conveyed an impression of his own importance.

The personage inclined her head and then appeared to address a general question to her fellow passengers. Iris noticed how her proud gaze swept each face and that her voice had a ring of authority.

Following her lead the professor interrogated every person in turn – only to receive the inevitable shake of the head which seemed the chief language of the country.

Remembering her own experience, Iris whispered to Hare, 'Can't they understand him?'

He replied by a nod which told her that he was listening closely and did not wish to be disturbed. Thrown on her own resources she made her own notes and was amused to remark that – in spite of being accustomed to teach mixed classes – the professor was scared of the ladies, including the little girl.

Very soon he confined his questions to the businessman, who answered with slow deliberation. He was obviously trying to be helpful to a foreigner, who might have difficulty in understanding him. In the end he produced his card and gave it to the professor, who read it, and then returned it with a bow of thanks.

In spite of the general atmosphere of politeness Iris grew impatient and tugged Hare's arm.

'Is he finding out anything about Miss Froy?' she asked.

She was unpleasantly surprised by his grave face.

'Oh, it's rather involved,' he told her. 'All about where is the pen of the aunt of my gardener!'

Her confidence began to cloud as she grew conscious of an unfriendly atmosphere. The Baroness did not remove her eyes from her face during her short speech, to which the professor listened with marked respect. At its end she made a sign to the doctor, as though ordering him to support her statement.

Hitherto he had been a silent witness of the scene. His white impassive face and dead eyes made him resemble one newly returned from the grave, to attend a repeat performance of the revue of life before eternal damnation.

But as he began to talk at his patron's bidding he grew vital and even vehement, for he used his hands to emphasise his words.

When he had finished speaking the professor turned to Iris. 'You appear to have made an extraordinary mistake,' he said. 'No one in this carriage knows anything about the lady you *say* is missing.'

Iris stared at him incredulously.

'Are you telling me I invented her?' she asked angrily.

'I hardly know what to think.'

'Then I'll tell you. All these people are telling lies.'

Even as she spoke Iris realised the absurdity of her charge. It was altogether too wholesale. No rational person could believe that the passengers would unite to bear false witness. The family party in particular looked solid and respectable, while the father was probably the equivalent of her own lawyer.

The professor was of the same opinion, for his manner grew stiffer.

'The people whom you accuse of being liars are citizens of good standing,' he said, 'and are known personally to the Baroness, who vouches for their integrity. The gentleman is not only a well-known banker in the district, but is also the Baroness's banker. The young lady' – he glanced warily at the blonde – 'is the daughter of her agent.'

'I can't help that,' protested Iris. 'All I know is that I owe Miss Froy for my tea. She paid for me.'

'We can check up on that,' interrupted Hare. 'If she paid, you'll be so much to the good. Just count up your loose cash.'

Iris shook her head. 'I don't know how much I had,' she confessed. 'I'm hopeless about money. I'm always getting refer-to-drawer cheques.'

Although the professor's mouth turned down at the admission, he intervened in proof of his sense of fair play.

'If you had tea together,' he said, 'the waiter should remember your companion. I'll interview him next, if you will give me a description of the lady.'

Iris had been dreading this moment because of her clouded recollection of Miss Froy. She knew that she had barely glanced at her the whole time they were together During tea she had been half-blinded by the sun, and when they returned to the carriage she had kept her eyes closed on account of her headache. On their way to and from the restaurant-car, she had always been either in front or behind her companion.

'I can't tell you much,' she faltered. 'You see, there's nothing much about her to catch hold of. She's middle-aged, and ordinary – and rather colourless.'

'Tall or short? Fat or thin? Fair or dark?' prompted Hare.

'Medium. But she said she had fair curly hair.'

' "Said"?' repeated the professor. 'Didn't you notice it for yourself?'

'No. But I think it looked faded. I remember she had blue eyes, though.'

'Not very enlightening, I'm afraid,' remarked the professor.

'What did she wear?' asked Hare suddenly.

'Tweed. Oatmeal, flecked with brown. Swagger coat, finger-length, with patch pockets and stitched cuffs and scarf. The ends of the scarf

were fastened with small blue bone buttons and she wore a natural
tussore shirt-blouse, stitched with blue – a different shade – with a
small blue handkerchief in the breast-pocket. I'm afraid I didn't notice
details much. Her hat was made of the same material, with a stitched
brim and a Récamier crown, with a funny bright-blue feather stuck
through the band.'

'Stop,' commanded Hare. 'Now that you've remembered the hat,
can't you make another effort and put a face under it?'

He was so delighted with the result of his experiment that his
dejection was ludicrous when Iris shook her head in the old provoking
manner.

'No, I can't remember any face. You see, I had such a frantic headache.'

'Exactly,' commented the professor dryly. 'Cause and effect, I'm
afraid. The doctor has been telling us that you had a slight sunstroke.'

As though awaiting his cue the doctor – who had been listening
intently – spoke to Iris.

'That blow of the sun explains all,' he said, speaking in English, with
slow emphasis. 'It has given you a delirium. You saw someone who is
not there. Afterwards, you went to sleep, and you dream. Then,
presently, you awake and you are much better. So you saw Miss Froy
no more . . . She is nothing but a delirium – a dream.'

13

A Dream Within a Dream

At first Iris was too surprised to protest. She had the bewildered
sensation of being the one sane person in a mad world. Her astonishment turned to indignation when the professor caught Hare's eye and
gave a nod of mutual understanding.

Then he spoke to Iris in a formal voice.

'I think we may accept that as final. If I had known the circumstances
I should not have intervened. I hope you will soon feel better.'

'We'd better clear and let Miss Carr get some quiet,' suggested Hare,
with a doubtful grin.

Iris felt as though she were being smothered with featherbed
opposition. Controlling her anger she forced herself to speak calmly.

'I'm afraid it's not so simple as that. As far as I'm concerned the
matter's by no means ended. Why should you imagine I'm telling a lie?'

'I do not,' the professor assured her. 'I am convinced it is your mistake.

But, since you've raised the point of fairness, you must admit that the weight of evidence is against you. I have to be fair . . . Can *you* explain why six persons should lie?'

Iris had a sudden flash of intuition.

'I can't,' she said, 'unless one person started the lie, and the others are backing her up. In that case it's only her word against mine. And as I'm English and you're English and this concerns an Englishwoman, it's your duty to believe *me*.'

As she spoke Iris challenged the Baroness in an accusing stare.

Although the personage heard the charge with complete composure, the professor coughed in protest. 'You mustn't confuse patriotism with prejudice,' he said. 'Besides your insinuation is absurd. What motive would the Baroness have for telling a lie?'

Iris's brain began to swim.

'I don't know,' she said weakly. 'It's all such a mystery. No one could want to injure Miss Froy. She's too insignificant. Besides, she was proud of having no enemies. And she told me herself that the Baroness had been kind.'

'What have I done?' asked the Baroness blandly.

'She said that there was a muddle about her place and you paid the excess-fare for her to travel in here.'

'That was charming of me. I'm gratified to hear of my generosity. Unfortunately I know nothing of it. But the ticket-collector should be able to refresh my memory.'

The professor turned to Iris dutifully. 'What am I to do?' he asked. 'You are making things rather difficult by persisting in this attitude. But, if you insist, I will question the man.'

'I'll dig him out,' offered Hare.

Iris knew that he wanted a chance to escape. She felt that his sympathies were with her while he withheld his faith.

After he had gone the professor began to talk to the Baroness and the doctor, presumably for the sake of further practice. Suspicious of every glance and inflection, Iris believed that he was explaining the delicacy of his position and stressing the absurdity of the charge, for the Baroness looked almost as benevolent as a sated tigress that kills just for the sport.

She was glad when Hare – his rebellious tuft sticking out like a feather – battled his way down the corridor, followed by the ticket-collector. He was a sturdy young man in a very tight uniform, and he reminded Iris of a toy soldier with a blob of crimson on each broad cheek and a tiny black waxed moustache.

As he entered the Baroness spoke to him sharply and then waved to the professor to continue.

By this time Iris's nerve was shattered; she was so sure that the ticket-collector would prove another victim to mass-hypnotism that she was prepared when Hare made a grimace.

'He's telling the old, old story,' he said.

'Of course he is.' Iris tried to laugh. 'I expect he was one of her peasants. He looks bucolic. She seems to own the lot – including you and the professor.'

'Now, don't get het up,' he urged. 'I know just what you are feeling, because I've been through this myself. I'll tell you about it, if I can dislodge this young lady.'

The little girl, who had been making precocious eyes at Hare, responded to his invitation to move with shrugs and pouts of protest. All the same she reluctantly went back to her original place, while he squeezed into the corner originally occupied by the elusive spinster.

'Cheer up,' he said. 'Unless your Miss Froy was invisible, other people in the train must have seen her.'

'I know,' nodded Iris. 'But I can't think. My brain's too sticky.'

The professor, who was just leaving the compartment, caught the drift of Hare's argument, for he turned back to speak to Iris.

'If you can produce some definite proof of this lady's existence, I'm still open to conviction. But I sincerely hope that you will not expose us and yourself to further ridicule.'

Iris felt too limp for defiance.

'Thank you,' she said meekly. 'Where shall I find you?'

'In the reserved portion.'

'We're sharing a bunny-hutch,' supplemented Hare. 'Didn't you know we're rich? We started a prosperity chain.'

'I hate that man,' burst out Iris when the professor had gone.

'Oh, no,' protested Hare, 'he's not a bad old fossil. You've got him scared stiff because you're young and attractive.'

Then the grin faded from his lips.

'I want to bore you with a true story,' he said. 'Some years ago, I was playing in an international at Twickenham. Just before the match both teams were presented to the Prince of Wales and he shook hands with all of us. Well, after I'd scored the winning try – I had to slip that in – I got kicked on the head in a scrum and passed out. Later on, when I was fairly comfortable in a private ward at the hospital, the nurse came in, all of a flutter, and said there was a special visitor to see me.'

'The Prince?' asked Iris, trying to force an intelligent interest.

'The same. Of course, he didn't stay more than a minute. Just smiled at me and said he hoped I'd soon be all right and he was sorry about my accident. I was so steamed up I thought I wouldn't sleep a wink, but I dropped off the instant he had gone. Next morning the nurses said, "Weren't you pleased to see your captain?" '

'Captain?'

'Yes, the captain of the team. It was definitely *not* the Prince . . . And yet I saw him as plainly as I see you. He shook hands with me and said something nice about my try. He was *real*. And that's what a spot of head trouble can do to the best of us.'

Iris set her lips obstinately.

'I thought you believed in me,' she said. 'But you're like the rest. Please go away.'

'I will, because I'm sure you ought to keep quiet. Try and get some sleep.'

'No. I've got to think this out. If I let myself believe all of you, I should be afraid I was going mad. And I'm not. I'm *not*.'

'Now take it easy.'

'What a soothing nurse you'd make! You only want a silly cap. Listen.' Iris dropped her voice. 'I'm extra in the dark, because I couldn't understand these questions. Do you really *know* the language?'

'Better than English now. And it was so elementary that even the professor couldn't slip up. Sorry – but there are no holes anywhere . . . But you look all in. Let me get you a life-saver.'

'No. Miss Froy promised she'd get me something and I prefer to wait for her.' Her defiant eyes told Hare that she was nailing her colours to the mast. Since he regarded Miss Froy as a kind of ghost, he did not think that Iris would derive benefit from anything she might bring, so he resolved to renew his offer later. Meanwhile he could serve her best by leaving her alone.

Just as he was going he remembered something and beckoned Iris into the corridor.

'There was just one bit I didn't tumble to,' he confessed. 'The Baroness spoke to the ticket chap in a dialect which was Chinese to me.'

'Then that proves they come from the same district,' cried Iris triumphantly.

'Hum. But as we don't know what she said it's not too helpful. Salaams. See you later.'

After Hare had gone Iris crouched in her corner, rocking with the vibration of the train. It was clattering through a succession of short tunnels and the air was full of sound, as though a giant roller were flattening out the sky. The noise worried her acutely. She had scarcely eaten all day and was beginning to feel exhausted. But although she was unused to being ill, and was consequently frightened, she was far more alarmed by the jangling of her brain.

She started violently when a nursing-sister appeared in the doorway and beckoned to the doctor. She hardly noticed the relief of his absence, because her thoughts raced in a confused circle round the central incident of the blackout.

'I was on the platform one second – and the next second I went out. Where did I go? Was the waking up in the waiting-room, and all those women, and the funny little old porter – was all that *real*? Of course it was, or I should not be on the train . . .

'But I met Miss Froy *afterwards*. They say she's only my dream. So, if she's a dream, it means that I've dreamed the waiting-room and the train and that I'm not on the train at all. I'm not awake yet . . . If it was true, it would be enough to drive anyone mad.'

She resolutely fought back the rising tide of hysteria.

'But it's absurd. I am awake and I'm here in this train. So I *did* meet Miss Froy . . . Only I'm up against some mystery and I have to fight a pack of lies. All right, then, I *will*.'

At this stage her concern was for herself, rather than for Miss Froy. She had been spoiled since her birth, so it was natural for her to be selfish; and because that self was a gay and charming entity, the world had united to keep her fixed at her special angle.

But now her ego was getting involved with the fate of an obscure and unattractive spinster. Once again she began to review the incidents of their meeting. And then, suddenly, her clouded brain cleared and a sealed cell in her memory became unblocked.

The Baroness looked at her as she sprang from her seat. 'Is madame worse?' she asked.

'Better, thanks,' replied Iris. 'And I'm going to test some English memories, just for a change. I'm going to talk to some English visitors from my hotel who saw me with Miss Froy.'

14

Fresh Evidence

Now that she was about to establish Miss Froy's existence, Iris began to wonder what had become of her. When she remembered her exhaustive search of the train it seemed positive that she could not be there. But it was also impossible for her to be anywhere else.

The corridors and carriages were thronged with tourists, so that she could not open a door or window to jump out without attracting immediate attention. It was equally certain that no one could make a parcel of her and dump her on the permanent way without becoming an object of general interest.

There was no place for her to hide – nor could Iris conceive any motive for such a course. In short, she was protected from any form of injury – accidental or intentional – by the presence of a cloud of witnesses.

In despair Iris shelved the problem.

'She can't be proved missing until it's proved that she was there in the first place,' she argued. 'That's my job. After that, the others must carry on.'

As she remembered the professor's standard for reliable evidence she felt she could understand a showman's pride in his exhibits. Her witnesses must satisfy the most exacting taste – being British to the core.

The Baroness looked at her when she opened her bag and drew out her pocket-mirror and lipstick. Although her detachment was complete and her face void of expression, she somehow conveyed an impression of secret activity, as though she were spinning mental threads.

'She's pitting her brain against mine,' thought Iris, in a sudden flurry. 'I must get in first.'

Directly she began to hurry she went to pieces again. Her hands shook so that she painted her mouth with a streak of vivid red – more suggestive of crushed fruit than the crimson blossom after which the tint was named. Unable to find her comb she gave up the attempt and dashed out into the corridor.

Men stared at her and women muttered complaints as she pushed them aside without apology. As a matter of fact she was hardly conscious of them, except as so many obstacles in her way. After so much delay, every wasted moment was a personal reproach. In her excitement she could only see – a long way off – the blurred figure of a little spinster.

She must hurry to reach it. But faces kept coming in between her and her goal – faces that grinned or scowled – the faces of strangers. They melted away like a mist, only to give place to other faces. There was a flash of eyes and teeth – a jam of bodies. She thrust and struggled, while her cheeks burned and a wave of hair fell across her cheeks.

When at last she won through to the clearer stretch of corridor, the sight of the professor – smoking, while he looked through the window – reminded her of the conventions. She felt ashamed of her haste and she spoke breathlessly.

'Do I look like a jigsaw? It was that devastating crowd. They wouldn't let me through.'

The professor did not smile, for in spite of a picturesque attraction, her wild hair and brilliant colour produced a wanton effect which did not appeal to him.

Neither did Mr Todhunter approve of her appearance, as he criticised her through the open door of his coupé. Although he claimed to be a judge of feminine charm, he was of the type that prefers a lily-pond to a waterfall. He never lingered before an unframed picture, for he exacted the correct setting for beauty. Abandon was only permissible in a negligée and definitely bad form on a train journey. Although he had often seen Iris when she looked like a member of an undress beauty chorus, he had never noticed her until the evening when she wore a becoming frock.

'Who's the girl?' asked the bride as she flicked over the pages of a pictorial paper.

He lowered his voice.

'One of the mob from the hotel.'

'Help.'

In the next coupé Miss Rose Flood-Porter raised her head from the soft leather cushion without which she never travelled. Her movement roused her sister from her doze, and she, too, strained to listen.

Unconscious of her audience Iris spoke to the professor in a high excited voice.

'Your marvellous witnesses have let you down. They were all telling lies. The six of them.'

He looked at her burning cheeks with cold concern.

'Is your head worse?' he asked.

'Thanks, I'm perfectly fit . . . And I can prove Miss Froy was with me, because the English visitors from my hotel saw her, too. We'll get in touch with the English Consul when we reach Trieste and he'll hold up the train for a thorough examination. Oh, you'll see.'

Iris thrilled at the prospect of her triumph. At that moment she seemed to see the Union Jack fluttering overhead and hear the strains of the National Anthem.

The professor smiled with dreary patience.

'I'm waiting to be convinced,' he reminded her.

'Then you shall be.' Iris swung round to find herself facing Mr Todhunter. 'You'll help me find Miss Froy, won't you?' she asked confidently.

He smiled down indulgently at her but he did not reply at once. It was the pause of deliberation and was characteristic of his profession.

'I shall be delighted to co-operate with you,' he told her. 'But – who is Miss Froy?'

'An English governess who is missing from the train. You must remember her. She peeped in at your window and you jumped up and drew down the blind.'

'That is exactly what I should have done in the circumstances. Only, in this case, the special circumstances did not arise. No lady did me the honour to linger by my window.'

His words were so unexpected that Iris caught her breath, as though she were falling through space.

'Didn't you *see* her?' she gasped.

'No.'

'But your wife called your attention to her. You were both annoyed.'

The beautiful Mrs Todhunter, who had been listening, broke in with none of her habitual languor.

'We are not a peepshow and no one looked in . . . Do you mind if we shut the door? I want to rest before dinner.'

The professor turned to Iris with forced kindness.

'You're tired,' he said. 'Let me take you back to your carriage.'

'No.' Iris shook off his hand. 'I won't let the matter rest. There are others. These ladies – '

Dashing into the next coupé where the Misses Flood-Porter now sat upright in dignity, she appealed to them.

'You'll help me find Miss Froy, won't you? She's *English*.'

'May I explain?' interposed the professor as the ladies looked to him for enlightenment.

Iris could hardly control her impatience as she listened to the cultured drawl. Her eyes were fixed on the solid fresh faces of the sisters.

Then Miss Rose spoke. 'I have no recollection of your companion. Someone may have been with you, but I was not wearing my glasses.'

'Neither was I,' chimed in Miss Flood-Porter. 'So you can understand that we shall not be able to help you. It would be against our principles to identify someone of whom we were not sure.'

'Most unfair,' commented Miss Rose. 'So, please, don't refer to us. If you do, we must refuse to interfere.'

Iris could hardly believe her ears.

'But isn't it against your principles not to raise a finger to help an Englishwoman who may be in danger?' she asked hotly.

'Danger?' echoed Miss Rose derisively. 'What could happen to her on a crowded train? Besides, there are plenty of other people who are probably more observant than ourselves. After all, there is no reason why we should be penalised because we are English.'

Iris was too bewildered by the unexpected collapse of her hopes, to speak. She felt she had been betrayed by her compatriots. They might boast of wearing evening dress for the honour of their country, but they had let down England. The Union Jack lay shredded in tatters and the triumphant strains of the National Anthem died down to the screech of a tin whistle.

She hated them all so fiercely that when the vicar's wife put her head round the door she could only glare at her.

Mrs Barnes gave a general smile as she explained her presence.

'My husband is sleeping now, so I thought I'd run in for a chat. When we travel, I'm first in command, which is a new experience for me and only comes once a year.'

She spoke eagerly as though to justify her husband's weakness. Then she turned to Iris, who was following the professor from the coupé.

'Don't let me drive you away.'

'Nothing could keep me.' Iris spoke with bitter hopelessness. 'Of course, you didn't see Miss Froy?'

'Was that the little lady in tweed, with a blue feather in her hat?' asked Mrs Barnes. 'Why, *of course*, I remember her, and her kindness. We were so grateful for the tea.'

15

Transformation Scene

Her relief was so overwhelming that Iris felt on the verge of tears as she turned to the professor. 'Are you convinced now?' she asked shakily.

The professor glanced at the vicar's wife with almost an apologetic air, for the lady was a familiar type which he admired and approved, when it was safely married to someone else.

'The question is unnecessary,' he said. 'It was simply a matter of getting corroborative evidence. I'm sorry to have doubted your word in the first place. It was due to the unfortunate circumstances of your sunstroke.'

'Well, what are you going to do?' insisted Iris.

Having made one blunder, the professor was not inclined to be precipitate.

'I think I had better consult Hare,' he said. 'He is an expert linguist and has quite a fair brain, although he may appear irresponsible at times.'

'Let's find him at once,' urged Iris.

In spite of her haste she stopped to speak impulsively to the vicar's wife.

'Thank you so very much. You don't know what this means to me.'

'I'm glad – but why are you thanking me?' asked Mrs Barnes, in surprise.

Leaving Miss Rose to explain, Iris followed the professor. Hare was frankly incredulous when they ran him to earth in the restaurant car.

'Bless my soul,' he exclaimed, 'Miss Froy popping up again? There's something about that good woman that keeps me guessing. I don't mind admitting that I never really believed in the old dear. But what's happened to her?'

The professor took off his glasses to polish them. Without them his eyes appeared weak, rather than cold, while the painful red ridges on either side of his nose aroused Iris's compassion. She felt quite friendly towards him, now that they were united in a common cause – the restitution of Miss Froy.

'The Misses Flood-Porter didn't want to be drawn in,' she declared. 'That was clear. But why did those six foreigners all tell lies about her?'

'It must be some misunderstanding,' said the professor nervously. 'Perhaps I – '

'No, you didn't,' cut in Hare. 'You were a clinking interpreter, professor. You didn't slip up on a thing.'

Iris liked him for the ready good nature which prompted him to reassure the professor because she was sure that privately he considered him a pompous bore.

'We'll have to play the good old game of Spot the Lady,' went on Hare. 'My own idea is she's disguised as the doctor. That black beard is so obvious that she's making it too easy . . . Or she may be pulling the train, dressed up as a ladylike engine. I'd put nothing past Miss Froy.'

Iris did not laugh.

'You're not amusing,' she said, 'because you seem to forget that, besides being a real person, she is still missing. We must *do* something.'

'Admittedly,' agreed the professor. 'But it's a perplexing problem, and I do not care to act without careful consideration.'

'He means he wants to smoke,' explained Hare. 'All right, professor. I'll take care of Miss Carr, while you squeeze out some brain juice.'

He grinned across the ash-dusted table at Iris, when the professor had gone.

'Have I got it right?' he asked. 'Is this Miss Froy a complete stranger to you?'

'Of course.'

'Yet you're nearly going crackers over her. You must be the most unselfish person alive. Really, it's almost unnatural.'

'But I'm not,' admitted Iris truthfully. 'It's rather the other way round. That's the amusing part. I can't understand myself a bit.'

'Well, how did it start?'

'In the usual way. She was very kind to me – helpful, and all that, so that I missed her when suddenly she wasn't there any more. And then, when everyone declared I dreamed her, it all turned to a horrible nightmare. It was like trying to explain that everyone was out of step but myself.'

'Hopeless. But why had you to prove that she was there?'

'Oh, can't you understand? If I didn't, I could never feel that anything, or anyone, was *real* again?'

'I shouldn't fly off the handle,' remarked Hare stolidly. 'I should know it was a post-symptom of brain injury, and therefore perfectly logical.'

'But you can't compare your own experience with mine,' protested Iris. 'You saw a real person and mistook him for the Prince. But I was supposed to have talked to the thin air, while the thin air answered back . . . I can't tell you what a *relief* it was when Mrs Barnes remembered her.'

She smiled with happiness as she looked out of the window. Now that she was safely anchored to a rational world again, after spinning amid mists of fantasy, the gloomy surroundings had no power to depress her. The afternoon had drawn in early, so that the period of twilight was protracted and it added the final touch of melancholy to the small town through which the express was slowly steaming.

Whenever they crossed a street, Iris could see mean shops, with pitifully few wares, cobbled roads and glimpses of a soupy swollen river through the gaps between the buildings. The houses – clinging to the rocky hillside, like tufts of lichen on a roof – seemed semi-obliterated by time and weather. Long ago, wood and plaster had been painted grey, but the rain had washed and the sun had peeled some of the walls to a dirty white. Every aspect betrayed poverty and desolation.

'What a horrible place,' shuddered Iris, as they passed tall rusty iron gates which enclosed a dock-grown garden. 'I wonder who can live here, besides suicides.'

'Miss Froy,' suggested Hare.

He expected an outburst, but Iris was not listening to him.

'When do we reach Trieste?' she asked.

'Ten past ten.'

'And it's five to six now. We mustn't waste any more time. We *must* find her . . . It sounds exactly like some sloppy picture, but her people are expecting her home. They're old and rather pathetic. And the fool of a dog meets every train.'

She stopped – aghast at the sound of her choked voice. To her surprise she found that she was actually affected by the thought of the parents' suspense. As emotion was treason to the tradition of the crowd, she felt ashamed of her weakness.

'I'll have that drink, after all,' she declared, blinking the moisture from her eyes. 'I feel all mushy – and that's absurd. Old people aren't nearly as pathetic as young ones. They're nearly through – and we've got it all to come.'

'You do want a drink,' agreed Hare. 'I'll dig out a waiter.'

As he was rising Iris pulled him back.

'Don't go now,' she whispered. 'There's that horrible doctor.'

The spade-bearded gentleman seemed to be searching for someone; and directly his glasses flashed over the young couple his quest was over. He crossed directly to their table and bowed to Iris.

'Your friend has returned to the carriage,' he said.

'Miss Froy?' Iris forgot her repulsion in her excitement. 'How marvellous. Where was she?'

He spread his hands and shrugged.

'All the time she was so near. In the next carriage, talking with my nurses.'

'Yes,' declared Iris, laughing, 'that's just where she would be. The first place I ought to have looked, and didn't.'

'Hum.' Hare rubbed his chin doubtfully. 'It's all very rum. Sure it's the right one?'

'She is the lady who accompanied madame to the restaurant-car,' replied the doctor. 'A little short lady – not young, but not very old, with a blue feather in her hat.'

'That's Miss Froy,' cried Iris.

'But why was there all the mystery?' persisted Hare. 'No one knowing a thing about her – and all that.'

'Ah, that was because we did not understand madame.'

The doctor shrugged deprecatingly. 'She talked so fast and she talked of an English lady. Now the lady is German, may be, or Austrian – I do not know – but she is not English.'

Iris nodded to Hare.

'I made the same mistake, myself, at first,' she told him. 'She looks anything and she speaks every language. Come on and you shall check up on her.'

The journey along the train was growing so familiar that Iris felt she could make it blindfolded. As she passed by the Barneses' compartment she peeped inside. The vicar looked grimly heroic, with folded arms and knotted brow, while his wife showed visible signs of strain. Her eyes were sunken in black circles, but she smiled bravely at Iris.

'Still looking for your friend?' she asked.

'No,' called Iris. 'She's found.'

'Oh, thank God.'

'I didn't like that holy woman,' Iris confided to Hare as they struggled on again, 'but her stock has simply soared with me. She's really kind.'

When they reached the reserved coupés, Iris insisted on collecting the professor, to whom she told her news.

'I want you to come, too, and meet my Miss Froy,' she said. 'She'll be thrilled when she hears of the sensation she's caused.'

'A desire to attract attention seems a feminine characteristic,' observed the professor acidly.

Iris only laughed with excitement as her heart gave a sudden bound.

'There she is,' she cried. 'There she is, at the end of the corridor.'

Once again she was overwhelmed by the derided human element as she saw the familiar little figure in the light tweed suit.

'Miss Froy,' she cried huskily.

The lady turned so that Iris saw her face. At the sight she recoiled with a cry of horror.

'That's not Miss Froy,' she said.

16

The Star Witness

As Iris stared at the face of a stranger, she was plunged back into the inky darkness of the tunnel. She believed that she had emerged into the daylight and her heart was still singing with the joy of deliverance. But she had been deceived by a ray of sunshine striking through a shaft in the roof.

The horror persisted. Blackness was behind her and before – deadening her faculties and confusing her senses. She felt that she was trapped in a nightmare which would go on for ever, unless she could struggle free.

Miss Froy. She must hold on to Miss Froy. At that moment she suddenly remembered her elusive face distinctly in its strange mixture of maturity and arrested youth, with blue saucer eyes and small features all scratched and faded faintly by time.

An impostor stood before her, wearing Miss Froy's oatmeal tweed suit. The face under the familiar hat was sallow – the black eyes expressionless. It looked wooden, as though it could not weep, and had never smiled.

Breaking out of her nightmare, Iris challenged her.

'You are *not* Miss Froy!'

'No,' replied the woman in English, 'I have not heard that name ever before. I am Frau Kummer, as I told you, when we had our tea together.'

'That's a lie. I never had tea with you. You're a complete stranger to me.'

'A stranger, certainly, such as one meets on a journey. But we talked together. Only a little because your poor head ached.'

'*Ah!*'

The significance of the doctor's exclamation was deliberately stressed. It made Iris quiver with apprehension, even while it put her on her guard.

'I mustn't let them get me down,' she thought. Then she turned desperately to the professor.

'This is *not* Miss Froy,' she said vehemently.

'The lady has told us that herself,' remarked the professor impatiently. 'In fact, with the exception of yourself, no one appears to have heard the somewhat uncommon name of "Froy".'

'But she's wearing her clothes,' persisted Iris, trying to keep her voice from quivering. 'Why? *Why?* What's become of Miss Froy? It's some conspiracy – and I'm afraid . . . She says we had tea together, but we didn't. The waiter knows. Send for him.'

To her dismay Hare did not bound off on his mission like a Hermes in nailed boots. Instead, he twisted his lip and looked sheepish.

'Why not call it a day and get some rest?' he suggested in the soothing tone which infuriated Iris.

No one believed her – and the combined force of their incredulity made her doubt herself. The darkness seemed to be closing round her again when she remembered her supporting witness – the vicar's wife.

'Mrs Barnes,' she said faintly.

'I'll fetch her,' offered the professor, who was anxious to put an end to the scene.

Although he was kind-hearted and eminently just – when he knew his bearings – he was prejudiced against Iris, because of an unfortunate incident which marred the close of his last term. One of his most brilliant pupils – a plain, sedate young person, about whose progress he had been almost enthusiastic – had suddenly lost control and involved him in a very unpleasant emotional scene.

When she came to his study to wish him goodbye, she had broken down completely, assuring him that she had worked solely to please him, and that she could not face the thought of their parting.

As he had insisted on keeping the door open, from motives of prudence, a version of the affair had been put into circulation, to his intense annoyance. Therefore he cursed his luck in being involved with another hysterical girl as he passed the coupé occupied by the Misses Flood-Porter.

Through the glass he could see Mrs Barnes, who had returned to finish her interrupted chat, so he entered.

'More trouble for you, I'm afraid,' he warned her. 'That very emotional young lady now wants you to identify someone. I wonder if you would mind coming with me to her compartment?'

'Certainly,' said Edna Barnes. 'Is it the kind little lady in parchment tweed speckled with brown and a blue feather in her hat?'

'Presumably. I seem to recollect the feather.' The professor looked down at her strained brown eyes and added kindly. 'You look very pale. Not ill, I hope?'

'Oh, no.' Mrs Barnes's voice was extra cheerful. 'It's my husband who is ill. But I'm bearing his pain for him, so that he can sleep.'

'Absent treatment?'

'Something of the kind, perhaps. When you're married – if there is a real bond – you share more than an income.'

'Well, I call it silly,' broke in Miss Rose. 'He's far stronger than you are.'

The professor, however, looked at her sweet face with additional respect.

'I don't like to worry you with this matter,' he said. 'In my opinion, the girl is hysterical and wants to be in the limelight. She says now that the lady is not the original one, who, according to her, is still missing.'

'We'll hope she is the right one, for your sake,' remarked Miss Flood-Porter placidly. 'If not, she'll keep you hanging about at Trieste, and you'll miss your connection to Milan.'

Mrs Barnes pressed her hand over her eyes.

'Oh, I hope not,' she cried. 'My husband wants to get this wretched journey over. Still, one has to do one's duty – whatever the cost.'

'But it's so futile,' declared Miss Rose. 'From your description, this missing governess is no chicken and an experienced traveller. She's either lying low and has given the girl the slip for some good reason of her own, or else it's all moonshine.'

'Indubitably the latter,' remarked the professor, as he accompanied Mrs Barnes out into the corridor.

Here they met the vicar who had come in search of his wife.

'This *is* my husband,' cried Mrs Barnes, her face lighting up. 'Did you think I'd deserted you, Ken?'

While they lingered to chat, Iris sat awaiting the return of Hare with the waiter. She had no real hope of the issue, since she had begun to regard all the officials as being tools of the Baroness. A mysterious power was operating on a wholesale scale to her own confusion. In proof of this, opposite to her was the horrible changeling who wore Miss Froy's clothing. Yet the incident was inexplicable, since she could find no motive for such clumsy subterfuge.

Every detail of the woman's figure corresponded so exactly with her recollection of Miss Froy, as she stared at the familiar blue bone buttons, that the first real doubt began to sap her confidence. She asked herself whether she were, in reality, the victim of some hallucination. Hare's story about the Prince of Wales proved that it was no uncommon experience.

She was feeling so limp that it seemed almost the easiest way out of her troubles. After all, she would have her work cut out to fight the constant threat of overhanging illness, without the additional worry of a problematical Miss Froy.

'I shall soon know,' she thought, as Hare returned with a waiter in tow.

'You said the chap with the fair hair,' he said to Iris. 'I've bagged the only blond in the whole collection. By the way, he is proud of speaking English.'

Iris remembered the youth directly she saw the straw-coloured plastered hair and slanting forehead. He wore glasses, and looked more like a student or clerk.

'Do you really understand English?' she asked.

'Certainly, madame,' he replied eagerly. 'I have my certificates, both for grammar and the conversational test.'

'Well, do you remember waiting on me at tea? Have you a reliable memory for faces?'

'Yes, madame.'

'Then I want you to look at this lady – ' Iris pointed to Kummer and added, 'Don't look at her clothes, but look at her face. Now tell me – is that the lady who was having tea with me?'

The waiter hesitated slightly, while his pale eyes grew momentarily blank. Then he nodded with decision.

'Yes, madame.'

'You're *sure*?'

'Yes, madame, I am positive sure.'

As Iris made no comment, Hare tipped the youth and sent him away. Although the interview had corresponded with his own forecast, he felt acutely uncomfortable. He glanced uneasily at the Baroness and the doctor, but their faces only registered enforced patience, as they waited for the end of the infliction.

Suddenly a muffled cry rang out from the next carriage. Instantly, the doctor sprang up from his seat and hurried back to his patient.

The sound was so unhuman and inarticulate, with its dulled yet frantic reiteration of 'M-m-m-m,' that Iris was reminded of some maimed animal, protesting against suffering it could not understand. She had forgotten about the poor broken body – trussed and helpless in the next carriage – lying in complete dependence on two callous women.

The recollection caused all her latent distrust of the doctor to flare up again. She asked herself what awaited the patient at her journey's end? Did she guess that she was being hurried to some operation – doomed to failure, yet recommended solely as an experiment, to satisfy scientific curiosity?

Iris had still sufficient sense to know that she was indulging in neurotic and morbid speculation, so she hurriedly smashed up the sequence of her thoughts. As a characteristic voice told her of the approach of the professor, she tilted her chin defiantly.

'Mrs Barnes remembered Miss Froy when all the rest pretended to forget her,' she said to Hare. 'I know she couldn't tell a lie. So I don't care two hoots for all the rest. I'm banking on *her*.'

Edna Barnes advanced, her arm linked within that of her husband, as though for support. As a matter of fact, he was really leaning on her, for the shaking of the train made him feel rather giddy. Although still resolute, his face showed something of the strain of a knight approaching the end of his vigil.

'I understand you want us to identify a friend of yours,' he said to Iris, taking command of the situation as a matter of course.

Then he looked down at his wife.

'Edna, my dear,' he asked, 'is this the lady?'

Unlike the waiter, Mrs Barnes did not hesitate. Her recognition was instantaneous.

'Yes,' she said.

The vicar came forward with outstretched hand.

'I am glad of this opportunity to thank you for your kindness,' he said.

Miss Kummer stolidly accepted the tribute paid to Miss Froy. Or – was she really Miss Froy? Iris felt a frantic beating as though of wings inside her head as she slipped down into a roaring darkness.

17

There was No Miss Froy

The immediate effect of Iris's faint was to steady her nerves. When she recovered consciousness, to find someone forcing her head down below the level of her knees, she felt thoroughly ashamed of her weakness. There was not a trace of hysteria in her voice as she apologised.

'Sorry to be such a crashing bore. I'm quite all right now.'

'Don't you think you had better lie down?' asked Mr Barnes. 'I'm sure the Miss Flood-Porters would be only too glad to lend you their reserved compartment.'

Iris was by no means so sure that the ladies measured up to the vicar's own standard of charity; yet she felt a great need of some quiet place, where she could straighten out the tangle in her brain.

'I want to talk to you,' she said to Hare, leaving him to do the rest.

As she anticipated, he jumped at the opportunity. 'Sorry to eject you, professor,' he said, 'but our bunny-hutch is booked for the next half-hour.'

'Delighted,' murmured the professor grimly.

After swallowing some brandy from the vicar's flask, Iris staggered up from her seat. Her knees felt shaky and her temples were still cold; but the brief period of unconsciousness had relieved the pressure on her heart, so that she was actually better.

As she and Hare – linked together, to the general inconvenience – lurched down the corridor, she noticed that the lights were now turned on. This arbitrary change from day to night, seemed to mark a distinct stage in the journey. Time was speeding up with the train. The rushing landscape was dark as a blurred charcoal-drawing, while a sprinkle of lights showed that they had reached a civilised zone, of which the wretched little town was the first outpost.

Now that the outside world was shut out, the express seemed hotter and smokier. At first the confined space of the coupé affected Iris with a sense of claustrophobia.

'Open the window wide,' she gasped.

'There's plenty of air coming in through the top,' grumbled Hare, as he obeyed. 'You'll be so smothered in smuts that your own mother wouldn't know you.'

'I haven't one,' said Iris, suddenly feeling very sorry for herself. 'But I'm not here to be pathetic. There's something too real and serious at stake . . . I want to remind you of something you said this morning at the railway station. You were having an argument with the professor, and I overheard it. *You* said trial by jury was unfair, because it depended on the evidence of witnesses.'

'I did,' said Hare. 'And I stick to every word.'

'And then,' went on Iris, 'the professor talked about reliable evidence, and he compared two women. One was English and county – the sort that collects fir-cones and things when she goes for a walk. The other had bought her eyelashes and was dark.'

'I remember *her*. Pretty woman, like a juicy black cherry.'

'But the professor damned her . . . And that's exactly what has happened now. I'd damned as a tainted witness, while he is prejudiced in favour of all those British matrons and Sunday-school teachers.'

'That's only because they're plain Janes, while you've quite a different face – and thank heaven for it.'

Hare's attempt to soothe Iris was a failure, for she flared up.

'I hate my face. It's silly and it means nothing. Besides, why should I be judged on face value if it goes against me? It's not fair. *You* said it wasn't fair. You told the professor it would lead to a bloody mix-up . . . You can't blow hot and cold. Unless you're a weathercock, you've simply got to stand by me.'

'All right, I'll stand by. What do you want me to do?'

Iris laid her hot palms on the sticky old-gold plush seat and leaned forward, so that her eyes looked into his.

'I say there *is* a Miss Froy,' she told him. 'You've got to believe *me*. But my head feels like a three-ring circus, and I've grown confused. Will you go over it with me, so that I can get it clear?'

'I'd like to hear your version,' Hare told her.

He smoked thoughtfully as she went over the story of her meeting with the alleged Miss Froy, up to the time of her disappearance.

'Well, you've got one definite fact,' he told her. 'What the – the lady told you about the big boss is right. I can make an accurate guess as to her employer. At this moment a certain noble Johnny is in the local limelight over charges of bribery, tampering with contracts and funny little things like that. The latest is he's accused of bumping off the editor of the revolutionary rag which brought the charges.'

He picked up a flimsy yellow sheet of badly printed newspaper.

'It's in the stop press,' he explained, 'but as he was at his hunting-lodge at the time, the final sensation's squashed. However, nobody will bother. It's quite true about the feudal system being in force in these remote districts.'

'But it proves me right,' cried Iris in great excitement. 'How could I know all about her employer, unless Miss Froy told me? And there's something else. When I told Miss Froy about my sunstroke the Baroness was listening. She couldn't know about it in any other way. So Miss Froy *was* there in the carriage with me.'

She looked so radiant that Hare hated to crush her confidence.

'I'm afraid,' he said, 'that it only proves that Miss Kummer was there. She told you about her employer, and perhaps a spot of family history when you were having tea with her. Later on, you mentioned your sunstroke to *her* . . . If you remember, when you came on the train, directly after your sunstroke, you were under the impression that all the other passengers were foreigners. Then you dozed and woke up all confused, and suddenly Miss Froy, an Englishwoman, comes to life.'

'But she had blue eyes and giggled like a schoolgirl,' protested Iris. 'Besides, there were her old parents and the dog. I couldn't have made *them* up.'

'Why not? Don't you ever dream?'

Dejectedly, Iris conceded the point.

'I suppose so. Yes, you must be right.'

'I must remind you,' continued Hare, 'that Kummer was positively identified by the parson as the lady who sent them their tea. Now, I'm the last person to be biased, because all my uncles and fathers are parsons, and I've met them at breakfast – but the church does imply a definite standard. We insist on parsons having a higher moral code than our own and we try them pretty hard; but you must admit they don't often let us down.'

'No,' murmured Iris.

'Besides that parson has such a clinking face. Like God's good man.'

'But *he* never saw Miss Froy,' Iris reminded him. 'He was speaking for his wife.'

Hare burst out laughing.

'You have me there,' he said. 'Well, that shows how we can slip up. He took the stage so naturally that he got us all thinking he was the witness.'

'If you're wrong over one thing, you can be wrong over another,' suggested Iris hopefully.

'True. Let's go into it again. You suggest that the Baroness got rid of Miss Froy – never mind how – and that the other passengers, being local people and in awe of the family, would back her up. So far, you are right. They would.'

'Only it seems such a clumsy plot,' said Iris. 'Dressing up someone quite different and passing her off as Miss Froy.'

'But that bit was an eleventh-hour twist,' explained Hare. 'Remember, you upset their apple-cart, barging in at the last minute. When you made a fuss about Miss Froy, they denied her existence, at first. You were just a despised foreigner, so they thought they could get away with it. But when you said that other English people had seen her, they had to produce someone – and trust to luck that your friends had never heard of Pelman.'

He was talking of Miss Froy as though he took her existence for granted. It was such a novelty, that, in her relief, Iris's thoughts slipped off in another direction.

'Can't you get that bit of hair to lie down?' she asked.

'No,' he replied, 'neither by kindness nor threats. It's my secret sorrow. Thank you. That's the first bit of interest you've shown in me.'

'Miss Froy is bringing us together, isn't she? You see, you believe in her too.'

'Well, I wouldn't go quite so far. But I promised to believe in *you* – false lashes and all – against the Flood-Porter Burberry. In that case, we must accept a plot, inspired by the all-highest, and carried out by his relative, the Baroness – in connection with the doctor to bump off Miss Froy . . . So, naturally, that wipes out all the native evidence – train-staff and all.'

'You are really rather marvellous,' Iris told him.

'Wait before you hand out bouquets. We pass on to that English crowd. The Misses Flood-Porter seem typical John Bulls. What are they like?'

'They've been to the right school and know the best people.'

'Are they decent?'

'Yes.'

'Then they'd do the decent thing. I'm afraid that is one up against Miss Froy . . . Now we'll pass the honeymoon couple – who are presumably not normal – and come to the vicar's wife. What about her?'

'I don't know.'

'Remember, you're on oath, and I'm believing you.'

'Well,' – Iris hesitated – 'I don't think she could tell a lie.'

'And I'm positive she wouldn't. I mix with publicans and sinners and know very little about saints. But, to me, she looks like a really good woman. Besides, she supported you the first time. That shows she has no axe to grind. She said Miss Kummer was the lady who accompanied you to tea. Don't you think we must believe her?'

'I suppose so . . . Yes.'

'Well, then, the weight of evidence is against Miss Froy. But since I've declared my distrust of evidence – however convincing it may sound – I'm going to wash out the lot. To my mind, the whole point is – motive.'

Iris saw Miss Froy fading away as Hare went on with his inquisition.

'I understand Miss Froy was quite small beer. Would she be mixed up in any plot?'

'No,' replied Iris. 'She was against the Red element.'

'And neither young nor pretty? So she wasn't kidnapped by the order of the high hat?'

'Don't be absurd.'

'Any enemies?'

'No, she boasted of being friends with everyone.'

'Hum. It's hardly a motive for murder, but was the family annoyed because she was going to teach in the opposition camp?'

'No. She told me how her employer shook hands with her when he said goodbye and thanked her for her services.'

'Well – is it clear to you now? Unless you can show me a real motive for a high-life conspiracy against a poor but honest governess, I'm afraid there's an end of Miss Froy. Do you agree?'

There was a long pause while Iris tried to battle against the current that was sweeping Miss Froy away. She told herself that so many people, with diverse interests, could not combine to lie. Besides, as Hare had said, what was the motive?

It was useless to struggle any longer and she let herself be swung out with the tide.

'You must be right,' she said. 'One can't go against *facts* . . . Yet, she was so real. And her old parents and the dog were real, too.'

She had the feeling that she had just slain something fresh and joyous – that fluttered and fought for life – as she added, 'You've won. There is no Miss Froy.'

18

The Surprise

Mrs Froy would have been furious had she known that anyone doubted her reality.

While Iris was sighing for the passing of a pleasant ghost, she was at home in the depths of the country, and entertaining friends in her drawing-room. It was a small room with diamond-paned windows – hung with creepers, which made it rather dark – but in spite of the shabby carpet, it was a gracious place, where odd period chairs fraternised with homely wickerwork, and a beautiful red lacquer cabinet lent the colour which the faded chintz could not supply.

Pots of fine golden chrysanthemums, grown by Mr Froy, screened the empty iron grate. The guests might have preferred a fire, for there was that slight chill – often associated with old country houses – suggestive of stone flags. Yet the sun could be seen, through the curtain of greenery, shining on the flower-beds outside; for, although the electric lamps were gleaming in the express, the daylight still lingered farther north.

Mrs Froy was short and stout, with grey hair and great dignity. In addition to having a dominant personality, today she felt extra full of vitality. It was born of her excitement at the thought that her daughter was actually on her way home.

The postcard was on the marble mantelshelf, propped up against the massive presentation clock. On its back was printed a crudely coloured picture of mountains, with grass-green bases and white tops, posed against a brilliant blue sky. Scribbled across the heavens, in a round unformed handwriting, was the message: 'Home Friday night. Isn't it topping?'

Mrs Froy showed it to her guests.

'Everything is "topping" to my daughter,' she explained with proud indulgence. 'I'm afraid at one time it used to be "ripping".'

A visitor looked at the string of consonants printed at the base of the picture – shied at them – and compromised.

'Is she *there*?' she asked, pointing to the line.

'Yes.' Mrs Froy reeled off the name rapidly and aggressively. She did it to impress, for it was only the home-interpretation of Winnie's address. But, on her return, their daughter would give them the correct pronunciation, and put them through their paces while they tried to imitate her own ferocious gargling.

Then the room would know more of the laughter on which it had thriven and grown gracious.

'My daughter is a great traveller,' went on Mrs Froy. 'Here is her latest photograph. Taken at Budapest.'

The portrait was not very revealing since it was expensive. It hinted at the lower half of a small vague face, and a hat which photographed very well.

'She looks quite cosmopolitan with her eyes covered by her hat,' remarked Mrs Froy. 'Now, this is the Russian one . . . This one was taken at Madrid, on her birthday . . . Here she is in Athens.'

The collection was chiefly a geographical trophy, for while Mrs Froy was proud of the printing on the mounts, she secretly resented the middle-aged stranger, who – according to her – was not in the least like her daughter.

She ended the parade by stretching to reach a faded portrait in a silver frame, which stood on a shelf. It was taken at Ilfracombe, and showed a young girl with a slim neck and a smiling face, framed by a mass of curling fair hair.

'This is my favourite,' she declared. 'Now, this really *is* Winnie.'

It was the girl who had taught in Sunday school, giggled at church-wardens, and refused her father's curates, before she spread adventurous wings and fluttered away.

But she always returned to the nest.

Mrs Froy looked again at the clock. She tried to picture Winnie in a grand Continental express, which stamped proudly all over the map of Europe. The poor girl would have to endure two nights in the train, but she always vowed she loved the experience. Besides, she knew all the little dodges of an experienced traveller to secure comfort.

Although a gregarious soul, Mrs Froy began to wonder when her guests would go. There had been a hospitable big tea round the dining-room table, with blackberry pie, and a guest had made a stain on the best tablecloth. Although she had guiltily pushed her plate over it, Mrs Froy had seen it. And since every minute's delay in rubbing salt into the mark would make its removal more difficult, she had found it difficult to maintain the myopia of a hostess.

Besides she wanted to watch the clock alone, and gloat over the fact that every minute was bringing Winnie's return nearer.

Although her fingers were itching to remove the tablecloth, after she had escorted her visitors to the gate she did not return immediately to the house. In front of her was the field where she gathered mushrooms every morning. It was vividly green, and the black shadows of the elms were growing longer as the sun dipped lower.

It was rather melancholy and lonely, so that she thought of her husband.

'I wish Theodore would come home.'

Apparently he heard her wish for he appeared suddenly at the far end of the meadow – his tall thin black figure striding over the grass, as though he were in competition with the elm-shadows.

Around him capered a dog which had some connection with the breed of Old English sheepdog; but his original line had slipped and he was suppressed in the family tree. During a recent hot spell, his shaggy coat had been clipped, transforming him to a Walt Disney creation.

Sock was the herald and toastmaster of the family. Directly he espied the little dumpy grey lady at the garden gate, he made a beeline towards her and circled round her, barking excitedly to tell her that the master was coming home.

Having done his duty at her end of the field, he tore back to Mr Froy with the glad news that the mistress of the house was waiting for him. As he gradually drew them together, both his owners were laughing at his elephantine gambols.

'It must be a great relief to the poor fellow, getting rid of that thatch,' said Mr Froy. 'He evidently feels very cool and light now.'

'He probably imagines he is a fairy,' remarked his wife. 'Look at him floating through the air like a puff of thistledown.'

'The dear old fool . . . Won't Winsome laugh?'

'Won't she?'

In imagination, both heard the joyous girlish peal.

'And won't she be thrilled with her room?' went on Mrs Froy. 'Theo, I've a confession. The carpet came when you were out . . . And I am only human.'

Mr Froy hid his disappointment.

'You mean, you've unpacked it?' he asked. 'Well, my dear, I deserved it for running away with Sock instead of staying and helping you to entertain your visitors.'

'Come upstairs and see it. It looks like moss.'

They had bought a new carpet for Winifred's bedroom, as a surprise for her return. It represented stringent personal economy, since with a rigid income, any extra purchase meant taking a bite out of the weekly budget. So he had cut down his allowance of tobacco and she had given up her rare visits to the cinema. But now that the forty days were over, these good things would have been nothing but ashes and counterfoils. The carpet remained – a green art-square.

When they reached the bedroom, Mr Froy looked round him with proud satisfied eyes. It was a typical schoolgirl's bedroom, with primrose-washed walls and sepia photogravures of Greuze's beauties – limpid-eyed and framed in dark-stained oak. The modern note was there also in photographs of Conrad Veidt and Robert Montgomery, together with school groups and Winnie's hockey-stick.

The faded yellow-rosebud cretonne curtains and bedspread were freshly washed and ironed; a cake of green soap was displayed on the washstand; and two green candles – never to be lit – were stuck into the glass candlesticks before the mirror of the toilet-table.

'We've made it look very nice,' said Mr Froy.

'Yes, but it's not finished yet.'

Mrs Froy pointed to the narrow oak bed, where two lumps at the top and the bottom told of hot-water bottles.

'It won't be finished until there's something inside that bed,' she said. 'I can't believe that in two nights' time I shall be slipping in to kiss her good-night.'

'Only the first night,' advised Mr Froy. 'Remember our daughter is the modern girl. Her generation avoids sentiment.'

'Yes, for all her heart, Winnie is modern,' agreed his wife. 'That is why she gets on so well with everyone – high and low. You may depend on it that even on her journey by now she has made some useful friends who may be helpful at a pinch. I expect she knows all the best people on the train. And by "best" I mean it in every sense of the word . . . I wonder where she is at this moment.'

Well for Mrs Froy that she did not know.

19

The Hidden Hand

In the professor's opinion, the Misses Flood-Porter were representative of the best people. At home he had the reputation of being unsociable and self-sufficient; but directly he travelled he developed a distrust of unfamiliar contacts and a timidity which sought instinctively the security of his own class.

He wanted to hear his own accent reproduced by someone – however uncongenial – who had been to his college, or lunched at his club, or who knew a cousin of one of his acquaintances.

As he smoked in the corridor after his banishment, he glanced rather wistfully at the compartment where the sisters sat. Miss Rose – although his senior – was sufficiently near his age to be a potential danger. But her face dispelled any fears of dormant hysteria. It was slightly underhung and the firm outline of her protruding lip and chin was reassuring.

Although he recoiled automatically when the elder lady caught his eye and invited him to come in, with a smiling gesture, he entered and sat down rather stiffly beside Miss Rose.

'Are you being kept out of your reserved carriage by that girl?' asked Miss Rose bluntly.

When the professor explained the situation both sisters were indignant.

'Fainted?' Miss Rose's tone was incredulous. 'She was laughing when she passed, arm in arm with that youth. It's all too mysterious for me. Only I sincerely hope she won't stir up a fuss and get us all hung up at Trieste, for nothing.'

'It's her dog,' explained the elder sister in an aside.

Miss Rose caught her lower lip between her teeth. 'Yes, it's Scottie,' she said defiantly. 'I'll own up I'm not quite normal over him. But he's so devoted to me – and he pines. The only other person I can trust him to is the butler.'

'Strange,' remarked the professor. 'My own dog has a marked aversion to butlers. Particularly, to my uncle's.'

The social temperature rose several degrees, and Miss Rose grew confidential.

'It's like this. Coles – our butler – is due to go on a cruise, directly I come back. It's a new experience for him and he is thrilled. If I'm overdue he will probably stay at home with Scottie, and, of course, I don't want him to lose his holiday . . . On the other hand, if he went, poor little Scottie would be frantic. He would feel he had lost every friend.'

'We have an excellent staff,' supplemented Miss Flood Porter, 'but, unfortunately, none of them likes animals.'

The professor's long face wrinkled up in a smile which made him resemble a benevolent horse.

'I can enter into your feelings,' he told them. 'I confess that my own dog makes me lose my sense of proportion. I rarely go abroad because I cannot take her with me, owing to quarantine regulations. But this year a complete change seemed indicated.'

The sisters exchanged glances.

'Isn't that strange?' declared Miss Flood-Porter. 'That is exactly our own position.'

Miss Rose flinched and changed the subject quickly. 'What's your dog?' she asked.

'Sealyham. White.'

The professor was sitting bolt upright no longer. Introduced by butlers, and their friendship cemented by the common ownership of dogs, he felt he was in congenial company. So he relaxed to gossip.

'A position of responsibility towards the extraordinary young lady seems to have been thrust upon me,' he said. 'She appears bent on making things very awkward for everyone. I understand she was staying at the same hotel as you . . . What opinion did you form of her?'

'Don't ask me,' said Miss Rose bluntly. 'I'm prejudiced. So, perhaps, I shouldn't be fair.'

Her sister made the explanation.

'We know nothing about *her*, but she was with a party of near-nudists, who drank all day and night and were a complete nuisance. The noise was worse than a pneumatic road-drill. And we came so far especially to get perfect rest and quiet.'

The professor clicked. 'I quite understand your feelings,' he said. 'The point is – did she strike you as hysterical?'

'I only know there was a disgraceful scene on the lake yesterday. Two women screaming about a man. She was one.'

'I'm not surprised,' commented the professor. 'At present she is either telling a pack of lies to get into the limelight, or she is suffering from slight delirium as a result of sunstroke. The latter is the charitable view. But it involves responsibility. After all, we are her compatriots.'

Miss Rose began to fidget. When she opened her case and drew out a cigarette, her fingers were not quite steady.

'Suppose – she *is* telling the truth?' she asked. 'It's *not* fair for us to leave the girl behind us at Trieste without any backing . . . I'm worried stiff not knowing *what* to do.'

Had Mrs Froy been listening, she would have clapped her gouty old hands. At last Miss Rose's attitude was coming into line with her expectations. The best people would be looking after Winnie. So no harm could possibly come to her . . . But all the same, 'Keep her safe – and bring her home to us.'

Unfortunately the professor was proof against the power of prayer. He wrinkled up his face in a sceptical grimace.

'Her story is too unfounded for me to credit it,' he said. 'But even if the vanished governess were not a myth, I cannot conceive any cause for anxiety on her behalf. Her disappearance must be voluntary, because if she had come to any harm, or met with an accident, it would have been notified at once by an eyewitness.'

'Exactly,' agreed Miss Flood-Porter. 'The train is so crowded that if she knew the ropes she could play hide-and-seek indefinitely with the ticket-collector.'

'Therefore,' summed up the professor, 'if she *is* hiding, she must have some strong personal reason for such a course. My own feeling is never to interfere with private issues. It would be extremely tactless and inconsiderate of us to start a general search for her.'

Miss Rose drew deeply at her cigarette.

'Then you don't think me definitely feeble to put Scottie's interests first?' she asked.

'I should consider that you were letting your dog down if you sacrificed him to such an absolutely preposterous issue,' replied the professor.

'That goes for me. Thank you, professor.' Miss Rose examined her firm pink hands. 'I'm smutty. I'd better wash.'

When she had lurched out into the corridor, Miss Flood-Porter spoke to the professor confidentially.

'I couldn't mention it before my sister – she is so sensitive on the subject – but we've just been through a nerve-shattering experience. And I don't see that we did a penn'worth of good . . . Am I boring you?'

'Not in the least.'

Miss Flood-Porter began her story of those events which played their part in shaping the conduct of the sisters, and so – indirectly – affected the destiny of a stranger.

'We live in a very quiet neighbourhood, close to the cathedral. It was ruined for everyone when a terrible person came to live there. A war profiteer – at least, I call them all that. One day, when he was scorching in his car – drunk, as usual – he knocked down a woman. We saw the accident, and our evidence got him six months' imprisonment, as it was a bad case.'

'I congratulate you on your public spirit.'

'I'm afraid we, too, were quite pleased with ourselves, until he came out. After that we were marked people. This man – aided by his two boys – persecuted us in every kind of way. Windows were smashed – flower beds raided – horrible things thrown over the garden walls – obscene messages chalked on the gates. We could never catch them in the act, although we appealed to the police and they had a special watch kept on the premises . . . After a time it got on our nerves. It did not matter where we were, or what we were doing, we were always listening for another crash. It affected my sister most, as she was terrified lest one of her pet animals might be the next victim. Luckily, before it came to that, the man left the town.'

Miss Flood-Porter stopped, overcome by the memories she had raised.

It began on the morning when she went out into the garden to find that her unique white delphiniums had been uprooted during the night. After that there was the ever-increasing tension – the constant annoyance – the cumulative pecuniary loss – the futility of repairs, when panes of glass were replaced only to be smashed again. It was like standing at a crossroads in windy weather and being buffeted by an invisible weathercock, which whirled round again after it had struck its blow. There were flutters of apprehension whenever the fiendish boys scorched by them on their bicycles, grinning with impudent triumph. And the time came when their nerve was worn down, so that their imaginations raced away with them and they grew fearful of worse evils in store.

It ended on the evening when Miss Flood-Porter found her sister Rose in tears. If the Rock of Gibraltar had suddenly shaken like a jelly, she could not have been more aghast.

She looked up to meet the professor's sympathetic eye.

'Can you blame us,' she asked, 'when I tell you that, after that, we made a vow never to interfere in anything again – unless it was a case of cruelty to animals or children?'

As Iris passed the window, in token that he was free to return to his own compartment, the professor rose.

'Tell your sister,' he advised, 'not to worry any more, but to get back to her dog as quickly as possible. No one is going to suffer in any way. In case of any further complications, you can trust me to take charge.'

A few minutes later, when Miss Flood-Porter repeated the message, Miss Rose was greatly relieved.

'Now I can go home to Scottie with a *clear* conscience,' she said. 'Anyone must have complete confidence in the professor.'

She forgot one important point. The professor was working on the basis that Miss Froy was a fiction of hysteria – while both the sisters had seen her in the flesh.

20

Strangers Intervene

After Miss Froy had shrivelled to a never-never, Iris was thrown back on herself again. When her first relief at shelving the riddle had passed, she grew worried by her own sensations. Her knees were shaky, while her head felt light and empty as a blown eggshell.

Miss Froy would have known that, in addition to the after-effects of sunstroke, the girl was exhausted for lack of light nourishment. At this juncture she was a dead loss to Iris, while Hare – with the best intentions – could only offer stimulants.

As she clung to the shaking handrail, fighting off recurrent spells of giddiness, Iris told herself that she must forcibly hold out until she reached Basle.

'It would be fatal if I collapsed,' she thought fearfully. 'Max is too young to be any good. Some busybody would push me out at the first station, and pack me off to the local hospital.'

And anything might happen to her there, as in Miss Froy's terrible story. Or did Miss Kummer tell it to her?

It was an ordeal to stand, but although she had insisted on leaving Hare – when she found that both talking and listening had become a strain – she shrank from the thought of return to her own compartment. It was too near the doctor and too remote from her compatriots. At the far end of the corridor she felt bottled up in enemy territory.

Besides – it was haunted by the ghost of a little tweed spinster, of whom it was not wise to think too long.

The high-pitched conversation of the Misses Flood-Porter – audible through the open door – was a distraction.

'I've written to Captain Parker to meet us with his car at Victoria, to push us through the customs,' said Miss Flood-Porter.

'Hope he'll be there,' fussed Miss Rose. 'If he fails us, we may lose our connection. And I've written to cook that dinner is to be ready at seven-thirty on the dot.'

'What did you order?'

'*Not* chicken. Definitely. It will be some time before I can endure one again. I said a nice cutlet of salmon and a small leg of lamb. Peas, if possible. If it is too late for them, French beans and marrow. I left the sweet to cook.'

'That sounds very good. I'm longing to eat a plain English dinner again.'

'So am I.'

There was a short pause before Miss Rose began to worry anew.

'I do hope there'll be no muddle over our wagons-lits at Trieste.'

'Oh, my dear,' cried her sister, 'don't suggest such a thing. I couldn't face the idea of sitting bolt upright all night. Didn't you hear the manager telephone for them?'

'I stood by him while he was doing it. Of course, I could not understand anything. But he assured me positively that they were being reserved for us.'

'Well, we must hope for the best . . . I've been looking through my engagement-book. It's the Bishop's last garden party, the day after we get back.'

'Oh, we *couldn't* miss that.'

Iris's half-smile was bitter as she listened to the characteristic chatter of two inexperienced women-travellers, who felt very far from their beaten track.

'And I expected *them* to risk losing their reservations and spoiling their dinner,' she thought. 'What a hope.'

Once again she flattened herself against the window, as the flaxen-haired waiter came down the corridor. Miss Rose saw him pass for she bounded out after him.

'Stop,' she cried in her most imperious tone. 'You speak English?'

'Yes, madame.'

'Then get me some matches, please. Matches.'

'Oh, yes, madame.'

'I wonder if he really understood her,' thought Iris, who had grown sceptical of everyone.

Her doubts were unfounded, for after a brief interval the waiter returned with a box of matches. He used one to light Miss Rose's cigarette and handed her the remainder with a bow.

'The engine-driver is fulfilling his obligations and the express will reach Trieste within the scheduled time,' he informed Miss Rose, who remarked, 'Oh, definitely good.'

He seemed anxious to oblige everyone. When Iris in her turn called out to him, he wheeled round smartly as though eager for service.

As he recognised her, however, a change came over his face. His smile faded, his eyes shifted, and he appeared to conquer an impulse to bolt.

All the same he listened obediently as she gave her order.

'I'm not going to the dining-car for dinner,' she told him. 'I want you to bring me something to my carriage – right at the end of the corridor. A cup of soup or Bovril, or Ovaltine. Nothing solid. You understand?'

'Oh, yes, madame.'

He bowed himself away. But he never brought the soup . . .

Iris forgot her order directly she had given it. A stream of passengers had begun to file steadily past her, crushing her against the side of the corridor. Since everyone was heading in the same direction, she glanced at her watch.

The time told her that the first dinner was about to be served.

'Only three hours now to Trieste,' she thought gladly – goaded no longer by the thought of wasted minutes.

Where she stood she was very much in the way of the procession, and since the majority was hungry, she was resented as an obstacle. She met with ruthless treatment, but it was useless to fight her way out against the human current. When she made the attempt she was nearly knocked down, as some of the rougher element began to push.

No one appeared to notice her plight as she tried to get out of the jam. The train was racing at top speed, and she was shaken and bruised as she gripped the rail. Terrified of being crushed, her palms were sticky and her heart leaped with panic.

At last the pressure was relaxed and she breathed more freely as the better-behaved passengers began to pass. Presently a combination of strokes, dots and dashes, in black and white, told her that the family party – linked together – was on its way to dinner. Free from the restraining presence of the Baroness, they talked and laughed, evidently in high spirits at the prospect of their meal.

Although the parents were sufficiently big to inflict some merciless massage as they squeezed past her, Iris was glad to see them, for she argued that they must be in the tail of the procession. Then the blonde slipped by – cool as a dripping icicle – with unshatterable composure and without one ruffled hair.

Although the corridor was now practically clear, Iris still lingered, unable to face the prospect of being alone in the carriage with the Baroness. To her relief, however, the personage herself came in sight, accompanied by the doctor. Sure of getting a seat in the dining-car – however late her entrance – she had waited for the mob to disperse.

As her vast black figure surged past Iris, a simile floated into the girl's mind. An insect and a relentless foot.

The doctor threw her a keen professional glance which noted each symptom of distress. With a formal bow he passed on his way, and she was able to bump and sway along the corridor, back to the empty carriage.

She had barely seated herself, after an involuntary glance at Miss Froy's empty corner, when Hare hurried in.

'Coming to first dinner?' he asked. 'I warn you, the second one will be only the scrapings.'

'No,' she told him, 'the waiter's bringing me some soup here. I've been in a rough-house and I simply couldn't stand the heat.'

He looked at her as she wiped her damp brow.

'Gosh, you look all in. Let me get you a spot. No? . . . Well, then, I've just had an intriguing experience. On my way here, a woman's trembling hand was laid on my sleeve and a woman's piteous voice whispered, "Could you do something for me?" I turned and looked into the beautiful eyes of the vicar's wife. Needless to say, I pledged myself to the service of the distressed lady.'

'Did she want a hot-water bottle for her husband?' asked Iris.

'No, she wanted me to send a telegram for her directly we reached Trieste. But now comes the interesting bit. I'm not to let her husband know or suspect anything. After that, I can't hint at the message.'

'Who wants to know it?' asked Iris dully.

'Sorry. I see you really are flat. I won't worry you any more. Chin-chin.'

Hare left the compartment, only to pop his head again round the corner of the door.

'There's the ugliest ministering angel I've ever seen in the next carriage,' he told her. 'But what I really came back for was this. Do you know who Gabriel is?'

'An archangel.'

'I see. You're definitely *not* in the know.'

As the time passed and no waiter appeared with her soup, Iris came to the conclusion that he was too rushed to remember her order. But she felt too limp to care. All that mattered were the crawling hands of her watch, which drew her imperceptibly nearer to Trieste.

As a matter of fact, the fair waiter possessed a heart of gold, together with a palm which twitched as instinctively as a divining-twig in the direction of a tip. He would have found time to rush in that cup of soup, whatever the demand on his resource. The only drawback was he knew nothing about the order.

Like most of his fellow-countrymen, he had been made a good linguist by the method of interchange between families of different nationalities. As he was ambitious, he felt that one extra language might turn the scale in his favour when he applied for a job. Accordingly, he learned English from his teacher, who had taught himself the language from a book of phonetic pronunciation.

The waiter, who was an apt pupil, passed his school examination and was able to rattle off strings of English phrases, but the first time he heard the language spoken by a Briton, he was unable to understand it.

Fortunately English tourists were rare and most of their conversation was limited to the needs of their meals. While his ear was growing accustomed, therefore, he managed to keep his job by bluff and by being a good guesser.

Miss Rose's unlighted cigarette gave him the clue that she wanted matches. Moreover her voice was loud and she was brief.

But in Iris, he met his Waterloo. Her low husky voice and unfamiliar words beat him completely. After his first nerve-racking experience, he could only fall back on the mechanical, 'Yes, madame,' and rush to take cover.

Before the other passengers returned to the carriage, Iris had another visitor – the professor. He took off his glasses to polish them nervously, while he explained the nature of his mission.

'Hare has been talking to me, and – frankly – he is worried about you. I don't want to alarm you. Of course, you are not ill – that is, not definitely ill – but we are wondering if you are fit to continue the journey alone.'

'Of course I am,' cried Iris in a panic. 'I'm perfectly fit. And I don't want anyone to worry on my account.'

'Yet, if you should collapse later, it would be decidedly awkward for you and everyone. I was discussing it with the doctor, just now, and he came to the rescue with an admirable suggestion.'

As he paused, Iris's heart began to flutter with apprehension, for she knew by instinct what the proposal would be.

'The doctor,' went on the professor, 'is taking a patient to a hospital at Trieste, and he offers to see you safely placed in a recommended nursing home for the night.'

21

Lies

As the professor made his proposal, Iris saw the opening of the trap. But he had forgotten the bait. She was a free agent – and nothing could induce her to walk inside.

'I will not go anywhere with that doctor,' she said.

'But – '

'I refuse to discuss it.'

The professor seemed about to argue, so she decided that it was no time for politeness.

'I can't pretend to be grateful for your interest,' she told him. 'I consider it interference.'

The professor stiffened at the last word.

'I have not the slightest wish to be intrusive,' he said. 'But Hare was genuinely concerned about you, and he asked me to use my influence.'

'No one can influence me to go with that horrible doctor.'

'In that case there is no more to be said.'

The professor was only too thankful to be rid of his responsibility. Since the girl was bent on antagonising those who held out a helping hand, there would be time for a smoke while he waited for the second dinner.

Iris did not like the professor's face, but his Harris-tweed back was British and reassuring. She realised with a pang that she was sending it away.

Acting on impulse she called him back.

'I won't go with that doctor,' she said. 'He's like death. But – supposing I *should* flop – which is absurd – I'd go with *you*.'

She thought she was making a concession, but at that there were two frightened people in the carriage.

'That's is impossible,' said the professor sharply, to hide his nervousness. 'The circumstances put it out of court. The doctor has made you a kind and helpful offer – which comes best from a medical man.'

He opened the door of the trap again, but she shook her head. She would never go inside. Unless – of course she were tricked.

It was a disquieting reflection, for she was beginning to think that she could trust no one. Even Hare had let her down. While he was, in reality, concerned about her condition, he had been facetious about

Mrs Barnes. According to him, she had asked him to send a telegram to some man called Gabriel, while her husband was to be kept in the dark.

Since it was impossible to connect the vicar's wife with a clandestine affair, Iris concluded that Hare had been trying to pull the wool over her eyes.

She resented the feebleness of the effort, especially as Mrs Barnes was connected with a poignant memory. It was she who had driven away Miss Froy and sent her groping back into limbo.

Iris could not forgive her for that, for she was missing badly the support which only the little governess could give. At this juncture, she knew she would be safe in those experienced hands. She felt terrified, sick, friendless – for she had burned her bridges.

Besides, whenever she thought about the mystery, she felt near the borderline of that world which was filled with shifting shadows – where fantasy usurped reality, and she existed merely in the Red King's dream. Unless she kept a firm grip on herself, her sanity might hang – or crash – on the fact of Miss Froy's existence.

There were others in that train full of holiday folk who were in a worse plight than herself. One was the invalid in the next carriage. Although she was chiefly unconscious, the flash of every lucid second held the horror of the shock which had stunned her into darkness. And if the moment lasted a fraction too long, there was time for a cloud of awful doubts to arise. 'Where am I? What is going to happen to me? Where are they taking me?'

Luckily, before these questions could be answered, the flare always died down again. So, therefore, she was better off than Edna Barnes, who was in full possession of her faculties while she endured a protracted martyrdom of mental suffering.

She had been completely happy in anticipation of their last mountain ramble when she saw the letter in the pigeon-hole of the bureau. Her mother-in-law's handwriting gave her a warning pang which broke slightly the shock of the contents of the note.

'I've been wondering what to do for the best,' wrote the excellent lady. 'I don't want to make you anxious during your long journey, yet, on the other hand, I feel I ought to prepare you for a disappointment. I had hoped to have Gabriel in perfect health for your return, and up to now he's been splendid. But now he has developed a cold in his chest. He is quite comfortable and the doctor says he is going on as well as can be expected. So there is no need for you to worry.'

Edna Barnes skimmed the letter in a flash which read between the lines. If her mother-in-law had composed it with a view to alarm her, she could not have succeeded better. All the familiar soothing phrases were there. 'No need to worry.' 'As well as can be expected.' 'Comfortable' – hospitable formulae for a hopeless case.

A cold on the chest could camouflage bronchitis or even pneumonia; and she had heard that a big strong baby, stricken by these complaints, was sometimes snuffed out after a few hours' illness. Her heart nearly burst as she wondered whether, at that moment, he were already dead.

Then her husband called out to enquire the contents of the letter. The answer had been 'Margaret Rose silk'.

She had lied with a fierce protective instinct to save him from her own agony. There was no need for two to suffer, if she could bear his pain for him. Screening her torment with her habitual smile, she racked her brains desperately for some reason to leave for England that same day.

Just as the vicar took the packet of sandwiches from her, preparatory to their start, she snatched at the excuse of Miss Rose Flood-Porter's warning dream.

Although he was disappointed, the vicar gave way to her in the matter. The sisters, too, decided to take no chances, when they heard that the vicar's wife had changed her plans owing to superstitious presentiments. As the honeymoon couple had previously decided to go, the exodus from the hotel was complete.

For the first time Edna Barnes was glad that her husband suffered from train-sickness. While he sat with closed eyes and gritted teeth, she had some respite from acting. Her only consolation was knowing that she was on her way home. Therefore, when she was threatened with the prospect of an enforced delay at Trieste, she felt desperate.

She was faced with the first real test of her principles – and her conscience won. Deception to save her husband from unnecessary suffering was a form of the lie *magnifique*. But now she told herself that the cause of humanity must come before family ties, because it was selfless. She was prepared to do her duty – whatever the cost – by Miss Froy.

But when she was assured by those whose judgement she could trust, that the peril was negligible, her resolution slipped. The cause was too inadequate to exact such a sacrifice. On the evidence, it was nothing but the trumped-up invention of a hysterical girl to attract notice. But Gabriel was ill. He needed her, and he won.

It was after she had identified Miss Kummer as Miss Froy that she suddenly realised the advantage of a willing young man who could send off a telegram to her mother-in-law. As she doubted whether she could receive the reply without her husband's knowledge – since her name might be bawled out by some official – she asked for the latest bulletin to await her at Calais. The sea-crossing would revive the vicar, while it would not be kind to keep him in the dark until he reached home.

Although her eyes were tragic, she smiled faintly at the thought of his unconsciousness. Like a big baby he was sorry for his aches and pains, but he knew nothing of what he was spared.

'Only a mother knows,' she thought.

This was exactly Mrs Froy's own conviction as she sat in the twilight and hungered for her child's return.

22

Killing Time

As a rule Mrs Froy lived on the sunny side of the street. This evening, however, the long black shadows of the elms seemed to have stretched out to reach her mind, for she was unaccountably depressed.

The sun no longer shone greenly through the creepers which muffled the windows, but she was accustomed to gloom. For reasons of economy, the lamp was never lit until the last possible moment. Neither was she influenced by the melancholy of the view from her bedroom, which overlooked a corner of the churchyard.

Having dwelt in rectories for so long, it was second-habit for the Froys to live close to the church. Whenever she looked out at the slanting tombstones of forgotten dead, she had trained herself to picture a spectacular resurrection, when the graves suddenly burst open and their glorified contents shot up into the air like a glittering shower of rockets.

This evening, when the green had all turned grey, she had her first misgivings.

'I wonder if it's healthy for us to sleep so near all those mouldering corpses.'

In ordinary circumstances she would have scoffed at her idea; but she could not dislodge the black monkey that sat on her shoulder. Vague misgivings and presentiments kept passing through her mind.

She told herself that she would be profoundly grateful when Winnie was safely home. Travel must be risky – otherwise railway companies would not issue insurance policies. Suppose Winnie were taken ill on the journey and had to be dumped in some foreign waiting-room.

Anything might happen to her – a smash, or even worse. One read of terrible things happening to girls travelling alone. Not that Winnie was actually a girl – thank goodness – but she was so young for her age.

At this point Mrs Froy took herself in charge.

'Only two nights more,' she reminded herself. 'You ought to be happy as a queen, instead of carrying on like a weeping-willow with a stomach ache. Now, you find out what's at the bottom of all this.'

Before long she believed she had worked back to the original cause of her depression. It was the blackberry stain on the best tablecloth, which had not yielded entirely to salt.

'Goose,' she said. 'It'll boil out in the wash.'

Making a face at the tombstones, she stumped out of the room and down the stairs in search of her husband.

Contrary to custom she found him in the parlour sitting in the dark.

'Lazybones, why haven't you lit the lamp?' she asked.

'In a minute.' Mr Froy's voice was unusually lifeless. 'I've been brooding. Bad habit . . . It's an extraordinary thing that Winsome has been away so often, yet this is the first time I've ever felt apprehensive about her safety. These Continental trains – I suppose I'm growing old. The ground is pulling me.'

Mrs Froy's heart gave a sudden leap as she listened. So he, too, had caught the warning whisper.

Without speaking, she struck a match, turned up the wick of the lamp, lit it, and fitted on the chimney. As she waited for the glass to warm through, she looked at her husband's face, visible in the weak glow.

It appeared white, bloodless and bony – the face of a man who should be going to bed in a damp corner under the window, instead of sharing her spring-mattress.

At the sight she exploded with the righteous wrath of a woman who is rough on shadows.

'Never let me hear you talk like that again,' she scolded. 'You're as bad as Miss Parsons. She's only sixty-six, yet the last time we came back from town together, she grumbled because the bus was full and she had to stand. I said, "My dear, don't let everyone know that you are not accustomed to court circles." And then I said, "Take my seat. I'm young."'

'Did the people in the bus laugh?' asked Mr Froy appreciatively.

In the circle of mellow lamplight his face had lost its pallor. Before she replied, his wife pounced on the window-cords and rattled the green window-curtains together, shutting out the bogie-twilight.

'Yes,' she said, 'they simply roared. Then someone started to clap. But when I thought the joke had gone far enough, I stopped it . . . I *looked* at them.'

Although Mrs Froy was proud of her gifts as a comedian, her sense of dignity was stronger. Her head was held high, as though she were still quelling her audience, as she enquired, 'Where is Sock?'

'My dear, I'm afraid he is waiting outside until it is time to meet the train. I do wish I could make the poor fellow understand it's Friday.'

'I'll make him,' announced Mrs Froy. 'Sock.'

The big dog shambled in immediately, for although normally too spoiled to be obedient, he always respected a certain rasp in his mistress's voice.

Mrs Froy took three biscuits from the tin and laid them in a row on the fender-stool.

'Look, darling,' she said. 'Mother's got three biscuits for you. This is tonight, but Winnie's not coming tonight. This is tomorrow, but Winnie's not coming tomorrow. *This* is Friday, and Winnie's coming on Friday and you shall go and meet the train . . . Remember – *this* one.'

Sock looked up at her as though he were straining to understand – his amber eyes beaming with intelligence under his wisps of hair, for his head had not been shorn.

'He understands,' declared Mrs Froy. 'I can always talk to animals. Perhaps our vibrations are the same. I know what's in his mind and I can always make him know what is in mine.'

She turned back to the fender-stool and picked up the first biscuit.

'This is tonight,' she explained. 'Well, tonight's over. So you can eat tonight.'

Sock entered into the spirit of the game. While he was making a mess of crumbs on the mat, Mrs Froy spoke to her husband.

'That's an end of tonight for us, too,' she said. 'And good riddance. I wish you would remember that it's bad form to go halfway to meet troubles which are not coming to your house, and which have no intention of calling on you . . . What are you grinning at?'

Shaking with laughter, Mr Froy pointed to Sock, who was in the act of crunching the last biscuit.

' "He understands," ' he quoted with gentle mockery.

The sight of his face made Mrs Froy forget her momentary discomfiture. It looked years younger. There was no question now of where he ought to sleep that night.

She patted Sock, kissed his nose and flicked the biscuit crumbs from his coat.

'Yes,' she said tartly, 'he understands – and better than you do. Don't you see that he is trying to make the time pass quicker?'

Stake Your Counter

At that moment others besides Mrs Froy were anxious to speed up the march of time. Some were on the express which was being stoked up for its final spurt, to reach Trieste on time.

One of these – Mrs Todhunter – hid her impatience under a pose of nonchalance. Wherever she went, she attracted notice and she also excited feminine envy by her special atmosphere of romance. Apparently she had everything that a woman could want – beauty, poise, exquisite clothes, and a wealthy, distinguished bridegroom.

In reality she was feverishly eager to get back to her husband.

He was a stout middle-aged building-contractor, named Cecil Parmiter. When at home Mrs Laura Parmiter lived in a super-fine new house, with all those modern improvements which her husband introduced into the blocks of flats he built for others – and with none of their shortcomings. She had a comfortable income, a generous allowance, competent servants, leisure, a trusting affectionate husband and two large children. She had the additional detail of respectability.

Although she was the social queen of her set, she was secretly ambitious and discontented. During the rehearsals for a local pageant, when class-distinctions were levelled, she met a certain rising barrister – a visitor to the district, who had been roped into taking a part. He was a king and she was a queen – and the royal atmosphere lent a glamour to their meetings.

He was infatuated – temporarily – by her statuesque beauty and the facility with which she could quote passages from Swinburne and Browning, culled from her *Oxford Book of English Verse*. After a few meetings in London, under the seal of the apple, he swept her away with him on a passionate adventure.

Although she lost her footing, Mrs Laura's brain still functioned. She had a definite ulterior motive for her surrender. During a session of Browning lectures, she had read 'The Statue and the Bust' and had imbibed its spirit. She determined, therefore, to risk her counter on a bold fling – the chance of a double divorce.

After the preliminary patch of mud was crossed, she would take her rightful place in Society as the beautiful wife of a distinguished barrister. The world soon forgets – while she was confident that she could compel her husband to admit her moral claim to the children.

She lost . . . And Browning would have been proud of the spirit in which she took her toss.

The barrister was married to a sour elderly wife; but she possessed both a title and wealth. When Mrs Laura discovered that he had not the slightest intention of making their adventure a prelude to matrimony, her pride forbade her to show any disappointment.

Perhaps her nonchalance was easier to assume by reason of her own disillusionment. The passionate adventure had not matured according to its promise. It taught her that a professional man did not differ so greatly from a tradesman in essentials and that they looked much the same before shaving and without their collars.

Moreover, the barrister had a handicap from which the builder was immune. He was a hard snorer.

To make matters worse, while he was careless of his own failings, his standard for women was so fastidious that she found it a strain to live up to it. She could never relax, or be natural, without being conscious of his criticism or impatience.

Being practical, she determined to cut short the holiday and get back to her husband while the going was good. Fortunately, she had not burned any bridges. Her husband had bought her return ticket to Turin, and she had told him to expect no mail, since he was going on a sea trip to the Shetlands.

Her plan was to leave the barrister at Turin, where he had joined her on the outward journey, and to stay there, for a night, so that her luggage could display the hotel labels.

The end of it all would be a happy domestic reunion and a better understanding, for – by contrast – she had learnt to appreciate her husband's solidity. Thus one more matrimonial shipwreck had been averted by a trial-venture and a smashed code of morality.

As the Todhunters sat in their coupé, waiting for the second dinner to be served, they were a spectacle which attracted the interest of the tourists who straggled past the window. They must still be known by the name in which they had registered, since the barrister was too cautious to sign his own name.

It was 'Brown'.

However, his parents had done their best for him, and his title of 'Sir Peveril Brown' was sufficiently well-known to be dangerous – in addition to a striking profile which had been reproduced often in the pictorial press.

True to her character of Browning's good loser, Mrs Laura continued to play her part. Although her acquired drawl was replaced sometimes by her natural accent, she still looked choice and aloof as a beautiful princess – remote from the rabble. But her fingers kept tapping the greasy old-gold plush seat, while she glanced continuously at her watch.

'Still hours and hours,' she said impatiently. 'It seems as though we'll never make Trieste – let alone Turin.'

'Anxious to drop me?' asked Todhunter incredulously.

'I'm not thinking of you . . . But children get measles – and deserted husbands prove unfaithful. The world is full of pretty typists.'

'In that case, he'd have nothing on you, if it came to a show-up.'

She started at the word.

'*Show-up?* Don't give me the jitters,' she cried sharply. 'There's no chance of it, is there?'

He stroked his lip.

'I should say we are reasonably secure,' he told her. 'Still . . . I've handled some queer cases in my career. One never knows what will break. It was unfortunate that there were any English visitors at the hotel. And you are entirely too beautiful to remain anonymous.'

Mrs Laura shook off his hand. She wanted reassurance, not compliments.

'You told me there was no risk,' she said. Forgetting that her original scheme had been to force her husband to take action, she added bitterly, 'What a fool I've been.'

'Why are you suddenly so anxious to get back to your husband?' asked Todhunter.

'Well, to be brutally frank, we are all of us out for what we can get. And he can give me more than you can.'

'Haven't I given you a memory you'll never forget?'

Mrs Laura's eyes flashed angrily, and Todhunter laughed. He had grown rather bored by the languid beauty and her synthetic culture; but now that she had suddenly become alive, he was aware of the fact that she was slipping from him.

'I was only teasing you,' he said. 'Of course, no one will ever know about us. *I* could risk nothing like that . . . But we might have been in a jam if I had not thought a jump ahead when that girl asked me about the peeping woman.'

'Why,' asked Laura, who had only grasped the fact that Todhunter would never go an inch out of his way to champion an unattractive middle-aged woman.

'Why? Because she's disappeared. If I had not repudiated her, I should have had to make a statement at Trieste,' Todhunter laughed. 'Can't you see the headlines? "Englishwoman lost on Continental express." Photograph of Mr Todhunter who was on his honeymoon, when . . .

And thus and thus. It wouldn't be long before the English press got on to my identity. One of the penalties of fame – however limited.'

Mrs Laura did not look as impressed as he wished, for his words had raised a new issue.

Perhaps, after all, the game was not lost, because it was not yet ended. Although Todhunter had no intention of risking a scandal when he lured her away on this trip, she saw a chance to engineer one and so force his hand.

If she went to the professor and assured him of Miss Froy's existence, the result was bound to be future complications. There could be no doubt of the professor's probity and public spirit, which would enforce an investigation – whatever the cost to his personal convenience.

Her violet eyes suddenly glittered. As the beautiful bride of the alleged Todhunter, she was an important detail in the picture, and one that reporters would not overlook or suppress. She always made such an appealing photograph.

Afterwards there would be a sensational divorce case, and Sir Peveril – in honour bound – would be obliged to make her the second Lady Brown.

At the thought she drew a deep breath, for the wheel was still spinning.

Her counter was not yet lost.

24

The Wheel Spins

Mrs Laura sat and looked at the window which held the reflection of the lighted carriage, thrown on panels of rushing darkness. She smiled at her dimly-mirrored face – smoky-dark, with shadowed eyes and triumphant lips. The wheel was still spinning for her.

And since their fates were interlinked it was spinning also for Miss Froy. The little spinster was in a perilous plight, but she was an obstinate optimist. She clung to the hope that everything would come right in the end, and that at long last she would reach home.

Miss Froy loved her home with that intense perverted passion which causes ardent patriots to desert their native lands and makes men faithless to their wives. Like them, she left what she loved most – for the joy of the return.

This special absence had been a thrilling experience. During the first six months of exile, she had been excited by the novelty of living in semi-royal surroundings. Everything was so exaggerated and unreal that she had a confused sense of having strayed into some fairy tale. She wandered and lost herself amid a maze of pillared halls and gilded apartments. There seemed to be endless marble stairs, countless galleries – all duplicated in enormous mirrors, so that at least one half of the castle was illusion.

The scenery, in its breathless beauty, held the same bewildering quality of unreality. In her letters to her family she gave up the attempt to describe blue and purple mountains, whose white crests pierced the sky – boiling jade rivers – lush green valleys – towering precipices.

'There aren't enough adjectives,' she wrote. 'But it's all simply topping.'

True to schedule, however, when she cracked her seventh month of absence, her rapture suffered its first eclipse and she began to realise the drawbacks of living in a castle. To begin with she got lost no longer, and there were not so many marble staircases, since she had located the mirrors.

There were other unpleasant details, including fleas in the thick carpets and rich upholstery, for the hounds were many and the servants few.

Her vast bedroom, which was like a stage royal apartment, was comfortless and cold, since the enormous coloured porcelain stove – resembling a cathedral altar – was insufficiently stoked.

There were ten courses for dinner – but only one knife and fork, which the diner cleaned with bread.

All the men were handsome and respectful, but none seemed to realise that she was a curly-headed girl whose pet sport was refusing curates.

Before her last five months were up she became so homesick that her longing for a small stone house – backed by an apple orchard, and overlooking a country churchyard – grew to a passion. Sick of the theatrical scenery, she would have exchanged all the mountains and rivers for one corner of an English meadow with a clump of elms and a duck-pond.

The night before her return her excitement was so great that she could not sleep, in anticipation of her journey. She could not believe in it, although her luggage was packed and labelled. One suitcase held soiled linen, destined for a real good boil. She did her personal washing in the bathroom, by stealth, since she had seen too many pails emptied into the beautiful green river which was the communal laundry.

As she lay and tossed she heard the faint scream of an engine, muted by distance to an amplified mosquito-ping. It was the night express, which – when farther down the valley – woke up the homesick sleepers in the hotel and whistled their thoughts after it, as though it were a monstrous metallic Pied Piper.

Just as, later, it called to Iris, it now drew the little spinster from her bed. She ran to the window and was in time to see it shoot past the end of the gorge, like a golden rod of light slipping into grooves of darkness.

'Tomorrow night I shall be in an express, too,' she gloated.

It was a rapture to anticipate her long journey, stage by stage and frontier by frontier, until she reached a small dingy station which was merely a halt built amid empty fields. No one would meet her there, because her father was afraid that blundering Sock, in his ecstasy, might leap at the engine and try to lick its face too.

But they would be waiting for her farther down the lane – and her eyes grew misty at the thought of that meeting. Yet even then she would not reach her journey's end until she ran through a dim white gate and a starlit garden, to see the light streaming through an open door.

'Mater,' whispered Miss Froy, with a lump in her throat.

Then a sudden fear touched her heart.

'I've never been so homesick before,' she thought. 'Is it a warning? Suppose – suppose something happened – to keep me from getting home.'

Something did happen – something so monstrous and unexpected that she could not really believe in it. It was an adventure which could only be credited in connection with someone else.

At first she was certain that somebody would soon come to her aid. She told herself it was a fortunate circumstance that she had met the charming English girl. They were compatriots, and she could rely on her with utmost confidence, because – were the situation reversed – she knew she would tear the train apart, wheel by wheel, in order to find her.

But as the time crawled on and nothing happened, doubts began to flock into her mind. She remembered that the girl had a touch of sunstroke and was far from well. She might be worse, or even seriously ill. Besides it would be difficult to try to explain the circumstances when one was ignorant of the language.

There was an even worse possibility. Iris might have tried to intervene and been snatched up, too, in the great machine which had caught her up in one of its revolutions. At the thought, Miss Froy's lip grew beaded from desperation and fear.

Then, suddenly, she felt the braking of the train. Its clatter and roar died down to a grinding slither, and with a mighty jerk the engine stopped.

'They've missed me,' she thought triumphantly. 'Now they are going to search the train.'

And once again she saw the lights of home streaming through the open door.

As she waited in happy expectation she would have been surprised and gratified to know that the beautiful bride – who looked like a film star – was thinking of her.

Although she was only a pawn, she was the central figure in a plot to restore her liberty. At that moment the professor was standing in the corridor just outside Mrs Laura's coupé. She had only to call to him and Miss Froy's ultimate release would be put in train.

As there was plenty of time before Trieste was reached, she delayed in order to be quite certain of the wisdom of her decision. Once she had applied the match she could not stop the blaze of publicity.

In reality, however, her mind was made up. Although she had discovered the barrister's drawbacks, he was the original prize for which she had played. When she was Lady Brown, Sir Peveril would be merely a husband and she knew how to deal with this useful domestic animal. Hitherto she had been humiliated by the knowledge that his programme did not include marriage, and in her anxiety to impress him favourably, she had developed an inferiority complex.

Royal smashing tactics suited her better. Her voice was arrogant as she spoke to the barrister.

'What are we stopping for?' she asked, looking out at a squalid platform, dimly revealed by a few flickering lights.

'Frontier,' explained the barrister.

'Help. Have we got to get out and go through the customs?'

'No, we take on the officials here . . . What's that shock-headed lunatic up to?'

The barrister frowned as Hare raced into the telegraph office, shouting back the while to the guard who was yelling at him. It was evidently a first-class slanging match, but unintelligible to the English passengers who were deprived of its finer points.

As a matter of fact it had struck the bright young man that he could save his own valuable time at Trieste if he took advantage of the halt to send off Mrs Barnes's telegram to Bath, England. The idea, however, did not make him popular with his compatriots.

'Fool's holding us up,' growled the barrister, looking at his watch.

To his surprise Laura was perfectly calm at the menace to their timetable.

'Does it matter?' she drawled. 'We shall get there.'

'We might lose our connection. We've cut it pretty fine. That reminds me of something. I was wondering whether, in *your* interests, we had better part before we get into Italy. We might run up against someone we know.'

'Personally I should not compare Italy with Piccadilly Circus. Still, it's on the map. What do you want to do?'

'I could take the Trieste-Paris express. Could you manage by yourself at Milan?'

'Perfectly. I shall find someone. Or someone will find me. In any case, I can look after myself.'

There was a confident note in her voice – associated with the dismissal of cooks – for the professor had just gone back to his compartment. She rose from her seat, prepared to follow him, when the customs officials appeared at the end of the corridor.

That check was of vital importance to Miss Froy. As Laura did not wish to be interrupted, she waited for the professor's luggage to be examined. In the interval the barrister had sensed a situation which prompted a few leading questions.

'What makes you look so serious?' he asked.

'You forget, this may be serious for me.'

'In what way? We're not parting for ever, are we? I can meet you in London.'

'How nice.'

Now that her pride was no longer a buffer between the natural woman and self-expression, Laura felt mistress of the situation. She held the winning card.

'I'm wondering,' she said, 'if I can endure the name of "Brown" after being Mrs Parmiter.'

'Will the occasion arise?'

'Well, if there's a divorce, you could hardly let me down. It's not done, is it, darling?'

'But, my sweet, there will be no divorce.'

'I'm not so sure. I know you made it very plain to me that you would not give your wife the evidence to divorce you. But she'll read about us in the papers – and no woman could stand for that.'

'You seem very sure of your publicity. Perhaps you have a better knowledge of the possibilities than I have?'

The barrister glowered at her as though she were a hostile witness, for he had realised the threat which underlay her smiles.

She meant to try to rush a situation.

'I can reassure you on one point,' he said coldly. 'If your husband brings an action, you may lose your own charming name. But you will not be called upon to make the greater sacrifice. There is already one

Lady Brown . . . My wife will never divorce me.'

Laura stared at him incredulously.

'You mean, she'd take it lying down?' she asked.

'Does the posture matter? The point is that we have a complete understanding. It would be against our mutual interests ever to part company . . . But I think there is no real risk of publicity. Do you?'

He knew he had won and she knew it too. His cool level voice stirred up Laura's smouldering passion.

'If there was,' she said, 'it seems as if I was the only one that stood to lose. You boast that your wife won't divorce you. Well, my husband would. And I thank God for it. At least I am married to a real man with decent natural feelings.'

The barrister screwed his monocle in his eye in an instinctive effort to preserve his dignity.

'I'm afraid I've disappointed you,' he said. 'I had no idea that I had led you to hope for anything beyond a pleasant and unconventional holiday.'

Before Laura could speak, the customs officer entered their compartment and was very courteous and obliging over the luggage and passports of the distinguished Englishman and his beautiful bride.

After he had gone the professor appeared again in the corridor – still puffing at his pipe.

Laura shivered at the sight of him because he reminded her of what she had nearly lost by a premature disclosure. Her fine house, her social position, her respectability, and perhaps even her children would all have been swept away for a man who would not marry her.

'Thanks be I sounded him first,' she told herself.

Her gain was Miss Froy's loss. The express carried a ghost-passenger, whose passport – although in order – was never examined. An experienced traveller, she realised what had actually happened when the train began to move slowly for the second time.

'Frontier,' she thought.

But in the interval between picking up the customs officials and dropping them again, she swept through a cycle of emotions, as she shot up from midnight to sunshine, and then – through the gradual twilight of suspense, deferred hope and anxiety – sank back again into darkness.

The train rushed on.

25

'Strange Disappearance'

After the professor had left her Iris slumped down in her seat and listened to the choppy current of the train's frantic rhythm. The grimed glass was beginning to grow steamy, so that it was difficult to see anything outside the window, except an occasional line of lights when the express flashed through some small station.

Since Miss Froy had been proved non-existent by the laws of logic she felt too flat to be interested in her surroundings. She had not even sufficient spirit to remain angry with the professor for his interference.

'All travellers are selfish,' she reflected. 'It was those Miss Flood-Porters. They were afraid they might be saddled with me, so they got at the professor. I expect he consulted the doctor about what could be done.'

She straightened herself in an effort to relieve the aching of her back. The continual shaking of the train had worn her out, while her neck felt as though it were made of plaster of Paris and would crack in two if she jerked it. At that moment she longed for a comfortable bed where she could rest, far from the incessant rattle and din.

It was the doctor's suggestion – a good night's rest. Yet, although she began to doubt her own wisdom in trying to swim against the current, she remained set in her determination to oppose advice.

Presently Hare entered and sat opposite to her in Miss Kummer's seat.

'Well?' he asked hopefully. 'Going to stop off at Trieste?'

'No,' replied Iris stiffly.

'But are you sure you're fit to go on?'

'Does it matter to you?'

'No. But, all the same, I'm worried stiff about you.'

'Why?'

'Hanged if I know. It's not a habit of mine.'

Against her will Iris smiled faintly. She could not forget Miss Froy. The memory of her was a grumbling undercurrent, like the aching of a stopped tooth. Yet whenever Hare was present he acted in the same manner as a local application that deadened the pain. In spite of her misery there was a queer thrill in being alone with him on the same nightmare journey.

'Cheer up,' he said. 'You'll soon be home. Back with your colony of friends.'

The prospect seemed suddenly distasteful to Iris.

'I don't want to see one of them,' she declared petulantly. 'I don't want to get back. I've no home. And nothing seems worth while.'

'What do you do with yourself?'

'Nothing . . . Oh, play about.'

'With other chaps?'

'Yes. We all do the same things. Silly things. There's not one real person among the lot of us . . . Sometimes I get terrified. I'm wasting my youth. What's at the end of it all?'

Hare made no attempt to console her or answer her question. He stared out at the darkness with a half-smile playing round his mouth. When he began to talk, it was about himself.

'My life's very different from yours. I never know where I'm going next. But it's always rough. And things happen. Not always pleasant things . . . Still, if I could take you with me on my next job, you'd get a complete change. You'd go without every comfort a refined home should have – but I'd lay you odds you'd never feel bored again.'

'Sounds lovely . . . Are you proposing to me?'

'No. Just waiting to dodge when you start to throw custard pies at me.'

'But lots of men propose to me. And I'd like to go to a rough place.'

'Fine. Now I can go into it seriously. Got any money?'

'Some. Just chicken feed.'

'Suits me. I've none.'

They were scarcely conscious of what they said as they talked at random in the only language they knew – their light words utterly at variance with the yearning in their eyes.

'You know,' said Hare, breaking a pause, 'all this is rot. I'm only doing it to take your mind off things.'

'You mean – Miss Froy?'

'Yes, confound the woman.'

To his surprise Iris changed the subject.

'What sort of brain have you?' she asked.

'Fair to middling, when it's lubricated. It works best on beer.'

'Could you write a detective thriller?'

'No. Can't spell.'

'But could you solve one?'

'Every time.'

'Then suppose you give me a demonstration. You've been very clever in proving Miss Froy could not exist. But – if she did – could you find out what *might* have happened to her? Or is it too difficult?'

Hare burst out laughing.

'I used to think,' he said, 'that if ever I liked a girl, I'd be cut out by some beautiful band conductor with wavy hair. I'm hanged if I thought I'd have to play second fiddle to an ancient governess. Time's revenge, I suppose. Long ago, I bit one. And she was a good governess . . . Well, here goes.'

He lit his pipe and furrowed his brow while Iris watched him with intense interest. His face – no longer slack and careless – was hardened into lines of concentration, so that he looked almost a different man. Sometimes he ran his fingers through his hair, when his rebellious tuft sprang up rampant, and sometimes he chuckled.

Presently he gave a crow of triumph.

'I've got it to fit. Bit of jiggery-pokery in parts, but it hangs together. Now would you like to hear an original story called "The Strange Disappearance of Miss Froy"?'

Iris winced at the light tone.

'I'd love to,' she told him.

'Then you're for it. But, first of all, when you boarded the train, was there one nun next door to you, or two?'

'I only noticed one as we passed the carriage. She had a horrible face.'

'Hum. My story demands a second one, later on.'

'That's convenient, because there is another one. I met her in the corridor.'

'Seen her since?'

'No, but I shouldn't notice one way or another. There's such a jam.'

'Good. That proves that no one would be likely to notice whether there was one nun, or two, connected with the invalid outfit. Especially as it's corked up at the end of the corridor. You see, I've got to play about with these blessed nuns, so they're very important.'

'Yes. Go on.'

'I haven't started yet. The nun part was preamble. Here really goes . . . Miss Froy is a spy who's got some information which she's sneaking out of the country. So she's got to be bumped off. And what better way than on a railway journey?'

'You mean – they've thrown her on the rails going through a tunnel?' asked Iris faintly.

'Don't be absurd. And don't look so wan. If they chucked her on the line her body would be found and awkward questions asked. No, she's got to *disappear*. And what I was getting at was this. On a journey, a lot of valuable time will be wasted before it can be proved even that she is missing. At first her people will think she's lost a connection or stopped at Paris for a day or two, to shop. So, by the time they get busy, the trail will be stone cold.'

'But they wouldn't know what to do. They're old and helpless.'

'Tough luck. You're making my tale positively pathetic. But even if they are influential and know the ropes, when they begin to make enquiries they'd find themselves up against a conspiracy of silence.'

'Why, is the whole train in the plot?'

'No, just the Baroness, the doctor and the nuns. Of course, there'd be a passive conspiracy of silence, as I mentioned before. None of the passengers, who are local folk, would dare to contradict any statement of the Baroness.'

'But, don't forget the Baroness said something to the ticket collector which you couldn't understand.'

'Is this my yarn or yours? But – perhaps you're right. There may be a railway official or two in it. In fact, there must have been some dirty work at the crossroads over her reserved seat. They had to be sure that she would be in the Baroness's compartment, and at the end of the train.'

'Next door to the doctor, too . . . But what's *happened to her*?'

In spite of her resolution to keep cool, Iris clenched her fingers in suspense as she waited.

'Aha,' gloated Hare. 'That's where my brain comes in . . . Miss Froy is lying in the next compartment to this, covered with rugs, and disguised with bandages and trimmings. Her own mother wouldn't know her now.'

'How? When?'

'It happened when you obligingly dropped off to sleep. Enter the doctor. He asks Miss Froy if she could render some slight service to his patient. I'm sure I don't know why he should rope her in as he's got a nurse on tap. But she'll go.'

'I know she would.'

'Well, directly she enters the compartment she gets the surprise of her life. To begin with all the blinds are drawn down and the place is in darkness. She smells a rat, but before she can squeal the three of them set on her.'

'The three?'

'*Ja*, the patient is one of the gang. One of them pinions her, the other throttles her so she can't shout, and the doctor is busy giving her an injection, to make her unconscious.'

Iris felt her heart hammer as she pictured the scene. 'It *could* happen,' she said.

Hare gave her a delighted beam.

'Wish I had you to listen to my golf-stories. You've got the right reaction to lies. Artistic ones, of course . . . By the way, one of the nuns is a man. The one with the ugly face.'

'I believe she is.'

'Don't be so prejudiced. All men aren't ugly. Well, Miss Froy is now down and out, so they're able to bandage her up roughly, and stick a lot of plaster over her face, to disguise her. Then they tie her up, gag her, and lay her out, in the place of the false patient, who was already dressed in uniform, only she was covered with rugs. So she's only to pull off her plaster and stick a veil over her bandaged head, to look the perfect nun. Number two.'

'I saw a second one in the corridor,' nodded Iris.

'But, by now, you've unearthed some English people who will remember Miss Froy, and you've roped in the parson's wife. As I think I explained before, the conspirators have to produce someone, and trust to bluff. So, down comes the blind again, while the second nun – the one who posed as the original patient, dresses herself in Miss Froy's clothes.'

As Iris remained silent Hare looked rather depressed.

'Admittedly feeble,' he said, 'but the best I can do.'

Iris scarcely heard him, for she was nerving herself to ask a question. 'What will happen to her when they reach Trieste?'

'Oh, this is the part my readers will adore,' explained Hare. 'She'll be put in an ambulance and taken to some lonely house, overlooking deep deserted water – a creek, or arm of the river, or something. You know the sort of thing – black oily water lapping a derelict quay. Then she'll be weighted, and all that, and neatly dumped among the mud and ooze. But I'm not altogether ruthless. I'll let them keep her drugged to the bitter end. So the old dear'll know nothing about it . . . Here. What's up?'

Iris had sprung to her feet and was tugging at the door. 'Everything you say may be true,' she panted. 'We mustn't waste time. We must do something.'

Hare forced her back to her seat.

'Here – you,' he said. Already she meant everything to him but he'd completely forgotten her name. 'This is simply a yarn I made up for you.'

'But I must get to that patient,' cried Iris. 'It's Miss Froy. I must see for myself.'

'Don't be a fool. The patient next door is *real*, and she's been smashed up. If we forced our way into that carriage and started to make any fuss the doctor would order us out. And quite right too.'

'Then you won't help me?' asked Iris despairingly.

'Definitely no. I'm sorry to keep harping on it, but I can't forget your sunstroke. And when I remember my own experience and how I mistook my own footer captain – '

'For the Prince of Wales. I know, I know.'

'I'm frightfully sorry I led you on. I only told you how things *might* be worked. But I'm just like the old lady who saw a giraffe for the first time. Honestly, "*I don't believe it.*" '

26

Signature

'Of course,' agreed Iris dully, 'you were just making it up. What a fool I am.'

As she tried to stifle her disappointment someone – farther down the corridor – began to speak in an unnaturally loud voice. The words were unintelligible to her and sounded like an incantation for rain; but Hare's face lit up.

'Someone's got a wireless set,' he said springing up. 'It's the news. Back in two shakes.'

When he returned he told Iris what he had heard.

'Another good murder sensation gone west. The medical evidence on the editor states he was shot about midnight – while the high hat had left for his hunting lodge directly after dinner. So they can't hang it on him. Pity.'

As he spoke something floated across Iris's memory, like one of those spirals of cobweb which are wafted on the air on still autumn mornings. She started up as Hare looked at his watch.

'Nearly time for the second dinner,' he told her. 'Coming?'

'No. But the others will be coming back.'

'What's the odds? Are you frightened of them?'

'Don't be absurd. But they make a little clump, all together, this end. And I – I don't like being so near that doctor.'

'Not frightened then. Well, our compartment will be empty while the professor and I are having dinner. I am willing to sublet it, at a nominal rent, to a good tenant.'

After he had gone Iris felt the old limpness stealing over her. A long-drawn howl, as though some damned soul were lamenting, followed by the rattle of machine-gun fire, told her that they were passing through a tunnel. It suggested a gruesome possibility.

Suppose – at that minute – a dead body were being thrown out of the train.

She reminded herself that Hare's story was fiction and managed to drive it from her mind. But another tale – which she had read in a

magazine and which was supposed to be authentic – slipped in to take
its place.

It was about two ladies who arrived by night at a Continental hotel,
on their way back from an Oriental tour. The daughter carefully noted
the number of her mother's room before she went to her own. When
she returned some time later, she found no trace of her mother, while
the room itself had different furniture and a new wallpaper.

When she made enquiries, the entire staff, from the manager downwards, assured her that she had come to the hotel alone. The mother's
name was not in the register. The cab-driver and the porters at the
railway terminus all supported the conspiracy.

The mother had been blown out like a match.

Of course there was an explanation. In the daughter's absence the
mother had died of plague, contracted in the East. The mere rumour
would have kept millions of visitors away from the exhibition about to
be held in the city. With such important interests at stake a unit had to
be sacrificed.

Iris's hands began to grow clammy as she wondered whether Miss
Froy's disappearance might not be a parallel on a very small scale. In
her case it would not involve a vast and complicated organisation, or a
fantastic conspiracy – merely the collusion of a few interested persons.

And Hare had shown her how it *could* have been worked.

She began to try to fit the facts to the theory. To begin with, although
the Baroness was wealthy, she was sharing a compartment with the
proletariat. Why? Because she had decided to take her journey at the
last minute and was unable to make a reservation? In that case, the
Flood-Porters and the Todhunters could not have secured coupés.

Then was it meanness? Or was it because she wanted a special
compartment at the end of the corridor, next to the doctor's carriage,
where they would not be seen nor disturbed?

Further – was it chance that the rest of the seats were occupied by
local people whose destinies she controlled to a great extent?

The questions hung in the air while a cloud of fresh suspicions
quivered into Iris's mind. It was an extraordinary fact that the blinds
remained undrawn in the invalid's compartment. She was left on show –
so to speak – to declare the goods. Was that to prepare the way for a
version of the old strategy – to hide an object in some place where it was
visible to everyone?

Only – what had poor little Miss Froy done? Hare was right when he
declared that he was influenced mainly by the question of motive. As far
as Iris could tell she had discharged her duties so faithfully that her
august employer had personally thanked her for services rendered.

Suddenly Iris caught her breath with excitement.

'That was *why*,' she whispered.

The personage was supposed to be in his hunting-lodge at the time of the murder. Yet Miss Froy, by tactlessly lying awake, had surprised him coming from the one and only bathroom, where presumably he had been washing before he flitted.

She had destroyed his alibi.

Her knowledge would be a positive danger in view of the fact that she was returning to teach the children of the Red leader. Everyone knew that she was a confirmed gossip and rattle. She would be proud of the personage's confidence and advertise it. And, as a British subject – with no axe to grind – her testimony would have weight against a mass of interested evidence.

When the personage shook hands so graciously with her, he was sealing her doom.

Iris pictured the hurried family conference at dawn – the hasty summons to the necessary confederates. Telephones would be humming with secret messages. In view of the urgency, it followed of necessity that Miss Froy's suppression could not be the perfect crime.

She tried to control the gallop of her imagination.

'Maximilian – Max' – she had not forgotten his name, since 'Hare was too long' – 'spun me a yarn. He was stretching the facts to make them fit in. Perhaps I'm doing the same. It's futile to palpitate about someone who may not exist. After all, as they say, she may be only a delusion . . . I do wish I could be sure.'

Her wish was granted in a dramatic manner. The carriage had grown hot and the steam on the window was turning gradually to beads of moisture, which were beginning to trickle downwards.

Iris followed the slow slide of one of these drops from the top down to a grimy corner of the uncleaned pane.

Suddenly she gave a start as she noticed a tiny name which had been written on the smoked glass.

Leaning over she was able to decipher the signature. It was 'Winifred Froy'.

27

The Acid Test

Iris stared at the name, hardly able to believe that her eyes were not playing her a trick. The tiny neat handwriting was round and unformed as that of a schoolgirl, and suggested the character of the little governess – half prim adult and half arrested youth.

It was proof positive that Miss Froy had sat recently in the corner seat. Iris vaguely remembered that she was knitting when she first entered the carriage. When she scrawled her name on the grimy glass with the point of one of her pins, she was working off some of the gush of her holiday mood.

'I *was* right, after all,' thought Iris exultantly.

It was an overwhelming relief to emerge from the fog of her nightmare. But her exhilaration was blotted out almost immediately by a sense of impending crisis.

She was no longer fighting shadows – but facing actual danger.

A terrible fate awaited Miss Froy. She was the only person on the train who realised the peril. And time was slipping remorselessly away. A glance at her watch showed that it was ten minutes past nine. In less than an hour they would arrive at Trieste.

Trieste now assumed a terrible significance. It was the place of execution.

The train was rushing at tremendous speed, in a drive to make up lost time. It rattled and shrieked as it swung round the curves – shaking the carriages as though it cared nothing for its human load. Iris felt that they were in the grip of an insensate maddened force, which, itself, was the victim of a relentless system.

The driver would be fined for every minute over the scheduled time of arrival. The sense of urgency made Iris spring up from her seat, only to stagger back again at a sudden wave of faintness. She felt a knocking inside her head and stabbing pains behind her eyeballs as the result of her unguarded movement. With a vague hope that it might act as an opiate she lit a cigarette.

A babel of voices in the corridor told her that the passengers were returning from dinner. The family party, with the blonde, came first. They were all in excellent spirits after their meal and took no notice of Iris, who glowered at them from her corner. She resented their passive conspiracy, even though they were ignorant of any threat to Miss Froy, and were pleased only to be of some slight service to the Baroness.

They were followed by the woman who wore Miss Froy's tweed suit and feathered hat. At the sight of the impostor, Iris's temperature rushed up again as she asked herself whether this were actually the second nursing-sister whom she had met in the corridor.

Both had dull black eyes, a sallow skin and bad teeth; but the peasants in the railway waiting-room had looked much the same. As it was impossible to reach any conclusion, Iris rose and dashed out into the corridor.

She was strung up to action and intended to storm the next carriage. But blocking her way and almost filling the narrow space was the gigantic black figure of the Baroness. As she towered above her, Iris realised that she was bottled up in the danger-zone of the train – away from everyone she knew.

She felt suddenly helpless and afraid as she looked away from the grim face to the shrieking darkness rushing past the window. The maniac shrieks of the engine and the frantic shaking of the train increased her sense of nightmare. Once again her knees began to shake and she had a terrible fear that she was going to faint.

Her horror of becoming insensible and so being at their mercy made her fight the dizziness with every ounce of her strength. Licking her dry lips, she managed to speak to the Baroness.

'Let me pass, please.'

Instead of giving way, the Baroness looked at her twitching face.

'You are in pain,' she said. 'That is not good, for you are young and you travel without friends. I will ask the nurse here for a tablet to relieve your head.'

'No, thank you,' said Iris firmly. 'Please, will you stand on one side?'

The Baroness took no notice of her request, or of her refusal. Instead, she shouted some imperious command which brought the callous-faced nurse to the doorway of the invalid's carriage. Iris noticed subconsciously that the Baroness's words did not conform to a conventional request, but were a peremptory order for prompt action.

The glass of the patient's window was also growing steamy from heat, but Iris tried to look inside. The still form laid out on the seat appeared to have no face – only a white blur.

As she asked herself what lay underneath the bandages, the nurse noticed her interest. She pounced forward and gripped the girl's arm, as though to pull her inside.

Iris looked at the brutal mouth, the dark shading round the lips and the muscular fingers, whose backs were covered with short black hairs.

'It *is* a man,' she thought.

Terror urged her to an elemental action of self-defence. She was scarcely conscious of what she did as she pressed the end of her smouldering cigarette against the back of one of the hands. Taken by surprise, the nurse relaxed her grip with what sounded like an oath.

In that instant Iris pushed past the Baroness and dashed down the corridor, fighting her way against the stream of returning diners. Although they opposed her advance, she was glad of their presence, because they formed a barrier between her and the Baroness.

As her terror waned, she began to realise that everyone in the train seemed to be laughing at her. The guard openly sneered as he twisted his little black spiked moustache. There was a white flash of teeth and hoots of smothered laughter. The passengers evidently considered her slightly mad and were amused by a funny spectacle.

Their derision made Iris aware of the situation. She felt self-conscious and ashamed as though she were in an unclothed kind of dream.

'Heavens, what have I done?' she asked herself. 'That nurse only offered me some aspirin, or something. And I burned her hand. If they're really on the level, they will think me mad.'

Then her terror flared up again as the thought of Miss Froy.

'They won't listen to me. But I *must* make them understand about her . . . This train seems a mile long. I'll never get there . . . Faces. Grinning faces . . . Miss Froy . . . I must be in time.'

She seemed imprisoned in some horrible nightmare, where her limbs were weighted with lead and refused to obey her will. The passengers blocked her way, so that she appeared to recede two steps where she advanced one. To her distorted imagination, the faces of these strangers were caricatures of humanity – blank, insensible and heartless. While Miss Froy was going to be murdered, no one cared for anything but dinner.

After an age-long struggle through several sections of the train – when the connecting-passages turned to clanking iron concertinas, which tried to catch her and press her to death – she reached the restaurant-car. As she heard the clink of china and the hum of voices, her brainstorm passed and she lingered in the entrance – her returning sense of convention at war with elemental fear and horror.

Soup was being served, and the diners were spooning it up vigorously, for they had been waiting a long time for their meal. In her lucid interval, Iris realised the hopeless prospect of trying to convince hungry men who had only just begun their dinner.

Once again she ran the gauntlet of faces as she reeled down the gangway. Two waiters, whispering to one another, tittered, and she felt sure that they were sneering at her.

The professor, who shared a table with Hare, saw her first, and an expression of apprehension flitted across his long face. He was chatting to the doctor, who had lingered over his coffee and liqueur, since the places for the second dinner were not all filled.

Iris felt chilled by her reception when they all stared at her in silence. Even Hare's eyes held no welcome, as he watched her with a worried frown.

In desperation she appealed to the professor.

'For heaven's sake go on with your soup. Don't stop – but please listen. This is of deadly importance. I know there is a Miss Froy. I know there's a conspiracy against her. And I know *why*.'

The professor gave a resigned shrug as he continued spooning his soup. As Iris poured out her incoherent story, she was herself appalled by the weakness of her arguments. Before she finished she despaired of convincing him. He listened in stony silence, and was obviously absorbed by the exact proportion of salt to add to his soup.

At the end of the tale he raised his brows interrogatively as he glanced at the doctor, who broke into some rapid explanation. Watching their faces with anxious eyes, Iris could tell that Hare was disturbed by what was said, for he cut into the conversation.

'That's not her yarn. It's mine. I spun it for a lark, and the poor kid sucked it in. So, if anyone's loopy, it's – '

He broke off, suddenly aware of what he had revealed. But Iris was too distraught to notice implications.

'Won't you come now?' she entreated the professor.

He looked at his empty plate which the waiter had placed in readiness for the fish course.

'Can't it wait until after dinner?' he asked wearily.

'*Wait?* Won't you understand. It's deadly, terribly urgent. When we reach Trieste it will be too late.'

Again the professor mutely consulted the doctor, who stared fixedly at Iris as though he were trying to hypnotise her. When at last he spoke, it was in English for her benefit.

'Perhaps we had better come at once to see my patient. I'm sorry that your dinner should be spoiled, professor. But the young lady is in a very highly-strung condition. It may be – safer – to try and reassure her.'

Wearing the expression of a martyr to his sense of justice, the professor unfolded himself from his seat. Once again the little procession staggered in single file along the corridors of the reeling train. As they neared the end, Hare turned and spoke to Iris in a fierce whisper.

'Don't be a blasted fool and start anything.'

Her heart sank as she realised that his advice was too late. The nursing-sister was already displaying her hand for the benefit of the doctor and the professor. Iris noticed vaguely that she had wrapped a handkerchief around her wrist as though she wished to conceal the wound from too close a scrutiny.

Then the doctor turned to her and spoke in soothing syrupy accents.

'My dear young lady, wasn't it rather – impetuous – to burn my poor nurse? And all because she offered you a harmless tablet to relieve the pain of your head . . . See, professor, how her face twitches.'

Iris shrank as he touched her forehead with a cold forefinger to illustrate his meaning.

Suddenly she remembered that when one is losing a defensive game, the only hope is to attack. Plucking up her courage, she managed to steady her voice.

'I cannot be sorry enough about the burn. It's no excuse to say I was hysterical. But there was some excuse for my being so. There is so much that I cannot understand.'

The doctor accepted her challenge.

'Such as – ?' he asked.

'Well, the professor tells me you offered to take me to a nursing home at Trieste.'

'The offer is still open.'

'Yet you are supposed to be rushing a patient to hospital for a dangerous operation. How could you possible bother yourself with a complete stranger? . . . It makes one wonder exactly how serious her injuries are. Or if she has any at all.'

The doctor stroked his beard.

'My offer was made merely to relieve the professor of an unwelcome responsibility, which is in my line and not in his. But I am afraid that you exaggerate your own importance. My intention was to give you a seat in the ambulance which took us to the hospital. After we had gone inside with our patient, the driver would follow his instructions and drive you to some recommended nursing home. It was not for professional service – but merely to give you a bed, so that you could continue your journey after a good night's sleep.'

The proposal sounded so reasonable that Iris could only fall back on her second question.

'Where is the other nurse?'

The doctor paused perceptibly before his reply.

'There is only one nurse.'

As she looked at his impassive face, partly screened by his black spade-beard, Iris knew instinctively that it was useless to protest. The result would be the same – denials on every side. No one but herself would have seen that second nurse. Just as no one would accept Miss Froy's signature as genuine – supposing that it had not been already destroyed by condensation.

The doctor spoke to the professor.

'I am sorry to detain you further,' he said, 'but here is a young lady who believes very terrible things. We must try to convince her of her *delusions*.'

He crossed to the shrouded form of his patient and pulled up a corner of one of the rugs, displaying a neat pair of legs.

'Can you identify these stockings or these shoes?' he asked.

Iris shook her head as she looked at the thick silk stockings and regulation brown-calf single-strap shoes.

'You know I can't,' she said. 'But you might have better luck if you would raise just one bandage and let me see her face.'

The doctor grimaced with horror.

'Ah,' he said, 'I see you do not understand. I must tell you something that is not pretty. Listen.' He touched the swathed forehead with a butterfly flick of his fingertips. 'There is no face here at all. *No face*. Only lumps of raw flesh. Perhaps we shall make quite another face, if we are lucky. We shall see.'

His fingers moved on and hovered for a second over the bandage which covered the eyes of the figure.

'We await the oculist's verdict on these,' he said. 'Till then, we dare not expose them to a flicker of light. It may be a case of total blindness, for one eye is but pulp. But science can work marvels.'

He smiled at Iris and continued. 'But most terrible of all is the injury to the brain. I will not describe it, for already you look sick. First of all we must attend to that. Afterwards – the rest, if the patient still lives.'

'I don't believe you,' Iris told him. 'It's all lies.'

'In that case,' said the doctor smoothly, 'you can convince yourself. You have only to tear one little strip of plaster from the face, to see . . . But if you do, I warn you that bleeding will start again and the patient will die instantly from shock . . . You will be charged with murder and you will be hanged . . . But since you are so sure of the face which is under these bandages, you will not hesitate . . . *Will* you tear off this strip?'

Iris felt Hare's fingers closing over her arm, as she hesitated. Her instinct told her that the doctor was putting up a bluff, and that she ought to grasp at even the hundredth chance to save Miss Froy's life.

Yet the doctor had done his work too well. The thought of that mutilated face spouting fountains of blood made her shrink back. After-wards? The rope – or Broadmoor for life. It was too horrible a prospect to contemplate.

'I – I can't,' she whispered.

'Ah,' sneered the doctor, 'you talk, but you are not so brave.'

For the first time it struck Iris that he had never intended to risk his patient. Had he done so, he would have committed professional suicide. Both he and the nurse were on guard, to anticipate her movements.

All the same, he had some ulterior object in view, for he seemed disappointed.

At the time Iris was too sick at heart over her own cowardice to question further. She realised that she had two enemies in the carriage. The doctor – and herself.

28

Raise Your Hand

Iris started from her daze to realise that the professor was talking of dinner.

'If you would hurry back to the dining-car, Hare,' he said hopefully, 'you might explain to the waiter that we've missed the fish course.'

'He'd only say it was "off",' Hare told him. 'They've got to rush the second dinner through before we make Trieste.'

'Tut, tut.' The professor clicked. 'In that case, we had better return at once. Perhaps you would go on ahead and order extra portions of meat, since we've gone without our fish.'

'Not their fault. We walked out on the fish. But I'll see what can be done about it.'

Hare checked himself and turned to Iris rather doubtfully.

'Do you mind?' he asked.

She gave an hysterical laugh, for it had just struck her that although the professor was confident of his ability to conduct her investigation, he could not risk his linguistic talent where vital interests were concerned.

'Go back, for pity's sake,' she said. 'Nothing matters but dinner, does it?'

The professor, whose lean face had brightened at the prospect of food, resented her reproach. Although famished, he felt he must defend his own reputation for meticulous justice.

'Are you being quite fair?' he asked. 'We've paid a stiff price for a meal, so we are entitled to claim – at least – a portion of it. And you must admit we have not spared time or convenience in trying to convince you of your mistake.'

She shook her head, but she was oppressed by a weight of hopelessness. There seemed nothing more to be done to help Miss Froy. Any attempt at interference would only expose her to the risk of reprisal.

It was not cowardice alone that made her fear the power of the doctor, but common sense. Since she was the sole person on the train who believed in Miss Froy's existence, it stood to reason that she could be of use to her only if she were a free agent.

Her one chance lay in convincing the professor that there was a real need of further investigation. Although she disliked him, he possessed those qualities which counted in such a crisis. He was pig-headed, coolly humane, and rigidly just. If he were morally certain that he was right, nothing could shake him, and he would plug away at his objective in the face of all opposition.

It was bad luck that – at the moment – he was concentrating on his dinner.

Her curdled brain cleared just as he was about to leave the carriage.

'Professor,' she said, 'if I'm right, when you get back to England you'll read about a missing Englishwoman – Miss Froy. When you do, it will be too late to save her. Won't it haunt you for the rest of your life that you wouldn't listen to me *now*?'

'I might regret it,' admitted the professor, 'only the occasion is not likely to arise.'

'But if you'll only do something – a very little thing – later you won't have to be sorry at all. And you won't have to cut short your dinner.'

'What is it that you want me to do?'

'Go with the doctor to the Trieste hospital and watch while a bandage or strip of plaster is removed. Just enough to show you that there is genuine injury.'

Although the professor was staggered by the suggestion, he considered it slowly with habitual conscientiousness. It encouraged Iris to follow up her advantage with a fresh argument.

'You must admit, *I* can do nothing. I'm not a lunatic and it might mean manslaughter. Besides, the doctor wouldn't let me. So it boils down to this. His precious test means nothing at all.'

At her words, the first distrust of the doctor entered the professor's mind. It was visible in his puckered face and drumming fingers. He always counted the cost before he entertained any project, although it was typical of his high sense of duty that it could not deter him.

In this case the drawbacks were numerous, the chief of them being finance. Although he was no spendthrift, his standard of living at Cambridge took all his salary, and he had to encroach on his capital for holidays. To get a complete mental change he went away at least three times a year, so he had to practise economy.

As the most expensive part of this special trip was the long railway journey, he had booked through one of the cheaper tourist agencies which specialised in cut-prices. Therefore, his ticket would not allow for his breaking the journey anywhere.

To make matters more difficult he was short of cash, since his dislike of communal travel had made him yield to the temptation of sharing a coupé with Hare on the return journey.

There was another and more urgent reason why he should not stop at Trieste for the night. Delay would involve the sacrifice of a cherished engagement. He had been invited to spend the following weekend with an elderly peer – an intellectual recluse – who lived in a remote corner of Wales. If he reached England on Saturday, instead of Friday, it would be too late.

The doctor watched him closely as he frowned and tapped his cheek-bones.

'Is it not convenient for you to stop at Trieste?' he asked.

'Definitely inconvenient.'

'I am sorry. Because, in my own interest, I must beg of you to do what this young lady asks.'

'Why?' asked the professor, incensed by this double assault on his weekend.

'Because I am growing convinced that there must be some reason for this poor young lady's distress. It is always "Miss Froy". Is that a common name in England, like "Smith"?'

'It is not familiar to me.'

'But she had heard it before – and in connection with some terrible experience. I do not know what has happened. But I think that there really is a lady called "Miss Froy", and that some harm has happened to her. I think, too, that this poor young lady knew, but the shock has driven away all memory.'

'Absurd,' interrupted Iris. 'I won't – '

'Shut up,' whispered Hare fiercely.

He had listened with close attention, for he was beginning to wonder whether the doctor had not found the true explanation of Iris's delusion. She had been unconscious until just before she managed to catch the train. Although the explanation was sunstroke, it might have been supplied through the agency of some interested person, who wanted to confuse her recollection.

'You will understand,' went on the doctor, 'that I do not wish to be under any suspicion, if – later – a lady might be declared missing.'

'It's a preposterous idea,' said the professor. 'Besides, the hospital authorities would back you up.'

'But how am I to prove that it is this patient I bring to them, and not some substitute? But if you, professor, would accompany me to the hospital and wait for the surgeon's initial examination, there can be no further question. It is your high reputation that I crave for my protection.'

The professor smiled bleakly, for he was very hungry. Although he was an excellent bridge player, he had no knowledge of poker. Consequently the doctor's offer seemed to him proof positive that there was not even the flimsiest foundation for Iris's fantastic theory.

'I think you are carrying professional caution too far,' he said. 'Miss Carr' – unlike Hare, he was used to memorising names – 'has declared that she went to the dining-car with one lady whom she called "Miss Froy" – and that lady has since been identified as a Miss Kummer . . . She is not well, which accounts for her mistake . . . In the circumstances, there is no shred of evidence that the real Miss Froy – if there is such a person – is on the train at all.'

'Then, in case of future trouble, may I apply to you to support any statement I might make?' asked the doctor.

'Certainly. I will give you my card.'

The professor wheeled round and turned dinnerwards.

Hare divined that Iris was on the verge of an explosion.

Hitherto he had managed to restrain her by the warning pressure of his hand on her arm, but she was at the end of her patience.

'Don't throw a scene,' he implored. 'It's no good. Come back to the coop.'

Instead of obeying she raised her voice.

'*Miss Froy*. Can you hear me? Hold up your hand if you can.'

29

Trieste

Miss Froy heard her. She held up her hand.

Although she was blinded by her bandage, she had recognised Iris's voice among a murmur of other sounds. In a confused fashion she realised that people were talking; but their tones were blurred and broken, as though they were far away – giving the impression of an imperfect long-distance call.

She tried to speak to them, but could not because of her gag. Once before she had contrived to move it partially, with frenzied pressure – remembering the while how her father used to tease her about the power of her tongue. She put every ounce of strength into that cry for help, but it was an uncouth incoherent sound, like an animal in pain.

No one heard her – and her captors had wedged the gag tighter, increasing her discomfort. Her arms were bound to her body above the elbows, and her legs were tied together at the ankles by a surgical bandage. The doctor made no attempt to hide it when he exposed her shoes and stockings for identification. He knew that among such a profusion of strappings, one more or less would never be remarked.

However, her hands were free from the wrists, because the supply of bindings had given out, and – in any case – they were powerless to do more than wave feebly. Miss Froy's heart fluttered with joy as she told herself that her clever girl knew that an instantaneous response to her appeal, however slight, would show that the patient recognised her name and was giving proof of identity.

So she spread out her fingers – fan-wise – and flapped them in the air in a pathetic SOS.

Then once again her mind, which she was unable to control, slid away. It was cobwebbed and smeared from drugs, but every now and again a corner would clear, like the transparent red stains of juice that veins the scum of boiling jam. In these lucid moments a whirl of memories returned, but in the end her mind always went back to that first moment of shock.

It was incredible – monstrous. She had been sitting in her compartment when the doctor had entered and asked if anyone would help him raise his patient. He explained that the nurse had gone away for a few minutes and the poor creature in his charge had grown restless, as though she were uncomfortable.

It was second-nature to Miss Froy to respond. She was not only always ready to be of service, but she was also anxious to see the crash casualty at closer quarters, besides learning perhaps more about the accident. It would be something with which to thrill the family when she related her adventures on Friday night.

When they entered the patient's compartment the doctor asked her to raise the head while he lifted the body. It was with specially deep sympathy that she bent over the prostrate form, because she was reminded of the contrast between them.

'She's smashed,' she thought, 'and I'm well and happy. I'm going home.'

Suddenly a long pair of white linen-clad arms shot out and clutched her throat.

The helpless patient was gripping her windpipe in a merciless grip. In that appalling moment she remembered a Grand Guignol horror, when an electrified corpse had strangled the man who had galvanised it to synthetic life. Then the pressure tightened, lights flashed under her eyelids, and she knew no more.

For some time the eclipse had been total. Then, gradually, there were infinitesimal rifts in the darkness of her senses. She became conscious that she was trussed, gagged and blinded, while muffled voices discussed her fate.

It was not a cheerful prospect. Although she was ignorant of her crime, she had an inkling of her sentence. It was connected with an ambulance which would meet them at Trieste. But it would take her to no hospital.

Yet in spite of cramp and thirst, of bodily anguish and mental torment, she never gave up hope.

It was said in the family that she followed Aunt Jane. In her lifetime, this Victorian lady had wanted a talking-doll, a tricycle, an operatic career, a husband, a legacy. She got none of these things, but she never discarded a single wish, nor doubted that each would be granted – in the end.

When the end came, she was seventy-seven and a pensioner on family charity; yet she closed her eyes with as lively a faith in the talking-doll as in the legacy which would grant her a leisured life and a dignified death.

Aunt Jane helps to explain why Miss Froy remained tolerably calm in the face of each fresh disappointment. Mercifully, however, her clear moments were of brief duration. Most of the time she was in a drugged dream, during which she was forever trying to get home.

She always managed to reach the gate and saw the lighted garden path with its exaggerated hollows – when a displaced pebble revealed a pit. The turf borders and the pink and purple Chinese asters were unnaturally vivid in the lamplight, while the pungent scent of early chrysanthemums hung on the frosty air.

But although she was so near that she could see the cracked red tile in the passage, she knew that something was wrong, and that she would never reach the door . . . It was when she was struggling out of one of these tantalising visions, that she heard Iris calling her name and telling her to hold up her hand.

Unfortunately she did not know that there was a bad block in her system of communication. None of the channels were clear, so that her brain did not register the message from her ears until after the doctor – in a state of indignant horror – had literally swept his visitors out into the corridor. Even after that, some time elapsed before her nerve-centres were linked up with the intelligence department, and by then it was too late.

The blinds had all been drawn down, so there was no one besides the nurse to witness the futile signal of her fluttering fingers.

Outside the door the doctor wiped his face in his agitation.

'That was a terrible thing to do,' he said, his voice vibrating with passion. 'I was wrong to let you in at all. But I never dreamed you would be so imbecile as to try and injure my poor patient.'

As Iris shrank involuntarily before his rage, he appealed to the professor.

'You can understand, professor, that absolute quiet is essential for my patient. The grave injury to the head – '

'How can she get quiet on a railway journey?' broke in Iris, as the engine plunged into a tunnel with an ear-splitting yell.

'That is something quite different,' explained the doctor. 'One can sleep through traffic. It is the slight unaccustomed sound which wakens one from sleep. If she had heard you she might have been called back, while I am doing my utmost – in mercy – to keep her unconscious.'

'I quite understand,' the professor assured him. 'And I regret this has happened.' His voice was glacial as he spoke to Iris. 'You had better get back to your carriage, Miss Carr.'

'Yes, come on,' urged Hare.

Iris felt that they were all against her. In sudden defiance she launched a lone offensive.

'Directly we reach Trieste I am going to the British Embassy,' she told them.

They were brave words, but her head was swimming and her knees shook so violently that she felt incapable of carrying out her threat. All the same, her intentions filled her with an illusion of power. Then Hare tackled her in his old international form and carried her along the corridors with the impetus of a tidal-bore, while the professor plodded in the rear.

'My only hope is we shall get some sort of a dinner,' was his parting remark to the doctor.

Iris was too bewildered by what had happened to resist Hare's high-handed treatment. She could not understand why there had been no response to her cry. It shook her confidence and made her feel that her moral cowardice in failing to expose the mystery patient was justified.

Yet even if she were a genuine accident case, the danger which threatened Miss Froy was not dormant. When she was back in the coupé she presented Hare with an ultimatum.

'Are you with me or against me? Are you stopping at Trieste?'

'No,' replied Hare firmly. 'Neither are you.'

'I see. Then you didn't mean what you said about liking me – and all that.'

'I certainly meant – all that.'

'Well, if you don't come with me to the Embassy, I'm through with you.'

Hare tugged at his collar miserably.

'Can't you realise I'm your only friend?' he asked.

'If you were a friend you'd prove it.'

'Wish I could, only I haven't the spunk. As your best friend, I ought to knock you out, so that you'd stay put for the next twenty-four hours, and rest your poor old head.'

'Oh, I hate you,' stormed Iris. 'For heaven's sake, go away.'

In the next compartment the Misses Flood-Porter overheard scraps of the dialogue.

'That girl certainly contrives to get some excitement out of a railway journey,' remarked the elder sister astringently.

While the young people were quarrelling about her, Miss Froy was lying rigid, with still hands. It had gradually dawned upon her that she had no audience, so her demonstration was wasted. However, she had one crumb of comfort when Iris mentioned appealing to the British Consul. She had heard that cry of defiance through the closed door.

Presently she realised that the hint had not been wasted. There was a low rumbling conference inside the carriage.

'Trieste,' remarked a masculine voice. It belonged to the doctor's chauffeur, who was wearing the incongruous uniform of a nursing-sister. 'What now?'

'We must waste no time at Trieste,' replied the doctor. 'We shall have to drive all night, like hell, to get back to protection.'

'But – where will you dump the body now?'

The doctor mentioned a place. 'It is on our road,' he explained. 'The wharf is deserted – and the eels swarm.'

'Good. They will be hungry. Very soon there will be no face to tell tales, if it should be found later . . . Will you dump the clothes and baggage there too?'

'Fool. They would be a certain means of identification. No, we take them with us in the car. You will incinerate them without delay directly we get back.'

Although her brain was so misty, some vibration of her senses made Miss Froy aware that they were talking about her. She shuddered instinctively at the thought of black stagnant water, thick with mud and scummed with refuse. She had such a violent dislike of corruption.

But she missed the real implication.

The chauffeur went on to anticipate difficulties.

'What if anyone makes enquiries at the Trieste hospitals?'

'We shall explain that the patient died in transit.'

'But if they demand to see the corpse?'

'They will see it. There will be no difficulty about that, once we are back. The mortuary will provide me with a female corpse which I will mutilate.'

'Hum. I wish I was safely at home. There is still that girl.'

'Yes,' remarked the doctor, 'it is extraordinary how the English will regard themselves as the policemen of the world. Even a girl has the habit. But it is a mistake to think them a stupid nation. That professor has a good brain, and he is no fool . . . But luckily, he is honourable, and believes that all the world must be honourable, too. He will support all I say.'

'Still, I wish I was back,' harped the chauffeur.

'The risk is great,' his employer reminded him. 'So, also, is the reward.'

The drone of masculine voices which drummed against Miss Froy's semi-sealed ears – like the hum of a spinning wheel – ceased. The chauffeur thought of the garage he would buy, while the doctor planned to retire from practice.

He did not relish his present commission, but the ruling family claimed his loyalty and self-interest forbade disobedience. Directly the Baroness had sent for him, privately, by night, he had evolved the best scheme he could devise on the spur of the moment to clear an obstacle from the illustrious pathway.

He knew why he had been chosen, for he, himself, would not use a delicate surgical instrument to cut a tarry string. His reputation was smutted because of recent mishaps at the local hospital. His scientific curiosity was keener than his wish to exterminate disease, and he was under suspicion of having prolonged operations unduly, and at the expense of life.

From the beginning the venture had been unlucky, because of the interference of the English girl. But for her, the little plan would have worked perfectly, by reason of its simplicity, and the small number of confederates. He knew that he and his chauffeur would take their lives in their hands when they scorched homewards through dangerous passes, rounding dizzy precipices on one wheel, in their effort to race the express back to their native territory.

But once they were back, every emergency would be forestalled. An adequate explanation would be forthcoming to any enquiry. No one would have any awkward knowledge to disclose and every wire that connected the dead patient with Miss Froy would be cut.

'Will you dump the English girl in the sewer, too?' asked the chauffeur suddenly.

'No,' replied the doctor. 'Further complication would be dangerous. But when we reach Trieste she will not be in a position to make further trouble for us.'

Miss Froy heard his words and, for the first time, her optimism failed her. With a wave of agonised longing she thought of the family at home, for she had sent them her timetable, and she guessed they would be tracing it on the map.

True to her forecast, at that moment they were thinking of her. They had done their best to fight their unusual depression, for they had lighted a fire – composed principally of fir-cones – and had been guilty of an extravagant supper – scrambled eggs.

Sock lay on the rug watching the flames. In spite of the welcome warmth, he was still subdued after his disappointment, for he had rushed off against orders to meet the train, with a hope new-born.

Mr Froy looked at his wife and noticed that the underlip of her small firm mouth was pendulous and that she sagged in her chair. For the first time he saw plainly that she was his senior, and that he, too, had grown old.

Then he glanced at the clock.

'Winsome's nearly come to the end of her first stage homewards,' he told his wife. 'She'll soon reach Trieste.'

Mrs Froy passed the information on to the dog.

'Sock, the little mistress is really on her way home now. Every minute she is coming nearer – nearer – nearer. In another half-hour she'll be at Trieste.'

Trieste.

30

Recantation

The waiter managed to salvage some dinner for the professor and Hare, who ate through the courses in silence. As they were finishing their cheese and biscuits, the doctor entered the dining-car and seated himself at their table.

'I am sorry to disturb you,' he said, 'but I want a little conference about the young English lady.'

The professor stifled an exclamation, for he feared that Iris had broken out in some fresh indiscretion.

'Coffee, please,' he said to the waiter. 'Black . . . Well – what is the trouble *now*?'

'As a medical man I find myself faced with a responsibility,' explained the doctor. 'The lady is in a dangerous mental state.'

'What grounds have you for your conclusion?' asked the professor, who never accepted a statement without data.

The doctor shrugged.

'Surely it is obvious to the meanest intelligence that she is suffering from a delusion. She invents someone who is not here. But there are other signs. She is highly excitable – suspicious of everyone – inclined to be violent – '

As he noticed Hare's involuntary grimace, he broke off and turned to the younger man.

'Pardon. Is the young lady your affianced?'

'No,' grunted Hare.

'But perhaps a lover – or a dear friend? Yet it would not surprise me to hear that she has been very angry recently with you. Has she?'

'I'm not really popular at present,' admitted Hare.

'Thank you for the confidence, for it confirms my diagnosis. It is always a sign of mental malady when they turn upon those they love best.'

He could tell he had captured Hare's sympathy as he continued.

'There is no real danger if we can take a precaution. It is essential at this stage that her brain should be rested. If she could have a long sleep, I am confident she will wake up quite well again. But if we let her persist in working herself up into a fever, the mental mischief may be – irreparable.'

'I think there is something in that, professor,' agreed Hare. 'It's exactly what I've been thinking myself.'

'What do you propose?' asked the professor cautiously.

'I should suggest,' replied the doctor, 'that you persuade her to swallow a harmless sedative which I can give you.'

'She will object.'

'Then it should be given by force.'

'Impossible. We cannot control her wishes.'

'Then, perhaps, you could trick her into taking it?'

As the professor remained mulishly silent, the doctor half rose from the table.

'I can assure you,' he said, 'that I have more than enough responsibility of my own to shoulder, with my patient. I only felt it my duty to warn you. We doctors are pledged to the service of humanity – whether we receive fees or no. But now that I have explained the position, I can leave the decision to you. My own conscience is clear.'

The doctor was on the point of departing with dignity, when Hare called him back.

'Don't go, doctor. I feel the same as you about this. I've had personal experience of delusions, with concussion.' He turned eagerly to the professor. 'Can't we wangle it somehow?'

The professor's long upper lip seemed to lengthen in his disapproval.

'I could not be a party to such a course,' he said. 'It would be gross interference with Miss Carr's personal liberty. She is a free agent.'

'Then – you'd prefer to observe "good form" and see her go to the bughouse?' asked Hare indignantly.

The professor smiled acidly.

'My own impression is,' he told them, 'that there is not the slightest danger of that. I have had experience of such cases. My work brings me into contact with neurotic young women. To my mind, Miss Carr is merely hysterical.'

'Then – what do you propose?' asked Hare.

'I think a salutary shock will probably bring her to her senses.'

Reinforced by his meal, the professor felt master of the situation. He finished his coffee and liqueur, flicked a crumb from his waistcoat, and rose in a leisurely manner.

'*I* will reason with Miss Carr,' he said.

He strolled out of the dining-car and lurched along the corridors. As he passed the coupé occupied by the Misses Flood-Porter, he was tempted to resign his mission and join them in a little chat. The ladies looked so composed and immaculate – for they were well in advance in their preparations for arrival at Trieste – that he was hopeful that further conversation would reveal some mutual friend.

Resolute in his self-imposed duty, however, he entered his carriage and seated himself opposite to Iris. His first glance told him that she had been lighting cigarette after cigarette, only to throw them away, barely smoked. Although her action was merely a sign of nervous tension, he looked with distaste at the litter of spent matches on the floor and seats.

'Will you take some advice offered in a friendly spirit?' he asked, speaking to her as though she were a fractious child.

'No,' replied Iris mutinously. 'I want to hear the truth, for a change.'

'The truth may be a bit of a shock. But you've asked for it, so you shall have it . . . The doctor has just told me that, as a result of your sunstroke, you are – very slightly, and only temporarily – deranged.'

The professor honestly believed that he was dealing with a neurotic girl who was telling lies from a love of sensation, so he watched her reaction with complacent confidence. When he saw the horror in her eyes, he felt his experiment was justified.

'Do you mean – *mad*?' she asked in a whisper.

'Oh, dear, no. Nothing to be frightened of. But he is not happy about your safety as you are travelling alone. He may be forced to take steps to ensure it, unless you can manage to keep perfectly quiet.'

'What steps?' asked Iris. 'Do you mean that nursing home? I should resist. No one can do anything to me against my will.'

'In the circumstances, violence would be most unwise. It would only confirm the doctor's fears. But I want to make the position quite clear to you. Listen.'

The professor sawed the air with his forefinger and spoke impressively.

'You have only to keep calm and everything will be all right. No one will interfere with you in any way, unless you remind them of your existence. To be brutally frank, you've made yourself a public nuisance. It's got to stop.'

The professor was not so unhuman as he seemed. His own unpleasant experience with his infatuated student had prejudiced him against emotion, but he thought he was acting in Iris's interests.

Therefore he could have no idea of the hell of fear into which he plunged her. She was white to her lips as she shrank into the corner of the carriage. She was afraid of him – afraid of everyone in the train. Even Hare seemed to have entered into the conspiracy against her. The whole world appeared roped into a league that threatened her sanity.

Lighting yet one more cigarette with shaking fingers, she tried to realise the position. It seemed clear that she had blundered into important issues and that, consequently, she had to be suppressed. The professor had been sent to bribe her with immunity in return for her silence.

Even while she rejected compromise angrily, she had to face the cold truth. She had not a ghost of a chance against these influential people. If she persisted in her hopeless quest to find Miss Froy, the doctor would merely pull wires and whisk her away to some nursing home in Trieste.

She remembered Miss Froy's tale of the woman who had been held in a private mental asylum. The same might happen to her. Any opposition on her part would be used as evidence against her sanity. They could keep her imprisoned and under the influence of drugs, until she really crashed under the strain.

It would be some appreciable time before anyone missed her. She was not expected in England, for she had not troubled to engage rooms at a hotel. Her friends would believe that she was still abroad. When at last her lawyers or the bank made enquiries, it would be too late. They would trace her to the nursing home, and arrive to find a lunatic.

In her distraught state, she plunged herself into a morass of distorted fears and exaggerated perils. But although her reason was nearly submerged by a tidal wave of panic, one corner of her brain still functioned on common-sense lines.

It convinced her that Miss Froy's rescue was an utterly hopeless proposition.

'Well?' asked the professor patiently, as she tossed away her unsmoked cigarette.

Suddenly Iris thought of the familiar Calais–Dover express – the white cliffs – Victoria Station – with almost frantic longing. She felt homesick for England and the cheery casual crowd of her friends. Before her eyes, in letters of fire, flashed the familiar slogan – SAFETY FIRST.

'Well?' repeated the professor. 'Have you come to your senses?'

Utterly worn out and paralysed with fear, Iris slipped into the trough of lost hopes. She reminded herself that Miss Froy was merely a stranger whom she had tried to help. To persist merely meant a double – and useless – sacrifice.

'Yes,' she replied dully.

'You'll make no more scenes?' went on the professor.

'No.'

'Good . . . Now, will you admit to me that you invented Miss Froy?'

Iris felt plunged into the hell of Judas Iscariot and all traitors as she made her denial.

'Yes. I invented her. There's no Miss Froy.'

31

A Cup of Soup

The doctor looked after the professor as he went from the dining-car.

'That is a very clever man,' he said dryly. 'He would cure illness by a scolding. Yet he may be right. Indeed, for the first time in my career, I hope I shall be proved wrong.'

He watched Hare's frowning face closely and asked, 'What is your opinion?'

'I know he's making a damnable blunder,' growled the young man.

' "He that knows, and knows that he knows," ' quoted the doctor, ' "he is wise" . . . Well – what then?'

'Hanged if I know.'

'Ah, you feel, perhaps, that the professor is cleverer than you?'

'I feel nothing of the kind. Our lines are different.'

'Then probably you are not used to exert authority?'

'Oh, no. I've only got to control hundreds of toughs – and some of them ready on the draw.'

'Then, frankly, I do not understand your hesitation. Unless, of course, you fear the young lady's anger when she discovers she has been tricked. She has what you call "spirit", and what I call "temper", since I have a very sweet wife myself . . . Well, it is for you to decide whether you prefer the angry words of a sane woman to the gentle smile of an imbecile.'

'Don't rub it in,' muttered Hare. 'I've got to *think*.'

'There is not much time left,' the doctor reminded him.

'I know. But – it's the hell of a risk.'

'Not at all. Here is my card. I will write a declaration on it that the drug is harmless, under penalty of heavy damages, should the lady be ill afterwards as a direct result . . . I will do more. You shall have a sample to take back to England, so that you may have it analysed.'

Hare pulled at his lip. He knew that the doctor's offer was fair, yet he could not shake off his distrust of the unknown.

The doctor seemed to read his thoughts.

'Perhaps,' he said, 'you hesitate because I am not Dr Smith, of London, England. Yet, if you were in a strange city and had a raging toothache, you would seek relief from the first dentist. Remember, a man's name on a brass plate, with certain letters after it, is a profession's guarantee of good faith to the public.'

He let the argument sink in while Hare continued to maltreat his face and hair. Presently he glanced at his watch, and then thrust his wrist before the young man's eyes.

'See the time. I must go back to my patient.'

Hare sprang up as though galvanised.

'One minute, doctor. How could we give the stuff?'

The doctor knew that the bridge had been crossed as he hastened to explain.

'That poor young lady has had no dinner,' he said reproachfully. 'Surely you will bring her a small cup of soup, since there will be no opportunities on the Italian train, until they couple the breakfast-car.'

'Chump,' exclaimed Hare, hitting his head. 'I never thought that she'd be hungry . . . But if she is asleep, how will I manage changing trains at Trieste?'

'Ah, my dear sir, you must not expect miracles. You are too impatient. The drug will not take full effect until she is in the Italian train. Then, she will sleep and sleep. But at Trieste she will merely be very dull, very heavy, very docile. And' – the doctor's eyes narrowed – 'she will be far too torpid to worry about any phantom lady.'

'Suits me all right . . . I'll take a chance.'

The doctor accompanied him to the kitchen-car and fought a battle with the protesting chef. In the end medical authority won the day. Not long afterwards, Hare, with anxious eyes and tightly compressed lips, began his fateful journey along the corridors, holding a half-filled bowl.

But he carried so much more than soup. Within the narrow circle of the cup lay the destiny of a woman.

As he staggered on his way – by a coincidence due to the time, in a small stone house in England, Mrs Froy's thoughts turned to nourishment.

'I do hope Winnie will eat something before she gets to Trieste,' she said to Mr Froy. 'Her dinner won't stand by her all through the night. Besides she is always too excited to eat on a journey. She merely pecks her first supper at home.'

Her husband gave a guilty smile, for he knew the reason for Winnie's lack of appetite.

Meanwhile, Hare was still scared by the responsibility of his step. While he assured himself that he was actually carrying a gift of sanity to Iris, he could not rid himself of apprehension. Tormented by indecision, he proposed a foolish test for himself.

'If I don't spill any it's going to be OK. But if I do, I'll cry off.'

He crabbed slowly along, with utmost care and caution, while the train seemed to put on an extra spurt of speed. The soup splashed furiously against the rim of the cup – forever on the point of brimming over. Yet, in some extraordinary manner, it always whirled within its confines.

Hare was reminded of a simple circus trick he used to practise – as a boy – with a hoop and a glass of water. Apparently the same principle operated now, and the soup could not be spilt from sheer velocity of motion.

But just before he reached the reserved portion of the train he came to grief completely. As he was crossing the connecting passage, a small boy – rushing from the pursuit of a smaller girl – charged into him and received a baptism of soup, together with an undesirable name.

Hare broke off in his malediction to wipe his fingers.

'That's torn it,' he muttered. 'Well, it's out of my hands now.'

Meanwhile Iris was actually in the grip of a brainstorm. When the professor left her she was numb with fear. Some vital mainspring in her brain seemed to have snapped, reducing her mind to a limp tangle. Miss Froy was a lost cause – so she denied her. But nothing was left but a void, without aim or hope or self-respect.

'I was her only chance,' she told herself. 'And now I've crashed too.'

The knowledge was torture which she tried vainly to forget. But vivid little thumbnail pictures persisted in flashing before her closed eyes. Two bent old people, huddled in a lighted doorway – waiting. Sock – a woolly blunderbuss – rushing off to meet a mistress who would never come home.

She was most affected by the thought of the dog, for she assumed the senility of the aged parents. She told herself that the shock would probably kill them both, since they would be too devoted – or too used to each other – to survive singly. And then – what would become of the dog, stranded and hungry in a country cottage?

She worked herself into a positive fever about him. As her temperature rose, her head began to ache so furiously that it seemed to bang in a series of small explosions which kept time with the frantic revolutions of the wheels.

'You're *get*–ting near. You're *get*–ting near.'

And then the rhythm changed and began to chop out a devil's tattoo. 'Nearer – nearer – nearer – *nearer* – NEARER.'

Nearer to Trieste. The express was in the relentless grip of the schedule. The pulsations of the engine throbbed through Iris like the shaking arteries of an over-driven heart. It rocked and roared over the rails – a metal monster racing an invisible rival.

It had to beat Time.

When Hare came into the carriage she hardly raised her eyes, and did not speak to him.

'Still hating me?' he asked.

'I only hate myself,' she said dully.

He looked furtively at her twitching face and burning cheeks, which, to his mind, confirmed the doctor's diagnosis of dangerously overstrung nerves, while he assured himself that – since he could not give her that essential sock on the jaw – he was rendering her a real service.

'I've brought you some soup,' he said guiltily.

She shrank from it even while she thanked him.

'Sweet of you – but I couldn't touch it.'

'Try. It'll make a new man of you.'

'All right, then. Leave it, will you?'

'No, that's too old a dodge. The instant I go you'll chuck it out of the window. Well – I'm not going.'

Iris clutched her head.

'I feel so sick,' she pleaded.

'Lack of nourishment. Listen, my child, there's a history of the try-try-again kind connected with that simple bowl of soup. I slaughtered the chef to get it in the first place. Then, on my way here, some wretched kid bowled the whole lot over . . . I said, "Kismet". And then I said, "She's had nothing all day and she'll have nothing until tomorrow's breakfast." And I went all the way back and slaughtered another chef, all to bring you a second cup.'

'Oh, well – ' sighed Iris helplessly. 'But have I got to be grateful?'

She swallowed the first spoonful with reluctance, grimacing as though it were a nauseous draught; then she paused, while Hare waited in acute suspense. 'What is it?' she asked. 'It's got a horribly druggy taste.'

'It's the same soup I wolfed down at dinner. That's all I know,' lied Hare.

'Well, I'd better get it over.'

Raising the cup to her lips, she gulped it down with a shudder.

'You'll feel better soon,' Hare assured her as he took the empty bowl from her nerveless hands.

For some time they sat in silence, while he watched her stealthily, hoping to detect the first sign of drowsiness. He knew that drugs affect people differently, and that it was difficult to gauge the right dose for Iris, because of her abnormal condition.

'If anything goes wrong,' he thought desperately, 'I'll have to take the rap.'

At intervals he heard the whine of the professor's voice, as he strained it in an effort to be audible above the uproar of the train. He was in the next compartment, improving an acquaintance with the Misses Flood-Porter, which he hoped to authorise with the discovery of a third-party link.

'You live in Somersetshire,' he remarked. 'It is a county where I have stayed often. I wonder if we know any mutual friends.'

'I hate every single person living there,' said Miss Rose vehemently, sweeping away any claimants to friendship.

'Stag-hunting,' supplemented Miss Flood-Porter.

Relieved by the explanation the professor began gently and skilfully to extricate a few worthy persons from under the wholesale ban. He was rewarded when the ladies recognised a name.

'Oh, yes. Charming people. Great friends of ours.'

The contact was complete and they all shouted against each other.

Iris recognised the voices for, after a time, she spoke to Hare.

'That's the professor, isn't it? I wish you'd tell him I want to sleep but can't because he's making too much noise. And slip in something about him being a public nuisance, will you? He'd appreciate it. Because that's what he called me.'

The speech was so unexpectedly jaunty, that Hare stared at her in surprise. He did not know whether he were imagining changes, but her eyes were less strained, while her face seemed to have lost the glazed flush of fever.

'That doctor's sold me a pup,' he thought wrathfully. 'She is not settling down. She's gingering up. At this rate she'll be fighting-mad at Trieste.'

As a matter of fact their little conspiracy was hampered by their ignorance of working conditions. On the rare occasions when Iris was unwell, her response to treatment was almost immediate. In her abnormal state she was now beating her own speed record. Although its effects were bound to be short-lived, she was feeling miraculously restored by the nourishment, while the drug was beginning imperceptibly to soothe her brainstorm, like the first film of oil spreading over a rough sea.

She was conscious of a glow of spurious strength, followed by a rush of confidence, as she climbed out of the traitors' hell into which she had hurled herself.

'Lost causes are the only causes worth fighting for,' she told herself.

In her relief at her own restoration, she smiled at Hare, who grinned back at her.

'Didn't I tell you you'd feel better after that nice good strong nourishing soup?' he asked.

'It tasted as though it was made from a mummy – but it has picked me up,' she admitted. 'My head's clearer. I realise now that the professor was right. I've made an awful fool of myself.'

Hare chalked up a good mark to the properties of the drug.

'You mean – you've chucked Miss Froy off the train?' he asked incredulously.

'Please, don't bring her up again. Of course, there's no such person. I told the professor so.'

Iris felt a momentary pang as she looked into his guileless eyes.

'It's a shame to trick him,' she thought.

She had resolved on a secret stratagem. She would sham docility, to avert suspicion. When Trieste was reached, she would contrive to give them the slip and hire a taxi, in which to follow the ambulance. They would not suspect any outside interest in their movements, since she was definitely out of the running.

Having warned the taxi-driver in advance to memorise the address to which Miss Froy was taken, she would drive furiously back to the British Embassy. She had always found Italians gallant and susceptible, so she was sure of enlisting their sympathies and getting immediate action.

Her jammed brain was now clicking on with amazing speed. She told herself that the success of her plan depended on whether she could fool them all. She must return to her own carriage, which was full of the doctor's spies, and sham the requisite limp submission.

'I mustn't overdo it,' she thought. 'They might want to fuss over me if they thought I was ill.'

She counted on the confusion when the passengers, with their luggage, changed trains at the terminus. Hare must be sent off on some errand, since he was her only obstacle. The rest of the travellers would remain true to type and look after their own interests.

She raised her eyes and met Hare's earnest gaze. He was thinking of the nice long sleep which awaited her in the Italian train.

'It's a shame to trick her,' he thought.

32

The Dream

Although it was still some distance from Trieste, the train was already astir with the projected bustle of its arrival. Passengers were beginning to lock opened suitcases and to pull on their coats and hats. Infected by the unrest, the leisurely professor left the Misses Flood-Porter and entered his own coupé.

'I don't want to disturb you,' he hinted to Iris., 'but we shall soon reach Trieste.'

Iris showed none of her former morbid reluctance to return to her own carriage.

'I must get my suitcase,' she said, eager to impress the professor with her obedience.

He rewarded her with an approving smile. For the last time she made the shaky journey along the train. Nobody laughed at her or took any notice of her, for everyone was too preoccupied with their own affairs. Suitcases and bags had already been lifted down from racks and stacked outside the carriages, increasing the congestion. Mothers screamed to collect those children who were still chasing each other in the corridors. They washed their chocolate-grimed mouths with corners of moistened handkerchiefs. Banana skins were thrown out of the windows – newspapers bundled under the seats.

The heat and the jam were so oppressive that Iris was actually glad to reach her own compartment. But before she could enter, she shrank back as the doctor came out of the invalid's carriage. His face looked dry and white as the pith of willow above the black blotch of his spade-beard, and his eyes – magnified by his glasses – were dark turgid pools.

As he looked at her, she felt that it was useless to try to deceive him. Like an expert chess player he would have forseen any possible move of her own and would be prepared with a counter stroke.

'Is madame better?' he asked.

'Oh, yes. I'm merely slack. Everything seems an effort. And once I sit down I shan't want to move again.'

Iris was encouraged by the success of her strategy when the two men exchanged a glance of understanding. She went inside her compartment, but no one appeared to take any interest in her return. The mother and child were reassembling the contents of the family suitcases, while the blonde made an elaborate toilet. The father had taken charge of the Baroness' dressing-bag and was evidently prepared to act as temporary courier.

Iris sat and watched them until the spectacle of noses being powdered and waves reset reminded her of her own need to repair. It was essential to make a good impression at the Embassy. She opened her bag languidly and drew out her compact, yawning the while with sudden drowsiness. Blinking her eyes violently, she began to apply powder and lipstick.

But before she could finish, her lids were drooping so continuously that she could not see properly. To her dismay, she realised that she was being overwhelmed with waves of sleep.

They were too powerful to resist, although she struggled vainly to keep awake. One after another they swept over her, piling up in a ceaseless procession.

The other passengers began to waver like shadows. Outside, Trieste was visible as a quivering red glow on the night sky. The engine thundered and panted in a last stupendous effort to breast that invisible tape stretched in front of the buffers. Alongside, skimmed the vast shadow, with beating wings and swinging scythe.

There was exultation in the stokehold and driver's cabin, for they were actually ahead of the schedule. Time was beaten, so they relaxed their efforts and slackened speed gradually in readiness for the final stretch.

Iris's head had fallen forward and her eyes were closed. Then a dog barked in the distance, jerking her awake. As she stared out of the window with clouded gaze, a few scattered lights speckling the darkness told her that they were on the outskirts of Trieste.

In that moment she thought of Miss Froy.

'Trieste,' she agonised. 'I must keep awake.'

Then, once again, everything grew blurred and she sank back in her corner.

When Hare returned to the carriage his jaw dropped at the sight of her huddled figure. He called to the doctor, who merely rubbed his bony hands with satisfaction.

'Excellent,' he said. 'She has responded with most extraordinary rapidity.'

'But how will I get her out at Trieste?' demanded Hare.

'You will have no trouble. You can wake her at a touch. This is merely preliminary – what you call a cat's-sleep. She will be merely somewhat dazed.'

The doctor turned away, but paused to give a word of advice.

'Better leave her alone until you have secured porters. If you wake her too soon she may sleep again. Each time it will be for longer.'

Hare took the hint and stood in the corridor, staring out of the window. The reflection of the lighted train flowing over the masonry of roofs and walls transformed them to the semblance of quivering landscape and water. In every carriage luggage was being lowered. Voices shouted for service. The fleeting friendships of a railway journey were being at once sealed and broken in handshakes and farewells.

Iris slept . . .

In the coupé of the bridal pair, the barrister – Todhunter, for a few minutes longer – was doing his utmost to reconcile a gesture of renunciation with a strategic retreat.

'Shall we say goodbye now?' he suggested. 'Before we are surrounded with a cloud of witnesses.'

Mrs Laura ignored his overture.

'Goodbye,' she said, carefully curling her lashes upwards. 'Thanks for your hospitality. It's been a cheap holiday for me. Cheap in every sense.'

In the next coupé the Misses Flood-Porter were facing a major tragedy. It was Miss Flood-Porter who threw the bombshell.

'Rose, did you see the brown suitcase put in the van?'

'No.'

'Then I believe it's been left behind. It was pushed under the bed, if you remember.'

Their faces were rigid with horror, for their purchases had been packed together for conscientious declaration.

'I was counting on Captain Parker to get them through the customs for us,' lamented Miss Rose. 'But it may be in the van.'

'It may. We can do nothing but hope for the best.'

Iris slept on . . .

When she was a child she suffered from an unsuspected inferiority complex, due to the difference between her lot and that of other children. Although pampered by adults she was exposed to the secret hostility of some of her companions. She was not equal to reprisals, but, at night, her inhibitions found expression in dreams of power, when she sacked the toy-stores and sweet-shops of London with glorious immunity.

Time brought its revenge and Iris got on top of her own little world. But now the professor's hostility, the antagonism of the doctor and Baroness, together with the derision of the other passengers, had combined with her sunstroke to make the old inferiority complex flare up again. The result was that she passed from unconsciousness into one of her childish dreams of power.

She thought she was still on the express and on her way to rescue Miss Froy. The corridors were hundreds of miles long, so that it took her centuries to complete what passed within the limit of a minute. The doctor and a crowd of passengers kept trying to oppose her passage, but she had only to push back their faces for them to dissolve like smoke.

She was mowing them down in swathes when she was aroused by the scream of the engine. Shouts and sudden flashes of light told her that they were rushing into Trieste.

Instantly she staggered to her feet – half-awake and half in a dream – and walked directly into the next compartment.

Her action took everyone by surprise. No one expected it as it was believed that she was asleep. The doctor and the disguised chauffeur were looking out of the window, watching for the arrival of the ambulance. But Hare – who was chatting to the guard – saw her enter, and he made a frantic effort to stop her.

He was too late. Still under the influence of her dream of power and secure in her knowledge of immunity which raised her high above the fear of consequences – Iris rushed towards the invalid and tore the plaster from her face.

The doctor had made the final mistake of an unlucky venture when he gave her the sleeping-draught. Had she carried out her threat to go to the Embassy, she might have encountered incredulity and delay. But the drug had given her the courage to do the impossible thing.

As the criss-cross of strips peeled off and dangled in her fingers like a starfish, Hare held his breath with horror. Then the guard behind him gave a whistle of astonishment as, instead of spurting blood and raw mutilated flesh, the healthy though reddened skin of a middle-aged woman was revealed. Iris gave a low cry of recognition. *'Miss Froy.'*

33

The Herald

Two days later Iris stood on the platform of Victoria Station, watching the dispersal of the passengers. Among the first to leave were the Misses Flood-Porter. Confident in their right to preferential treatment, they stood aloof with pleased expressions, while an influential gentleman, with an authoritative voice and an infallible method with officials, shouted and shepherded their luggage through the customs.

Once, by mistake, they looked at Iris, but they were too preoccupied to bow. This was England, where she went out of their lives.

They were very gracious, however, to Mrs Barnes, when she came to wish them goodbye. Her face was radiant with happiness born of a telegram which she had received at Calais.

COLD QUITE GONE STOP GABRIEL QUITE WELL AGAIN

In spite of her impatience to get home to him she lingered to listen to the last snatch of gossip from the sisters.

'Wasn't it *peculiar* about the honeymoon couple?' asked the elder Miss Flood-Porter. 'I know he wasn't on the Venice train, because I looked. And she got off at Milan – alone.'

'Yes,' nodded Mrs Barnes. 'I know my husband wouldn't like me to say it – but it makes you wonder if they were really married.'

'Of course they weren't,' scoffed Miss Rose. 'I'm precious glad we had nothing to do with them. If there had been a divorce action later on, *we* might have been subpoenaed as witnesses.'

'Exactly,' agreed her sister. 'It just shows how careful one should be when one is abroad. We always keep to our rule *never* to get mixed up in other people's business.'

Iris smiled rather bitterly at the conscious virtue in their voices. It reminded her of what she had suffered as a result of their policy of superb isolation. With a shrug she turned her back on the affectionate leave-taking to watch instead the long thin white beams – as of a myriad searchlights – thrown by the sun through the smoky glass roof.

Although she was still shaky she felt quick with fresh life – glad to be back – glad to be alive. While Hare was scouting round the piles of luggage, her thoughts slipped back to the journey. Her memories were dim, with many blanks.

There was a blackout at Trieste, where she crashed completely, and she did not become conscious of her surroundings until she was rushing through the darkness in the Italian train. Someone with lustrous black eyes looked after her, while Hare came and went. She slept most of the time, but whenever she woke she was conscious of happiness.

The carriage was crowded with other passengers, all shouting, smoking and gesticulating. She could not understand a word, but she felt in perfect tune and sympathy with all of them. There was so much happiness in the world and the prospect of joyous reunions. The barriers of language were down, so that they were not alien nationalities but fellow-citizens of the world, united by common values.

In the morning she discovered another passenger in the carriage – a little drab, middle-aged woman, with a small lined face and vivid blue eyes.

Iris gave a cry of rapture as she hugged her.

'Miss Froy. You horrible little brute to give me all that trouble . . . Oh, darling, darling.'

In spite of the joy of reunion, Miss Froy proved a bad exchange for the Italian stranger. Her fussy attentions, her high tinkling laugh, her incessant chatter, became such a strain that Hare had to scheme for intervals of release.

For all the drawbacks, however, there was a sense of great adventure and high hope about the journey. The wind seemed to blow them along when they travelled across the flat stretches of France. Everything moved with them – streaming smoke and fluttering clouds. The wide fields and white sky swam in light, so that they felt that they were sailing through a magic country.

Although she was better Hare refused to answer any of Iris's questions.

'Tell you in London,' he always said.

She reminded him of his promise when he returned with her suitcase, duly chalked.

'I can't wait another minute,' she told him.

'Righto,' he agreed. 'Take a pew.'

Squatting together on a luggage truck and smoking cigarettes, they escaped the clamour and she listened to his story.

'It was all very tame. No rough-house – no nothing. The guard was a hero. He knew just what to do, and the doctor and the two nurses went like lambs. You see, they'll probably only be charged with attempted abduction.'

'What happened to the Baroness?' asked Iris.

'Oh, she just sailed out, twice her natural size. No connection at all with the next carriage . . . But she'll pull wires and wangle their discharge. Wheels within wheels, you know.'

Iris felt indifferent to their fate.

'What did the others say when they heard about Miss Froy?' she enquired eagerly. 'After all, I was right – and everyone was out of step but me.'

'To be quite candid,' said Hare, 'it all went in one ear and out the other. We had a close shave at Venice and some of the Miss Flood-Porters' luggage was missing. They were in such a panic about it that they were prostrate afterwards. And the parson's wife was very worried about her husband.'

'But the professor?'

'Well, he's the sort that doesn't like to be proved wrong. When he saw Miss Froy running about like a two-year-old, he thought it was all exaggerated. I overheard him saying to Miss Flood-Porter, "People generally get what they invite. I cannot imagine anything of the kind happening to Miss Rose." '

'Neither can I . . . Everyone seems to be saying goodbye. Here's my Miss Froy.'

Hare hurriedly made his escape just in time to avoid the little woman. She looked wonderfully fit and seemed actually rejuvenated by her terrible experience.

Although she had grown so irritated by the touch of those hard, dry hands, Iris felt a pang of regret now that the parting was near.

'I'm stopping in London for a few hours,' confided Miss Froy. 'Selfridges, my dear. Just wandering. Topping.'

She looked after Hare as he chased a taxi, and lowered her voice.

'I'm just making up my story to tell them at home. Mater will be *thrilled*.'

'But do you think it wise to tell her?' objected Iris. 'At her age it might prove a shock.'

'Oh, you mean about me.' Miss Froy shook her head and gave Iris the conspiratorial wink of one schoolgirl to another. 'I'm going to keep mum about *that*. She'd throw a fit and she wouldn't let me go back.'

'Shall you?' gasped Iris.

'Of course. I shall have to give evidence at the trial, very likely. Besides, all the exciting things seem to happen abroad.'

'You're a marvel . . . But what is the story you're making up?'

Miss Froy grew suddenly young.

'It's about you – and your romance. Is it true?'

Iris did not know herself until that minute.

'Yes,' she replied. 'I'm going with him on his next trip.'

'Then I'm first to congratulate you. And one day perhaps you'll congratulate me . . . And now I must fly to send off my wire.'

Not long afterwards, a telegram was received at the little grey stone house. Mr and Mrs Froy read it together, and later each read it privately to Sock.'

HOME EIGHT TEN STOP TOO TOPPING STOP WINNIE

*   *   *

That evening Mrs Froy stood at the window of Winnie's bedroom. Although she could not see the railway station, she got a glimpse of one amber signal lamp through a gap in the trees.

Everything was ready for her daughter's return. The table was laid in the dining-room and decorated with vases of white dahlias and claret-tinted carrot-tops. The hot-water bottles had been removed from the bed. The rarely-used lamp had been lit in the hall, and the front door thrown open in readiness, so that a strip of light carpeted the mossy garden path.

The supper was keeping hot in the oven. Mrs Froy always cooked sausages and mashed potatoes for the first meal, under the mistaken impression that it was Winnie's favourite dish. It had been, some thirty years ago – but Winnie never had the heart to undeceive her.

Outside the window was darkness and silence. The stars were frosty and the keen air held the odour of autumnal bonfires. Then, suddenly, the stillness was torn by the scream of the distant train.

Mrs Froy could trace its approach by the red cloud quivering about the belt of elms which hid the station. She knew when it stopped, because the engine panted and blew off some steam. It rattled on again, leaving her guessing. She wondered whether it had brought Winnie. Perhaps she had lost her connection in London. She could see nothing – hear nothing – for she was growing deaf and her eyes were beginning to fail.

The surrounding darkness baffled her and cheated her with un-redeemed promises. Figures advanced through the gloom, but just as her heart leaped in welcome – they always changed back to trees. She strained vainly to catch the first sound of voices – her husband's deep tones and a girl's high-pitched treble.

As she held her breath in suspense, somewhere in the distance a dog barked. Again and again, in frantic excitement. Then through the open gate and up the lighted path charged the clumsy shape of a big shaven dog – capering like an overgrown puppy – whirling round in circles – leaping at his shadow – falling over himself in his blundering haste.

It was the herald who had rushed on ahead, to tell her that the young mistress had come home.

The Spiral
Staircase

1

The Tree

HELEN REALISED that she had walked too far just as daylight was beginning to fade.

As she looked around her, she was struck by the desolation of the country. During her long walk, she had met no one, and had passed no cottage. The high-banked lanes, which blocked her view, were little better than steep mudslides. On either hand rose the hills – barren sepia mounds, blurred by a fine spit of rain.

Over all hung a heavy sense of foreboding, as though the valley awaited some disaster. In the distance – too far away to be even a threat – rumbled faint, lumpy sounds of thunder.

Fortunately Helen was a realist, used to facing hard economic facts and not prone to self-pity. Of soaring spirit, yet possessed of sound common sense, she believed that those thinly veiled glimpses of hell – heaviness of body and darkness of spirit – could be explained away by liver or atmosphere.

Small and pale as a slip of crescent moon, she was only redeemed from insignificance by her bush of light-red springy hair. But, in spite of her unostentatious appearance, she throbbed with a passion for life, expressed in an expectancy of the future which made her welcome each fresh day and shred the interest from every hour and minute.

As a child, she pestered strangers to tell her the time, not from a mere dull wish to know whether it was early or late, but from a genuine curiosity to see their watches. This curiosity persisted when she had to earn her own living under the roofs of fortunate people who possessed houses of their own.

Her one dread was being out of work. She could estimate, from experience, the scores of replies which had probably been received as a result of the advertisement for a lady-help at Professor Warren's country house; she guessed, as soon as she arrived at The Summit, that it was its very loneliness that had helped to remove her from the ranks of the unemployed.

The house was tucked away in a corner, somewhere at the union of three counties, on the borderline between England and Wales. The nearest town was twenty-two miles away – the nearest village, twelve.

No maid would stay at such a forsaken pocket – a pocket with a consequent hole in it – through which dribbled a steady stream of domestic labour.

Mrs Oates, who, with her husband, helped to fill the breach, summed up the situation to Helen, when they met, by appointment, in the Ladies' Waiting Room at Hereford station.

'I told Miss Warren as she'd *have* to get a lady. No one else would put up with it.'

Helen agreed that ladies were a drug in the market. She had enjoyed some months of enforced leisure, and was only too grateful for the security of any home, after weeks of stringent economy – since 'starvation' is a word not found in a lady's vocabulary. Apart from the essential loneliness of the locality, however, it was an excellent post, for she had not only a nice room and good food, but she took her meals with the family.

The last fact counted, with her, for more than a gesture of consideration, since it gave her the chance to study her employers. She was lucky in being able to project herself into their lives, for she could rarely afford a seat at the cinema, and had to extract her entertainment from the raw material of life.

The Warren family possessed some of the elements of drama. The professor, who was a widower, and his sister and housekeeper Miss Warren were middle-aged to elderly. Helen classified them as definite types, academic, frigid and well bred, but largely devoid of vital human interest. Their stepmother, however, old Lady Warren – the invalid in the blue room – was of richer mould. Blood and mud had been used in her mixture, and the whole was churned up, thrice daily, by a dose of evil temper.

She was the terror of the household; only yesterday, she had flung a basin of gruel at her nurse's head. It had been her natural and ladylike protest against this nourishing substitute for the rare steak, which she preferred but was unable to chew. As her aim was excellent, it had achieved the desired result; that morning Oates had driven the departing nurse into the town, and was coming back, in the evening, with a fresh target.

Helen, who had not yet been brought into contact with the old lady, rather admired her spirit. The household was waiting for her to die, but she still called the tune. Every morning, Death knocked politely on the door of the blue room and Lady Warren saluted him in her customary fashion with a thumb to her nose.

Besides this low-comedy relief, Helen suspected a triangular situation, as represented by the professor's son, his daughter-in-law and the resident pupil, whom the professor was coaching for the Indian Civil Service. The son – a clever, ugly youth – was violently and aggressively in love with his wife, Simone. She was an unusually attractive girl, with money of her own, and a wanton streak in her composition.

To put it mildly, she was an experimentalist with men. At present, she was plainly testing her powers of seduction on the pupil, Stephen Rice – a good-looking casual young sprig, rejected by Oxford. Helen liked him instinctively, and hoped he would continue to resist the lady.

Although her curiosity hovered around The Summit and its inmates, her duties were her chief interest. The reminder that she had a new job to hold down made her pull a face as she glanced at her watch.

Already the first shadows were beginning to creep, as prelude to the lighting of the lamps. Very soon it would be dark.

A long walk stretched between her and The Summit. She could see the house, in the distance, blocked with solid assurance against the background of shrouded hills. But dividing them yawned a bowl of empty country, which dipped down for about a mile into a tree-lined hollow before it climbed up a corresponding slope to the young plantation on the opposite crest.

In spite of her stoicism, Helen's heart sank faintly at the prospect of toiling back through that choked dell. Since she had come to The Summit, she had been struck by the density of the surrounding under-growth. When she looked out of the windows, at twilight, the evergreen shrubs on the lawn seemed actually to advance closer to the walls, as though they were pioneers in a creeping invasion.

Feeling secure as in a fortress, she enjoyed the contrast between the witched garden and the solid house, cheerful with lights and voices. She was inside and safe. But now, she was outside, and nearly two miles away.

'Idiot,' she told herself, 'it's not late. It's only dark. *Scram.*'

As she was denied the employer's privilege of abuse, she got even by saying exactly what she liked to herself. She whipped up her courage by calling herself a choice collection of names as she began to run cautiously, slipping on the slimy camber of the lane, since the rutted middle was too stony for safety.

She kept her eyes fixed on her goal, which seemed to be sinking gradually into the ground as she dipped lower and lower. Just before she lost sight of it, a light gleamed out in the window of the blue room.

It seemed to her a signal, calling her back to a special duty. Every evening, at twilight, she had to go around the house, locking the doors and putting the shutters over the windows. Hitherto, she had derided the job as involving excessive precaution; but, here, in the tenebrous solitude, it assumed an unpleasant significance.

There was a connection between it and a certain atmosphere of tension – excitement in the kitchen, whispers in the drawing-room – which emanated from a background of murder.

Murder. Helen shied instinctively at the word. Her mind was too healthy to regard crime as other than fiction, which turned newspapers into the sensational kind of reading-matter which is sold on railway-station bookstalls. It was impossible to believe that these tragedies happened to real people.

She forced herself to think of a safer subject.

'Suppose I won the Irish Sweep.'

But, as the lane dropped deeper, its steep banks shutting out the light, she found it difficult to focus her mind on mere supposititious wealth. Simple pleasures appealed to her more at that moment – the safety of the kitchen at The Summit, with Mrs Oates and the ginger cat for company, and dripping-toast for tea.

She made another start.

'Suppose I won the Irish Sweep. *Someone's got to win*. Out of all the millions of people in the world, a few people are *marked out* to win fortunes. Staggering.'

Unfortunately, the thought introduced another, equally stupendous.

'Yes. And out of all the millions of people who die in their beds, a few are marked out to be murdered.'

She switched off the current of her thoughts, for before her crouched the black mouth of the hollow.

When she had crossed it earlier in the afternoon, she had been chiefly concerned with picking out a fairly dry passage over the rich black mould formed by leaf-deposits. She had only marked it down as a sheltered spot in which to search for early primroses.

But the promise of spring was now only a mockery. As she advanced, the place seemed an area of desolation and decay, with windfalls for crops. In this melancholy trough – choked with seasonal litter – sound was reduced to furtive rustles; light was shrunken to a dark miasma, through which trees loomed with the semblance of men.

Suddenly, murder ceased to be a special fiction of the press. It became real – a menace and a monstrosity.

Helen could no longer control her thoughts as she remembered what Mrs Oates had told her about the crimes. There were four of them – credibly the work of the same maniac, whose chosen victims were girls.

The first two murders were committed in the town, which was too far away from The Summit for the occupants to worry. The third took place in a village, but still comfortably remote. The last girl was strangled in a lonely country-house within five miles of Professor Warren's residence.

It was an uncomfortable reminder that the maniac was growing bolder with success. Each time he penetrated closer into the privacy of his victim.

'The first time, it was just a street-murder,' thought Helen. 'Then, he hid in a garden. After that, he went inside a house. And then – right upstairs. You ought to feel safe there.'

Although she was determined not to yield to panic and run, she ceased to pick her way between cart-ruts filled with water and plunged recklessly into muddy patches, whose suction glugged at the soles of her shoes. She had reached the densest part of the grove, where the trees intergrew in stunting overcrowding.

To her imagination, the place was suggestive of evil. Tattered leaves still clung to bare boughs, unpleasantly suggestive of rags of decaying flesh fluttering from a gibbet. A sluggish stream was clogged with dead leaves. Derelict litter of broken boots and rusty tins cropped out of a rank growth of docks and nettles, to mark a tramp's camping-place.

Again Helen thought of the murders.

'It's coming nearer – and nearer. Nearer to us.'

Suddenly, she wondered if she were being followed. As she stopped to listen, the hollow seemed to be murmurous with faint sounds – the whisper of shrivelled leaves, the snapping of twigs, the chuckles of dripping water.

It was possible to fancy anything. Although she knew that if she ran her imagination would gallop away with her, she rushed across the soft ground, collecting poultices of mud on the soles of her boots.

Her heart was pounding when the opposite lane reared itself in front of her, like the wall of a house. The steepness however proved deceptive, for, around the first bend, it doubled, like a crooked arm, to relieve the steepness of the gradient.

Once more, Helen's normal courage returned, for her watch told her that she had won her race against time. The precious new job was safe. Her legs ached as she toiled upwards, but she cheerfully reminded herself that a merry heart goes all the way – that the longest lane has a turning – that every step was bringing her nearer home. Presently she reached the top of the rise, and entered the plantation, which was thinly planted with young firs and larches and carpeted with fallen needles. At its thickest part, she could see through it, and, suddenly, she caught sight of The Summit.

It was no longer a distant silhouette, but was so close that she could distinguish the colour of the window-curtains in the blue room. The vegetable garden sloped down to the wall which bounded the plantation, and a coil of rising smoke, together with a cheerful whistle told her that the gardener was on the other side, making a bonfire.

At the sight of her goal, Helen slackened her pace. Now that it was over, her escapade seemed an adventure, so that she felt reluctant to return to her dreary routine. Very soon she would be going round locking up in readiness for curfew. It sounded dull – already she had forgotten that in the darkness of the hollow she had realised the importance of those shutters.

The rising wind spattered her face with rain, and increased her sense of rebellion against four walls and a roof. She told herself that it was blowing up for a dirty night as she walked towards the front gate.

At its end, the plantation thinned down to a single avenue of trees, through which she could see the stone posts of the entrance to The Summit, and the laurels of the drive. As she watched, fresh lights glowed through the drawing-room windows.

It was the promise of tea – calling her home. She was on the point of breaking into a run, when her heart gave a sudden leap.

She was positive that the farthest tree had moved.

She stopped and looked at it more closely, only to conclude that her fancy had tricked her. It was lifeless and motionless, like the rest. Yet there was something about its shape – some slight distortion of the trunk – which filled her with vague distrust.

It was not a question of logic – she only knew that she did not want to pass that specific tree.

As she lingered, in hesitation, her early training asserted itself. She began to earn her living, at the age of fourteen, by exercising the dogs of the wealthy. As these rich dogs were better-fed, and stronger than she was, they often tried to control a situation, so she was used to making quick decisions.

In this instance, her instinct dictated a short way home, which involved a diagonal cut across boggy ground, through a patch of briars, and over the garden wall.

She carried through her programme, in the minimum of time, and with little material damage, but complete loss of dignity. After a safe, but earthy, landing in the cabbage-bed, she walked around to the front door. With her latchkey in the lock, she turned, for a last look at the plantation, visible through the gates.

She was just in time to see the last tree split into two, as a man slipped from behind its trunk, and disappeared into the shadows.

2

The First Cracks

The surge of Helen's curiosity was stronger than any restraining emotion. It compelled her to rush down the drive, in an effort to investigate the mystery. But when she reached the gate she could see only lines of trunks, criss-crossing in confusing perspectives.

Forgetful of her duties, she stood gazing into the gloom of the plantation while a first star trembled through a rent in the tattered clouds.

'It was a man,' she thought triumphantly, 'so I was right. He was hiding.'

She knew that the incident admitted the simple explanation of a young man waiting for his sweetheart. Yet she rejected it, partly because she wanted a thrill, and partly because she did not believe it met the case. In her opinion, a lover would naturally pass the time by pacing his beat or smoking a cigarette. To her, the rigid pose and the lengthy vigil, while the man stood in mimicry of a tree, suggested a tenacious purpose.

It reminded her of the concentrated patience of a crocodile, lurking in the shadow of a river bank to pounce on its prey.

'Well, whatever he was doing, I'm glad I didn't pass him,' she decided as she turned to go back to the house.

It was a tall grey stone building of late-Victorian architecture, and it looked strangely out of keeping with the savage landscape. Built with a flight of eleven stone steps leading up to the front door and large windows, protected with green jalousies, it was typical of the residential quarter of a prosperous town. It should have been surrounded by an acre of well-kept garden, and situated in a private road, with lamp-posts and a pillar-box.

For all that, it offered a solidly resistant front to the solitude. Its state of excellent repair was evidence that no money was spared to keep it weatherproof. There was no blistered paint, no defective guttering. The whole was somehow suggestive of a house which, at a pinch, could be rendered secure as an armoured car.

It glowed with electric-light, for Oates's principal duty was to work the generating plant. A single wire overhead was also a comfortable reassurance of its link with civilisation.

Helen no longer felt any wish to linger outside. The evening mists were rising so that the evergreen shrubs which clumped the lawn appeared to quiver into life. Viewed through a veil of vapour, they looked black and grim, like mourners gathering at a funeral.

'If I don't hurry, they'll get between me and the house, and head me off,' Helen told herself, still playing her favourite game of make-believe. She had some excuse for her childishness, since it seemed her sole relaxation was now to be a tramp through muddy blind lanes instead of three hours at the cinema.

She ran eagerly up the steps, and after a guilty glance at her shoes, put in some vigorous footwork on the huge iron scraper. Her latchkey was still in the lock, where she had left it before her swoop down the drive. As she turned it, entered and heard the spring lock snap behind her, shutting her inside, she was aware of a definite sense of shelter.

The house seemed a solid hive of comfort, honeycombed with golden cells, each glowing with light and warmth. It buzzed with voices, it offered company, and protection.

In spite of her appreciation, the interior of The Summit would have appalled a modern decorator. The lobby was floored with black and ginger tiles, on which lay a black fur rug. Its furniture consisted of a chair with carved arms, a terracotta drainpipe, to hold umbrellas, and a small palm on a stand of peacock-blue porcelain.

Pushing open the swing-doors, Helen entered the hall, which was entirely carpeted with peacock-blue pile and dark with massive mahogany. The strains of a wireless struggled through the heavy curtain which muffled the drawing-room door, and the humid air was laden with the scent of potted primulas blended with that of orange-pekoe tea.

Although Helen's movements had been discreet, someone with keen hearing had heard the swing of the lobby doors. The velvet folds of the portière were pushed aside, and a voice cried out in petulant eagerness. 'Stephen, you – Oh, it's *you*.'

Helen was swift to notice the drop in young Mrs Warren's voice.

'So you were listening for him, my dear,' she deduced. 'And dressed up like a mannequin.'

Her glance of respect was reserved for the black-and-white-satin tea-frock, which gave the impression that Simone had been imported straight from a London restaurant *thé dansant*, together with the music. She also followed the conventions of fashion in such details as artificial lips and eyebrows superimposed on the original structure. Her glossy black hair was sleeked back into curls, resting on the nape of her neck, and her nails were polished vermilion.

But in spite of long slanting lines, painted over shaven arches, and a tiny bow of crimson constricting her natural mouth, she had not advanced far from the cave. Her eyes glowed with primitive fire, and her expression hinted at a passionate nature. She was either a beautiful savage, or the last word in modern civilisation, demanding self-expression.

The result was the same – a girl who would do exactly as she chose.

As she looked down, from her own superior height, at Helen's small, erect figure, the contrast between them was sharp. The girl was hatless, and wore a shabby tweed coat, which was furred with moisture. She brought back with her the outside elements, mud on her boots, the effect of wind on her cheeks and glittering drops on her mop of ginger hair.

'Do you know where Mr Rice is?' demanded Simone.

'He went out of the gate, just before me,' replied Helen, who was a born opportunist, and always managed to be present at the important entrances and exits. 'And I heard him saying something about "wishing goodbye".'

Simone's face clouded at the reminder that the pupil was going home on the morrow. She turned sharply, when her husband peered over her shoulder, like an inquisitive bird. He was tall, with a jagged crest of red hair, and horn-rimmed glasses.

'The tea's growing stewed,' he said, in a high-pitched voice. 'We're not going to wait any longer for Rice.'

'I am,' Simone told him.

'But the teacake's getting cold.'

'I adore cold muffin.'

'Well – won't you pour out for me?'

'Sorry, darling. One of the things my mother never taught me.'

'I see.' Newton shrugged as he turned away. 'I hope the noble Rice will appreciate your sacrifice.'

Simone pretended not to hear, as she spoke to Helen, who had also feigned deafness.

'When you see Mr Rice, tell him we're waiting tea for him.'

Helen realised that the entertainment was over, or rather, that the scene had been ruthlessly cut, just when she was looking forward to a rejoinder from Simone.

She walked rather reluctantly upstairs, until she reached the first landing, where she paused to listen outside the blue room. It always challenged her curiosity, because of the formidable old invalid who lay within, invisible but controlling, like some legendary character.

As she could hear the murmur of Miss Warren's voice – for the stepdaughter was acting as deputy nurse – she decided to slip into her room, to put it ready for the night.

The Summit was a three-storeyed house, with two staircases and a semi-basement. There was a bathroom on each floor but no water during a drought. The family – consisting of old Lady Warren, the professor, and Miss Warren – slept on the first floor, while the spare-rooms were on the second. The top attics housed the domestic staff – when any – and, at present, was only occupied by the Oates couple.

Newton now counted as a visitor, for he and his wife had the big red room, on the second floor, while his old room, which connected with the bedrooms of Lady Warren and the professor, was turned into the nurse's sitting-room.

As Helen opened the door of Miss Warren's room, a small incident occurred which was fraught with future significance. The handle slipped round in her grip, so that she had to exert pressure in order to turn the knob.

'A screw's loose,' she thought. 'Directly I've time I'll get the screw-driver and put it right.'

Anyone acquainted with Helen's character would know that she always manufactured leisure for an unfamiliar job, even if she had to neglect some legitimate duty. It was the infusion of novelty into her dull routine which helped to keep undimmed her passionate zest for life.

Miss Warren's room was sombre and bare, with brown wallpaper, curtains and cretonne. An old-gold cushion supplied the sole touch of colour. It was essentially the sanctum of a student, for books overflowed from the numerous shelves and cases, while the desk was littered with papers.

Helen was rather surprised to find that the shutters were fastened already, while the small green-shaded lamp over the bureau gleamed like a cat's eye.

As she returned to the landing, Miss Warren came out of the blue room. Like her brother, she was tall and had a commanding figure, but there the resemblance ended. She appeared to Helen as an overbred and superior personality, with dim flickering features and eyes the hue of rainwater.

In common with the professor, however, she seemed to resent the gaze of a stranger as an outrage on her privacy; yet, while her remote glance sent Helen away on a very long journey, the professor's annihilated her.

'You're late, Miss Capel,' she remarked in her toneless voice.

'I'm sorry.' Helen looked anxious, as she wondered if her precious job were in peril. 'I understood, from Mrs Oates, that I was free till five. It's my first afternoon off since I came.'

'That is not what I meant. Of course, I am not reproaching you for any breach of duty. But it is too late for you to be returning from a walk.'

'Oh, thank you, Miss Warren. I *did* go farther than I intended. But it did not grow dark till the last mile.'

Miss Warren looked at Helen, who felt herself slipping into the distance.

'A mile is a long way from home,' she said. 'It is not wise to go far, even by daylight. Surely you get sufficient exercise working about the house? Why don't you go into the garden to get fresh air?'

'Oh, but Miss Warren,' protested. Helen, 'that is not the same as a good stretching walk, is it?'

'I understand.' Miss Warren smiled faintly. 'But I want you, in turn, to understand this. You are a young girl, and *I* am responsible for your safety.'

Even while the warning seemed grotesque on Miss Warren's lips, Helen thrilled to the intangible hint of danger. It seemed to be everywhere – floating in the air – inside the house, as well as outside in the dark, tree-dripping valley.

'*Blanche*.'

A deep bass voice – like that of a man, or an old woman – boomed faintly from the blue room. Instantly, the stately Miss Warren shrank from a paralysing personality to a schoolgirl hurrying to obey the summons of her mistress.

'Yes, mother,' she called. 'I'm coming.'

She crossed the landing, in ungainly strides, and shut the door of the blue room behind her, to Helen's disappointment.

'I'm getting a strange contrast in my types,' she thought, as she slowly walked up the stairs to the next landing. 'Mrs Newton is torrid, and Miss Warren frigid. Hot and cold water, by turns. I wonder what will happen in case of fusion?' She liked to coin phrases.

She also enjoyed the reflection that she was brought into daily contact with two bachelors – the pupil and the old lady's doctor, who made regular calls – and a widower, thus reviving a lost art. Those derided Victorians, who looked upon every man as a potential husband, certainly extracted every ounce of interest from a dull genus.

Yet, while she respected the professor's intellect, and genuinely looked forward to the visits of the young Welsh doctor, she resolved to go on buying Savings Certificates for her old age. For she believed in God – not in Jane Eyre.

She was on the point of entering her room, when she noticed that a light was shining through the glass transom of one bachelor's room. It drew her, as a magnet, to his door.

'Are you inside, Mr Rice?' she called.

'Come and see for yourself,' invited the pupil.

'I only wanted to know if the light was being wasted.'

'Well, it's not. Come in.'

Helen obeyed the invitation. She was used to two kinds of behaviour from men: they either overlooked her altogether, or paid her exaggerated attention, in private.

Of the alternatives, she preferred to be insulted; she could always give back as good as she got, and she was braced by any kind of personal experience.

She liked Stephen Rice, because he treated her exactly as he treated other girls – with a casual frankness. He was smoking as he pitched clothing into an open suitcase, and he made no apology for his state of undress, as his underwear satisfied his own standard of decency. Although he did not appeal to Helen, who liked a man's face to betray some trace of intellect, or spirit, he was generally accepted as unusually handsome, on the evidence of heavy regular features and thick waving hair, which grew rather too low on his brow.

'Like dogs?' he asked, shaking out a confusion of ties.

'Let me,' remarked Helen, taking them from him, with kind firmness. 'Of course I like dogs. I've looked after them.'

'Then that's a bad mark to you. I loathe women who boss dogs. You set them showing off in parks. Like the blasted centurion, who said come and he cometh. I always want to bite them, since the dogs are too gentlemanly to do their own job.'

'Yes, I know,' nodded Helen, who agreed, on principle, when it was possible. 'But my dogs used to boss *me*. They had a secret understanding all to pull at once, in different directions. The wonder is I didn't develop into a starfish.'

Stephen shouted with laughter.

'Good for them. Like to see something special in the way of dogs? I bought him today, from a farmer.'

Helen looked around the untidy room.

'Where is he?' she asked. 'Under the bed?'

'Is that where you sleep? Inside the bed, you cuckoo.'

'Oo. Suppose he has fleas?'

'Suppose he hasn't? Come, Otto.'

Stephen raised a corner of the eiderdown, and an Alsatian peeped out.

'Bit shy,' explained Stephen. 'I say, what price old Miss Warren when she sees him? She won't allow a dog inside the house.'

'Why?' asked Helen.

'Afraid of them.'

Oh, no, she *can't* be. It's the other way round. People are afraid of her, because she's so formidable.'

'That's only her make-up. She's a hollow funk. Put her in a jam, and she'd smash.' She's got the wind up now, over this murdering gent. By the way, are you afraid of him?'

'Of course not.' Helen laughed. 'Perhaps, I might be a bit if I was alone. But no one could feel nervous in a house full of people.'

'I don't agree. It all depends on the people. You'll always find a weak link. Miss Warren is one. *She'd* let you down.

'But there's safety in numbers,' persisted Helen. 'He wouldn't dare to come here. D'you want any sewing done?'

'No, thank you, my dear. The godly Mrs Oates has kept me sewn up. In more senses than one, by the way. Now, there's a character, if you like. You can *bank* on her – if there's not a bottle about.'

'Why – does she drink?'

Stephen only laughed in reply.

'Look here, you'd better clear out,' he advised, 'before Miss Warren raises hell. This is the bachelor's room.'

'But I'm not a lady. I'm Staff,' explained Helen indignantly. 'And they're waiting tea for you.'

'You mean, Simone is waiting. Old Newton is wolfing down the teacake.' Stephen pulled on his coat. 'I'll take the pup down with me. Introduce him to the family, and make us two to one in the muffin handicap.'

'Surely you don't call that large thing a pup,' cried Helen, as the Alsatian followed his master into the bathroom.

'He's quite young, really.' Stephen's voice was positively tender. 'I love dogs – and hate women. Reason? Remind me to tell you the story of my life.'

Helen felt slightly forlorn when his whistle died away in the distance. She knew she would miss the pupil. But a second glance around the untidy room reminded her that his absence would mean less work, so she resolved to leave all regret to Simone.

Her tea was calling her downstairs to the kitchen. Not stopping to clear away any litter, she hurried to her own room, and took off her coat and shoes. As the order for closed shutters only included the basement, ground-floor and first-floor, her own casement banged open in the wind.

In spite of her haste, she could not resist the luxury of lingering there, looking out over the valley, just to enjoy the sense of contrast. She could see only a spongy blackness. It seemed to stir and creep before the breath of the breeze. Not a gleam shone from any window of the sparsely sprinkled cottages.

'I wonder where I stood, looking across at The Summit,' she mused. 'It seemed such a long way off, then. And now, I'm inside, safe.'

She was visited by no prescience to warn her that – since her return – there had been certain trivial incidents which were the first cracks in the walls of her fortress. Once they were started, nothing could stop the process of disintegration; and each future development would act as a wedge, to force the fissures into ever-widening breaches, letting in the night.

3

A Fireside Story

Helen went down to the kitchen by the back way – a spiral of steep steps, broken up into flights at each floor by a small landing, where a door connected it with the main staircase. It was covered with the original linoleum – brown-and-biscuit, and small-patterned – like an old-fashioned tile, but still in excellent condition.

To Helen, this dingy back way down represented the essence of romance. It was a delicate filament connecting her with the glamour of the past, and revived memories of spacious and leisured days.

She had been brought up in a tiny mansion flat, with no room to keep a maid, a hat-box or a cat. The perambulator was housed in the bath-room, and the larder was thoughtfully built in the only spare recess, which happened to be next to the stove.

When Helen reached the basement-hall, she could hear the welcome rattle of china and see the glow of the kitchen fire through the frosted-glass panels of the door. Mrs Oates was drinking tea from her saucer as she made herself another piece of toast.

She was a tall, strapping woman, broad-shouldered and muscular, with an ugly, underhung face. She did not wear uniform, and her afternoon skirt was protected by an apron of red and black Welsh flannel.

'I heard you running down all them steep steps,' she said. 'You're free to use the front.'

'Yes I know' replied Helen. 'But backstairs remind me of my granny's house. The servants and the children were never allowed to go up the front way, because of wearing out the carpet.'

'Go on,' remarked Mrs Oates politely.

'Yes, indeed, and it was the same with the jam. Pots and pots of it, but the strawberry and raspberry were only for our elders. All the children had to eat was rhubarb or ginger-and-marrow. How cruel we grown-ups were then.'

'Not you. You should say "them grown-ups".'

' "Them grown-ups",' repeated Helen meekly, accepting the correction. 'I've come to invite myself to tea, as your husband is away.'

'And you're welcome.' Mrs Oates rose to get down fresh china from the Welsh dresser. 'I see as how you know the tricks of the trade. You want a brown pot to draw the flavour from the leaves. I'll get out the drawing-room cake for you.'

'Shop-cake? Not on your life. I want kitchen dough-cake. You don't know how all this appeals to me, Mrs Oates. I was thinking of this, about an hour ago, in very different circumstances.'

She looked around her with appreciative eyes. The kitchen was a huge room, with an uneven floor, and corners where shadows collected. There was no white enamel, no glass-fronted cabinet, no refrigerator; yet the shabby hearthrug and broken basket-chairs looked homely and comfortable in the glow from the range.

'What an enormous cavern,' said Helen. 'It must make a lot of work for you and your husband.'

'Oh, it don't worry Oates.' Mrs Oates's voice was bitter. 'All the more places for him to muck up and me to clean up after him.'

'It looks fine. All the same, Miss Warren would have a fit if she saw there were no shutters.'

As she spoke, Helen glanced at the small windows, set high up in the walls. They were on a level with the garden, and through the mud-speckled glass, she could see a faint stir of darkness, as the bushes moved in the wind.

'It's only just turned dark,' said Mrs Oates. 'They can wait till I've finished my tea.'

'But don't you feel nervous, down here all by yourself?'

'D'you mean *him*?' Mrs Oates's voice was scornful. '*No*, miss, I've seen too many work-shy men to be scared of anything in trousers. If he tried any of his funny business on me, I'd soon sock him in the jaw.'

'But he *is* a murderer,' Helen reminded her.

'He's not likely to trouble us. It's like the Irish Sweep; someone wins it, but it's never *you* and never *me*.'

They were consoling words and made Helen feel safe and comfortable as she crunched her toast. The grandfather clock ticked pleasantly and the ginger cat purred on the best patch of rug.

Suddenly she felt in the mood for a thrill.

'I wish you would tell me about the murders,' she said.

Mrs Oates stared at her in surprise.

'Why, they was in all the newspapers,' she said. 'Can't you read?'

'I naturally keep up with all the important things,' Helen explained. 'But I've never been interested in crime. Only, when it's a local murder, it seems slack to know nothing about it.'

'That's right,' agreed Mrs Oates, as she relaxed to gossip. 'Well, the first girl was murdered in town. She did a dancing-turn, with no clothes on, at one of the Halls, but she was out of a job. She was in a public, and had one over the eight. They seen her go out of the bar, just before time. When the rest come out, she was lying in the gutter, dead. Her face was as black as that bit of coal.'

Helen shuddered.

'The second murder was committed in the town, too, wasn't it?' she asked.

'Yes. She was a housemaid, poor thing. It was her evening out, and when her master came out into the garden, to give the dog its run, he found her all doubled up, on the drive, choked, like the other. And no one heard a whisper, though it was quite close to the drawing-room windows. So she must have been took by surprise.'

'I know,' nodded Helen. 'There were shrubs on the lawn, that looked like people. And suddenly, a shrub leaped on her.'

Mrs Oates stared at her, and then began to count on her fingers.

'Where was I? Let me see. One, two, three. Yes, the third was in a public-house, and it put everyone in a proper scare, because he'd come out into the country. The young lady in the bar had just popped into the kitchen, to swill a few glasses under the tap, and they found her there, two minutes after, choked with her own teacloth. There was people in the bar. But no one heard a sound. He must have crept in through the back door, and jumped on her from behind.'

Helen listened with a sense of unreality. She told herself that these things had never really happened. And yet they toned in too well with the damp darkness of the valley, where trees crept up to windows, until it was possible to imagine confused faces peering down into the kitchen. Suddenly she felt sated with secondary horrors.

'Don't tell my any more,' she implored.

But Mrs Oates was wound up to a finish.

'The last,' she said, 'was five miles from here, as the crow flies. A pure young girl, about your own age. She was a nursery governess in some big family, but she was home for her holiday and she was going to a dance. She was up in her bedroom, and drawing her beautiful party-frock over head, when he finished the job for her. Twisted the lovely satin frock all round her neck, as it ate right into her throat, and wrapped it all over her face, so that she never saw another mortal thing on earth. Looking at herself in the glass, she was, and that was her last sight, which shows these beauty competitions don't get you far.'

Helen did her best to curb the surge of her imagination by picking on the weak spots in the tale.

'If she was looking at herself in the glass, she'd see him too, and be warned. And if her dress was over her head how could she see herself? Besides her arms would protect her throat.'

All the same, she could not help making a mental picture of the scene. Because her own possessions were so few, perhaps, she had a keen sense of property, and always exercised a proprietary right over her room, even if someone else paid the rent.

She imagined that the murdered governess occupied a bedroom much like her own at The Summit – brightly lit and well furnished. It was cluttered with girlish treasures, symbolic of the crossroads – childish relics and womanhood's trophies, like restaurant souvenirs. Hockey sticks jostled with futuristic, long-bodied dolls; photographs of school-groups stood beside that of the latest heart-throb. Powder, vanishing-cream – and the distorted satin shape on the carpet.

'How did he get in?' Helen asked, desperately anxious to prove that this horror could not be true.

'Quite easy,' Mrs Oates told her. 'He climbed up the front porch, just under her bedroom window.'

'But how could he tell she would be there alone?'

'Ah, but he's a loony, and they know everything. He's after girls. Believe me, or believe me not, if there was a girl anywhere about, he'd smell her out.'

Helen glanced apprehensively at the window. She could vaguely distinguish glistening twigs tossing amid dim undergrowth.

'Have you locked the back door?' she asked.

'I locked it hours ago. I always do when Oates is away.'

'Isn't he rather late getting back?'

'Nothing to make a song about.' Mrs Oates glanced at the clock, which told her its customary lie. 'The rain will turn them steep lanes to glue, and the car's that old, Oates says he has to get out and carry it up the hills.'

'Will he carry the new nurse too?'

Mrs Oates, however, resented Helen's attempt to introduce a lighter note.

'I'm not worrying about her,' she replied, with dignity. 'I could trust Oates alone with the very highest in the land.'

'I'm sure you could.' Helen glanced again at the greyness outside the window. 'Suppose we put the shutters up and make things look more cheerful?'

'What's the good of locking up?' grumbled Mrs Oates, as she rose reluctantly. 'If he's a mind to come in, he'll find a way. Still, it's got to be done.' But Helen enjoyed the task of barring the windows. It gave her a sense of victory over the invading night. When the short red curtains were drawn over the panes, the kitchen presented the picture of a delightful domestic interior.

'There's another window in the scullery,' remarked Mrs Oates, opening a door at the far end of the kitchen.

On the other side loomed the blackness of a coalmine. Then Mrs Oates found the switch and snapped on the light, revealing a bare clean room, with blue-washed walls, a mangle, a copper and plate-racks.

'What a mercy this basement is wired,' said Helen.

'Most of it's as dark as a lovers' lane,' Mrs Oates told her. 'There's only a light in the passage, and switches in the storeroom and pantry. Oates did say as how he'd finish the job properly, and that's as far as he'll ever get. He's only got one wife to work for him, poor man.'

'What a labyrinth,' cried Helen, as she opened the scullery door and gazed down the vista of the passage, dimly lit by one small electric-bulb swinging from the ceiling halfway down its length. The light revealed a section of stone-slabbed floor and hinted at darker recesses lost in obscurity.

On either side were closed doors, dingy with shabby brown paint. To Helen's imagination they looked grim and ominous as sealed tombs.

'Don't you always feel a closed door is mysterious?' she asked. 'You wonder what lies on the other side.'

'I'll make a guess,' said Mrs Oates. 'A side of bacon and a string of Spanish onions, and if you open the storeroom door you'll find I'm not far out. Come along. That's all here.'

'No,' Helen declared. 'After your nice little bedtime tales, I shan't sleep until I've opened every door and satisfied myself that no one's hiding inside.'

'And what would a shrimp like you do if you found the murderer?'

'Go for him, before I'd time to think. When you feel angry, you can't feel frightened.'

In spite of Mrs Oates's laughter, Helen insisted on fetching a candle from the scullery and exploring the basement. Mrs Oates lagged behind her as she made an exhaustive search of the pantry, storeroom, larder, boot-closet and the other offices.

At the end of the passage, she turned into a darker alley, where the coal-cellars and wood-house were located. She flashed her light over each recess, stooping behind dusty sacks and creeping into corners.

'What d' you expect to find?' asked Mrs Oates. 'A nice young man?'

Her grin faded, however, as Helen paused before a locked door.

'That's one place as you, nor no one else, will ever get into,' she said grimly. 'If the loony gets inside *there*, I'll say good luck to him.'

'Why?' asked Helen. 'What is it?'

'The wine-cellar – and the professor keeps the key. It's the nearest you'll ever get to it.'

Helen, who was a total abstainer, through force of circumstance, realised that since she had been at The Summit no intoxicant had been served with the meals.

'Are they all teetotallers here?' she asked.

'There's nothing to hinder the professor having his glass,' said Mrs Oates, 'seeing as he keeps the key. But Oates and the young gentlemen have got to go to the Bull for their drop of tiddley. And Mr Rice is the only one as has ever asked me if I have a mouth.'

'What a shame not to allow you beer, with all your heavy work,' sympathised Helen.

'I get beer-money,' admitted Mrs Oates. 'Miss Warren's just got a bee in her bonnet about no drink served in the house. But she's like the professor, no trouble so long as you leave her with her books. She's not mean – only you mustn't do a thing what's worth doing. That's her.'

That was exactly how Miss Warren had struck Helen – a grey studious negation.

Mrs Oates relieved her feelings by kicking the cellar door, before they turned away.

'I've promised myself one thing,' she said solemnly. 'It's this: if ever I come across the key of this cellar, there'll be a bottle short.'

'And the fairies will have drunk it, I suppose?' smiled Helen. 'Come back to the fire. I've something thrilling to tell you.'

When they were back in the kitchen, however, Mrs Oates began to chuckle.

'You've something to tell me. Well, I've something to show you. Look at these.'

She opened one of the cupboards in the dresser, and pointed to a line of empty bottles.

'What Mr Rice calls "dead men". Many's the bottle of gin or stout he's brought back from the Bull.'

'He's kind,' admitted Helen. 'There's *something* about him. Pity he's such a rotter.'

'He's not as black as he's painted,' said Mrs Oates. 'He was sent down from his school in Oxford for mucking about with a girl. But he told me, one night, as he was more sinned against than sinning. He's not really partial to girls.'

'But he flirts with Mrs Newton.'

'Just his fun. When she says "A", he says "B". That's all.'

Helen laughed as she looked into the glowing heart of the fire. Unknown to her, fresh cracks had been started in the walls of her fortress. As she stroked the ginger cat, who responded with a startling rumble, her recent experience seemed very remote.

'I promised you a tale,' she said. 'Well – "believe me or believe me not" – when I was coming through the plantation, I met – the strangler.'

It was certain that she did not believe her own story, although she exaggerated the details in order to impress Mrs Oates. It was such a thin-spun theme – a man hiding behind a tree, with no sequel to prove a dark motive.

She was not the only one to be incredulous. In a cottage halfway up the hillside, a dark-eyed girl was looking at herself in a small fly-blown mirror. Her face was rosy from moist mountain air, and her expression was eager and rebellious.

Here was one who grabbed at life with both hands. She perched a scarlet hand-knitted beret at a perilous angle on her short black hair, powdered her cheeks and added unnecessary lipstick to her moist red lips, humming as an accompaniment to her actions.

As she looked around the small room, with the low bulging white-plaster ceiling and cracked walls, the limp muslin curtain before the shuttered window, her desire grew. She told herself that she was sick of confinement and the cheesy smell of indoors. She had stayed in, night after night, until she was fed up, and willing to chance any hypothetical criminal. She yearned for the cheery bar of the Bull, with a young man or two, a glass of cider and the magic of the wireless.

She buttoned up her red leather coat and put on Wellington boots before her stealthy descent down the creaking stairs. When she slipped through the cottage door her heart beat faster, but only with excitement. She was as used to the narrow, pitchy lane, which dropped down precipitously to the valley, as a Londoner is to Piccadilly. Familiarity with loneliness had robbed it of any terror, just as immunity from attack had resulted in perfect nerve. Without fear or foreboding, she hurried down the stony hillside in sure-footed haste.

When she reached the plantation, she knew that she was within fifteen minutes of her goal. A bare mile of level ground separated her from the bar of the Bull. Civilisation was represented by The Summit, which was so close to her that she could hear the broadcast strains of Jack Hylton's band.

Like most Welsh girls, she had a true ear and a musical voice. She took up the tune, jumbling the words but singing with the passionate exaltation due to a revivalist hymn.

> 'Love is the sweetest thing –
> No bird upon the wi–ng . . . '

The rain drove down upon her face in steady slanting skeins through the partial screen of the larches, and the hard ground under her feet was growing slimed, in spite of its carpet of spines. Happy, healthy and unwise, she hurried to meet the future. Careless of weather, and one with the elements, she sang her way through the wood – youth at its peak.

Her sight was excellent, so that she could distinguish the lane of single trees where the plantation thinned towards its end. But her imagination was more blunted than Helen's, so that she did not notice that one of the trees was apparently rootless, for it shifted behind the trunks of its fellows.

Had she remarked it, she would have distrusted the evidence of her eyes. Common sense would have told her that trees do not move from their stations. So she hurried on, and sang yet louder.

> 'I only pray that life may bring
> Love's sweet story to you.'

When she reached the last tree, it suddenly changed into a man. Its branches were clutching arms. But still she did not believe.

For she knew that these things do not happen.

4

Ancient Lights

'The tree moved,' declared Helen, finishing her story in the safety of the kitchen. 'And – to my horror – I saw that it was a man. He was waiting there, like a tiger ready to spring on his prey.'

'Go on.' Mrs Oates was openly derisive. 'I've seen that tree, myself. Often seen him, I have, waiting for Ceridwen, when she used to work here. And he was never the same tree twice.'

'Ceridwen?' repeated Helen.

'Yes. She lives in a cottage halfway up the hill. A pretty girl, but she would mix her cloths. Old Lady Warren couldn't abide her. She said as how her feet smelt, and when she dusted under her bed, her ladyship used to wait for her, with her stick, until she crawled out, so as to fetch her a clout on the head.'

Helen burst out laughing. Life might ignore the invalid, but she remained acutely conscious and appreciative of the eternal comedy.

'The old darling gets better and better,' she declared. 'I wish you'd give me the job of dusting under her bed. She'd find me a bit too quick for her.'

'So was Ceridwen. She used to bait the old girl, shooting out when she wasn't expecting her. But she got her, in the end. She fetched her such a crack that her father came and took her away.'

'She certainly makes – What's that?'

Helen broke off to listen. Once again the sound was repeated – an insistent tapping on a window-pane. Although she could not locate it, it seemed to be not far away.

'Is someone knocking?' she asked.

Mrs Oates listened also.

'It must be the passage window,' Mrs Oates said. 'The catch is loose. Oates did talk of mending it.'

'That doesn't sound too safe,' objected Helen.

'Now, miss, don't worry. The shutter's put up. No on can get in.'

But, as the wind rose, the monotonous rattle and beat continued, at irregular intervals. It got on Helen's nerves, so that she could not settle down to her tea.

'It's a miserable night,' she said. 'If that tree was waiting for Ceridwen, I don't envy her.'

'He's caught her by now,' chuckled Mrs Oates. 'She won't be noticing weather no more.'

'There it goes a again . . . Have you a screwdriver?' Helen's eyes lit up as she spoke, for she had a mania for small mechanical jobs. 'You see, Mrs Oates, this sound will irritate you,' she explained. 'And then you'll spoil the dinner. And then we shall have indigestion. I'll see if I can't put it right.'

'What a one you are to look for work,' grumbled Mrs Oates, as she followed Helen through the scullery.

The smallish window was at the end of the passage close to the scullery door. As Helen unbarred the shutter, a gust of wind struck it, like a blow, and dashed drops of rain against the streaming glass.

Together, the big woman and the small girl stood, peering out into the garden. They could see only a black huddle of shrubs and a gleam of thrashing boughs.

'Doesn't it look creepy?' said Helen. 'I wonder if I can fix this catch. Have you any small nails?'

'I'll see if I can find some. Oates is a terror for nails.'

Mrs Oates lumbered through the scullery, leaving Helen alone staring out into the wet garden. There were no bushes, on this side, to give the impression of a crawling greyness creeping towards the house; the night seemed to have become solid and definite – clear-cut chunks of threatening blackness.

It inspired a spirit of defiance in Helen.

'Come on – if you dare,' she cried aloud.

The answer to her challenge was immediate – a piercing scream from the kitchen.

Helen's heart leaped at the thin terror-stricken wail. There was only room for one thought in her mind. The maniac was lurking in hiding, and she had sent the poor unsuspecting Mrs Oates into his trap.

'He's got her,' she thought, as she caught up the bar and dashed into the kitchen.

Mrs Oates greeted her with another scream, but there was no sign of the source of her terror, although she was on the verge of hysteria.

'A mouse,' she yelled. 'It went over there.'

Helen stared at her in blank incredulity. 'You *can't* be frightened of a little mouse. It isn't done. Old stuff, you know.'

'But they make me crawl all over,' whimpered Mrs Oates.

'In that case, I suppose murder will have to be committed. A pity. Here, Ginger, Ginger.'

Helen called, in vain, to the cat, who continued to wash with an affectation of complete detachment.

Mrs Oates apologised for him. 'He's a civil cat, but he can't abide mice. Oates would swat it.'

'If that's a hint, *I'm* not going to swat it. But I'll frighten it away.'

With her sensitised reaction to any situation, she was conscious of anticlimax when she went down on her knees and began to beat the floor with her bar. Just whenever the drama seemed to be working up to a moment of tension, the crisis always eluded her and degenerated into farce.

Not until the night was over could she trace the repercussions of each trivial incident and realise that the wave of fear which flooded the house washed back to an insignificant source.

She could see her quarry – a small and rather attractive rodent – frisking in the distance, with the assurance of an old resident.

'Where's its hole?' she whispered.

'In that corner,' panted Mrs Oates. 'Oates did say as how he'd stop it up.'

Helen was driving the mouse homewards when she started at the sound of footsteps on the back stairs.

'Who's that?' she cried.

'Not him,' laughed Mrs Oates. 'When he comes you'll not hear him on the way. He'll creep. That sounds like Mr Rice.'

As she spoke the door was pushed open, and Stephen Rice, carrying a suitcase, entered the kitchen. He stared at the sight of the demure Miss Capel on her knees, with her hair falling in a mane across her eyes.

'What's this?' he asked. 'Red Indians, or a crawling party? Count me in.'

'I'm chasing a mouse,' explained Helen.

'Great sport. I'll help.'

'No, I don't want to catch it.' Helen rose and placed the bar on the table. 'I think he's gone now.'

Stephen sat down and looked around him.

'I always feel at home, here,' he said. 'It's the one room I like in this horrible house. Mrs Oates and I hold our prayer-meetings here.'

'Where's your dog?' asked Helen.

'In my room. Miss Warren did not come to tea, unfortunately. So the row's postponed.'

'Why d' you have one at all?' asked Helen. 'You're leaving tomorrow. I expect Miss Warren would prefer not to know.'

'No.' Stephen stuck out his prominent chin. 'I'd rather come out in the open. Noble of me, when I know the heroic Newton will enlighten her darkness in any case.'

'He wouldn't tell?' cried Helen incredulously.

'Wouldn't he? To be frank, Otto was not a blazing success. The poor lad is not used to afternoon tea. Like his master, he's happier in the kitchen.'

'But Mrs Newton must have fallen for him,' insisted Helen, who argued along the familiar lines of 'Love me, love my dog.'

'If she did, she controlled her passion.' Stephen opened his empty suitcase and turned to Mrs Oates. 'Where are the empties?' he asked. 'I thought I'd lift them now, and lug them over to the Bull tonight, to save that poor delicate husband of yours.'

'And I suppose you want to say goodbye to your young lady there?' Mrs Oates winked at Helen, who – enlightened by her previous gossip – understood the allusion to the daughter of the licensee of the Bull. Apparently, this young lady was not only the patron-saint of the bar, but the magnet that drew the sparse male population of the district.

Mrs Oates took advantage of her privileged position to ask another more personal question.

'And what will your other lady say, if you spend your last night away?'

'My other – what?' demanded Stephen.

'Mrs Newton.'

'Mrs Newton Warren is a respectable married lady. She will naturally pass the evening in the company of her lawful husband, working out mathematical problems.

'Did you have a good tea?'

Helen did not hear the question, for she suddenly glimpsed an exciting possibility.

'Did Miss Warren have her tea up in the bedroom?' she asked.

'I suppose so,' replied Stephen.

'Then she's been up there for ages. I wonder if I might, offer to relieve her?'

'If you do,' advised Stephen, 'see that she's supplied with cushions. Unless, of course, you're expert in dodging.'

'But does she always throw things at people?' asked Helen incredulously.

'It's the only way she knows of expressing her temperament.'

'Well, it doesn't matter. I think she sounds so *alive* for an old woman. I admire that.'

'You'll be disillusioned,' prophesied Stephen. 'She's a vile-tempered old cuss, with horrible manners. When I was presented to Her Majesty, she was eating an orange, and she spat out all the pips – to impress me.'

He broke off to laugh at a sudden recollection.

'All the same,' he said, 'I'd love to have seen her chuck the basin at that pie-faced nurse.'

'But, surely, that was an accident. She couldn't have known she was going to hit her.'

Mrs Oates looked up, with streaming eyes, from her task of peeling onions. 'Oh, no, miss,' she said. 'Lady Warren wouldn't miss. When she was younger, she spent all her time tramping over the fields, shooting rabbits and birds. They said she went to bed with her gun.'

'Then she's been here a long time?' asked Helen.

She believed that her curiosity was about to be given a real meal, for Mrs Oates's manner hinted at gossip.

Stephen rolled a cigarette, the cat purred on the rug, the mouse washed his face in the safety of his hole. Inside was firelight and tranquillity – outside, the rising storm.

A gust of wind smashed against the corner of the house, and spattered the unbarred shutter before the passage window with the remnants of its original fury. Slowly, as though pushed open by invisible fingers, the casement swung outwards over the garden. The house was open to the night. It looked in, through the gap, and down the darkness of the passage. The far end stretched away into shadows. Round the bend, was the warren of the offices – a honeycomb of cells, where a man could hide.

Inside the kitchen, Mrs Oates electrified her audience.

'They do say,' she said dramatically, 'as old Lady Warren shot her husband.'

'No,' gasped Stephen and Helen together.

'Yes,' declared Mrs Oates. 'It's an old wives' tale now, but my mother told me all about it. Old Sir Roger was just such a one as the professor, quiet and always shut up with his books. He made a lot of money with some invention. He built The Summit, so as to have no neighbours. And Lady Warren couldn't abide it. She was always nagging him about it, and they had one awful quarrel, in his study. She was overheard to threaten to shoot him for vermin. A few minutes later he was found shot dead, with her rook rifle.

'Looks pretty bad,' murmured Stephen.

'Yes, everyone thought she'd stand in the dock,' agreed Mrs Oates. 'There was some nasty questions asked at the inquest. She said as how it was an accident, and her clever lawyer got her off. But there was so much feeling about it that she went abroad – though she'd have gone, anyhow, as she fair hated the house.'

'Was it shut up afterwards?' asked Helen.

'No, the professor left Oxford, and came here, and he's been just the same as his father before him – always staying in and never going out. Old Lady Warren only came back when she said she was ill.'

'What's the matter with her?' asked Helen.

Mrs Oates pursed up her lips and shook her head.

'*Temper*,' she said firmly.

'Oh, but Mrs Oates, she must be ill, to have a nurse, and for the doctor to keep her in bed.'

'He reckons she's less trouble there. And she reckons she can give more trouble there. It's a fair game for her to drive the nurses away, so as to get fresh ones in to bully.'

'But Miss Warren told me that the professor was anxious about her heart,' persisted Helen.

'Ah, but a man don't forget the mother, that bore him,' declared Mrs Oates, lapsing into sentiment.

'But she's only his stepmother,' objected Stephen. 'She has no children. Still, she must be expected to croak because the vultures are gathering. Simone told me that the old girl has made a will, leaving her money to charities. She has a nasty perverted taste and apparently likes Newton. Anyway, she makes him an allowance, which will cease at her death. That's why he's down here.'

'His pa sent for him,' explained Mrs Oates.

Helen thought of the professor's glacial eye and Miss Warren's detached manner. It was impossible to believe that they were swayed by financial considerations.

'Hello,' said Stephen suddenly, as he swung himself up from his chair. 'What's this?'

He drew from under him a wooden bar, which Helen took from him, rather guiltily.

'Sorry,' she said. 'It belongs to the shutter in the passage. I'm glad you reminded me of it. I'll try and fix the window.'

After what she had heard, she felt eager to finish the job and get upstairs, to the blue room, as quickly as possible. She made a makeshift fastening with some string and a peg, and then hurried back to the kitchen.

To her surprise, Stephen was peeling onions with Mrs Oates.

'She always makes me work,' he complained. 'It's her way of explaining away a man in the kitchen when Oates comes home. I say, isn't he very late? I bet you a fiver he's run off with the pretty new nurse.'

Mrs Oates snorted.

'If she's like the last, she'd have to hold his nose to get him to kiss her. Are you really going to sit with Lady Warren, miss?'

'I am going to ask if I may,' replied Helen.

'Then, take my warning, and be on the watch out against her. It's my belief she's not as helpless as they make out, by a long way. I'm sure she can walk, same as me. She's got something up her sleeve. Besides, have you heard her voice, *when she forgets*?'

Helen suddenly remembered the bass bellow from the sickroom. Here was a situation charged with mystery and drama. In her eagerness to be in the thick of it she almost ran to the door.

'I've tied up the window,' she said. 'Now, we're safely locked up for the night.'

5

The Blue Room

As Helen mounted the stairs to the blue room, she felt an odd stir of expectancy. It took her back to childhood days, when she neglected her toys in favour of an invisible companion – Mr Poke.

Although she played by herself for hours, in a corner of the communal sitting-room, it was plain to her parents that she was not indulging in a solitary game. She did everything with a partner. And at twilight, when the firelight sent tall shadows flickering on the walls, she carried on an interminable conversation with her hero.

At first, her mother disliked the disquieting nature of the company kept by her small daughter; but when she realised that Helen had discovered the best and cheapest of playfellows – imagination – she accepted the wonderful Mr Poke and used to ask questions about his prowess, to which there was no limit.

The staircase was lit by a pendant globe, which swung from a beam which spanned the central well. The first floor was between this light and the illumination from the hall, so that the landing was rather dark. Facing the flight of stairs, was an enormous ten-foot mirror, framed in tarnished gilt carving and supported by a marble console table.

As Helen approached it, her reflection came to meet her, so that a small white face rose up from the dim depths of the glass, like a corpse emerging from a deep lake on the seventh day.

The thrill which ran through her veins, in response, seemed to her an omen. Miss Warren came to the door in answer to her knock. Her pale face looked haggard and devitalised after hours of imprisonment with her stepmother.

'Has the new nurse come?' she asked.

'No.' Helen was aggressively cheerful. 'And we don't expect her for hours and hours. Mrs Oates says the rain has made the hills difficult for the car.'

'Quite,' agreed Miss Warren wearily. 'Please let me know directly she arrives. She must relieve me as soon as she has had something to eat.'

It was Helen's chance – and she took it.

'Might I sit with Lady Warren?' she asked.

Miss Warren hesitated before her reply. She knew that it would be against her brother's wish to entrust Lady Warren to an untrained stranger; but the girl seemed reliable and conscientious.

'Thank you, Miss Capel,' she replied. 'It would be kind. Lady Warren is asleep, so you will only have to sit very still, and watch her.'

She crossed the landing to her own room, and then turned to give further advice.

'If she wakes and wants something you can't find, or if you are in any difficulty, come, at once, to me.'

Helen promised, even while she was conscious that she would appeal to Miss Warren only as a last resort. She meant to cope with any situation on her own initiative, and she hoped that the need would arise.

The tide of her curiosity was running strongly when, at long last, she entered the blue room. It was a huge, handsome apartment, furnished with a massive mahogany suite, made sombre by reason of the prevailing dark-blue colour of the walls, carpet and curtains. A dull red fire glowed in the steel grate. Although its closeness was mitigated with lavender-water, the atmosphere smelt faintly of rotten apples. Lady Warren lay in the big bed. She wore a dark-purple quilted silk dressing-jacket, and her head was propped high with pillows. Her eyes were closed and she was breathing heavily.

Helen's first glance told her that Stephen was right in his description. There was no sign of grand character in this bedridden old woman. The lines which scored her face, like an ancient map, were all plainly traced by bad temper and egotism. Her grey hair was cut short in a thick untidy shock and her nose was suspiciously red.

Stealing across the floor, Helen sat down in the low chair by the fire. She noticed that each coal was wrapped in white tissue paper, so that the scuttle appeared to be filled with snowballs. As she knew this precaution was a means to ensure quiet, she took the hint, and remained motionless, as though she were furniture.

Lady Warren's breathing continued with the volume and regularity reminiscent of a steam-engine. Presently Helen began to suspect that it was a special performance for her benefit.

'She's not really asleep,' she thought. 'She's foxing.'

The breathing went on – but nothing happened. Yet Helen was aware of the quiver of her pulse which always heralded Mr Poke's approach.

Someone was watching her.

She had to turn her head round, in order to look at the bed. When she did so, Lady Warren's lids were tightly closed. With a joyous sense of playing a new game, Helen waited for a chance to catch her unawares.

Presently, after many feints and failures, she proved too quick for Lady Warren. Looking up unexpectedly, she caught her in the act of spying. Her lids were slit across by twin black crescents of extraordinary brightness, which peered out at her.

They shut immediately, only to open again, as the invalid realised that further subterfuge was vain.

'Come here,' she said, in a faint fluttering voice.

With a memory of Mrs Oates's warning, Helen advanced warily. She looked a small and insignificant person – a pale girl in a blue pinafore-dress which made her fade into the background.

'Come nearer,' commanded Lady Warren.

Helen obeyed, although her eyes wandered to the objects on the bed-table. She wondered which missile the invalid might choose to hurl at her head, and stretched out her hand for the biggest medicine bottle.

'Put that down,' snarled her ladyship faintly. 'That's *mine*.'

'Oh, I *am* sorry.' Helen spoke eagerly. 'I'm like that. *I* hate people to touch my things.'

Feeling that there was a link between them, she stood boldly by the bed, and smiled down at the invalid.

'You're very small,' remarked Lady Warren, at last breaking her silence. 'No style. Very unimpressive. I thought my grandson would have shown better taste when he chose a wife.'

As she listened, Helen remembered that Simone had refused to enter the blue room, although Newton had urged her to do so.

'He showed excellent taste,' she said. 'His wife is marvellous. I'm not her.'

'Then – who are you?' asked Lady Warren.

'The help. Miss Capel.'

A ripple of some strong emotion passed over the old woman's face, leaving the black crescent eyes fixed and the lips hanging apart.

'She looks afraid,' thought Helen. 'But what's she afraid of? It – it must be me.'

Lady Warren's next words, however, gave the lie to this exciting possibility. Her voice strengthened.

'Go away,' she shouted, in the bass voice of a man.

Startled by the change, Helen turned and ran from the invalid, expecting every second to feel the crash of a bottle on her head. But, before she reached the door, she was recalled by a shout.

'You little fool, come back.'

Quivering with expectation at this new turn, Helen crossed to the bed. The old lady began to talk in such a faint whine that her words were almost inaudible.

'Get out of the house. Too many trees.'

'Trees?' repeated Helen, as her mind slipped back to the last tree in the plantation.

'Trees,' repeated Lady Warren. 'They stretch out their branches and knock at the window. They try to get in. When it's dark, they move. Creeping up to the house. Go away.'

As she listened, Helen felt a sense of kinship with the old woman. It was strange that she, too, had stood at the window, at twilight, and watched the invasion of the misted shrubs. Of course, it was all imagination; but that fact alone indicated common ground of the Mr Poke variety.

In any case, she wanted to use the trees as a liaison between Lady Warren and herself. It was one of her small failings that, although she liked to succeed in her own line, she liked still better to make common cause with others. She proceeded to try and make a conquest of Lady Warren.

'How strange,' she said. 'I've thought exactly the same as you.'

Unfortunately, Lady Warren resented her words as impertinence.

'I don't want to hear *your* thoughts,' Lady Warren whined. 'Don't dare to presume, because I'm helpless. What's your name?'

'Helen Capel,' was the dejected reply.

'How old are you?'

'Twenty-three.'

'Liar. Nineteen.'

Helen was startled by her acumen, as her employers had always accepted her fictional age. 'It's not exactly a lie,' she explained. 'I feel I'm entitled to put on my age, because I'm old in experience. I began to earn my own living when I was fourteen.'

Lady Warren showed no signs of being impressed.

'Why?' she asked. 'Are you a love-child?'

'Certainly not,' replied Helen indignantly. 'My parents were married in church. But they couldn't provide for me. They were unlucky.'

'Dead?'

'Yes.'

'Then they're lucky.'

In spite of her subordinate position, Helen always found the necessary courage to protest when any vital principle of her creed was challenged.

'No,' Helen protested. 'Life is wonderful. I always wake up just glad to be alive.'

Lady Warren grunted before she continued her catechism.

'Drink?' she asked.

'No.'

'Any men?'

'No chance – worse luck.'

Lady Warren did not join in her laugh but stared at Helen so rigidly that the black slits of her eyes appeared to congeal. Some scheme was being spun amid the cobwebs of her mind.

The clock ticked away the silence and the fire fell in, with a sudden spurt of flame.

'Shall I put on more coal?' asked Helen, anxious to break the spell.

'No. Give me back my teeth.'

The request was so startling that Helen positively jumped. But the next second, she realised that Lady Warren was only referring to her dentures, which were in an enamel cup on the bed-table.

She looked away tactfully while the august invalid fished them out of the disinfectant with her fingers and adjusted them to her gums.

'Helen,' she cooed, in a new dove-like voice, 'I want you to sleep with me, tonight.'

Helen looked at her, aghast, for the change in her was both grotesque and astonishing. The denture forced her lips apart in a stiff artificial grin, which gave her a hideous resemblance to an old waxwork.

'You were afraid of me without my teeth,' Lady Warren told her. 'But you won't be afraid now. I want to take care of you, tonight.'

Helen licked her lips nervously. 'But, my lady,' she said, 'the new nurse will sleep with you tonight.'

'I'd forgotten the new nurse. Another slut. Well, I'll be ready for *her*. But *you're* to sleep with me. You see, my dear, you're not safe.'

As she smiled, Helen was suddenly reminded of the grin of a crocodile. 'I *couldn't* pass a night alone with her,' she thought, even while she was conscious that her fear was only of her own creation. It was obviously absurd to be afraid of a bedridden old woman.

'I'm afraid I can do nothing without Miss Warren's instructions,' she said.

'My stepdaughter's a fool. She doesn't know what's going on in this house. Trees always trying to get in. Come here, Helen.'

As Helen stooped over the bed, she felt her hand caught in a strong grip.

'I want you to get me something,' whispered Lady Warren. 'It's in the cupboard at the top of the wardrobe. Get on a chair.'

Helen, who was enjoying the rare flavour of an adventure, decided to humour her.

She climbed on to one of the heavy chairs and stood on her toes in order to open the door of the cupboard.

She felt a little doubtful of the commission, as she groped with her hand in the dark recess. It was evident that Lady Warren was using her as a tool to procure forbidden fruit. With a memory of her inflamed nose, she suspected a hidden bottle of brandy.

'What is it?' she called.

'A little hard thing, wrapped in a silk scarf,' was the disarming reply.

As she spoke, Helen's fingers closed upon something which answered to the description.

'Is this it?' she asked, springing to the ground.

'Yes.' Lady Warren's voice was eager. 'Bring it to me.'

In the short journey to the bed, Helen was gripped with a sudden fear of the thing she held. Even through the scarf, its shape was unmistakable. It was a revolver. She remembered Lady Warren's dead rabbits – and also a husband shot dead by accident.'

'I wonder if it's loaded,' she thought fearfully. 'I can't even tell which is the dangerous end. I mustn't let her have it. Mrs Oates warned me.'

'Bring it to me,' commanded Lady Warren. She made no attempt to disguise her excitement. Her fingers shook with eagerness, as she stretched out her hands.

Helen pretended not to hear. With affected carelessness, she laid down the revolver on a small table – at a safe distance from the invalid – before she advanced to the bed.

'Now, you mustn't get worked up,' she said soothingly. 'It is so bad for your heart.'

Fortunately Lady Warren's attention was distracted by her words.

'What does the doctor say about me?' she asked.

'He says your vitality is wonderful,' replied Helen.

'Then he's a fool. I'm a dead woman. But I'm not going to die till I'm ready.'

Her lids closed, so that her eyes were visible only as narrow black rims. Her shrivelled face seemed to become a worn-out garment, and she spoke in the reedy voice of a burnt-out force.

'I've a job. Keep putting it off. Weak of me. But it's a job no one likes. Isn't it?'

Helen guessed immediately that she referred to her will.

'Yes,' she replied. 'Everyone puts it off.'

And then, because she could not resist her interest in the affairs of others, she added a bit of advice.

'But we all of us have to do it. It *must* be done.'

But Lady Warren was not listening.

The eclipse was rapidly passing, for her eyes grew alert as they slanted across to the small bundle on the table.

'Bring it to me,' she said.

'No,' replied Helen. 'Better not.'

'Fool. What are you afraid of? It's only my spectacle case.'

'Yes, I know it is. I'm ever so sorry, my lady, but I'm only a machine.

I have to obey Miss Warren's orders. And she told me I was only to sit and watch.'

It was plain that Lady Warren was not used to opposition. Her eyes blazed, and her fingers hooked like talons as she clawed her throat.

'Go,' she gasped. 'Get – Miss – Warren.'

Helen rushed from the room – almost glad of the attack, since the crisis of the revolver was postponed. As she reached the door, she looked back and saw that Lady Warren had collapsed upon her pillows.

A second later, the invalid raised her head. There was a stir amid the bedclothes, two feet, in bedsocks, emerged from under the eiderdown and Lady Warren slipped out of bed.

6

Illusion

Her heart beating fast with mingled exhilaration and fear, Helen hurried to Miss Warren's room. For the first time in her life, she was up against unknown possibilities. Unlike the other houses in which she had worked, The Summit provided a background.

It was true that Mrs Oates had heartlessly plucked the mystery from the last tree in the plantation, so that Helen was forced to accept him as the yokel lover of a rustic beauty; yet there remained material for macabre drama in the savage muffled landscape and the overhanging shadow of murder.

The old woman, too, with her overtures and her gleaming artificial smile, supplied a touch of real horror. She might be only a bedridden invalid, but the fact remained that she was under suspicion of having sent her husband prematurely to heaven or to hell.

Her sting might be drawn, but her desires were still lethal. Helen had proof of this in the incident of the revolver.

Her thoughts, however, reverted to practical matters when as she turned the handle of Miss Warren's room it once again slipped round in her grasp.

'I really must get at it the instant I have a chance,' she promised herself.

Miss Warren was sitting at her bureau, under the green light. Her eyes were fixed upon her book.

'Well?' she asked wearily as Helen entered.

'I'm sorry to disturb you,' began Helen, 'but Lady War – '

Before she could finish her sentence, Miss Warren was out of her chair, and crossing the room with the ungainly gait of a giraffe.

In her element, Helen followed her to the blue room. Lady Warren was lying as she had left her, with closed eyes and puffing lips. The revolver, wrapped in the silk handkerchief, was still on the kidney table, the width of the room away from the bed.

Yet there was some change. Helen, who was observant, noticed the fact at once, and in her second survey traced it to its cause. When she had gone to fetch Miss Warren, the bedclothes were disordered. Now the sheet was drawn down over the eiderdown as neatly as though it had been arranged by a hospital nurse.

'Miss Capel,' said Miss Warren, who was bending over the prostrate figure of her stepmother, 'fetch the oxygen-cylinder.'

Helen, who was always ready to experiment with unfamiliar things, hurried to lug it across to the bed. She thoughtfully unscrewed the top, and managed to get a whiff of air, like a mountain breeze, before she surrendered it to Miss Warren.

Presently, Lady Warren revived under their joint ministrations. To Helen's awakening suspicions, it was an artistic performance, with calculated gradations of sighs, groans and fluttering lids.

Directly her eyes were open, she glared at Helen. 'Send her away,' she said weakly.

Miss Warren caught Helen's eye. 'Please go, Miss Capel. I'm sorry.'

Forgetful of her pose, Lady Warren turned on her stepdaughter, like some fishwife. 'Idiot. Send her packing. Tonight.'

She closed her eyes again, and murmured, 'Doctor. I want the doctor.'

'He'll be here presently,' Miss Warren assured her.

'Why is he always late?' complained the invalid.

'Because he likes to see how you are last thing,' explained Miss Warren.

'It's because he's a slacker,' snarled Lady Warren. 'I must change my doctor, Blanche. That girl wasn't Newton's wife. Why doesn't *she* come to see me?'

'You are not strong enough for visitors.'

'That's not it. *I* know. She's *afraid* of me.'

The idea seemed to please Lady Warren for her face puckered up in a smile. Helen, who was watching from a safe distance, thought that she looked positively evil. In that moment, she could almost believe in the story of a murdered husband.

Her eye fell on the nurse's small single-bed.

'I wouldn't be that nurse, for all the money in the world,' she shuddered.

Suddenly, Miss Warren became aware that she was still in the room, for she crossed over to her corner.

'I can manage by myself, Miss Capel.'

Her tone was so cold that Helen tried to justify herself.

'I hope you don't think I did anything to annoy her. She changed all of a sudden. At first, she took a fancy to me. Indeed, she kept asking me to sleep with her, tonight.'

Miss Warren's expression was incredulous, although her words were polite. 'I am sure that you were kind and tactful.'

Her glance towards the door was a hint of dismissal, and Helen turned to go; but her head was humming with confused suspicions which fought for utterance. Although experience had taught her that interference is usually resented, she felt that she must warn Miss Warren.

'I think there is something you ought to know,' she said, lowering her voice. 'Lady Warren asked me to get her something from the little cupboard above the wardrobe mirror.'

'Why do you consider that important?' asked Miss Warren.

'Because it was a revolver.'

Helen achieved her effect. Miss Warren looked directly at her, with a startled expression.

'Where is it now?' she asked.

'On that table.'

Miss Warren swooped down upon the small bundle with the avidity of some bird of prey. Her long white fingers loosened a fold of the silk wrapping. Then she held it out, so that Helen might see it.

It contained a large spectacle case.

As she stared at it, Helen was forcibly struck by an exciting possibility.

'That is not the same shape,' she declared. 'I felt the other. It had jutting-out bits.'

'What exactly are you hinting at?'

'I think that, when I went to fetch you, Lady Warren hid the revolver and put this in its place.'

'And are you aware that my mother has heart-disease, and has been unable to move for months?'

All hope of being taken seriously died as Helen looked at Miss Warren's sceptical face. Its fluid lines seemed to have been suddenly arrested by a sharp frost.

'I'm sorry if I've made a mistake,' she faltered. 'Only, I thought I ought to keep nothing back.'

'I am sure you were trying to be helpful,' Miss Warren told her. 'But it only hinders to imagine stupid impossibilities.' She added, with a grim smile, 'I suppose, like all girls, you go to the cinema.'

In the circumstances, her reproach was laden with painful irony. She seemed as divided from Helen as if she came from another era.

'She's prehistoric,' thought the girl. Her small figure appeared actually shrunken as she went out of the blue room. Besides being cheated out of the recognition which was her due, she did not feel satisfied with Miss Warren's acceptance of the revolver incident.

'The customer is always right,' she reminded herself, as she walked down the stairs. 'But there's one comfort. Now that Lady Warren's soured on me, there will be no more talk about sleeping in her room.'

Luckily, in spite of her discouragement, her sense of duty remained unimpaired. As Oates was late, she decided to take on his job of laying the dinner-table.

At the sound of footsteps, the drawing-room door was opened, and Simone looked out – her eyes parched with longing. Instantly, her husband's head reared itself over her shoulder, like a serpent.

Simone showed no signs of discomfiture. She merely shrugged and smiled. 'So faithful,' she murmured, as she closed the door.

Braced by this glimpse of the clash of human passions, Helen went into the dining-room. For the first time, she felt a certain degree of sympathy with Simone.

'It would get on my nerves to be followed about like that,' she thought.

It was evident that Newton's jealousy was reaching saturation-point, but with Stephen's departure, he would probably become normal again. Meantime, he plainly meant to give his wife no opportunity of a final interview with the pupil.

In Helen's eyes, his obsession amounted almost to mania, as she considered the stolid indifference with which Stephen opposed Simone's passion. He did not run from her pursuit, he merely shoved her away. Even then, he was in the kitchen, helping Mrs, Oates. He had been offered romance – and he chose onions.

The dining-room was the finest room in The Summit, with an elaborate ceiling of dark carved wood, and a massive fireplace and overmantel to correspond.

The great windows were screened with thick crimson curtains, while dark-red paper covered the walls.

Helen crossed to the walnut sideboard, where the glass and silver was kept, and took a tablecloth from one of the drawers.

From years of practice, Helen could lay a table in her sleep. As she mechanically sorted out spoons and forks, her mind was busy in speculation. Although she was denied the privilege of discussion with her employer on the subject, she was positive that, during her absence, there had been some monkey-work in the blue room.

'I'm sure Mrs Oates is right,' she thought. 'Lady Warren is not bedridden. She got up, and then she tried to cover her tracks by tidying the bed. Well, she overdid it. I'd like to talk it over with Dr Parry,'

Dr Parry was clever, young and unconventional. The first time he met Helen, he had shown a direct interest in her welfare, which she had accepted as professional concern. He asked her personal questions, and seemed apprehensive about the influence of her surroundings on her youth.

What appealed to her most was his unprofessional gossip about his patient.

'Her heart's in a shocking state,' he told her. 'Still, hearts are sporting organs. She might climb Snowdon and be all right, and the next time she sneezed it might finish her off. But – she keeps me guessing. I sometimes wonder if she is so helpless. To my mind, she is an aged surprise-packet.'

Helen remembered his words as she trotted to and fro between the table and the sideboard. But her ears still burned whenever she recalled the irony of Miss Warren's voice.

'Well, I've warned her,' she thought. 'It's her pigeon. But I would like to know where that revolver is. You won't catch me in that room again, if I can help it.'

Although she tried to listen for the sound of the car, the fury of the storm prevented her from hearing the hum of the engine. It was not until she caught Mrs Oates's welcome to her husband that she realised that the new nurse had come.

She rushed across the room and opened the door, but was too late to see the woman's face, for she was in the act of following her guides through the entry to the kitchen stairs. Her back view, however, was impressive, for she was unusually tall.

Helen felt a burst of confidence.

'She's not a weak link, anyway,' she decided. 'She'd be an awkward customer for *him* to tackle.'

As she lingered in the hall, she remembered the loose handle of Miss Warren's door. She had watched where Oates kept his handful of tools, and discovered that it was wherever he had used them. With this clue to guide her, she found the box stuck away in a corner of the boot-closet, in the hall.

As this was not a legitimate job, she crept up the stairs to the first-floor landing, and knelt before the door. She had hardly begun her investigations, when a sudden sound made her look up.

As she did so, she was the victim of an illusion. She was sure that the door across the landing, leading from the back stairs, opened and shut again, giving her a glimpse of the face of a stranger.

It passed, like the dissolving memory of a dream, yet it left a horror in her mind, as though she had received a vision of elemental evil.

Then, while she stared in stunned bewilderment, she realised that a door had actually opened and that the professor was advancing towards her.

'It must have been the professor,' she thought. 'It must. I believe it looked like him. Some trick of light or shadow altered his expression. It's so dark here.'

Even while she clung to this commonplace explanation, her reason rejected it. At the back of her mind remained a picture of the spiral of the back stairs. The two staircases of The Summit offered special chances to anyone who wished to hide.

She reminded herself that no one could get in during the daytime. Besides, the house was so full of people that it would be impossible for anyone to escape notice. The intruder would have to know the habits and timetable of all the inmates.

Suddenly she remembered that Mrs Oates had commented on the super-normal cunning of a criminal maniac.

He would know.

A shiver ran down her spine, as she wondered if she ought to tell the professor of her experience. It was her duty, if any unauthorised person was secreted in the house. But, as she opened her lips, the memory of her recent encounter with Miss Warren made her afraid of appearing officious.

Although the professor's eyes seemed to reduce her to the usual essential gases, the sight of his conventional dinner clothes acted as a tonic. His shirt-front gleamed, his black tie was formal, his grey hair was brushed back from his intellectual brow.

Although he was rigid where his sister was fluid, he inspired her with the same sense of alienation.

Suddenly aware that he might suspect her of spying through a bed-room keyhole, she broke into an explanation of the defective door-handle.

'Tell Oates to see to it, please,' he said, with an absent nod.

Shaken by the incident, Helen resolved to test her nerve by a descent of the back stairs. When she opened the landing door, and looked down the spiral, it was a daunting sight, corkscrewing down to depths of darkness. But her courage did not desert her until the last flight, which she nearly leaped, at a sudden memory of a seared, distorted face.

7

The New Nurse

When Helen entered the kitchen, she was greeted by explosions of spluttering fat. The table was crowded with materials for dinner in different stages of preparation, and while vegetables bubbled on the range, Mrs Oates fried fish, juggled with her saucepans and dried her husband's wet things over the boiler. In spite of the seeming confusion, she took her many tasks in her stride, without loss of head or temper.

Oates, in his grey woollen cardigan, was eating a huge meal in the corner his wife had cleared for him. He was a good-natured giant of a man, with the build of a prizefighter.

At the sight of his small honest eyes, Helen's heart leaped in real welcome. Like his wife, he was to her a tower of strength.

'I'm so glad you've come back,' she told him. 'You're as good as three men about the house.'

Oates smiled sheepishly as he tried to return the compliment.

'Thank you for laying my table, miss,' he said.

'Is it still raining heavily?' asked Helen.

'Not near so much,' interposed Mrs Oates bitterly. 'Oates brought most of it in with him.'

Oates poured Worcester Sauce over his fish, and changed the subject.

'Wait till you see what I've brought back with me,' he chuckled.

'You mean – the new nurse?' asked Helen.

'Yes, the little piece I picked up at the Nursing Home. By the look of her, she's as good as another man.'

'Is she nice?'

'As nasty a bit of work as ever I've come across. Talks with plums in her mouth, and kept me in my place. Well, if she's a lady, I'm Greta Garbo.'

'Where is she?' enquired Helen curiously.

'I put a meal for her in your sitting-room,' replied Mrs Oates.

'My room?'

Mrs Oates exchanged a smile with her husband. Helen's sense of ownership was a perpetual source of amusement to them, because of her small stature.

'Only for tonight.' she said soothingly. 'After her wet ride, I thought she'd rather not wait for the regular dinner.'

'I'll go and welcome her,' decided Helen, even while she knew that 'inspect' would be a more appropriate word.

Her own sanctum – a dingy semi-basement room, on the other side of the kitchen – was originally intended for the servants' hall, in the days before the dearth of domestic help. Its walls and ceiling had been washed butter-yellow, in an attempt to lighten the gloom, and it was shabbily furnished with the overflow of the rest of the house.

Because it had been assigned to Helen, she clung to it with jealous tenacity. Although she took her meals with the family, in recognition of the fact that her father had done nothing for his living, the corresponding fact that she herself was a worker cut her off from the privilege of relaxing in the drawing-room.

As she entered her refuge, the nurse looked up from her tray. She was a tall broad-shouldered woman, and was still wearing her outdoor nursing-uniform of conventional navy blue. Helen noticed that her features were large and reddened, and her eyebrows bushy and set close together.

She had nearly finished her meal and was already smoking, between mouthfuls.

'Are you Nurse Barker?' asked Helen.

'How do you do?' Nurse Barker spoke in a voice of heavy culture, as she laid down her cigarette. 'Are you Miss Warren?'

'No, I'm the help, Miss Capel. Have you everything you want?'

'Yes, thanks.' Nurse Barker began to smoke again. 'But I would like to ask a question. Why am I put in the kitchen?'

'It's not,' explained Helen. 'It's my own sitting-room.'

'Do you take your meals here, too?'

'No. I take them with the family.'

The sudden gleam in the older woman's deep-set eyes told Helen that she was jealous. Although it was a novelty to be an object of envy, her instinct advised her to smooth Nurse Barker's ruffled feelings.

'The nurse has her own private sitting-room, on the first floor, which is far superior to the basement,' she said. 'Your meals are served there. Only tonight we thought you'd rather not wait, as you must be cold and tired.'

'I'm more.' Nurse Barker spoke in tones of tragic intensity. 'I'm *horrified*. This place is off the map. I never expected such a lonely spot.'

'You knew it was in the country.'

'I expected the usual country-house. They told me my patient was Lady Warren, which sounded all right.'

Helen wondered whether she ought to warn Nurse Barker what was in store for her.

'I'm afraid you may find her a bit strong-willed,' she said. 'The last nurse was frightened of her.'

Nurse Barker swallowed a mouthful of smoke, in professional style. 'She won't frighten *me*. She'll find it won't pay to try her tricks. I keep my patients in order. Influence of course. I believe in kindness. The iron hand in the velvet glove.'

'I don't think an iron hand sounds very kind,' remarked Helen. She looked up, with a sense of relief, as Mrs Oates entered. She had temporarily removed her greasy overall, and was looking forward to gratifying her social instinct.

'The dinner'll keep now, till it's time to dish-up,' she announced. 'I popped in to see if you would fancy a bit of pudding, nurse. Plum-pudding, or a bit of gooseberry-pie?

'Are the gooseberries bottled?' asked Nurse Barker.

'No, no, our new December crop, fresh-picked from the garden.'

'Then – neither, thanks,' said Nurse Barker.

'Well – a nice cup of tea?'

'No, thanks.' Nurse Barker's accent grew more refined as she asked a question. 'Is there any stimulant?'

Mrs Oates's eyes gleamed, and she licked her lips.

'Plenty in the cellar,' she said. 'But the master keeps the key. I'll speak to him about it, if you like, nurse.'

'No, thank you. I prefer to tell Miss Warren my own requirements. It is extraordinary that she has not come downstairs to interview me. Where is she?'

'Sitting up with her ladyship. I wouldn't be in too great a hurry to go up *there*, nurse. Once you're there, you've got to stay put.'

Nurse Barker pondered Mrs Oates's advice.

'I understood it was a single-handed case,' she said. 'But I've come straight off duty. I only came to oblige the matron. I ought to have a good night's rest.'

She turned to Helen. 'Are you a good sleeper?' she asked.

'Ten to seven,' boasted Helen unwarily.

'Then a bad night won't hurt you. *You'll* have to sleep with Lady Warren tonight.'

Helen felt a pang of horror.

'Oh no,' she cried. 'I *couldn't*.'

'And why not?'

'I – Well, it sounds absurd, but I'm afraid of her.'

Nurse Barker looked pleased at the admission.

'Nonsense. Afraid of a bedridden old woman? I never heard anything so fantastic. I'll arrange it with Miss Warren.'

Helen had a spasm of shrinking aversion as she thought of Lady Warren's artificial grin. She had something to smile about now. She alone knew where she had hidden her revolver.

Suddenly, she wondered what would be the outcome if the nurse insisted on her night in bed. As she looked around her with troubled eyes, she thought of the young doctor. If she appealed to him, she was sure that he would not fail her.

'Well, we'll see what the doctor says about it,' she said.

'Is the doctor young?' asked Nurse Barker.

'Youngish,' replied Helen.

'Married?'

'No.'

Mrs Oates winked at Helen, as Nurse Barker opened her bag and drew out a mirror and lipstick. She coated her tips with a smear of greasy crimson.

'You understand,' she said, turning to Helen, 'I interview the doctor. That is professional etiquette. You are not to talk to him about the patient.'

'But I don't talk to him about her,' protested Helen.

'About what, then?' asked Nurse Barker jealously.

'Aha, what *don't* they talk about?' broke in Mrs Oates. 'Something saucy, you may depend on it. Miss Capel's a terror with the gentlemen.'

Although Helen knew that Mrs Oates only wanted to tease the nurse, the sheer novelty of the description made her feel gloriously triumphant, and capable – like her famous namesake – of launching ships.

'Mrs Oates is only pulling your leg,' she told the nurse – responsive to the vague warning that she must not make an enemy. 'But the doctor's rather a darling. We're friends. That's all.'

Nurse Barker looked at Mrs Oates. 'What a curious house this is. I expected a staff of servants. *Why* are there none?'

'Funny thing,' came the reply, 'but as long as this place has been built there's been a trouble to get girls to stay here. Too lonely, for one thing. And then it got an unlucky name with servants.'

'Unlucky?' prompted Nurse Barker, while Helen pricked up her ears.

'Yes. It's an old tale now, but right back in Sir Roger's time, one of the maids was found drowned in the well. Her sweetheart had jilted her, so it was supposed she'd threw herself down. It was the drinking-well, too.'

'Must have caused disgusting pollution,' murmured Nurse Barker.

'So it did. And then, on top of that, was the murder. Kitchen-maid it was, found dead in the house with her throat slit from ear to ear. She was always hard on tramps and used to like to turn them from the door, and one was heard to threaten to do her in. They never caught him. But it got the house a bad name.'

Helen clasped her hands tightly.

'Mrs Oates,' she asked, 'where, exactly, was she murdered?'

'In the dark passage, where the cellars are,' was the reply. 'I wouldn't tell you, just now, but Oates and I always call that bit "Murder Lane".'

As she listened, it occurred to Helen that Lady Warren's rambling talk about trees breaking into the house was built on a solid foundation. When she was a young woman, she had been soaked to the marrow in this damp solitude. She had stood at her window staring out into the winter twilight, while the mist curled to shapes, and trees writhed into life.

One of the trees – a tramp, savage and red-eyed – had actually slipped inside. No wonder, now that she was old, she relived the scene in her memory.

'When did this happen?' she asked.

'Just before Sir Roger's death. Lady Warren wanted to give up the house, as they couldn't get no servants, and it was rows all the time till the accident.'

'And has the professor servant-trouble, too?' enquired Nurse Barker.

'Not till now,' replied Mrs Oates. 'There's always been old and middle-aged bits as wanted a quiet home. They've kept things going until these murders started the old trouble again.'

Nurse Barker licked her lips with gloomy relish. 'One of them was quite close to The Summit, wasn't it?' she asked.

'A few miles off.'

Nurse Barker laughed as she lit a fresh cigarette. 'Well, I needn't worry,' she said. 'I'm safe, as long as she is here.'

'Do you mean Miss Capel?' asked Mrs Oates.

'Yes.'

Helen did not like being picked out for this special distinction. She felt sorry that she had stepped into the limelight with the announcement of her alleged power to attract men.

'Why pick on me?' she protested.

'Because you are young and pretty.'

Helen laughed, with a sudden sense of fresh security.

'In that case,' she said, '*I'm* safe, too. No man would ever look at me, while the professor's daughter-in-law is by. She is young, too, and oozes sex-appeal.'

Nurse Barker shook her head, with a smile full of dark meaning. 'No,' she insisted. '*She* is safe.'

'Why?' asked Helen.

In her turn, Nurse Barker put a question. 'Haven't you noticed it for yourself?'

Her hints were so vague and mysterious that they got under Helen's skin. 'I wish you would come out in the open,' she cried.

'I will, then,' said Nurse Barker. 'Haven't you noticed that the murderer always chooses girls who earn their own living? Very likely he's a shell-shock case who came back from the war to find a woman in his place. The country is crawling with women, like maggots, eating up all the jobs. And the men are starved out.'

'But I'm not doing a man's work,' protested Helen.

'Yes, you are. Men are being employed in houses, now. There's a man, here. *Her* husband.' Nurse Barker nodded to indicate Mrs Oates. 'Instead of being at home, you're out, taking a wage. It's wages from somebody else. That's how a man looks at it.'

'Well – what about yourself?'

'Nursing has always been the preserve of women.'

Mrs Oates made an effort to relieve the tension as she rose from her chair. 'Well, I'd better see what mess one man's made of the dinner. Upon my word, nurse, to hear you talk, you might be a man yourself.'

'I can see through their eyes,' said Nurse Barker.

Helen, however, noticed that Mrs Oates had scored a bull, for Nurse Barker bit her lips, as though she resented the remark. But she kept her eyes fixed upon the girl, who felt herself shrink under the relentless stare.

Her common sense returned at the sound of Mrs Oates's loud laugh. 'Well, anyone what wants to get our little Miss Capel will have to get past Oates and me first.'

Helen looked at her ugly face, her brawny arms. She thought of Oates with his stupendous strength. She had two worthy guardians, in case of need.

'I'd not afraid of getting preferential treatment,' she said.

As though she had some uncanny instinct, Nurse Barker seemed to know exactly how to raise up the spectre of fear.

'In any case,' she observed, 'you will have Lady Warren to keep you company. You are sleeping with her tonight.'

Helen heard the words with a horrible sense of finality. Lady Warren knew that Helen would have to come. Her smile was like that of a crocodile, sure of prey which never failed to materialise.

The old lady would be waiting for her.

8

Jealousy

While Helen grappled with the problem of how to make the doctor understand her aversion to night-duty – so that he might back her up with the necessary authority – the triangle was working up to a definite situation. Had she known it, she would at present have been indifferent to any evidence of marital friction. For the first time in her life, she was removed from her comfortable seat in the theatre, and pushed on to the stage.

The more she thought of the prospect of sleeping in the blue room, the less she liked it. It was a case for compliance or open rebellion; with the latter she risked not only dismissal, but a probable forfeiture of salary. She was positive that Miss Warren would side with the nurse, for her short spell as her deputy had been both repugnant and inconvenient.

Nurse Barker's status in the household, as a trained professional woman, was far higher than the help's. If she declared an ultimatum, Helen must inevitably go to the wall. Moreover, in spite of his apparent interest in her, she had an uneasy suspicion that – as a matter of etiquette – the doctor must support the nurse.

'If he fails me, I'll just have to grit my teeth and see it through,' she thought. 'But, first, I'll make a desperate appeal to his higher nature.'

Although there seemed to be no connection between her own grim drama of fear and the teacup tempest in the drawing-room, the repercussions of that trivial tempest were to be of vital importance to her safety.

For the moment, the drawing-room and kitchen seemed worlds apart. As Helen was grating nutmeg, Simone tossed her cigarette into the fire and rose, with a yawn. Instantly her husband's head shot up from behind his book.

'Where are you going?' he asked.

'To dress. Why?'

'Merely an opening gambit for conversation. Your unbroken silence is uncivilised.'

Simone's eyes flashed under her painted brows.

'You do nothing but ask questions,' she said. 'I'm not used to cross-examination – and I resent it. And another thing. I object to being followed.'

Newton stuck out his lower lip as he threw away his own cigarette.

'But your way happens to be my way, my dear,' Newton told her. 'I'm going up to dress, too.'

Simone spun round and faced him.

'Look here,' she said, 'I don't want to throw a scene here, because of the professor. But I warn you once and for all, *I've had enough of it.*'

'And I warn you, too,' he told her, 'I've had enough of you and Rice.'

'Oh, don't be a fool and start that Middle Ages stuff all over again. You've nothing on me. I'm free to do as I like. I can chuck you – and I will, too – if you persist in being impossible. I've my own money.'

'Perhaps, that's why I'm anxious to keep you,' said Newton. 'Don't forget, this family runs to brains.'

The anger faded from Simone's face and she looked at her husband with a flicker of real interest. Swayed by her senses and desires, she had deliberately neglected her own intellect. She despised cleverness in a woman, since she believed she needed only instinct in order to explore every part of the territory – man.

Because it was an unfamiliar dimension, she respected a masculine brain. She married Newton, in spite of his ugly face, for the sake of the uncharted region behind his bulging forehead. Intensive spoiling had made her care only for the unattainable quality he possessed.

Her series of affairs with ardent undergraduates had made no impression on her, because they were too easy. Newton could have held her, had he maintained his pose of indifference.

Unfortunately, his jealousy of Stephen Rice's good looks had dragged him down from his heights and into the arena.

There was mutual dislike between them, on the score of an old episode which had got Rice sent down from Oxford. For this reason, Stephen played Simone's game whenever her husband was present, on purpose to annoy him.

At the drawing-room door, Simone turned and spoke to her husband. 'I'm going upstairs, *alone.*'

Newton stared at her, and then sullenly sank down again in his chair. A minute later, he threw down his book and walked softly up the stairs as far as the first landing, where he stood, listening.

Simone had reached the second floor, but she did not enter the red room. Instead, she scraped with her finger on the panel of Stephen's door.

'Steve,' she called.

Stephen was stretched on the bed, smoking, while the Alsatian lay beside him, his head on his master's chest.

At the sound of Simone's voice, Stephen grimaced to him as a sign to him to remain silent.

The dog showed the lining of his ears, while his eyes rolled, revealing their whites. Simone knocked loudly and rattled the door-handle.

'Don't come in,' shouted Stephen. 'I'm dressing.'

'Then hurry. I want to see you.'

Simone sauntered back to the big red room, to find her husband already in possession.

'No luck?' he asked casually, as he took off his coat.

'I told you not to follow me,' she said.

'I didn't. I merely moved, in obedience to the natural law. Even glaciers travel – although we don't see them do it.'

'If you travelled at their rate, I shouldn't complain.'

Simone crossed to the wardrobe and took out the black velvet dinner gown which she had worn since her arrival at The Summit.

Rejecting it in favour of a backless gown of pale-pink angel-skin, she drew the shining material over her head.

'Excellent taste for a family dinner, in the wilds,' sneered Newton.

Simone looked at him defiantly. 'I'm not wearing it for the benefit of your family,' she told him.

She felt his eyes upon her, watching every stage of the making-up process.

'A touch of perfume behind the ears,' he advised. 'No man can resist it.'

'Thanks for the reminder.'

Simone finished her toilette – eyes brilliant with temper and her lips compressed. When she went out of the room, she deliberately flung the door wide open, so that her husband could hear her footsteps cross the landing to the bachelor's room.

'Steve,' she called. 'I want to speak to you.'

'Oh – all right.'

The pupil appeared, looking both crumpled and sulky.

'Your hair's untidy,' said Simone, putting up her hands to part his heavy wave.

'Don't.' He shook his head impatiently. 'I detest fiddling.'

'But I like doing it.'

'Then keep on doing it, my dear.'

Stephen ceased to protest, for the reason that he heard Newton's footsteps behind him. He looked round at him with a malicious grin.

'You'll get the benefit of this, Warren,' he said. 'Your wife's practising on me.'

The veins swelled on Newton's temples as he watched his wife's bare arms clasped around Stephen's neck. With a laugh and a backward sweep of her hand, she rumpled his hair until it stood up in a mop.

'There – you're finished,' she declared.

Newton burst into a hoot of amusement at Stephen's discomfiture.

'He looks like Harpo,' he said. 'I hope my wife will continue to use you as her model, so long as she spares me that.'

Simone glanced at her husband's stubborn crest.

'Where's the difference?' she asked. 'Stephen, you've not admired my new dress.'

Although the young man had not even noticed her finery, he stressed his admiration for Newton's benefit.

'*Well*. I'm bowled over. Beautiful – and most revealing. I'll never mistake you for a nun again.'

Newton's mouth tightened and his glasses magnified the ugly gleam in his eyes. Stephen was self-conscious and truculent as Simone slowly revolved to display a back which had been pronounced perfect.

The scene appeared an ordinary exhibition of primitive behaviour, complicated by a frustrated sense of ownership. Yet each released current of human passion was another tributary to swell the tidal-wave which, later, would sweep Helen away, like a straw on flood water.

Newton turned aside, with an affected shrug.

'I'm afraid my wife's dresses have not the same novelty for me,' he said, 'Oh – by the way, Rice – what have you done with that dog?'

'He's in my bedroom,' snapped Stephen.

'In a bedroom? Really, than going too far. It's hardly fair to the lady of the house. If you take my advice, you'll put him in the garage for the night.'

'I'll take nothing from you,' snarled Stephen.

'Not even my wife? Many thanks.'

Whistling in apparent unconcern, Newton strolled down the stairs, without a backward glance.

Stephen bristled with defensive instinct, although he knew that Newton's attitude was reasonable. 'Hanged if I'll park the pup in that draughty hole,' he stormed. 'He stays here – or I go with him,'

'For heaven's sake, forget the dog,' exclaimed Simone. 'Tell me if you really like my dress.'

'What there is of it,' remarked Stephen, reverting to type, since Newton had gone. 'I'm keen on seeing how a boxer strips, when I've backed him; but I don't care for bare backs out of the ring.'

'You brute,' Simone cried, 'I put it on for you. I want you to remember our last night. And *me*.'

'Sorry, my dear,' said Stephen lightly, 'but I'm going to the Bull after dinner.'

Simone's eyes blazed with sudden passion.

'You're going to see that tow-headed barmaid,'

'Whitey? Yes. But I'm going to see something else, too. Beer. Glorious beer.'

'Stay with me, instead. You're the only man I've ever had to ask before.'

Stephen stuck out his lip, like a spoiled child. He wanted an evening of masculine society – the freedom and alcoholic good company of the little country inn. The landlord's flaxen-haired daughter was merely incidental to his pleasure, because she filled his tankard.

He also wanted to get rid of Simone.

Had he known, he could have done so by a show of humility, or an avalanche of attentions. But when he turned away from her, he snapped yet another link of the chain which connected Helen with safety.

Almost running into his room, he slammed the door behind him, and threw himself on the bed. 'Women are the devil,' he told the Alsatian. 'Never get married, my lad.'

In an evil temper, Simone flounced down the stairs. On the landing, she met Mrs Oates who was showing Nurse Barker to her patient's' room. At the sight of the ferocious-looking woman, her expression slightly cleared, for her jealousy was so inflamed that she would have resented an attractive nurse.

'Young Mrs Warren,' whispered Mrs Oates, as she knocked at the door of the blue room.'

Nurse Barker grunted, for she recognised the type. 'Nymphomaniac,' she said.

'Oh, no, she's quite sane,' declared Mrs Oates. 'Just flighty.'

Miss Warren opened the door – a film of welcome in her pale eyes. 'I'm glad you've come, nurse,' she said.

'Yes, I expect you're glad to pass on the job to me,' observed Nurse Barker. 'Can I see the patient?'

She stalked after Miss Warren into the blue room and stood beside the bed, where Lady Warren lay in a shrunken heap, with closed clay-coloured lids. 'I do hope she'll take a fancy to you,' ventured Miss Warren nervously.

'Oh, we'll soon be friends,' said Nurse Barker confidently. 'I've a way with old people. They want kindness with firmness. They're just like children, at the other end.'

Lady Warren suddenly opened an eye which was not in the least childlike, unless it was that of an infant shot out of an eternity of sin.

'Is that the new nurse?' she asked.

'Yes, mother,' replied Miss Warren.

'Send her away.'

Miss Warren looked helplessly at the nurse. 'Oh dear,' she murmured, 'I'm afraid she's taken another dislike.'

'That's nothing,' said Nurse Barker. 'She's being a bit naughty, that's all. I'll soon win her over.'

'Send her away,' repeated Lady Warren. 'I want the girl back.'

Nurse Barker saw her chance of redeeming her unpopularity.

'You shall have her, tonight,' she promised.

Then she drew Miss Warren aside.

'Is there any brandy in the room?' she asked. 'I'm medically ordered to take a little stimulant.'

Miss Warren looked disturbed.

'I thought you understood this is a teetotal house,' she said. 'As you know, you are paid a higher salary.'

'But it's not safe to have no brandy in a sickroom,' insisted Nurse Barker.

'My mother depends on oxygen,' explained Miss Warren. 'It is her life . . . Still . . . Perhaps . . . I'll speak to the professor.'

Driven before the towering form of Nurse Barker, she drifted across the landing, like a withered leaf in the eddy of an east wind.

The professor appeared at his bedroom door, in answer to his sister's tap. He greeted the nurse with stony courtesy, and listened to her request.

'Certainly you may have brandy, if you require it,' he said. 'I will go down, at once, to the cellar, and send a bottle up to your room.'

Helen, who was helping in the kitchen, glanced curiously at Mrs Oates when the professor asked her for a candle.

'I shall want you to hold it,' he said. 'I'm going to the wine-cellar.'

Although the request amounted to mental cruelty, Mrs Oates hastened to obey. The electric pendant lit the passage only as far as the bend; around the corner it was quite dark. She walked ahead of the professor, to guide him, and when she reached the door of the cellar stood, holding her candle aloft, like a pilgrim who had reached Mecca.

The key turned in the lock, and Mrs Oates and the professor entered the sacred place. Naked greed swam in the woman's eyes as her master selected a bottle from a bin.

As she gazed at it thirstily, the professor glanced at the thermometer which hung on the wall.

'That temperature cannot be right,' he said, thrusting the bottle into her hands. 'Hold this while I read it in a better light.'

In a short time he returned from the passage, and relocked the cellar door. This time, he led the way back to the kitchen, while Mrs Oates walked respectfully in his rear. As she passed through the scullery, she ducked down for a second beside the sink.

The professor placed the bottle of brandy on the kitchen table and spoke to Helen.

'Please take this up to the blue room, immediately, after Mrs Oates has drawn the cork.'

When they were alone Helen sympathised with Mrs Oates.

'It's a shame. Why don't you keep back just a tablespoonful, to drink Lady Warren's health?'

'I wouldn't dare,' Mrs Oates told her. 'That nurse would know, and split on me. Besides, it would be sin to water down such lovely stuff.'

Helen admired the fortitude with which the woman surrendered the bottle into her hands.

'Run off with it, quick,' she said, 'but be sure not to drop it.'

Directly she was alone, the secret of her courage was revealed. Lumbering into the scullery, she groped for something she had hidden under the sink.

Opportunity had knocked at her door, and she had been swift in her response. When she returned to the kitchen, she smiled triumphantly at her spoil before she hid it away among the empties in her cupboard.

It was a second bottle of brandy.

9

The Old Woman Remembers

When Helen carried the brandy up to the blue room, Nurse Barker opened the door, in answer to her tap. In her white overall – her dark-red face framed in its handkerchief headgear – she looked like a gigantic block of futuristic sculpture.

'Thank you,' she said. 'This will help me to get some sleep. I must have one good night if I have to carry on this case, single-handed.'

There was a sinister glint in her deep-set eyes as she added: 'I have arranged for you to sleep here, tonight. Miss Warren was present, so she understands the agreement, and the old girl – Lady Warren – ' she hastened to correct her slip – 'raised no objection.'

Helen thought it was wiser to let any protest come from an official quarter. 'Yes, nurse,' she said. 'But I must hurry to dress.'

'Oh, you dress for dinner, do you?'

The woman's tone was so strained – her glance so spiked – that Helen was glad to get away.

'She's jealous,' she thought. 'And Miss Warren's a coward. They're both weak links. I wonder what my special failing is.'

Like the majority of the human race, she was blind to her own faults, and would have protested vehemently against the charge of curiosity, although Mrs Oates already knew the origin of several trivial mishaps.

When she entered her bedroom, she recoiled with a violent start at the sight of a black shape, which appeared to be swinging into her window.

Snapping on the light, she saw that she had been misled by the branches of a tall cedar which was being lashed by the gale. Although it seemed so near, the tree was too far away for any athlete to leap from it into her room; but every gust swept the boughs towards the opening in an unpleasantly suggestive manner.

'That tree looks as if it was trying to force its way in,' thought Helen. 'I'll have to shut that window.'

When she fastened the casement, she noticed how the rain streamed down the glass like a waterspout. The garden lay below in sodden blackness, amid the tormented landscape over which the elements swept mightily.

She was glad to draw the curtains and gloat over the comfort of her splendid room. It contained the entire furniture of the bedroom of the first Lady Warren. When she had exchanged it for her dwelling in the family vault, it was still new and costly, so that time, combined with lack of use, had done little to dim its grandeur.

Miss Warren, on her return from Cambridge, had made a clean sweep of her mother's belongings to a spare room, in preference for stark and rigid utility; but Helen gladly accepted its superfluity of ornament and its colour-scheme of terracotta and turquoise-blue, for the novelty of thick carpet and costly fabrics.

The original owner's photograph had the place of honour on the marble mantelshelf. It was taken probably in the 1880s, and represented an amiable lady, with a curled fringe, too little forehead and too many chins.

Above her rose the mirror. Its base was heavily painted with bulrushes, water-lilies and storks.

As Helen thought of the ordeal which threatened her, she wished that Sir Roger had remained faithful to the dead.

'If *she'd* lived, she'd have been a dear old lady,' she thought. 'Still, I asked for it. You couldn't keep me out of that room to start with.'

The need to win over Dr Parry became so urgent that she adopted Simone's tactics. As a rule, she wore a sleeveless white summer frock for dinner; but, tonight, she resolved to put on her only evening-dress for the first time. It was a cheap little gown bought in Oxford Street during the sales. All the same, the artistic – if hackneyed – contrast of its pale-green colour with the flaming bush of her hair made her smile at her reflection in the big swinging cheval-glass.

'Ought to fetch him,' she murmured, as she hurried downstairs in sudden dread, lest he should have arrived in her absence.

She was still faced with the problem of making an opportunity to see him alone; for, of necessity, she was at the call of the household, owing to the elastic nature of her duties. But she had learned how to hide in the commission of her work; and no SOS could reach her when she was afflicted with temporary deafness.

'The lobby,' she decided. 'I'll take down a damp cloth, and wipe the dust from the palm.'

When she reached the landing on the first floor, the door of the blue room was opened an inch, to reveal a section of white and the glint of Nurse Barker's eye. Directly she saw that she was observed, the woman shut the door again.

There was something so furtive about that secret examination that Helen felt uneasy.

'She was waiting for me,' she thought. 'There's something very queer about that woman. I wouldn't like to be alone with her in the house. *She'd* let you down.'

As her instinct was always to explore the unfamiliar, she turned in the direction of the blue room. Nurse Barker saw that her ambush was discovered, and she opened the door.

'What d' you want?' she asked ungraciously.

'I want to warn you,' replied Helen.

She broke off, conscious that Nurse Barker was looking at her neck with hungry gloating eyes.

'How white your skin is,' she said.

'Red hair,' explained Helen shortly.

As a rule, she was sorry that she did not attract general attention; now, for the first time in her life, she shrank from admiration.

'Did you say you wanted to warn me?' asked Nurse Barker.

'Yes,' whispered Helen. 'Don't play Lady Warren too low.'

'What d' you mean?'

'She's hiding something.'

'What?'

'If you're as clever as she is, you'll find out,' replied Helen, turning away.

'Come back,' demanded Nurse Barker. 'You've either said too much, or not enough.'

Helen smiled as she shook her head.

'Ask Miss Warren,' she advised. 'I told her, and got nicely snubbed for my pains. But I felt I ought to put you on your guard.'

She started at the rumble of a deep voice from inside the blue room. 'Is that the girl?'

'Yes, my lady,' replied Nurse Barker. 'Do you want to see her?'

'Yes.'

'I'm sorry.' Helen spoke quickly. 'I can't stop now. I've got to help with the dinner.'

Nurse Barker's eyes glittered with a sense of power.

'Why are you so *afraid* of her?' she sneered.

'You'd be afraid, too, if you knew as much as I do,' hinted Helen.

Nurse Barker grasped her by the wrist, while her nostrils quivered.

'The dinner can wait,' she said. 'Miss Warren's instructions are that Lady Warren *must* be humoured. Come in.'

Helen entered the blue room with a sinking heart. Lady Warren lay in bed, propped up with pillows. She wore a fleecy white bed-jacket. Her shock of grey hair was neatly parted in the middle, and secured with pink bows. It had obviously been Nurse Barker's first job to deck her patient out like a sacrificial lamb. Helen knew that some grim sense of humour had made the old lady submit to the indignity. She was luring the nurse into a false sense of security, only to make the subsequent disillusionment the harsher.

'Come here,' she said, in a hoarse whisper. 'I want to tell you something.'

Helen felt herself gripped and drawn downwards, so that Lady Warren's hot breath played on her bare neck.

'A girl was murdered in this house,' said Lady Warren.

'Yes, I know.' Helen spoke in a soothing tone. 'But why do you think about it? It happened so long ago.'

'How do you know?' rapped out Lady Warren.

'Mrs Oates told me.'

'Did she tell you that the girl was thrown down the well?'

Helen remembered that in Mrs Oates's version, a more gory method was employed. The well figured in the suicide incident. It struck her that Mrs Oates had exaggerated the truth in order to achieve the sensational interest of a murder.

'Perhaps it was an accident,' she said aloud.

Lady Warren lost her temper at the attempt to calm her.

'No,' she bellowed, 'it was murder. I saw it. Upstairs, from a window. It was nearly dark, and I thought it was only a tree in the garden. Then the girl came, and it moved and threw her in. I was too late. I couldn't find a rope . . . Listen.'

She drew down Helen's head almost on to the pillow.

'You are that girl,' she whispered.

Helen felt as though she were listening to a forecast of her own fate; but she caught Nurse Barker's eye in an attempt to delude her that she was humouring the invalid, in professional style.

'Am I?' she said lightly. 'Well, I'll have to be very careful.'

'You little fool,' panted the old woman. 'I'm warning you. Girls get murdered in this house. But you sleep with me. I'll take care of you.'

Suddenly Helen thought she might trap her to reveal the hiding-place of the revolver.

'How will you do it?' she asked.

'I'll shoot him.'

'Fine. But where's your gun?'

Lady Warren looked at Helen with a gleam of crocodile cunning in her eyes.

'I haven't a gun,' she whined. 'I had one once, but they took it away. I'm only a poor old woman. Nurse, she says I have a gun. Have I?'

'Of course not,' said Nurse Barker. 'Really, Miss Capel, you've no right to distress the patient.'

'Then I'll go,' declared Helen thankfully. She added, in an undertone, 'You asked me a question, just now. You've had your answer. You know now what to look for.'

At the door, she was arrested by Lady Warren's bass bellow.

'Come back, tonight.'

'Very well, I will,' she promised.

To her surprise her nerves were quivering from the episode as she went down into the hall.

'What's the matter with me?' she wondered. 'I believe I shall go goofy if the doctor doesn't get me out.'

She looked anxiously at the grandfather clock. Dr Parry lived several miles away, so he always paid his last call at The Summit, in order to get back to his dinner.

He had never been so late before. A slight foreboding stole over Helen as she listened to the fury of the storm. When Miss Warren drifted by, like a woman in a dream, she appealed to her.

'The doctor's late, Miss Warren.'

Miss Warren looked at the clock. She was already dressed for dinner, in her usual mushroom-lace gown.

'Perhaps he's not coming,' she said indifferently.

Helen gave a gasp of dismay. With the egotism of an employer, who never connected a young girl with an independent existence, Miss Warren believed that Helen's concern was on account of the family.

'My mother's condition is static,' she explained, 'although the end is inevitable. Dr Parry has given us instructions how to act, in case of sudden failure.'

'But why shouldn't he come tonight?' insisted Helen. 'He *always* comes.'

'The weather,' murmured Miss Warren.

A rush of wind crashing against the corner of the house illustrated her meaning with perfect timing. Helen's heart turned to water at the sound.

'He won't come,' she thought. 'I shall have to sleep in the blue room.'

10

The Telephone

Helen had to sleep in the blue room. Everyone in The Summit had accepted the situation. Feeling that preparing an ambush in the lobby would be a waste of time, since she was certain that Dr Parry would not come, she walked dejectedly towards the kitchen stairs.

She was intercepted by Newton, who slouched out of the morning-room.

'I hear you've made a conquest of my grandmother,' he said. 'Congratulations. How is it done?'

The interest in Newton's eyes invigorated Helen and made her feel mistress of a difficult situation.

'I don't have to tell *you*,' she replied.

'You mean I'm her blue-eyed boy,' said Newton. 'That may be. But it doesn't take me far when financial interests are at stake. I can't live on sugar.'

Hitherto, Helen had been somewhat in awe of Newton, who completely ignored her as a social entity. She was there merely to do a job, and he supposed that she – like all the other girls – would go at the end of the month, if she lasted as long.

The novelty of his attention stimulated her confidence.

'Do you mean the will?' she asked boldly.

He nodded. 'Will she – or won't she?'

'We talked about it,' said Helen, inflated with her own importance. 'I advised her not to keep putting it off.'

Newton gave a shout of excitement. 'Aunt Blanche. Come here.'

Miss Warren was wafted by some terrestrial wind out of the drawing-room, in obedience to her nephew's call. For some inexplicable reason, the shambling short-sighted youth seemed to sway the affection of his own womanfolk, even if he failed to hold his wife.

'What is it?' she asked.

'Epic news,' Newton told her. 'Miss Capel has worked faster in five minutes than the rest of us in five years. She's got gran to talk about her will.'

'Not exactly that,' explained Helen. 'But she said she couldn't die, because she had a job to do – an unpleasant job, which everyone puts off.'

'Good enough,' nodded Newton. 'Well, Miss Capel, I only hope you will go on with the good work, if she's wakeful tonight.'

Even Miss Warren seemed impressed by the fresh development, for she looked, more or less directly, at Helen.

'Extraordinary,' she murmured. 'You seem to have more influence over her than anyone else.'

Helen walked away, conscious that she had been betrayed by her impulse to play to the gallery. Now that the family had a direct personal interest in her relations with Lady Warren, she could only expect their opposition if she appealed to them against being sentenced to the blue room.

But she continued to hold her head high, as though sustained by popular support, on her way to execution, even while she shrank from thought of the scaffold. In her last minute, she would be alone.

When she reached the kitchen, she was instantly aware that Mrs Oates was in no mood for gossip, while Oates was keeping out of his wife's way, in a significant manner.

Regardless of Helen's finery, Mrs Oates pointed to a steaming basin on the table. 'Just blanch these for the tipsy-cake,' she said. 'I'm behind with my dinner. And Oates keeps dodging under my feet until I don't know if I'm up in the air or down a coalmine.'

In a chastened mood, Helen sat down and gingerly popped almonds out of their shrivelled brown skins. She had accepted the fact of the doctor's absence so completely that she ignored the sound of a bell ringing in the basement hall.

It was Mrs Oates who glanced at the indicator.

'Front door,' she snapped. 'That'll be the doctor.'

Helen sprang to her feet and rushed to the door. 'I'll let him in,' she cried.

'Thank you, miss,' said Oates gratefully. 'I haven't my trousers on.'

'Disgraceful,' laughed Helen, who knew he referred to the fact that he put on his best trousers and a linen jacket in order to carry in the dinner.

Again hope soared, as she flew up the stairs and opened the front door, letting in a sheet of torrential rain, driven before the gale, as well as the doctor.

He was strongly-built, and inclined to be stocky, with short blunt clean-shaven features. Helen beamed her welcome, while he – in turn – looked at her with approval.

'Is this Gala Night?' he asked.

His gaze held none of the uncomfortable rapacity of the nurse's eyes, so that Helen rejoiced in her new evening frock. But Dr Parry was more concerned by the hollows in her neck than struck by the whiteness of her skin.

'Odd that you are not more robust,' he frowned, 'with all the house-work you do,'

'I've not been doing any lately,' explained Helen.

'I see,' muttered Dr Parry, as he wondered why voluntary starvation, in the case of a slimming patient, should fail to affect him, since the result was the same.

'Like milk?' he asked. 'But, of course, you don't.'

'Don't I? I'd be a peril if I worked in a dairy.'

'You ought to drink a lot. I'll speak to Mrs Oates.'

The doctor drew off his leather motoring coat and flung it on the chair.

'Dirty weather,' he said. 'It made me late. The roads are like broth. How is Lady Warren tonight?'

'Just the same; she wants me to sleep with her.'

'Well, if I know anything about you, you'll enjoy doing that,' grinned the doctor. 'Something new.'

'But I'm *dreading* it,' wailed Helen. 'I'm just depending on you to tell them I'm not – not competent.'

'Heebie-jeebies? Has the house got you, too? Are you finding it too lonely here?'

'Oh, no, it's not just nerves. I've got a *reason* for being afraid.'

Eager to unburden herself, Helen held the doctor's attention while she told him the story of the revolver.

'It's a rum yarn,' he said. 'But I'd believe anything of that old surprise-packet. I'll see if I can find out where she's hidden it.'

'And you'll say I'm not to sleep with her?' insisted Helen.

But things were not going to be as simple as that, for Dr Parry rubbed his chin doubtfully.

'I can't promise. I must see the nurse first. She may really need a good night, if she's come straight off duty. I'd better be going up.'

He swung open the doors leading to the hall. As they crossed it, he spoke to her in an undertone.

'Buck up, old lady. It won't be loaded. In any case, her eye will be out, after all these years.'

'She hit the nurse,' Helen reminded him.

'Sheer fluke. Remember, she's an *old* woman. Don't bother to come up.'

'No, I'd better introduce you formally to the nurse,' insisted Helen, who was anxious not to infringe professional etiquette.

But the glare in Nurse Barker's eye, when she opened the door in answer to Helen's knock, told her that she had blundered again.

'I've brought up Dr Parry,' said Helen.

Nurse Barker inclined her head in a stately bow.

'*How* long have you been here, doctor?' she asked.

'Oh, five minutes or so,' he replied.

'In future doctor, will you please come straight to the bedroom?' asked the nurse. 'Lady Warren has been worried, because you were late.'

'Certainly, nurse, if it's like that,' said the doctor.

Helen turned away with a sinking heart. The woman seemed to dominate the young doctor with her will even as she appeared to tower over him physically – an optical illusion, due to the white overall.

Simone – in all the glory of her sensational gown – swept past her in the hall. Even in the midst of her own worries, Helen noticed that she was literally awash with emotion. Her eyes sparkled with tears, her lips trembled, her hands were clenched.

She was in the grip of frustrated desire, which converted her into a storm-centre of rage. She was angry with Newton – because he was an obstacle; angry with Stephen – because he was unresponsive; angry with herself – because she had lost her grip.

And all these complex passions were slowly focusing on one person whom she believed to be the other woman in the case. She was obsessed with the idea that Stephen was turning her down for the sake of the flaxen-haired barmaid at the Bull.

The help, in spite of her new frock, might have been invisible, for she passed her without the slightest notice. And when Helen reached the kitchen, Mrs Oates received her with uncharacteristic gloom.

It seemed as though the atmosphere of The Summit was fraught with toxicity.

'You won't have to hold back dinner much longer,' said Helen in the hope of cheering Mrs Oates. 'The doctor will soon be gone.'

'It's not that,' remarked Mrs Oates glumly.

'Then what's the matter?'

'Oates.'

'What's he done?'

'Nothing. But he's always here, night and day, so that a woman can't never be alone. Don't you never get married, miss.'

Helen stared at her. She had always admired the good nature with which Mrs Oates accepted her husband's laziness and supplemented his efforts. Although he did not pull his weight, she always made a joke of it, while a rough, but real, affection turned their partnership into a very companionable one.

'It's for better, or worse,' said Helen tactfully, 'and I can understand Mr Oates grabbing you, because he could see with you it would be "better". Now, I can't see the man who'd marry Nurse Barker. I wonder if she drinks.'

'Eh?' asked Mrs Oates absently.

'Well,' shrugged Helen, 'she was probably right to insist on having the brandy, even if Miss Warren does say that the oxygen is Lady Warren's life.'

Mrs Oates only stared at Helen – her brow puckered as though she were grappling with a complicated sum in vulgar fractions. Presently, however, she finished her calculations, and gave her own jolly laugh.

'Well, you don't often see me under the weather, do you?' she asked. 'And, talking of husbands, the best is bad, but I've got the best. Now, my dear, just listen for the doctor. Directly he goes, I want to slip upstairs with a bit of pudding for the nurse.'

Helen vaguely resented the attention as treachery towards herself.

'Take her tipsy-cake, to go with her brandy,' she advised.

'Now, somebody's on her hind-legs,' Mrs Oates laughed. 'But she's got to go through the night on only a snack. She may look like a slab of stale fish, but a nurse's life is a hard one.'

Helen felt ashamed of her resentment as she waited at her listening-in station on the kitchen stairs. She was still puzzled by Mrs Oates's changes of mood, for she was not temperamental by nature. For no apparent reason, she was swaying to and fro, like a weathercock. Whence came the mysterious wind which was blowing on her?

'There's something wrong about this house, tonight,' decided Helen.

Hearing Dr Parry's voice in the distance, she shouted to Mrs Oates and dashed up into the hall. Directly he saw her, Dr Parry came to meet her. His face was red and he bristled with suppressed anger.

'Miss Capel,' he said, using the formal voice of a stranger, 'if there is any question of your sleeping with Lady Warren tonight, understand, I will not sanction it.'

Helen realised, at once, that Nurse Barker had overreached herself with her high-handed methods. Although her heart sang at her release, experience had taught her the advantage of appealing to the fount of authority.

'Yes, doctor,' she said meekly. 'But if Nurse Barker goes to Miss Warren, she'll get her own way.'

'In that case,' he said, 'I'll go straight to the professor. No woman shall bully-rag me. If there's any opposition to my orders, some other doctor can take the case. I only hang on, because my own mother – the dearest soul – had a tongue which would raise a blister on a tortoise's back. For her sake, I've a bit of a weak spot for the old b – blessing.'

Helen drew back when they reached the professor's study.

'Come in with me,' said the doctor.

In spite of her awe of the professor, Helen obeyed eagerly. The curiosity which would have propelled her to visit any strange and savage beast in its lair, made her anxious to see her employer in his privacy.

She was struck by the resemblance to Miss Warren's room in that the furniture was merely incidental to the books and papers – supplemented in the case of the professor by files and shelves of volumes of reference. There was no trace of the comfort usually characteristic of a man's den – no shabby varsity chair, no old slippers or tobacco-jar.

The professor sat at his American roll-top desk, his fingertips pressed against his temples. When he looked up, his face appeared blanched and strained.

'Headache?' asked the doctor.

'Uh-huh,' was the reply.

Helen bit her tongue to keep back her impulsive offer of aspirin, as she felt that professional advice should take preference.

'Take anything?' asked Dr Parry casually.

'Yes.'

'Good. The new nurse wants Miss Capel to relieve her, tonight. I forbid it. Lady Warren's heart is in a bad way, and she is in too critical a condition to be left in the charge of an untrained girl. Will you see that this order stands?'

As he listened, the professor kept his fingers pressed over his eyeballs.

'Certainly,' he agreed.

When they were outside, Helen turned to the doctor, her eyes limpid with gratitude.

'You don't know what this means to me,' she said. 'You – '

She broke off at the shrilling of the telephone-bell. As the instrument was in the hall, she rushed to answer it.

'Hold on, please,' she said, beckoning to Dr Parry. 'The call's for you. Someone's ringing up from the Bull. He asked if you were here.'

With her abiding interest in the affairs of others, she tried to reconstruct the inaudible part of the conversation from listening to Dr Parry's end of the line.

'That you, Williams?' he asked. 'What's the trouble?'

His casual tone dulled to incredulity and then sharpened to a note of horror.

'What? . . . Impossible . . . What a horrible thing. I'll come at once.'

When he hung up, his expression testified to the fact that the telephone-message had proved a shock. While Helen waited for him to speak, Miss Warren came into the hall.

'Was that the telephone-bell?' she asked vaguely.

'Yes,' replied Dr Parry. 'Do you remember a girl – Ceridwen Owen – who used to work here? Well, she's dead. Her body has just been discovered in a garden.'

11

An Article of Faith

As Helen heard the name, she remembered the gossip in the kitchen. Ceridwen was the pretty sluttish girl, who used to dust under Lady Warren's bed, and whose lovers waited for her outside the house with the patient fixity of trees. She believed she had actually seen one of them in the plantation, whose vigil had certainly proved in vain.

'Rum thing,' said Dr Parry. 'Williams says that when Captain Bean got home from market he lit a match to find the keyhole. That's how he chanced to see her – huddled up in a dark corner of his garden. He ran, at once, hell-for-leather to the Bull, and asked Williams to ring my house. My housekeeper told them to try The Summit.'

'Very shocking,' observed Miss Warren. 'I suppose it was some sort of seizure. Her colour was unusually high.'

'I'll soon find out,' Dr Parry assured them. 'What beats me is this. The captain's cottage is only the other side of the plantation. Why didn't he come over here, instead of running nearly a mile to the Bull?'

'He had quarrelled with my brother. The professor pointed out a scientific slip in one of his articles. And I believe there was trouble with Mrs Oates over some of his eggs.'

Dr Parry nodded with complete comprehension. Captain Bean was a morose and hot-tempered recluse, who would reject Einstein's theory and the charge of supplying a bad egg with equal fury. He kept a small poultry-farm, worked about his cottage, and wrote articles on the customs and religions of native tribes in unfrequented quarters of the globe.

Dr Parry knew that his life of isolation tended to a lack of perspective, which would exaggerate a trifling grievance to the intensity of a feud; and he guessed that he would prefer to plough through torrential rain rather than ask his neighbour for the use of his telephone.

'I'll cut across the plantation,' he said. 'It will be quicker. I'll come back for my bike.'

The booming of the dinner-gong speeded his parting, but he left a sense of tragedy behind him. When the family was gathered around the table in the dining-room, the subject of Ceridwen cropped up with the soup.

Newton and his wife were not interested in the death of a domestic, but Stephen remembered her.

'Wasn't she the lass with the dark come-hither eye and a wet red mouth?' he asked. 'The one Lady Warren coshed?'

'An animal type,' remarked Miss Warren. She hastened to add, in a perfunctory voice, 'Poor girl.'

'Why – poor?' asked Newton aggressively. 'We should all envy her. She has achieved annihilation.'

' "Healed of her wound of living, shall sleep sound," ' murmured his aunt, adapting the quotation.

'No!' declared Newton. 'Not sleep. Too chancey a proposition. One might wake again. Rather – "I thank with brief thanksgiving whatever gods there be, that no life lasts for ever, that dead men rise up never, that even the weariest river – " '

'Oh, dry up,' broke in Stephen. 'Even a river does that, when it's been in the sun.'

'But unfortunately, I am not drunk,' said Newton. 'No one could be, in this house.'

'There's always the Bull,' Stephen reminded him.

'And a devastating barmaid,' said Simone, with meaning in her voice.

'Oh, Newton knows Whitey all right.' Stephen grinned. 'But I've cut him out. I always do that, don't I, Warren?'

Helen was glad of any interruption, however uncomfortable. It had been distasteful to listen to a dreary Creed of Negation when every cell in her body rejoiced in life. What had hurt her even more was the hint at a denial of the soul.

Her innate sense as hostess made Miss Warren rouse herself from her dream. Although she was unconscious of Stephen's provocative grin, Simone's slanting glances of passion and Newton's scowl, she was aware of some poisoned undercurrent. She changed the subject, after looking across at the professor, who sat with his eyes covered by his hand.

'Is your head aching again, Sebastian?' she asked.

'I hardly slept last night,' he said.

'What are you taking, chief?' enquired Newton.

'Quadronex.'

'Tricky stuff, Better be careful of your quantities.'

A sarcastic smile flickered round the professor's dry lips.

'My dear Newton,' he said, 'when you were an infant you squalled so ceaselessly that I had to administer a nightly sedative, for the sake of my work. The fact that you survive is proof that I need no advice from my own son.'

Newton flushed as Stephen burst into a shout of laughter at his expense.

'Thank you for nothing, chief,' he muttered. 'I hope you manage your own affairs better than you did mine.'

Helen bit her lip as she looked round the table. She reminded herself that these people were in many ways her superiors. They were better-educated than herself, and had money and leisure. The Warrens had intellect and culture, while Simone had travelled and had knowledge of the world.

She always sat silent through a meal, since it would require moral courage for her to take any part in the general conversation. Miss Warren, however, usually made some attempt to include her.

'Have you seen any good films, lately?' she asked, choosing a subject likely to appeal to a girl who never read *The Times*.

'Only films of general interest,' replied Helen, whose recent visits to a cinema had been confined to the free show at Australia House.

'I saw *The Sign of the Cross*, just before I left Oxford,' broke in Simone. 'I adored Nero.'

The professor showed some signs of interest.

'*The Sign of the Cross*?' he repeated. 'Have they revived that junk? And does the proletariat still wallow in an orgy of enthusiasm over that symbol of superstition?'

'Definitely,' replied Simone. 'The applause was absurd.'

'Amusing,' sneered the professor. 'I remember seeing the play – Wilson Barrett and Maud Jeffries took the leading parts – with a fellow-undergraduate. This youth was devoted to racing and completely unreligious. But he developed a sporting interest in the progress of the Cross. It appealed to him as a winner, and he roared and clapped in its scene of ultimate triumph, while the tears rained down his face in his enthusiasm.'

The general laughter was more than Helen could bear. Suddenly, to her own intense surprise, she heard her own voice.

'I think that's – *terrible*,' she said shakily.

Everyone stared at her in surprise. Her small face was red, and puckered up, as though she were about to cry.

'Surely a modern girl does not attribute any virtue to a mere symbol?' asked the professor.

Helen felt herself shrivelled by his gaze, but she would not recant.

'I do,' she said. 'When I left the convent, in Belgium, the nuns gave me a cross. It always hangs over my bed, and I wouldn't lose it for anything.'

'Why not?' asked Newton.

'Because it stands for – for so much,' faltered Helen.

'*What* – exactly?'

Helen felt tongue-tied, under the battery of eyes.

'Everything,' she replied vaguely. 'And it protects me.'

'Archaic,' murmured the professor, while his son continued his cross-examination. 'What does it protect you from?' he asked.

'From all evil.'

'Then as long as it hung over your bed I suppose you could open your door to the local murderer?' laughed Stephen.

'Of course not,' declared Helen, for she stood in no awe of the pupil. 'The cross represents the power which gave me life. But it gave me faculties to help me to look after that life for myself.'

'Why, she believes in providence, too,' said Simone.

'She will tell us next she believes in Santa Claus.'

Hard-pressed, Helen looked around the table. She seemed ringed about with gleaming eyes and teeth, all laughing at her.

'I only know this,' she declared in a trembling voice, 'if I was like all of you I wouldn't want to be alive.'

To her surprise, support came from an unexpected quarter, for Stephen suddenly clapped his hands. 'Bravo,' he said. 'Miss Capel's got more spunk than the lot of us put together. She's taken us on, five to one, and she's only a flyweight. Hang it all, we ought to be ashamed of ourselves.'

'It is not a question of courage,' observed the professor, 'but of muddled thinking and confused values which is definitely hurtful. You, Miss Capel, are assuming man to be of divine origin. In reality, he is so entirely a creature of appetites and instincts that – given a knowledge of his key interest – anyone could direct his destiny. There is no such thing as the guidance of providence.'

Newton thrust his head forward, his eyes gleaming behind his spectacles.

'Rather interesting, chief,' he said. 'I'd like to have a shot at developing a crime picture on those lines. No crude sliding-panels or clutching hands. Make one character do something which would set the rest into motion, so that each would do the natural and obvious thing.'

'You have some glimmering of my meaning,' approved his father. 'Man is but clay, animated by his natural lusts.'

Suddenly Helen forgot her subordinate position – forgot that she had a new job to hold down. She sprang to her feet and pushed back her chair.

'Please excuse me, Miss Warren,' she said, 'but I can't stay – and listen – '

'Oh, Miss Capel,' expostulated Newton, 'we were merely arguing. There was nothing personal intended.'

Before he could finish, Helen was out of the room and rushing down the kitchen stairs. She found Mrs Oates in the scullery, busy stacking dirty dishes.

'Oh, Mrs Oates,' she wailed, 'I've made such a fool of myself.'

'That's all right, my dear, so long as nobody else makes a fool of you,' was the consoling reply. 'Now, I want Oates to help me with the washing-up. So suppose you take up the coffee for him?'

Helen's courage returned with her reviving curiosity. She wanted to see what effect her outburst had created on her audience.

'Oh, well, I suppose I'd better get it over,' she sighed. But when she carried the coffee-tray into the drawing-room, she realised that the episode was already forgotten.

The young people took their cups mechanically, as they heatedly debated the alleged attractions of a celebrated film star. Miss Warren was cutting the pages of a new scientific journal, while the professor had retired to his study.

Suddenly Mrs Oates appeared in the doorway.

'The nurse is downstairs and wants a word with the master,' she said.

'He cannot be disturbed,' Miss Warren told her.

'But it's important. It's her ladyship's life.'

Everyone looked up at the dramatic statement. The household had waited so long for the old terror upstairs to die that it had grown to accept her as immortal. Helen's thoughts flew to the unmade will, and the vital importance of getting her signature before she struck her colours.'

'Is she sinking?' asked Newton.

'No, sir,' replied Mrs Oates. 'But the nurse says as we are out of oxygen.'

12

The First Gap

Newton broke the stunned silence.

'Who's responsible for such infernal carelessness?' he asked.

Miss Warren and Helen exchanged glances of mingled guilt and condemnation. While neither was exactly clear in her own conscience, each wanted to shift the responsibility on to the other. As employer, Miss Warren was allowed the first thrust.

'Miss Capel, didn't you screw the cap on the cylinder, after use?' she asked.

'No, because you sent me out of the room.'

'But, surely you did so, before you went?'

'I couldn't, because you had the cylinder.'

Helen spoke with firmness, for the reason that she was not quite clear. Fortunately, Miss Warren was equally confused.

'Had I?' she murmured. 'Yes, I believe I was giving oxygen to Lady Warren. But I have a dim recollection of screwing on the cap.'

'What's the good of arguing?' broke in Newton. 'The thing is, to get in a second supply as soon as possible.'

'Yes, that is the essential point,' she said. 'I will speak to the professor.'

Helen followed her into the study, to find that Nurse Barker had got there before them. Her voice had lost some of its culture as she talked volubly to the professor.

'It is unusual to come to a case and find such slackness,' she said. 'I'd like to know who's responsible.'

As she spoke, she fixed her deep-set eyes on Helen.

'*I* am,' replied Miss Warren quietly.

She appeared indifferent to Helen's look of gratitude, as she spoke to her brother.

'I suppose we must order another cylinder, at once.'

'Oh, there's no great hurry,' broke in Nurse Barker. 'She will go through the night quite well, on brandy. She – '

'Allow me to speak, please, nurse.' The professor raised his hand in protest. 'The doctor told me this evening that Lady Warren's condition is critical.'

'A green country doctor?' sneered Nurse Barker. 'She's not as bad as that. I know when a patient is going to die, and it's when I say she is.'

'The doctor's opinion stands,' said the professor coldly. 'I will telephone for another cylinder to be rushed out, at once.'

'The factory will be closed,' objected Miss Warren.

'And they'll never send it out to this wilderness, in such a storm,'
added Nurse Barker.

'In that case, someone must fetch it.' The professor spoke decisively.
'Lady Warren's life shall not be risked for the sake of sparing someone
a little trouble.'

Helen listened rather guiltily, for she feared that Dr Parry had stressed
the gravity of the case for her sake.

'Does Lady Warren know that the doctor said I'm not to sleep in her
room tonight?' she asked, anxious to have the matter clinched by the
professor's authority.

'Did he say that, too?' demanded Nurse Barker, a militant gleam in
her eye.

The professor pressed his brow with an impatient gesture, which
made Helen realise that Nurse Barker – in rousing his antagonism –
was proving her own unconscious ally.

'The doctor expects a crisis,' he explained, 'so naturally a trained
nurse must be in attendance.'

'Why don't you have a second nurse?' asked Nurse Barker.

'We have not the accommodation,' replied Miss Warren.

'Yes, you have. *She*' – Nurse Barker nodded at Helen – 'can sleep in
an attic. Besides, the bachelor's room will be empty tomorrow.'

Helen stared at this revelation of a perceptive talent which eclipsed
her own. In this brief time, the nurse – while apparently not leaving her
patient – had mapped the house.

'There is not enough work for two nurses,' said Miss Warren. 'The
other nurses have all assured me that Lady Warren sleeps nearly all
through the night, so that their rest has not been unduly disturbed.
Didn't the matron tell you that the salary is proportionate to the
demands?'

Nurse Barker grew suddenly meek.

'Yes, thank you,' she said, 'I'm quite satisfied with the conditions.'

The professor turned to his sister. 'I will telephone myself,' he said,
going into the hall, followed by Miss Warren.

Left alone with Nurse Barker, Helen broke an awkward silence. 'I'm
sorry. But you see, I'm not trained.'

'And I am.' Nurse Barker's voice was corrosive. 'To be "trained",
means that I'm made of iron, and can eat leavings, and do without sleep,
and work twenty-five hours to the day.'

'It's a shame. But it's not my fault.'

'Yes it is.' Nurse Barker pounced fiercely. 'You hung about to get at that doctor first, and you coached him what to say. Oh, you needn't think you can get the better of *me*. There's little I don't see, and what's left over I smell. We've not finished with this. If I turn the last trick – and I've something up my sleeve – you may yet sleep tonight in the blue room.'

Helen was not only scared by the uncanny penetration of the nurse, but she recognised the cruelty which made her hammer away at her fear of Lady Warren, like a torturer plucking at a nerve.

To break away from her company, she hurried into the hall, where the professor was speaking into the telephone. He raised his hand, as a signal for her to remain. Presently he hung up the receiver and spoke to her.

'They can't make a delivery until tomorrow, but they have promised to let my man have a cylinder tonight if he calls at any time up to eleven. Miss Capel, please let Oates know he is to start at once.'

Helen did not relish her job when she found Oates stretched before the kitchen fire, enjoying his first pipe after his day's work. She admired all the more his self-control, and the obedience which he had learned in his navy days.

He got up instantly, and began to lace up his boots.

'Just as I was looking forward to a nice lay-down on the bed,' he said. 'But that's life.'

'Shall I ask Mr Rice to go instead?'

'No, miss. Orders is orders, and the master said Oates. Besides, I wouldn't trust him with the car. No one but me knows how to ease my sweetheart up them hills.' He turned to his wife. 'Mind you lock up the back after me when I go out to the garage. Remember, you'll have to be double careful with me away.'

Helen felt a pang of dismay at the thought of losing Oates again so soon. Merely to look at his gigantic frame and amiable face, made her feel safe.

It did not improve matters to realise that she was partly responsible for her own trouble.

'If I'd gritted my teeth and said nothing to the doctor, Oates wouldn't have to be sent,' she thought. 'The professor said we did things ourselves. But did anyone make me do it?'

Suddenly she remembered how Nurse Barker had played upon her fears – and she shivered slightly.

'Oh, I do wish you weren't going,' she said to Oates.

'Same here, miss,' he replied. 'But you'll be all right, with two strong young gents, to say nothing of that nurse.'

'When will you be back?' asked Mrs Oates.

'It will be just as soon as I can make the grade.' He turned to Helen. 'Will you tell the master I'll sound the hooter and wait on the drive for a bit, in case he wants to speak to me.'

Helen delivered his message to the professor, who had returned to his study. Although he suppressed his irritation, she could see that he was fretted by the interruption.

'Thank you, Miss Capel,' he said. 'But Oates knows what to get, and where to go for it.'

Feeling that she wanted to speed his parting, although unseen, Helen went into the lobby, which was exposed to the full fury of the gale. As the wind shook the stout door with the impact of a mailed fist, and the rain gurgled down the pipes, she felt doubly sorry for Oates.

Presently she heard his hooter outside, and longed to open the door to wish him goodbye. But she remembered how the wind had swayed the light when she let in the doctor.

The engine of the old crock burst into a series of spluttering explosions and deepened to a roar before it gradually died away in the distance. With a pang of loneliness, Helen slipped through the swing doors.

She was just in time to witness a lively passage of arms between Miss Warren and Stephen Rice.

'Is it true,' demanded Miss Warren, 'that you have a dog in your bedroom?'

'Perfectly true,' replied Stephen flippantly.

'Take it out into the garage, at once.'

'Sorry. Can't be done.'

Miss Warren lost her habitual calm. 'Mr Rice,' she said, 'understand me, please. I *will not* have an animal in this house.'

'That's all right,' Stephen assured her. 'I'll push off tonight, and take my dog with me.'

'Where will you go?' asked Newton, who – lounging, with his hands in his pockets – was an appreciative spectator of the scene.

'Bull, of course. They'll put me up – and they'll be proud to have the pup.'

Simone gave a cry of protest.

'Don't be so childish, Steve. You can't go through this rain. You'd both be soaked.'

Stephen weakened as he gazed through the open door at the fire leaping in the drawing-room grate.

'I'll stay if the pup stays,' he said. 'If he goes, I go, too.'

'I'll speak to the professor,' cried Simone.

Her husband caught her by the arm. 'Don't worry the chief,' he said. 'He's about all in,'

Simone wrenched herself away and rushed into the study. Unlike the rest of the household, she stood in no awe of the professor. To her, he was merely an elderly gentleman to whom she paid a certain deference as her father-in-law.

In a few minutes, she appeared – her face radiant with triumph – to herald the professor.

'I understand,' he said, speaking to Stephen, 'that there is some difficulty about a dog. As mistress of my house, Miss Warren's prejudices are law. But – as it is for one night only – she will relax her rule.'

He turned to his sister. 'You understand, Blanche?' he asked.

'Yes, Sebastian,' was the low reply.

She went upstairs, while the professor returned to his study.

Suddenly Helen remembered her coffee. She never took any in the drawing-room, because the conventional cups were too small for her liking. Like a true pantry mouse, she always reboiled what was left in the pot, adding sufficient milk to make about a pint, which she drank in her own room. At the end of the official day, it was etiquette not to disturb Mr and Mrs Oates, whose kitchen became their private domain; so she always used her own saucepan and spirit stove.

Her room seemed a specially attractive refuge tonight, as, down in the basement, she seemed cut off from the worst of the storm. The light glowed on her golden walls and ceiling, like artificial sunshine. When she had settled down in her old basket-chair, she felt too comfortable to stir. Although the sound of stealthy footsteps, stealing down the back stairs, followed by a succession of dull thuds, piqued her curiosity, for once she was overcome by laziness.

There were faces forming in the red heart of the fire; they peered at her from between the coals, and she stared back at them. Her knees felt pleasantly warmed, and she was at peace with the world.

Presently she heard the footsteps again, ascending the back stairs. This time, her nature reasserted itself in a surge of frantic curiosity. Leaping up, she was just in time to see the hem of Miss Warren's mushroom-lace gown whisking round the bend of the landing.

Mrs Oates did not look exactly pleasant when she opened the kitchen door in answer to Helen's knock.

'*You?*' she said. 'I expected to see Marlene Dietrich. What's the idea of getting me up, just when I was off my feet?'

'I only wanted to know what Miss Warren was doing down here?' asked Helen.

'And you got me up – just for *that*? As if the mistress wasn't free to go through her own kitchen without leave from *you*.'

'But it's the very first time I've seen her down here,' insisted Helen.

'And, please, how long have you been here? Since anny-dominy?' demanded Mrs Oates, as she slammed the door.

In a chastened mood, Helen returned to her own room and lit her spirit stove, in order to re-boil the coffee. She was watching the brown bubbles foam up in the saucepan, when she heard the front-door bell. Turning out the flame, she rushed upstairs, hoping to be first to let in the doctor. She had a frantic fight to force the door open, for the wind seemed whirling in all directions; before she could throw it wide, Dr Parry slipped through the aperture, and slammed it behind him. Without a word, he fastened all the bolts, and put up the chain.

There was an urgency in his manner, and also in his silence, which excited her to a pitch of fearful expectation.

'Well?' she asked breathlessly. 'Why don't you say something?'

'It's a dirty night,' he said, taking off his dripping coat, while he looked at her with stern eyes.

'No, no,' she insisted. 'Tell me – have you found out the cause of that poor girl's death?'

'Yes,' was the grim reply. 'She was murdered.'

13

Murder

The news stunned Helen with such a shock of horror that she felt herself rock, while the house seemed to sway with her in the wind. When she was stationary again, she realised that the entire family had gathered in the hall, and was listening, with strained attention, to Dr Parry.

'She was strangled,' he said.

'When?' asked the professor.

'Impossible to tell within an hour or so. But I should say, roughly, about five or six o'clock.'

'Strangled,' repeated Miss Warren. 'Is it – the same kind of murder as the others?'

'Definitely,' replied the doctor. 'Only more ferocious. Ceridwen was a strong girl, and she put up a fight, which enraged him.'

'Then' – Miss Warren's face wavered painfully – 'if she was murdered in Captain Bean's garden, the maniac was quite close to us.'

'Closer than that,' said the doctor. 'The murder was actually committed in the plantation.'

A gasp of horror sobbed from Miss Warren's lips, while Simone grasped Stephen's arm. Even in the midst of her own terrible excitement,

Helen noticed that Mrs Newton was alive to the amatory possibilities of the situation, while her husband watched her with contracted eyes.

She felt herself slipping away on a backwash of recent memories. While she had stood, defenceless and stranded, staring at the stronghold of The Summit across a bowl of empty country, she was even then in the company of Murder. All the time It was creeping nearer – unseen, unheard. She might even have passed close to It, while It hid in the undergrowth of the gulley. But It had smelt her out – marked her down. It knew that she would have to come past, and It waited for her, in the plantation, in evil mimicry of a tree.

'What a wonderful escape,' she thought.

Now that the danger was over, she could almost exult in the adventure, were it not for the reminder that the tree had not been cheated of its ultimate prey. The thought of poor Ceridwen, going light-heartedly to a horrible fate, made her feel faint.

When the mist had cleared from her eyes, it was a relief to notice that the professor's face showed no sign of emotion. As he spoke in his habitual pedantic tones, she felt retrieved from a dark quivering landscape – split to reveal lightning glimpses of hell – and back in the comfortable interior of an English home.

'How do you establish the fact that this murder was committed in the plantation?' he asked.

'Because there were pine-needles in her clenched hands, and her clothing showed signs of having been dragged through a hedge. Of course, it is useless to try to follow the impulses of a diseased brain; but it seems rum to have taken such an unnecessary precaution. The body could easily have lain undiscovered in the plantation for many hours.'

'And it might not,' remarked the professor. 'You can depend on it, there was some process of reasoning behind the seeming absurdity.'

His son, who shared his dislike of their eccentric neighbour, gave a chuckle. 'Bean must have had a startling homecoming,' he said. 'A corpse propped up on his doorstep to let him in.'

'He was a bit upset.' Dr Parry spoke coldly. 'It was a nasty shock for a man of his age. Sudden death is not really amusing – least of all, to the victim.'

His dark eyes flashed angrily over the stolid faces of the young men, and Simone's vermilion lips, parted eagerly as though to sip sensation.

'I don't want to alarm you people,' he said. 'No, that's a lie. I *do* want to alarm you. Thoroughly. I want you all to realise that there is a criminal lunatic at large, who has tasted blood, and will probably lust for more. And he's somewhere near, quite close to you.'

'Will – will he try to break in here?' quavered Miss Warren.

'Don't give him a chance. I take it for granted that the professor will insist on everyone remaining in the house. It goes without saying that you will lock every door and window. Don't stint on your precautions – however ridiculous they may appear.'

'I have seen to all that. Ever since the – the governess,' Miss Warren told him.

'Good. It takes a clever woman to realise danger, and her responsibilities towards her juniors. You'll be all right. Oates, alone, could account for the chap, with one hand, if he should happen along.'

Again Helen was assailed by that odd pang of desolation as she listened to the professor's explanation of Oates's absence. She felt strangely depressed by the thought that Dr Parry, too, would soon be gone.

His practical, cheerful personality seemed to reduce even murder to rational proportions. It was an unnatural evil, which could be guarded against by natural means – which would prevail, since the defence was so much more powerful than the attack.

He presented an uncouth figure in contrast with the other men, who were all in immaculate evening-dress, but when he caught her eye and smiled at her, she knew, instinctively, that he could inspire both affection and trust.

Some bright elusive vision quivered before her eyes, filling her with happiness and hope. She felt she was on the verge of some discovery. But before she could collect her thoughts the doctor had turned to go.

'I must push off,' he said cheerfully. 'Professor. I know you understand the importance of all the men staying in tonight to protect these two girls.'

His glance included Simone, who responded with an alluring smile.

'Peter,' she said, leaning her chin on the professor's shoulder, 'you're not going to let the doctor go without offering him a drink?'

Before the doctor could refuse the unspoken invitation, Helen stepped into the breach.

'I've some coffee downstairs,' she said. 'Shall I bring some up?'

'The very thing,' remarked the doctor. 'But may I come down and dry off a bit while I mop it up?'

Helen could not resist a feeling of triumph over Simone, as Dr Parry clattered after her, down the kitchen stairs. While Simone's man strained at his chain, she had hers following in her wake.

Her sitting-room looked even more cheerful and restful when Dr Parry sat opposite to her, gulping coffee from a huge breakfast cup.

'What are you beaming about?' he asked abruptly.

'I ought not to,' she said apologetically. 'This is all so terrible. But – it is *living*. And I've done so very little of *that*.'

'What *have* you done?' he asked.

'Housework. Sometimes with children thrown in.'

'Yet you keep your tail up?'

'Of course. You never know what's just round the corner.'

Dr Parry frowned. 'Have you never heard that "curiosity killed the cat"?' he asked. 'I suppose, if you saw a smoking bomb, you'd feel bound to examine its fuse?'

'Not if I knew it was a bomb,' explained Helen. 'But I wouldn't know if it was, until I'd found out.'

'And *must* you find out?'

'Yes, you must – if you're *me*.'

'I give you up,' Dr Parry groaned. 'Haven't you enough wit to realise that there's a human tiger waiting to turn you into – what's left of Ceridwen. If you'd seen what I've just seen – '

'Oh, don't,' wailed Helen, her face suddenly pinched.

'But I want to frighten you. This sort of lunatic is usually normal in between his fits of mania. He might be living in this house with you, and you'd accept him, just as you accept young Rice or the professor.'

Helen shuddered.

'Might it be a woman?' she asked.

'No, unless she was abnormally strong.'

'In any case, I should be bound to know.'

'No, that is the paralysing part of it,' insisted the doctor. 'Just imagine the horror of seeing a friendly face – like my own – suddenly change into an unfamiliar mask – with murder glaring out of its eyes?'

'Are you trying to tell me someone in this house committed all the murders?' Helen asked. 'Well, I'd take on anyone here, except Oates. *He* would be awful, if he turned inside out. A sort of King Kong.'

Dr Parry lost his temper.

'You're making a joke out of it,' he said. 'But what happened to the girl who was frightened of a poor old woman?'

Helen shrivelled, instantly, at the memory.

'I want to thank you for that,' she said. 'You were a real sport. She's different. There's something unnatural about her. But I think that everyone should do all the things they shouldn't do – and then, they won't.'

Dr Parry laughed as he rose reluctantly from the old creaking basket-chair.'

'It takes a doctor to disentangle that,' he said. 'I imagine you refer to moral inoculation.'

'Yes,' nodded Helen. 'Like being vaccinated against smallpox.'

'And would you like to have an injection of your own vaccine?' he asked. 'Get drunk? Sniff snow? Have a weekend in Brighton?'

'Oh *no*,' objected Helen. 'Of course, I didn't mean myself. I'm always out of things.'

As Dr Parry looked at her, the meaning in his eyes underlined his words. 'I think, before long, you'll find yourself very much in the picture. Perhaps Welshmen are more impetuous than Englishmen. In fact, I'm ready to bet that, within six months, you'll be Mrs Jones, or Hughes, or – Parry.'

Helen purposely reversed the order of the names, as she smiled back at him.

'Taken,' she told him. 'If I'm not Mrs Parry, or Jones, or the other, I'll collect off you.'

'Done,' said the doctor. 'You'll lose. But now that I've got outside your coffee I must go.'

'No, wait,' said Helen, arrested by a sudden impulse. 'I want to tell you something first.'

In a few words she gave him a skeleton outline of her adventure with the tree. There was no need to colour any details to get her effect this time; Dr Parry's eyes were fierce and his lips set in a rigid line, in his attempt to hide his concern.

'I take back that bit about the bomb,' he said. 'Thank heaven, you've still got a scrap of the precious sense of danger.'

'Then you don't think me a fool for running away?'

'I think it was probably the wisest thing you've done in your life.'

Helen became thoughtful.

'It's a pity I didn't really see him,' she remarked. 'I mean, when he turned to a man. Do you think it is a local person, as he was waiting in the plantation?'

Dr Parry shook his head.

'No. This is obviously the fifth murder in a series of connected crimes. As the first two were committed in town, it is probable that the criminal lives there. What the police should do is to get acquainted with the timetable of some respected citizen, and find out if a handful of fringe is torn from his white silk scarf.'

'Do you mean there's a clue?' asked Helen.

'Yes. I found a hank of it inside Ceridwen's mouth. She must have torn at it, with her teeth, when they were struggling. She didn't make it easy for him – or he for her. Come with me, to let me out, and see that every bolt is shot.'

Helen obeyed, although she hated to see him go into the streaming darkness. The dripping laurels of the drive, and the clipped evergreens on the lawn, shook in the gale, as though straining at their roots.

She banged the door, hearing the click of the spring lock with a definite sense of security. The hall seemed calm as a millpond after the howl of the wind. There was serenity in the soft glow of its lighting – comfort and warmth in the thick pile of the peacock-blue carpet.

As the hall was empty, Helen ran downstairs to her own room, where Dr Parry's presence still seemed to linger. But she had barely seated herself before the fire when Mrs Oates's head appeared around the door.

'I'm warning you,' she said, in a hoarse whisper. 'There's something *queer* about that new nurse.'

14

Safety First

Helen stared at Mrs Oates, with vague misgiving. There was something unfamiliar in the woman's appearance which eluded her. Her face, still flushed from the heat of the fire, wore its usual expression of good-natured surliness, so that Helen was puzzled to account for the change.

'The nurse?' she repeated. 'She's rather a brute – but what's queer about her?'

'*Things*,' Mrs Oates nodded mysteriously. 'I've noticed them, but taken no notice. It comes back that I noticed them, and then I wonder what they were.'

'What things?' insisted Helen.

'Little things,' was the vague reply. 'I'd like a word with Oates. He could tell me.'

As her voice thickened, Helen suddenly traced the difference in her to its source. Something had gone out of her face; her lips hung loosely, so that her jaw had lost its suggestion of a bulldog grip.

She felt vaguely uneasy. One of her special guards was gone – and the other had changed. She had no longer the comforting assurance of Mrs Oates's protection.

A thread of meaning, however, ran through Mrs Oates's talk, and Helen found her attention gripped.

'I want to see Oates,' declared the woman, 'and ask him just where he picked up that nurse. A baby could diddle Oates. If someone cut off his head, and stuck on a cabbage, he'd never notice the difference, and no more would you.'

'But I'm sure he told us he took her from the Nursing Home,' Helen reminded her.

'Yes – and how? I know Oates. He'd drive up, and then, because he hadn't me to hop out and ring the bell for him, he'd just sound the hooter, and wait for things to happen. The first body in a cloak and veil what climbed inside the car would be good enough for him.'

'Hm,' mused Helen. 'Still, even if she is an impostor, she couldn't have committed the murder, because she was driving with him, in the car, when it was committed.'

'What murder?' asked Mrs Oates.

Helen was human enough to relish the importance of announcing tragic news which did not touch her personally.

But Mrs Oates's reception of Ceridwen's death was disappointing. Instead of being thrilled with horror, she accepted it as though it were an item in the weekly schedule.

'You don't say,' she muttered. 'Well, you mark *my* words. There'll be another murder before we're one night older, if we're spared to live as long.'

'Aren't you a little ray of sunshine?' exclaimed Helen.

'Well, I don't trust that nurse. Folks said as how the loony must have had a woman what used to talk to the girls and distract them so as he could spring.'

'You mean – a decoy?' asked Helen. 'I'll promise you this. If the nurse invites me to go for a little walk with her in the garden tonight, I won't go.'

'But she's not here for that,' said Mrs Oates. 'She's here to open the door to *him*.'

It was a most unpleasant idea, coming on the heels of Dr Parry's revelation. Helen awoke afresh to the loneliness of the storm-bound house. Even down in the basement, she could hear the fury of the gale, like a hurricane thudding against the shutters of the windows.

'I think I'll go upstairs and see what the others are doing,' she said, feeling that she needed a change of company.

The first person she met in the hall was Stephen Rice. He had opened the door of the closet where the coats were hung and had just unhooked his ancient Burberry from its peg.

'You're never going out in this storm,' she cried.

'Hush. I'm stealing off to the Bull. I need the company of my fellow working men to get the taste of this nasty affair out of my mouth. I might even try the experiment of a glass of beer. I'm the sort of desperate chap who'd try anything once.'

'I believe there's one thing you wouldn't,' said Helen, who felt strung up to a reckless pitch.

'Meaning?'

'Running off with another man's wife.'

Stephen followed Helen's glance towards the drawing-room.

'You never said a truer thing,' he nodded. 'No women for me.' Then he held out his hand. 'Sister, can you spare me a dime?'

Helen couldn't believe that he was really borrowing money from her, until he explained, 'I want to settle my score at the Bull. Buying the pup cleaned me out.'

'Where is the pup?' asked Helen.

'Up in my room, asleep on the bed. Sister, what about that dime?'

'I haven't got it,' faltered Helen. 'I don't get paid until the end of my month.'

'Tough luck. Another country off the Gold Standard. Sorry I asked. Nothing for it, now, but to touch Simone. She's plenty of chink.'

As he spoke Simone sauntered across the hall.

'Where are you going?' she demanded.

'First of all, I'm going to you, my dear, to borrow some cash. Then, I'm going to the Bull to hand over the said cash.'

Simone contracted her painted brows.

'You haven't got to invent an excuse for going to the Bull,' she told him. 'I know the special attraction.'

'Whitey?' groaned Stephen. 'For the love of Mike, stop harping on about her. She's a nice little girl. We're friends, and that's all.'

He broke off as Newton came out of the study.

'Will you all come into the study!' he said. 'The chief has an announcement to make.'

The professor was seated at his table, speaking in a low voice to his sister. His face wore a look of exhaustion, which was not lost on Helen.

She noticed, too, the glass of water and the small bottle of white tablets which stood at his elbow.

'I have something to say,' he announced, 'which applies to everyone. No one is to leave this house tonight.'

Simone flashed a look of triumph at Stephen, who began to splutter: 'Oh, but, sir, I have an important appointment.'

'Then you will not keep it,' the professor informed him.

'But I'm not a baby.'

'Prove it. If you are a man, you will realise that we are faced with a situation of actual danger and that it is the duty of every male member of this household to remain at home.'

Stephen continued to protest.

'I'd stay, like a shot, if there was any sense in it. But it's such bally rot. Of course, no woman should go out. But they are safe, at home. The chap wouldn't come inside the house.'

'Have you forgotten the girl who was murdered inside her bedroom?' broke in Miss Warren in a toneless voice.

'Her window was left open,' explained Stephen.

'But you heard what the doctor said?' insisted Miss Warren.

'And you've heard what *I've* said,' remarked the professor sternly. 'I'm master of this house, and I will not have the safety of anyone here imperilled by disobedience.'

Helen felt his glance hover for one moment over her, and her heart throbbed with gratitude.

'There is another precaution I wish observed,' went on the professor. '*No one* is to be admitted to the house tonight. If anyone knocks, or rings, he – or she – will remain outside. I forbid the unbolting of the door on any pretext whatsoever.'

This time objection came from Newton.

'That's rather drastic, chief,' he said. 'Anyone might come; the police, or someone with important news.'

The professor took up a paper as though he were weary of the discussion.

'Those are my orders,' he said. 'I am only concerned, tonight, with the safety of those under my roof. But I warn you. Anyone who goes outside the house – if only for a minute – *will not return*. The door will be locked on him, or her, and it will not be opened again.'

A host of disturbing possibilities flitted across Helen's mind. In particular, she had a vision of Dr Parry – on a special mission which concerned herself – standing outside in the rain.

'But, if we recognise the voice, will that alter things?' she asked timidly.

'Certainly not,' said the professor. 'Voices can be imitated. I repeat, you are to open to no one, man, woman or child.'

'Oh, but, professor, you *can't* mean a child?' cried Helen. 'If I heard a baby crying outside I'd just have to take it in.'

The professor smiled bleakly.

'You'd probably find your baby waiting to grip your throat,' he told her. 'Surely you've heard child-impersonators on the wireless whose imitations are faultless?'

'He could squeal his head off for all the effect he'd make on me,' said Stephen brutally. 'I was done out of my chance of a fortune by an unexpected Blessed Event in my family. And I promise you this, too. I wouldn't cross the room for any woman alive.'

The look which Simone threw him was a challenge which was intercepted by Newton. He gave a faint hoot of laughter.

'Ever heard of Shakespeare, Rice?' he asked caustically. 'Or of a quotation – "Methinks the lady doth protest too much"? We hear so much about your being a woman-hater, and see so little evidence.'

The professor rapped the table, as though he would silence a noisy council session.

'That is all,' he said. 'Miss Capel, will you please pass on my orders immediately to Mrs Oates and Nurse Barker?'

'Yes, professor,' said Helen.

Suddenly she was assailed by a fresh complication.

'What about Oates?' she asked.

'He will remain outside,' was the relentless reply. 'He can garage the car, and remain there, until the dawn.'

'But Lady Warren might want her oxygen?'

'Lady Warren must take her chance with the rest. I am committed to a policy of Safety First. Perhaps I understand the situation better than the rest of you. When I was in India, in my youth, I remember a tiger which prowled outside a cattle-enclosure. Again and again it broke through the defence, in spite of every precaution.'

He dropped his voice, as he added, 'There is a tiger, outside this house, *now*.'

As he spoke, there was the sound of loud knocking on the front door.

15

Secret Intelligence

The knocking ceased, and a bell was pealed which brought Helen instinctively to her feet.

'I'll answer the door,' she said.

She crossed the room before she realised the significance of her action. No one else had moved; but all were looking at her – their expressions impassive, scornful or amused, according to temperament.

The professor nodded at his sister – a sardonic gleam in his eye.

'The weak link,' he observed, in an undertone.

The significance of the phrase brought home to Helen its special application, so that she coloured to the roots of her hair. 'I'm sorry,' she faltered, 'but it's second-nature for me to answer a bell.'

'You gave us a demonstration of that,' said the professor acidly. 'I don't wish to be severe, but you must remember that forgetfulness, in this case, ranks with disobedience.'

The knocking was repeated, and again a bell pealed in the distance. Even knowing she was under observation, and on her guard, Helen found it an ordeal to stand by and do nothing.

'It's like watching milk boil over,' she thought, 'or seeing a child play with fire. Someone *ought* to do something. I'm sure it is all wrong.'

She noticed how the muscles of Miss Warren's face quivered at every blow, and her own nerves twitched in sympathy.

A third assault was made on the door. This time Stephen seemed conscious of the tension.

'Look here, sir, with due deference to you and all that, isn't this going a bit too far? Cutting all the wires, I mean. That may be the postman, with an unstamped letter for me, to say my Cousin Fanny has passed away having named me as her heir.'

The professor explained, with the dreary patience with which he enlightened a pupil's ignorance. 'I have just given an order, Rice. It would be reactionary conduct on my part to commit the same fault for which I've just rebuked Miss Capel. If once we begin to make exceptions to a precaution which is intended for the general safety, it ceases to have any value.'

'Yes, sir.' Stephen grimaced at a fourth, and louder assault on the knocker and bell. 'But it gets my goat not knowing who's outside.'

'Oh, my dear Rice, why didn't you say that in the beginning?' The professor's smile flickered and went out. 'Of course, it is the police.'

'Police?' echoed Newton. 'Why have they to come here?'

'A mere formality, since The Summit is in the radius of – of this affair. They will want to know if we can furnish them with any inform- ation. If they would accept a negative answer, and go, I would relax my rule in their favour.'

'But you can't keep them out, Sebastian,' cried Miss Warren.

'I have no intention of keeping them out. When they call tomorrow, they will be admitted. I'm master of my house, and I've wasted too much time already, tonight.'

Through his glasses, his eyes flashed hungrily over the papers on his desk.

Helen hoped fervently that Mrs Oates would answer the door, for the police seemed a direct answer to prayer. She had a mental vision of a compact body of solid, uniformed men, bringing with them the protection of the law.

Suddenly she thought that she might force the professor's hand.

'But I could tell them something,' she said.

'Miss Capel,' he said, in measured tones, 'have you any clear, concise knowledge that will be of definite use to the police? For instance – have you seen the criminal, so that you could describe him?'

'No,' replied Helen.

'Then, have you any idea as to who he is, or where he is?'

'No,' replied Helen, wishing she could sink into the floor.

'Well – have you any valuable theory?'

'No, but – but I think he hides behind trees.'

Simone led the suppressed laughter, in which even Miss Warren joined.

'Thank you, Miss Capel,' said the professor. 'I think the police can wait for your help until tomorrow morning.'

Helen's heart sank. It seemed it was always 'tomorrow', and she still dreaded the night which divided her from the dawn.

The professor, however, seemed to have some pity for her confusion, for he spoke to her in the voice of a considerate employer.

'Now, Miss Capel, will you be so kind as to tell Mrs Oates and Nurse Barker my decision.'

'Indeed, I will,' Helen assured him.

'I suppose gran doesn't know about the murder?' asked Newton.

'No,' replied Miss Warren, 'neither she nor the nurse can know. I'm the only person who has been upstairs since Dr Parry brought us the news. And I should certainly not dream of alarming her.'

'She *must not* be told,' commanded the professor.

The hall was silent when Helen passed through it. The professor had worn down the patience of the police, who happened to be represented by a single officer. After exposure to what was practically a waterspout, he drew his own conclusion from the barred windows, and decided to call by daylight. Apparently the fear of the maniac had spread from the cottages to the big houses of the neighbourhood.

When Helen reached the kitchen, to her surprise she was unable to enter. At first, Mrs Oates did not answer her tap; but presently a huge distorted shadow crossed the frosted glass of the door and a key turned in the lock.

Mrs Oates towered over her, with a confused red face and sleepy eyes.

'Must have lost myself,' she explained.

'But is it safe to go to sleep with the door locked?' asked Helen. 'Suppose your clothes caught on fire, and we couldn't get at you?'

'Yes, you could. Nearly all the locks here has the same key; only you can't turn them, because they're never used,'

'Naturally,' said Helen. 'You only lock your door in loose houses, and hotels. I've always taken pure situations, so I've never locked my door in my life.'

'Well, if I was you, I'd oil my key, and lock my door, tonight,' said Mrs Oates.

'How useful,' laughed Helen, 'if any other key would fit it.'

'But theirs would be rusty,' explained Mrs Oates.

When Helen delivered the professor's message, she jerked her head defiantly.

'Thank his lordship for nothing. Doors are not my work, and never was.'

As she retreated inside the kitchen, Helen caught her sleeve. 'Please, Mrs Oates, don't lock the door,' she entreated. 'I'd hate to feel I couldn't reach you. I'm such a fool, tonight. But I depend on you, more than anyone else in the house.'

'That's right.' Mrs Oates shot out her jaw in the old aggressive way. 'If anyone gets in, I'll knock his block off.'

With this comforting assurance ringing in her ears, Helen mounted the stairs to the blue room, which had regained some of its former fascination. The door slid open an inch to reveal Nurse Barker, as though she had been listening for her step.

'I've something to tell you,' Helen whispered. 'There's been another murder.'

Nurse Barker listened to every detail. She asked questions about Ceridwen's character, her duties about the house, her lovers. At the end of the story, she gave a short laugh.

'She's no loss. Her sort asks for it.'

'What d' you mean by "her sort"?' asked Helen.

'Oh, I know the type. You've not got to tell me. Sluttish. Little dark eyes, saying, "Come into a dark corner," to every man. A slobbery red mouth, saying, "Kiss me." A lump of lust.'

Helen stared as Nurse Barker reeled off the glib description, for she had not mentioned Ceridwen's personal appearance.

'Have you heard of Ceridwen before?' she asked.

'Of course not.'

'Then how did you know what she looked like?'

'Welsh.'

'But all Welsh girls are not like that.'

Nurse Barker merely changed the subject. 'As for the professor's orders about the doors, they are not necessary. Answering doors is not part of a nurse's duty. And I should certainly not risk my life by going outside in this storm. It is an insult to my intelligence.'

Helen felt more at her ease when Nurse Barker exalted her own

THE SPIRAL STAIRCASE

importance. She became a definite type, which, although unpleasant, was only too common in her experience. It did not pair with that mephitic shade – raised by Mrs Oates – the midnight hag, who crept down the stairs, when the household was asleep, to let in Murder.

'Nurse!'

At the familiar bass voice, Nurse Barker turned to Helen. 'I want to go down to the kitchen, to see about certain things,' she said. 'Could you stay with her?'

'Certainly,' replied Helen.

'Not frightened now?' sneered Nurse Barker. 'When did you have a change of heart?'

'I was just silly before,' explained Helen. 'I'm a bit run down. But now we've got something *real* to fight, fancies must go to the wall.'

With her old confidence, she entered the blue room, expecting a welcome. But Lady Warren seemed to have forgotten her former interest.

'What was all that knocking?' she asked.

'You've very keen hearing,' said Helen, while she tried to think of some explanation.

'I can see – hear – smell – feel – taste,' snapped Lady Warren, 'and better than you. Can you tell the difference between an underdone steak and one that is rare?'

'No,' replied Helen.

The next question raised a more unpleasant issue. 'Could you aim at the whites of a man's eyes, *and* pot them? . . . What was that knocking?'

'It was the postman,' explained Helen, lying to meet the professor's instructions. 'Oates has been sent out for fresh oxygen, as you know, and I was somewhere else; so no one heard him, at first.'

'Disgraceful organisation in *my* house,' stormed Lady Warren. 'You needn't stare. It's still *my* house. But I had servants in livery . . . Only they all left . . . Too many trees . . . '

The whimper in her voice was not assumed, and Helen knew that the past had gripped her again.

But even while she sympathised with this derelict of time, Lady Warren became several degrees more vital than herself; for she heard footsteps on the stairs which had been inaudible to Helen, and her eyes brightened in anticipation.

The door swung open, and the professor entered the bedroom.

Helen was interested to notice how the sex-instinct triumphed, even on the threshold of the grave, for Lady Warren's reception of her stepson was very different from her treatment of any woman.

'So, at last, you condescend to visit me?' she exclaimed. 'You're late, tonight, Sebastian.'

'I'm sorry, madre,' apologised the professor. He stood – a tall, formal figure – at the foot of the bed – in the shadow of the blue canopy.

'Don't go,' he whispered to Helen. 'I'm not remaining long.'

'But the post was late, too,' remarked Lady Warren, casually.

Helen's respect for the professor's intelligence was increased by his immediate grasp of her subterfuge.

'He was delayed by the storm,' he explained.

'Why didn't he push the letters through the slit?'

'There was a registered letter.'

'Hm . . . I want a cigarette, Sebastian.'

'But your heart? Is it wise?'

'My heart's no worse than yesterday, and you didn't make a dirge about it then. Cigarette.'

The professor opened his case. Helen watched the pair as he leaned over the bed, a lighted match in his fingers. The flame lit up the hollow of his bony hand, and Lady Warren's face.

Helen could tell that she was an experienced smoker by the way she savoured her smoke before blowing it out in rings.

'News,' she commanded.

In his dry voice, the professor gave her a summary, which reminded Helen of *The Times* leading article chopped up into mincemeat.

'Politicians are all fools,' remarked Lady Warren. 'Any murders?'

'I must refer you to Mrs Oates. They are more in her line than mine,' replied the professor, turning away. 'If you will excuse me, madre, I must get back to my work.'

'Don't overdo it,' she advised. 'You look very old-fashioned about the eyes.'

'I've not slept well.' The professor smiled bleakly. 'Were it not that I know it to be a popular fallacy, I should say I had not a single minute's sleep all night. But I must have lost consciousness for minutes at a stretch, judging by the chimes of the clock.'

'Ah, you're a clever man, Sebastian. The fools of nurses pretend that they wake if one of my hairs falls out – but they sleep like pigs. I could roll about, on wheels, and they wouldn't stir. Blanche, too. She dropped off in her chair when it was getting dark, but she'd never admit it.'

'Then you couldn't use *her* to establish an alibi,' said the professor lightly.

Helen wondered why the speech affected her disagreeably. Whenever she was inside the blue room she was affected by its poisonous atmosphere

'Where's Newton?' asked the old lady.

'He'll be coming up to see you soon.'

'He'd better. Tell him life is short, so he'd better not be late for the Grand Good-Night.'

The professor shook her formally by the hand and wished her a restful night. In obedience to his glance, Helen followed him outside the door.

'Impress on the nurse, when she returns, not to let Lady Warren know about what happened tonight.'

'Yes, I understand,' nodded Helen.

When she came back, Lady Warren was watching her intently, with black crescent eyes.

'Come here,' she said. 'Another murder has just been committed. Have they found the body?'

16

The Second Gap

As Helen listened, a herd of vague suspicions and fears galloped through her mind. Lady Warren spoke with the ring of authority. She was not guessing blindly; she knew something – but not enough.

It was this half-knowledge which terrified Helen. Had any of Dr Parry's audience told her about the murder, she would naturally have heard also about the discovery of the body in Captain Bean's garden.

Nurse Barker, alone, stood outside the circle of informed listeners. That fact did not necessarily assume a sinister significance. To use the professor's phrase, her alibi was established. When Ceridwen was being done to death, she was bumping in the old car towards The Summit in Oates's company.

Yet – if she had told her patient – she must have possessed some horrible specialised knowledge of the movements or intentions of the maniac which stopped short with the commission of the murder.

As Lady Warren gripped her wrist, Helen realised that it was useless to lie.

'How do you know?' she asked.

The old woman did not reply. She gave a hoarse gasp. '*Ah!* Then they've found her. That knocking was the police. I knew it. Tell me *all*.'

'It was Ceridwen,' Helen said. 'You remember? She used to dust under your bed, and you objected to her feet. She was strangled in the plantation, about teatime, and carried afterwards to Captain Bean's garden. He found her.'

'Any clue?'

'One. She tore a handful of fringe from the murderer's white silk scarf.'

'That's all. Go away,' commanded Lady Warren. She pulled up the sheet and covered her face entirely, as though she were already dead.

On her guard against foxing, Helen sat by the fire, where she could watch the bed. Although one fear had swallowed up the other – like two large snakes snatching at the same prey – she had an instinctive dread of exposing her back to Lady Warren.

To steady her nerves, she made a mental inventory of the situation

'There's the Warren family – four; then Mrs Oates, Nurse Barker, Mr Rice and me. Eight of us. We ought to be more than a match for one man, even if he's as clever and cunning as the professor says.'

Then her mind slipped back to a former situation, when she was nursery-governess in the house of a financier. With her phonographic memory for phrases, she reproduced one of his remarks to his wife. 'We want a merger. Separate interests are destructive.'

Her face grew graver as she thought of heated passions rising to boiling-point, and the strangling complications of the triangle. Had she known of the actual situation in the drawing-room, she would have been still more worried.

Stephen was affected most adversely by the confinement. He was not only specially rebellious against closed windows, but he was wary of Simone. Her ardent glances made him uncomfortable, as he remembered the Oxford episode, when he had been made the goat in another undergraduate amour.

He remembered that when the wretched girl had screamed, Newton had been first to come to her alleged rescue, and that he had always been censorious in his judgement – hence his refusal to believe in Stephen's innocence. Back then, the seeds of jealousy had been sown, although Simone had only expressed vague admiration for a regular profile.

It had been perversity on his part which made him become the professor's pupil, in order that his son might feel some sense of obligation – an impulse which he had repented, since the visit of the young couple to The Summit. He stopped his ceaseless pacing of the carpet, to address Newton.

'With due respect, and all that sort of bilge, to your worthy father, Warren, he doesn't get our angle. Our generation isn't afraid of any old thing – dead, alive, or on the go. It's being cooped up together, like rats in a drain, that *gets* me.'

'But I'm adoring it,' thrilled Simone. 'It's like a lot of married couples being snow-bound, in one hut. When they come out, just watch how they'll pair off.'

She seemed lost to all sense of propriety, as she stared at Stephen with concentrated eagerness, as though they were together on a desert island.

Completely unselfconscious, she ignored the presence of an audience. A spoilt brat, who'd been given the run of the toyshop, she simply could not understand why her desire for any special plaything should not be instantly gratified.

'What are your plans, Stephen?' she asked.

'First of all,' he told her, 'I shall fail in my exam.'

'Fine advertisement for the chief,' remarked Newton.

'After that,' continued Stephen, 'I shall probably go to Canada and fell timber.'

'Your dog will have to go into quarantine,' Newton reminded him spitefully.

'Then I'll stay in England, just to please *you*, Warren. And I'll come and have tea with Simone every Sunday afternoon, when you're having your nap.'

Newton winced, and then glanced at the clock.

'I must go up to gran. Any use asking you to come with me, Simone? Just to say good-night?'

'None.'

Raising his high shoulders, Newton shambled from the room.

When he had gone, Stephen made an instinctive movement towards the door. Before he could reach it, however, Simone barred his way.

'No,' she cried. 'Don't go. Stay and talk. You were telling me your plans – and they're pathetic. Supposing you had money, what would you do?'

'Supposing?' Stephen laughed. 'I'd do the usual things. Sport. A spot of travel. A flutter at Monte.'

'Does it appeal?'

'You bet. A fat lot of good it is talking about it.'

'But I have money.'

'How nice for you,' he said.

'Yes. I can do anything. It makes me secure.'

'No woman should feel too secure.' Stephen strained desperately to keep the scene on a light level. 'It makes her despise fate.'

Simone appeared not to hear him, as she came closer and laid her hands upon his shoulders. 'Steve,' she said, 'when you go away tomorrow, I'm coming with you.'

'Oh, no, you're not, my dear,' he said quickly.

'Yes,' she insisted. 'I'm mad about you.'

Stephen licked his lips desperately.

'Look here,' he said, 'you're jumpy and all worked-up. You're delirious. You don't mean one word. To begin with – there's old Newton.'

'He can divorce me. I don't care. If he doesn't, I still don't care. We'd have lots of fun together.'

Stephen cast a hunted glance towards the door. Fright made him brutal.

'I don't care for you,' he said.

The repulse had only the effect of making her more ardent.

'I'll soon make you care for me,' she said confidently. 'You're just a silly boy with inhibitions.'

Exultantly, she raised her face to his, her lips expectant of his kiss. When he shook her off, the first shade of doubt crept into her eyes.

'There's another woman,' she said. '*That's* why.'

Desperation made him lie.

'Of course,' he told her. 'There always is.'

He was both startled and relieved by her reception of his news. Her face lost its look of immaculate and finished artifice and crumpled up with elemental rage.

'I hate you,' she cried furiously. 'I hope you'll go to the dogs and die in the gutter.'

Rushing from the room, she banged the door behind her. Stephen took a deep breath and then thumped his chest.

'Thank the pigs,' he said piously.

But the incident left him worried. He wondered whether Simone contemplated some mean form of revenge. Assuring himself that it was no good meeting trouble halfway, as on the morrow he would be gone for good, he tried to escape into the excitement of a thriller.

Presently he became aware that his attention was no longer gripped. He kept raising his eyes from the pages, to listen. Above the howls of the gale rose a faint whine. It sounded like a dog in distress.

He bit his lip and frowned in perplexity. In spite of his objection, he realised that the professor's precautions were probably sound, and he was prepared to obey them to the last letter. But when the professor had referred to 'man, woman, or child' he had forgotten to include 'animal'.

Stephen frowned as he realised that he was up against an acid test. If this were a trap, some unknown brain had detected his blind spot, and knew how to exploit it.

'It's Newton,' he thought. 'He's trying to lure me outside, so I'll be shut out. The fool thinks he's got to protect his wife from me.'

Again the faint howl was borne on the wind, bringing him to his feet. But again he sat down.

'Hang it,' he muttered aloud. 'I won't. They shan't get at me. It's not fair to risk the women.'

He took up his novel, and tried to concentrate on what he read. But the lines of print were a meaningless jumble of words, because he was awaiting – and dreading – a repetition of the cry.

At last, it came – pitiful and despairing, as though the creature were growing weaker. Unable to sit still, he stole out into the lobby and unbolted the front door. As he put his head outside, the wind seemed about to tear off his ears, but it also bore the barking of a dog.

While it might be a faithful animal imitation, there was something familiar about the sound. Struck by a sudden suspicion, Stephen cautiously rebolted the door and hurried up to his room.

'Otto,' he cried, as he threw open the door.

But no dog leaped to welcome him. The bed was tidy and the room had been hurriedly put in order.

'The dirty tykes,' he said. 'They've run him out. This settles it. I clear out, too.'

Swearing under his breath, he hurriedly changed into his old tweeds and laced on thick shoes. Bag in hand, he clumped down the back stairs. No one saw him when he crossed the hall, but as he banged the front door behind him, Helen heard the slam.

Newton's visit to his grandmother had released her from her vigil, as the old lady had ordered her from the room. Although it was her usual bedtime, Helen decided to break her rule of early hours.

The whole household was upset; while boredom usually drove the family prematurely to their rooms, they all seemed restless tonight.

Mrs Oates, also, would be sitting up to let in her husband. Helen felt she had better share her vigil, in case she should drop off to sleep again and miss his ring. She flew to the front door, just in time to recognise Stephen as he retreated through slanting sheets of rain.

As the light flashed out over the gravel drive, he turned and shouted to her defiantly: 'Lock up. I'm never coming back.'

Helen hastened to slam the door and re-fasten the bolts.

'*Well*,' she said. 'The young rip.'

She was laughing over the incident when Nurse Barker came up from the kitchen.

'What was that noise?' she asked suspiciously.

'Mr Rice has gone,' Helen told her.

'Where?'

'He didn't tell me, but I can make a pretty good guess. He's been terribly keen to go to the Bull, to pay up and say goodbye.'

Nurse Barker's deep-set eyes glinted angrily.

'He's disobeyed the professor and risked our safety,' she stormed. 'It's criminal.'

'No, it's all right,' Helen assured her. 'I locked up after him, directly. And he's not coming back.'

Nurse Barker laughed bitterly.

'So it's all right, is it?' she asked. 'Don't you realise that now we have lost *our two best men*?'

17

When Ladies Disagree

As Helen stared at Nurse Barker, she was appalled by what she saw in her eyes. Anger had given way to a murky gleam of satisfaction, as though she welcomed the weakening of the defence.

Remembering that she was marked out for distinctive bait, the knowledge inspired the girl with defiance.

'We've still two men,' she said. 'And, five women – all able-bodied and strong.'

'Are *you* strong?' asked Nurse Barker, sneering down at Helen, from her superior height.

'I'm young.'

'Yes, you're young. You may remember that – before you're much older. And – perhaps – you may regret your youth.'

Helen tossed back her red mane impatiently.

'I suppose the professor ought to be told about Mr Rice,' she said.

'And, of course, you will tell him.'

'Why – me?' asked Helen.

'He's a *man*.'

'Look here, nurse,' Helen said, in her mildest voice, 'I think that bickering, just now, is silly. We all want to pull together. We don't want to keep harping on the nature of men. And I'm sure you don't want me to be the next victim. You're too good a sport.'

'I have no ill-feeling towards you,' Nurse Barker assured her in a low voice.

'Good,' said Helen. 'When you go up to Lady Warren, will you tell Mr Newton what's happened, and ask him to let his father know.'

Nurse Barker bowed her head, in stately assent, and began to mount the staircase. Helen stood in the hall, watching her flat-footed ascent, as the tall white figure gradually rose above her step by step.

'You can wear high Spanish heels, when you're small,' she thought, looking down, with satisfaction, at her own feet. 'She walks just like a man.'

She noticed that, as Nurse Barker receded, she appeared little more than a faint glimmer crossing the dimly-lit landing, as though some ghostly shape were rising from its churchyard bed. The illusion reminded her of her earlier experience, before dinner, when she had been appalled by a momentary vision of evil.

'It *must* have been the professor,' she assured herself. 'I fancied the rest.'

Suddenly she remembered the incident in greater detail. The professor had emerged from his bedroom just after she had the impression of a door being opened and then shut immediately.

'Odd,' she thought. 'The professor wouldn't open his door, and then slam it – and then open it again. There's no sense in that.'

Staring up at the landing, she noticed that the door of the professor's bedroom was close beside that of the back staircase. Someone might have looked out from the one, just as the other was opening, with the meticulous timing of a lucky coincidence.

The notion was not only absurd, but so disquieting that Helen refused to admit it.

'No one could have got into the house,' she told herself. 'It was all locked up when Ceridwen was strangled. But supposing there was some secret way in, then the murderer could have rushed from the plantation and been lurking on the back stairs when I saw him. Only, it was the professor.'

In spite of the seeming impossibility of anyone entering the fortress, she began to wonder if – for a minute or so – any chink had been left in the defence. At the back of her mind, something was worrying her . . . Something forgotten – or overlooked.

She had been unmethodical all the evening, breaking off in the middle of a job to start another. For example, she had not even begun to screw up the handle of Miss Warren's bedroom door. Before she had discovered how to tackle the difficulty, she had been interrupted by the professor, and had left her tools lying on the landing.

'Anyone might think I was untidy,' she thought. 'I'll go up again and experiment a bit.'

As the resolution formed in her mind it was swept aside by the spectacle of Newton hurrying down the stairs. His sallow face was flushed with excitement as he spoke to her.

'So the noble Rice has walked out on us?'

'Yes,' replied Helen. 'I was there when he went – and I locked him out.'

'Good . . . I suppose he was alone?'

'I only saw him on the drive. But it was very dark and confusing in the rain.'

'Quite.' Newton's eyes flickered behind his glasses. 'Do you mind waiting here, just for a minute?'

Helen knew what was in his mind as he galloped upstairs to the second floor, and she smiled over his groundless fear, even while she knew that she could have saved him his journey, but only at the expense of tact.

A minute later, he clattered down again, ostentatiously flourishing a clean handkerchief, to excuse his flight.

'My wife is a bit upset,' he remarked casually. 'Headache, and so on. Perhaps you'd see if you could do something for her, when you've time?'

'Certainly,' promised Helen.

Newton's smile was so unexpectedly boyish that Helen understood the secret of his popularity with his womenfolk.

'What a lot we Warrens expect for our money,' he said. 'I do hope you get a decent salary. You earn it. Now, we must tell the chief about Rice.'

Once again, Helen was flattered at being asked to help him. Although her sympathies were with Stephen, she had infinitely more respect for Newton. All the men seemed to be inviting her co-operation that night; instead of being in the wings, she was constantly on stage. It was true that she was there chiefly to feed the principals, and was not picked out by the limelight; but, in the circumstances, it seemed safer not to advertise. She even congratulated herself that Nurse Barker was not present to witness her entrance into the study, since personal triumph was not worth more friction.

The professor was lying back in his chair, with his eyes closed, as though in concentration. He did not open his lids, until Newton called his name. When he did so, Helen thought that his pupils looked curiously fixed and glassy.

Apparently, Newton shared her impression.

'Been mopping up the quadronex?' he asked.

The professor's stare reproved the impertinence.

'As I'm the financial head of this house,' he observed, 'I have to conserve my strength, for the benefit of my dependants. I must insure some sleep, tonight . . . Have you anything to tell me?'

His lips tightened as he listened to Newton's news.

'So. Rice rebelled against my restrictions?' he said. 'That young man may develop into a good citizen, ultimately, but, at present, I fear he is a Goth.'

'I should call him a throw-back,' remarked Newton.

'Still, he was a hefty barbarian,' his father reminded him. 'In his absence, Newton, you and I have more to do.'

'Which means I'm on my own, chief. You're a bit past tackling a maniac.'

Helen guessed that the professor was irritated by the remark.

'My brain remains at your service,' he said. 'Unfortunately, I was only able to pass on a section of it to my son.'

'Thanks, chief, both for the compliment and your help. I am afraid a formula for poison-gas hardly meets the case. We need brute-force.'

The professor smiled bleakly. 'My despised brain may yet prove the trump-card,' he said. 'Does Simone know that Rice has left?'

'Yes.' Newton bristled at the implication. 'What of it?'

'I leave that to you.'

'She's got a headache,' said Helen. 'Mr Warren has asked me to see to her.'

The professor's eyes slanted slightly inwards, as though he were trying to peer inside the lighted recesses of his brain.

'An excellent idea,' he said. 'Remember my daughter-in-law is temperamental. You may have to influence her, but don't irritate her.'

He whispered to his son, who nodded, and passed on the instruction. 'Miss Capel, it might be wiser not to leave her alone.'

Helen felt rather important as she went up to the red room, although she was slightly doubtful of the success of her mission. As she paused outside the door, she could hear the sounds of strangled sobbing. No notice was taken of her knock, so she entered, uninvited – to find Simone stretched, face downwards, on the bed.

'Oh, your lovely dress,' she cried. 'You'll ruin it.'

Simone raised her head, showing a tear-streaked face. 'I hate it,' she snarled.

'Then take it off. Anyway, you'll feel freer in a wrapper.'

It was second nature to Simone to be waited on, so she made no protest as Helen peeled the sheath-like gown over her head.

The younger girl took rather a long time in her selection of a substitute, from the wardrobe. The sight of so many beautiful garments aroused her wistful envy.

'What lover-ly things you have,' she said, as she returned to the bed, carrying a wisp of georgette and lace which was less substantial than the discarded gown.

'What's the good of them?' asked Simone bitterly. 'There's no man to see them.'

'There's your husband,' Helen reminded her.

'I said *man*.'

'Shall I get you some aspirin for your head?' asked Helen, who was determined to keep Simone's ailments on a strictly physical basis.

'No,' replied Simone. 'I feel foul. But it's not that. I'm so terribly unhappy.'

'But you've everything,' cried Helen.

'Everything. And nothing I want. My whole life has been one of sacrifice. Whenever I want something, it's taken from me.'

She coiled herself into a sitting posture, as a prelude to confidence. While her make-up was ruined, the tempest had swept harmlessly over her plastic coiffure, for her hair gleamed like unflawed black enamel.

'Has Stephen Rice ever flirted with *you*?' she asked.

'No,' replied Helen. 'And, if he did, I shouldn't tell you. Affairs should be kept private.'

'But, my good woman, how can they be? One goes out – balls, restaurants, and so on. And there's always the inevitable man.'

'I wasn't thinking of you,' said Helen. 'I was naturally speaking for myself.'

'*You?* Have you a lover?'

'Of course,' replied Helen recklessly, as she remembered Dr Parry's prophecy. 'I'm sorry, but I'm more interested in myself than you. Of course, I know that you have your photograph in the papers and that people talk about you. But to me, you're a type. I see lots like you, everywhere.'

Simone stared incredulously at Helen, whom she had only vaguely noticed as someone small, who wore a pinafore and shook a perpetual duster. Although she was staggered to realise that the nonentity was actually claiming individuality, she could not keep off her special subject.

'What do you think of Stephen?' she asked.

'I like him,' replied Helen, 'but I think he's a rotter. He shouldn't have left us in a jam.'

'*Left* us?' echoed Simone, springing up from her reclining posture

'Yes, he's gone for good. Didn't you know?'

Helen was rather startled by the effect of her news on Simone. She sat, as though stunned, her fingers pressed tightly over her lips.

'Where did he go?' she asked in a low voice.

Helen determined to make a thorough job of Simone's disillusionment.

'To the Bull,' she replied.

'To that woman, you mean.'

'If you mean the landlord's daughter,' Helen said, 'he was talking about her in the kitchen. He said he couldn't go away without wishing her goodbye.'

The next second, she realised her blunder, as Simone burst into a storm of tears. 'He's gone,' she cried. 'That woman has him. I want him so. You don't understand. It's burning me up. I must *do* something.'

'Oh, don't pine for him,' entreated Helen. 'He's not worth it. You're only making yourself cheap.'

'Shut up. And get out of my room.'

'I don't want to be where I'm not wanted,' Helen said stoutly. 'But I've orders not to leave you.'

Her speech roused Simone to white fury.

'So that's it?' she cried. 'You were sent to spy on me? That was clever of them. Oh, *thank* them from me. But why didn't I think of it for myself?'

'What do you mean?' asked Helen nervously.

'You'll see. Oh, you'll see.'

Helen watched in silent dismay as Simone whirled around the room, snatching at garments and dressing in frantic haste. She realised that the situation had passed from her control. She could no more arrest the inevitable catastrophe than subdue a runaway engine.

She cried out in protest, however, as Simone dragged on her fur coat.

'Where are you going?' she demanded.

'Out of this house. I won't stay to be watched and insulted.' Simone snatched up a handful of jewellery, thrust it inside her bag and turned to Helen. 'I'm going to my lover. Tell the professor I shan't be back tonight.'

'No, you shan't go,' declared Helen, trying to grip Simone's wrists. 'He doesn't want you.'

The struggle was short and desperate, but Simone was the stronger, besides being entirely reckless. Careless of consequences, she pushed Helen away with such force that the girl was thrown to the floor.

Although Helen was not hurt, she wasted a little time in assuring herself that such was actually the case. While she was rubbing her aching head, she heard the click of the key in the lock and realised that she was a prisoner.

18

The Defence Weakens

The sound brought Helen to her feet and sent her rushing to the door, even while she knew that she was too late. She tugged at the handle and battered on the panels, to relieve her feelings rather than with any hope of release.

It was a humiliating situation, and indignation was her strongest emotion. She had been thrown about, as though she were a dummy in a film. Worst of all, she had failed again in a position of trust. The thought quickened her sense of responsibility and made her rack her brain for some method of arousing the household – only to be forced back on the hopeless expedient of ringing the bell.

Even as she pressed the button, she knew that no one would come. The bell rang down in the basement-hall, where Mrs Oates would only hear it as a soothing accompaniment to her snores. Were she roused, she would ignore it, on principle.

Bells were none of her business. She did so much during her working-hours that she was forced, in self-defence, to guard her precious leisure. Helen remembered how she would point, either to her husband or the girl, and sing, 'The bells of Hell go ting-a-ling-a-ling for *you*, but not for me,' whenever she noticed an unanswered tinkle.

It was soon obvious that she did not intend to relax her rule on this occasion. Helen stopped prodding the button, and resigned herself to an indefinite wait.

At first, she had plenty of occupation, for she was able to satisfy her curiosity over Simone's wardrobe and toilet-aids; but she could not bring her usual interest to her investigations. Every silk stocking and pot of rouge reminded her of Simone. She was out in the storm – lashed on by a spluttering match of desire, which she had magnified to a torch of passion.

Helen reconstructed her – a luxury-product, spoiled, neurotic and useless. From her cradle, every wish had been gratified and every whim forestalled. She had been sheltered under a glass-case, lest life should blow too roughly upon her.

And, even then, the horror might be closing over her, shattering the glass and leaving her defenceless, to face reality.

Instead of protecting arms, she would see hands stretched out in menace. She would cry for help, and – for the first time in her life – she would cry in vain.

That was the vision which kept flashing across Helen's mind as she thought of Simone's peril. Although she had done her best, she still felt a sense of guilt. In order to prepare her story for the defence, she began to reconstruct the incident.

As she did so, she was again visited by a disquieting memory. This time, it was an auditory illusion. She was positive that she had heard the key click in the lock at the same time as she listened to the sound of Simone's frantic flight down the stairs.

'Someone else locked me in,' she whispered. 'Who? And why?'

She could only conjecture that Nurse Barker had been on the landing, probably attracted up there by the noise of the scuffle. If she had grasped the situation, her jealousy might have urged her to imprison Helen, in order to stamp her as an incompetent.

Suddenly Helen received a belated inspiration. Mrs Oates had told her that all the doors in The Summit were fitted with the same lock. In that case, Newton's dressing-room key should fit the bedroom keyhole.

She had some difficulty in wrenching it out, for it was rusted from desuetude. From her recent investigations, she knew where to find Newton's hair-oil; but before she began its lubrication, she decided to match it with the lock.

As she grasped the handle of the bedroom door, it slipped round in her fingers and the door swung open. Her lips, too, fell apart, as she stared out at the deserted landing.

'*Well,*' she gasped.

Faced with the prospect of a violent drop in favour, she ran downstairs, to raise the alarm. Although she had established the fact that she was the victim of a practical joke – or trick – it was impossible to prove it to her employers. She decided that it would be wiser to accept any blame and remain silent, only to find that no explanation was required. When she blurted out the news of Simone's flight, the Warren family was united in a solid front, to save the situation.

As the professor, Miss Warren and Newton looked at each other, the likeness between them was marked. The muscles of their thin overbred faces worked convulsively, betraying the violence of their emotion and the force of their self-control.

Although Newton's high voice broke in an occasional squeak, his manner remained as temperate as though the subject of discussion was the weather.

'You say, Miss Capel, that she went to the Bull, to find Rice,' asked the professor.

'Yes,' said Helen, avoiding looking at Newton. 'I fought with her, but – '

'Yes, yes. The question is – who will go after her, Newton. You or I?'

'I'm going,' replied Newton.

'No, darling,' urged Miss Warren. 'You're the younger man. Your father will have more authority. Your place is here.'

'You're in no danger,' Newton told her. 'But she's running a horrible risk.'

The professor laid his hand on his son's shoulder to steady him, and Helen noticed that his thin knotted fingers trembled slightly.

'I understand your feelings, Newton,' he said. 'But I think the chances are against your maniac being outside in this storm. If he's not back in his home, he will be sheltering in some barn. I am sure Simone will reach the Bull safely.'

'What a happy prospect.' Newton bit his lip. 'All the more reason for her husband to be there.'

'Perhaps you're right. But before you go we'd better discuss our line of procedure. We want to avoid a scandal'

'I don't want to divorce Simone.' Newton's voice cracked. 'I only want to get her away from that – from Rice.'

'Personally, I think she is in no danger from Rice,' remarked the professor. 'He is very definitely not an amatory type.'

'He locked that poor girl in his room at Oxford,' declared Newton heatedly.

'You forget, Newton, that I've been an undergraduate in my time. Such episodes can be staged. I've always kept an open mind on that charge. Wash out Rice. The question is – how to account for Simone running through the rain to a public-house?'

'A brainstorm, caused by nerves,' suggested Miss Warren. 'The murder would explain her condition.'

The professor nodded approval.

'I'm afraid you'll both have to put up at the Bull, for the night,' he said. 'They have no conveyance, and Simone could not return through the storm.'

'Couldn't you come back, Newton, when you've explained everything and made all arrangements for Simone?' asked Miss Warren.

Newton laughed as he thoughtfully buttoned his waterproof.

'Excellent. I could leave her in Rice's care. Don't worry, aunt. Expect us back tomorrow morning.'

Helen was assailed by a fresh pang of loneliness when the chain was refastened, after the exodus. As Newton went out of the house – his head thrust forward as though he were butting the storm – the partially-opened door revealed a section of chaos, interlaced with veins of slanting rain, spinning round in the shaft of electric-light.

After that glimpse of watery confusion, the atmosphere of the hall appeared stagnant, and clogged with femininity. All the virility had been drained out of it with the departure of the men. It was true that the professor remained, but he seemed exhausted by the excessive burden of responsibility.

'Mr Rice will have to come back tomorrow to fetch his dog,' said Miss Warren.

Helen's face brightened.

'Shall we free it, to roam the house?'

Miss Warren's face betrayed indecision. 'I fear and dislike all dogs,' she said. 'Still – the creature might be a protection.'

'I'm used to dogs,' Helen told her. 'May I feed him and then bring him down with me?'

'It has been fed, by Mrs Oates, before I took it out to the garage.' Miss Warren's gaze challenged her brother. 'Perhaps, Sebastian, you will bring it in?'

Helen pricked up her ears as the secret of the strange noises upon the back stairs was explained. Mrs Oates's reticence was but another proof of her loyalty to her employers.

The professor was looking at his sister; a faint smile tinged his lips.

'Typical, my dear Blanche,' he murmured. 'Is the door of the garage unlocked?'

'Locked. I have the key upstairs.'

As they waited for Miss Warren's return, Helen tried to conquer her dread of the professor. Like a kitten, which pats a suspicious object and then springs sideways, she could not resist an attempt to explore his mind.

'I admire Miss Warren's strength of character,' she said. 'Of course, she can't help being afraid of dogs.' She hastened to bring out the classic excuse of analogy. 'Lord Roberts was frightened of cats.'

'But my sister is not afraid in your sense of the word,' explained the professor. 'That is to say, she is not afraid of being bitten or worried by a dog. But she realises the danger of bacteriological infection which lurks in the parasites of animals.'

Helen did her best to reciprocate his intelligence.

'I know,' Helen said. 'There are millions of germs everywhere. Enough to kill all the people in the world. But – I understood that there were good germs to fight the bad germs.'

The professor's faint smile did not conceal his scorn.

'Even as your good angels strive with devils?' he enquired. 'There may be some combat, but, in the animal kingdom, the ultimate good does not prevail, as in your fairy-tale creed.'

Although she felt choked with nervousness, Helen continued the argument.

'If the destructive germs were the more powerful,' she said, 'we should all of us be dead.'

'We soon shall be dead. Longevity is only comparative, since many die young. Think of infant mortality, which is Nature's method of dealing with surplus population. Unfortunately, medical science has interfered with her good intentions to a certain extent. Still, death wins.'

Helen felt too overawed by the sardonic gleam in the scientist's eye to dare to argue further. She knew herself outclassed, even while her heart protested against his bleak pragmatic outlook.

'What is Miss Warren's special subject?' she asked timidly.

'She ranges. Her plane of vision is, consequently, different from your own. You see with eyes, but she sees through a microscope. Terrors which are lost to you are revealed to her.'

Helen rather liked the way the professor was trying to gloss over his sister's imperfections. She believed that, even as shadows on the sea betray the presence of rocks, so trifles indicate character.

Whatever his theological disbelief, the professor was staunch.

'How interesting,' she said politely.

'My sister is of too sensitised a nature to mix with the outside world,' went on the professor, 'yet her nerve is of iron. She did valuable work, during the war, at the front, which took daily toll of her reserves. Yet she never showed any sign of strain, and emerged with a fine record. That is one of the reasons why she insists on a teetotal household – so great is her horror of any kind of bestiality.'

'I think that was fine,' said Helen.

'It was. Especially, as you have already remarked, she suffers from a deficient pituitary gland.'

Helen did not understand his allusion, so she gazed with new respect at Miss Warren when she came down the staircase. In silence she handed her brother a key, and then walked into the library.

'Bolt the door after me, please,' said the professor, 'and remain here to let me in again.'

It was dreary waiting in the hall which was now so empty and silent. No sound of youthful voices or strains of wireless floated from the drawing-room.

'Thank goodness, I'll soon have the dog,' Helen thought.

Even that consolation was denied her. When – a little later – heralded by his knock, the professor was blown inside the lobby, he was alone.

'Rice has made good his threat,' he told her. 'I found the padlock on the garage door forced and the dog gone.'

Stripping off his dripping coat, he walked into his study.

Feeling doubly forlorn, Helen ventured to invade Mrs Oates's privacy. She knocked several times on the kitchen door without attracting any attention, although the light was shining through the frosted-glass panels.

She was on the point of turning away when she was startled by an unfamiliar thick voice.

'Come in, my dear.'

In spite of the genial invitation, Helen entered the kitchen with a sinking heart – not knowing what she feared.

Mrs Oates sat slumped back in her chair, like a sack of potatoes, a stupid smile on her red face.

In spite of her inexperience, Helen guessed that the ultimate disaster had befallen her. Her second guard had failed her. Mrs Oates was drunk.

19

One Over the Eight

As Helen looked at Mrs Oates, she felt in the grip of a bad dream. Everything had changed in the course of a few hours. It was impossible to believe that the kitchen was the same cheery place where she had drunk her tea.

It was not only comfortless and untidy, but actually darker, for no leaping fire helped to illuminate it. Crumbs and eggshells were strewn on the bare table. Even the ginger cat had deserted his rug for the peace of the empty drawing-room.

But the change in Mrs Oates was the worst feature of the transformation. An ugly woman at her best, she had lost the redeeming quality of her expression. The loyalty had been soaked from her eyes and the familiar lines of her face had melted together in an idiotic grin. When Helen gave her the latest bulletin of news, she received it with such indifference that the girl wondered whether she had actually grasped the fact of the wholesale desertion.

'Women can't get drunk decently,' she thought. It struck her that, in this special accomplishment, men remained supreme. Women equalled their records in other fields, but while a man, in his cups, could be amusing – or even brilliant – a drunken woman only relapsed into beastliness.

Yet, although she was disgusted by Mrs Oates's gross red face, she realised that she was only partially intoxicated. Since the catastrophe was not complete, it might be possible to appeal to her sense of trust and to pull her round again.

'Have you been drinking my health?' she asked.

Mrs Oates evinced exaggerated innocence.

'Funny, ain't you? Beer-money I get – I'll allow you that. But never a drop of tiddley.'

'Odd,' sniffed Helen. 'I thought I could smell brandy.'

'Must be that nurse, spilling her breath. She's been poking down here.'

Helen decided to try guile.

'Bad luck,' she sighed. 'I could do with a spot myself. Just to buck me up, after all the upset.'

She watched the conflict in Mrs Oates's inflamed face, as native kindliness struggled with greed and caution. In the end, generosity prevailed.

'And so you shall, you poor little squirt,' she declared.

Ducking down her head, she dived under her skirt, and drew out a bottle of brandy, which she placed triumphantly on the table.

'Help yourself,' she said hospitably. 'Plenty more where that comes from.'

'Where did you find it?' asked Helen.

'In the cellar, when the master went to look at the thermom-momm – '

As Mrs Oates continued to wrestle with the word, with a flicker of her old bulldog tenacity, Helen stretched out her hand for the bottle.

'You've drunk nearly half already,' she said. 'Hadn't you better save some for tomorrow?'

'No,' declared Mrs Oates solemnly. 'I can't taste nips. I must have swallows. I always finish a bottle.'

'But you'll get drunk, and then Miss Warren will sack you.'

'No, she won't. I done this before. The master only says she must put temptation out of my way and not give me another chance.'

Helen listened with the dismay of a card-player who has mistaken a small pip for a trump. A valuable trick – fear of the consequences – was lost to her.

It was obvious that Mrs Oates was sanguine with regard to the future. The Warren family balanced an occasional lapse against the value of her services.

'Still, put a little by for a rainy day,' she urged, as Mrs Oates's fingers closed around the bottle.

'For Oates to find? Not blooming likely. He'll know I've had one over the eight, and he's always out to block me. No. I'm going to hide it in the only safe place.'

'What rotten luck your husband had to go off,' wailed Helen tactlessly. 'Why should it happen tonight, of all nights?'

Mrs Oates began to laugh shrilly.

'I done that,' she crowed. 'I took up the pudding to the bedroom when I knew the nurse was busy with her ladyship, washing down the decks. I just gave the cap of the cylinder a twist as I was setting down the plate.'

'What made you think of it?' gasped Helen.

'You. You said it was her life. But if it hadn't worked I'd have thought up some other way to get rid of Oates.'

The nightmare oppression increased as Helen sat opposite Mrs Oates and watched her drain her glass. There seemed to be a conspiracy against her; yet when she traced back effect to cause, she could find no evidence of human malice.

There was nothing extraordinary in the fact that Mrs Oates should have a failing, and it was natural that her husband should try to check her; it therefore followed naturally that she should sharpen her wits to get him out of her way.

The same logic characterised the events which had been responsible for the dispersal of the young people. Stephen Rice was devoted to his dog and resented its banishment, while Simone had behaved in the normal manner of a spoiled neurotic girl whose desires had been thwarted. The professor, too, could not have done otherwise, when he authorised Newton to follow his wife.

Of course, there had been unlucky trifles which had been the levers which set the machinery in motion; but the responsibility for them was divided equally among the members of the household.

It was unfortunate that Stephen should have brought home a dog, in the first place, and doubly unfortunate when it clashed with Miss Warren's prejudice against all animals. The professor's lapse was also lamentable, although he could hardly credit Mrs Oates with the audacity of committing a theft under his nose.

Helen had to admit that she, too, had lent a hand in weaving this extraordinary tissue of consequences. She had influenced Dr Parry to exaggerate the gravity of Lady Warren's condition, while her unlucky remark about the oxygen had been the origin of Mrs Oates's brainwave.

Yet, even as she marshalled her arguments, she grew afraid. Something was advancing towards her – some vast slow movement of affairs, which she was powerless to deflect from its course.

Blind chance alone could not be responsible for this string of apparent accidents. Natural things were happening – but with unnatural complicity. The process was altogether too smooth and too regular; they timed too perfectly, as though some brain were directing their operations.

The sight of Mrs Oates slowly dissolving from a shrewd woman into a sot stung Helen to desperate action.

'Give me that,' she cried, seizing the bottle. 'You ought to be ashamed of yourself.'

She realised her mistake when Mrs Oates turned on her in a fury.

'Lay off that,' she shouted.

Helen tried to turn her action into a joke as she dodged around the kitchen, pursued by Mrs Oates.

'Don't be so silly,' she urged, still hugging the bottle. 'Try and pull yourself together.'

Red-eyed and panting, Mrs Oates penned her into a corner, snatched the bottle from her, and then slapped her cheek.

As the girl reeled back under the force of the blow, Mrs Oates gripped her shoulders and practically hurled her out of the kitchen.

'Good riddance to bad rubbish,' she muttered as she slammed the door. 'You keep out of here.'

Helen was glad to escape, for she recognised the need to enlist fresh help. Too timid to appeal to the professor, she went into the library. Miss Warren, who was hunched forward, poring over a book, did not welcome the interruption.

'I hope, Miss Capel, you've not disturbed me for a trifle,' she said.

'No,' Helen told her, 'it's important. Mrs Oates is drunk.'

Miss Warren clicked with disgust, and then glanced at the clock.

'There's nothing to worry about,' she said calmly. 'She will sleep it off tonight. Tomorrow she will do her work as usual.'

'But she has not quite passed out,' persisted Helen. 'If you were to speak to her now you might stop her.'

'I am certainly not going to argue with a semi-intoxicated woman,' said Miss Warren. 'And my brother's work is far too important to be interrupted. If you are wise, you will not interfere. This has happened before.'

Miss Warren took up her book again, to indicate that the interview was over.

Feeling utterly miserable, Helen wandered into the hall. At the sight of the telephone, however, her courage revived. It reminded her that while she had been feeling lonely as though marooned on a desert island, The Summit was still linked with civilisation.

'I'll ring up the Bull,' she decided. 'We ought to find out if Simone is safe. And then I'll ring up Dr Parry.'

She was conscious of the agony of suspense as she took the receiver from the hook. In this gale telephone poles must be crashing down all over the country. So many disasters had been caused that she quite expected to find that she was cut off.

To her joy, however, she heard the buzz of connection, and an operator's voice at the exchange asking what number she wanted. After a short interval, another voice, speaking with a strong Welsh accent, informed her that he was Mr Williams, landlord of the Bull.

In answer to her enquiries he told her that Mr and Mrs Newton Warren had arrived at the inn and were staying the night. He added that Mr Rice had left, with his dog, immediately after their arrival, presumably to make room for the lady.

'Where did he go?' asked Helen.

'To the parsonage. He said he knew the parson would put him up, seeing as he's partial to dogs.'

Feeling that she had family news to offer as her excuse, if she were surprised at the telephone, Helen looked up Dr Parry's number in the directory. Presently she heard his voice at the other end of the wire. It sounded tired, and not exactly enthusiastic.

'Don't tell me the old lady has thrown an attack. Have a heart. I'm only just started on my meal.'

'I want some advice,' Helen told him. 'There's no one else to ask but you.'

But at the end of her story she had not succeeded in convincing even herself of the gravity of the position. Everything sounded petty and the result of stress; and she was sure that Dr Parry shared her view.

'Bit of a landslide,' he said, 'but there's nothing you can do. Don't tackle Mrs Oates again.'

'Bit I *do* want to get her sober,' pleaded Helen. 'It's so lonely with no one.'

'Are you afraid?'

'N-no,' replied Helen.

'Because, if you are, I'll come over at once.'

As he expected, the offer braced Helen to a refusal. He was hungry, wet and dog-tired; although he was susceptible, at that moment a fire and his pipe appealed to him more than the brightest eyes.

'I know that watchtower of a house can't be too cheerful in a gale,' he said. 'But say your prayers and it won't come down. Of course, you've had a nasty shock, this evening, and you naturally feel lonely with those people walking out on you. Still, there's quite a respectable number left. Lock up, and you've nothing to fear.'

'Yes,' agreed Helen, starting at a violent crash outside one of the shuttered windows.

'If you went to bed now, and locked your door, could you sleep in this gale?' asked Dr Parry.

'I don't think so. My room's high up, and it's rocking like a cradle.'

'Then keep up the fire in your sitting-room, and make up a shake-down there. You'll hardly hear the storm. Before you know it, it'll be tomorrow morning.'

'And things look so different in the morning,' said Helen. It was easy to be brave with Dr Parry's cheerful voice resounding in her ears.

'Remember this,' he said. 'If you feel afraid, ring me up and I'll come over.'

With the promise to cheer her, Helen rang off. But as she looked around the hall her confidence died. The house seemed to sway with the gale, and the night to be full of sounds. A great voice roared down the chimney, until she felt she was on the verge of catching actual words. Feeling that any reception was better than loneliness, Helen went down to the kitchen again. To her relief, Mrs Oates beamed a welcome. Her colour had grown a trifle more congested, while the level of the brandy in the bottle had dropped.

'I mustn't irritate her,' thought Helen, as she sat down and patted Mrs Oates familiarly on the knee.

'We're friends, old thing,' she said. 'Aren't we?'

'Yes,' nodded Mrs Oates. 'Oates said, "Look after little miss." Them were his last words, before he was called away. "Look after little miss." '

'Oh, don't talk as if he was dead,' cried Helen.

Stroking Mrs Oates's hand the while, she began to talk persuasively. 'But how can you look after me if you're drunk?'

'I'm not drunk,' objected Mrs Oates. 'I can toe the line. And I can cosh anyone as dares to lay a finger on little miss,'

Rising, with only the slightest stagger, she walked across the room, sparring at shadow adversaries with such vigour that Helen felt comforted.

'If I can only keep her like this,' she thought, 'she's as good as any man,'

Mrs Oates stopped, blowing like a porpoise, to receive Helen's applause.

'I've been setting here,' she said, 'thinking. And thinking. I'm worrying about that nurse. Why does she speak with her mouth all choked up with breadcrumbs? What's the answer to that?'

'I don't know,' replied Helen.

'I do,' Mrs Oates told her. 'She's putting on a voice. Depend on it she's got another one of her own, same as the old lady upstairs. And she's putting on a walk. She's reminding herself not to tramp as if she was squashing beetles. Now, what do you make of that?'

'What do *you*?' asked Helen uncomfortably.

'*Ah*. Maybe she's not a woman – same as you and me. Maybe, she – '

As Mrs Oates broke off to stare, Helen turned and saw Nurse Barker standing at the open door.

20

A Lady's Toilet

Helen shrank back aghast, before Nurse Barker's stare. She had never before seen hatred – unmasked and implacable – glaring from human eyes.

It was only too obvious that Mrs Oates's words had been overheard; yet Helen made a feeble attempt to explain them away.

'We were just talking of Lady Warren,' she said. 'Isn't she an extraordinary woman?'

Nurse Barker brushed aside the subterfuge. In ominous silence she stalked over to the kitchen range and seized the kettle.

'No hot water,' she said.

'I'm so sorry, but the fire's gone out.' Helen apologised for Mrs Oates. 'If you can wait a few minutes, I'll boil up some on my spirit stove.'

'I need no help,' said Nurse Barker. 'I can do my own jobs. *And* finish them.'

The words were harmless, but she infused them with a hint of grim and settled purpose. With the same ominous significance, she looked first at the bottle on the table and then at Mrs Oates, who sagged in her easy-chair like a sack of meal.

'Brandy,' she remarked. 'In a teetotal house.'

Instantly Mrs Oates raised her glass defiantly. 'Good health, nurse,' she said thickly. 'May all your chickens come home to roost.'

Nurse Barker gave a short laugh.

'I see,' she said, 'I shall soon have *you* on my hands. Well, I shall know how to deal with you,'

Before Mrs Oates could retaliate, she had gone from the room.

'Well,' gasped Mrs Oates, sniffing vigorously, 'wot a nasty smell.

She'd better try no tricks on me, nor go telling tales, or I'll give her a thick ear. I won't be bullied by *that*.'

' "That"?' echoed Helen.

'Well, who's to say if it's a woman or a man?'

Again Helen was gripped with the nightmare horror of the situation as Mrs Oates sank her voice to a hoarse whisper. She had drained her glass again, in greedy gulps. It was only too clear that her guardian was slipping away from her, leaving her to solve the enigma of the nurse.

It was true that she had still the moral support of the professor and his sister; but they were too negligible to help. They seemed to retreat always to their distant horizons – aloof and invulnerable as shadows.

As a child, she had the reputation of never crying; but at this crisis she suddenly broke down.

'Oh, don't,' she cried piteously. 'I can't stand much more.'

As she began to cry, Mrs Oates looked at her with puzzled eyes.

'What's the matter, dearie?' she asked.

'I'm terrified,' confessed Helen. 'You keep on drinking. Soon, you'll be a log, and then you'll be in her power. You're asking for it. I'll do my best, of course – but she'd make three of me, and leave scrapings. And upstairs they won't believe a word I say, until it's too late.'

Helen spoke wildly, but her exaggeration had the desired effect of sobering Mrs Oates. In her turn she daubed lurid colours on her picture of the future.

'It's you she's after,' she said. 'She wants to do me in, to get at you. Well, we'll show her.'

Gulping with emotion, she pushed the bottle of brandy across the table. 'Put it somewhere where I can't reach it.'

Helen took a rapid survey of the kitchen, while Mrs Oates watched her with painful interest. She had repented her noble resolution before the girl started to climb up on to the tall dresser but was resigned. Helen had to pull herself up to the second shelf before she was able to hoist the bottle on to the top ledge: but directly it was out of Mrs Oates's reach, she felt a sudden glow of confidence.

Scrambling from her perilous perch, she began to make a bargain.

'You've been wonderful,' she said. 'If only you'll go on playing the game, I promise you shall finish that bottle tomorrow evening in my sitting-room. I'll keep Oates out, and I'll stand any racket.'

'Swear,' said Mrs Oates.

Helen went through the ritual of crossing her throat. 'Now, I'm going to make some strong coffee, to pull you round,' she said.

'Cawfee,' groaned Mrs Oates. 'If ever you get a man who lifts his elbow, heaven help the poor bloke.'

Helen actually whistled when she was in her sitting-room, for lighting the spirit stove revived memories of Dr Parry. Since he had gone she had experienced such a whirl of emotions that she had had no time to think of him. But as she reviewed the episode in retrospect it glowed with the dawn of happiness.

She remembered his eyes when he prophesied her marriage, and his recent promise to come to her aid if she were in need of him. At that moment she recalled her previous state of mind, when she had stood looking at the refuge of The Summit across the dark spread of intervening country. She felt that, now, she was gazing down the length of a pitchy tunnel to a golden glory which shone at its end. But between her and the dawn of a new day coiled the black serpent of the night.

The water boiled over and she made the coffee, filling a cup with strong dark fluid, which she carried to Mrs Oates.

'Here you are,' she said. 'Black as night and hot as hell.'

'Hell,' repeated Mrs Oates, as she held her nose and swallowed it in a draught.

'Mrs Oates,' asked Helen suddenly, 'is Dr Parry engaged?'

'Not yet, but may be soon,' replied Mrs Oates. 'I'm always asking him when he's going to get married and he always says he is waiting for a young lady as he can pick up and pitch over the moon.'

Although Mrs Oates's remark was under suspicion of being inspired by her audience, Helen smiled, and felt she must spread a little of her own happiness.

'I'll take some coffee up to the nurse,' she said. 'I'm afraid we hurt her feelings just now.'

When she reached the blue room, she knocked several times, but Nurse Barker did not appear.

After a slight hesitation, Helen cautiously opened the door an inch, and peeped into the room.

It was in semi-darkness, for the electric light had been switched off; only a faint bluish light from a shaded lamp, and the fitful glow from the fire illumined the gloom. Stealing over the thick carpet, she could make out the outline of Lady Warren's fleecy jacket between the bed-hangings of ultramarine. Apparently the old lady was asleep, for her snores whined up and down the scale.

Afraid of waking her, Helen could not warn Nurse Barker of her approach. The light shining through the partially opened door of the dressing-room told her that the nurse was inside.

Creeping closer, Helen took her unawares. She was apparently busy with her toilet, for she stood before the glass intently examining her reflection. As she rubbed a finger over her chin, Helen caught the gleam of some small glittering object in her doubled-up fist.

She started violently as Helen scraped on the panel of the door, and looked at the girl suspiciously.

'Well,' she said bitterly. 'This is the one place where I thought I might expect some privacy.'

'Yes, the arrangements are abominable,' agreed Helen. 'I thought you might like some coffee.'

'Thanks.'

Nurse Barker began to sip with studied refinement, which reminded Helen of a stage performance she had witnessed.

'But the man I saw gave a more natural female-impersonation,' she thought. She was so fascinated that she tried to find some excuse for lingering.

'As you saw, Mrs Oates has been drinking,' she said. 'Can you tell me of anything that will put her right?'

'Try an egg in Worcester sauce, and a hair of the dog that bit her,' advised Nurse Barker. 'What time do you go to bed?'

'About ten. But I'm not going to bed tonight.'

'Why?'

'Well, someone must sit up to let Oates in.'

Suddenly Nurse Barker pounced on the girl.

'So you've forgotten the professor's order already? He said you were to admit *no one*.'

Helen looked the picture of guilt as she remembered Dr Parry's promise. If he came, she did not intend to keep him outside.

'I did forget,' she confessed. 'Please don't tell the professor or Miss Warren.'

'I'll make no promises,' declared Nurse Barker. 'If you are not watched constantly, you will imperil the safety of everyone under this roof. It's bad enough having you here, at all – to draw him on us. For he's after *you*.'

At the reminder, Helen felt a tightening of her scalp.

'Why do you keep on trying to frighten me?' she asked.

'Because you forget.' Nurse Barker laid down her empty cup and approached Helen. 'There's another thing I've been saving up to tell you,' she added. 'I'm not satisfied about that Welsh doctor.'

'Dr Parry?' asked Helen incredulously.

'Yes, he's a queer, excitable type – unbalanced and neurotic. *He* might be a homicidal maniac.'

'Oh, don't be a fool,' Helen said.

'You know nothing about him,' went on Nurse Barker. 'These crimes are committed by some man who inspires the confidence of his victims, and who can move quickly from place to place. Well, think of the way he rushes all over the country on his motorbike – here, one minute – a mile away, the next. And everyone trusts the doctor.'

'Of course they do,' declared Helen hotly. 'I do, for one. I'd trust Dr Parry with my life. He's a darling. He's promised to come to The Summit, in this awful storm, if I feel nervous.'

Nurse Barker took a cigarette from her case and stuck it – unlit – in the corner of her mouth.

'You needn't trouble to send for him,' she sneered. 'He may come without waiting for an invitation.'

Helen turned towards the door.

'I won't disturb you any longer,' she said. 'Besides – I think you're goofy.'

Nurse Barker gripped her arm. 'You're afraid of me,' she said.

'I'm not.'

'What do you think of me?'

'I think you are very capable – and clever.'

'A fool?'

'Oh, anything but that.'

'Then,' said Nurse Barker, 'perhaps you will listen to me . . . unless you are a fool yourself. The man who commits these crimes is normal when the fit has passed. So you'll have no warning: You may meet him tonight. If you do, he'll be the biggest surprise of your life. And the last.'

As she listened Helen's heart gave a sharp double-knock, and her head swam, while Nurse Barker appeared to tower above her like a white pillar. She felt that she was losing her grip upon actuality. Everything was undergoing a hideous transformation. She did not know whom to trust – what to believe. In the confusion, friends masqueraded as enemies – humanity lost its familiar dimension.

What really worried her was the fact that Dr Parry had spoken to her in the same horrible language. She had a vision of his face changing before her gaze – his smile stiffening to a grimace – the red menace of murder glowing behind his eyes.

The mist cleared from her vision as Nurse Barker lit her cigarette. All her unwholesome dream was burned away, like a withered membrane, as one fear was killed by another. For the flame which reddened Nurse Barker's face revealed the shaven lip of a man.

21

Clearing the Way

The shock had the effect of steadying Helen's nerves. She had something definite to fight, instead of groping in the shifting horror of a nightmare. She had a problem for her brain to bite on, the need to think before she could decide on any course of action. Slipping through the darkened blue room, she went down to the hall.

Although the shaking of its one window, set high in the wall, reminded her of a storm at sea, it was less exposed than the sitting-rooms. It was also a point of vantage, where she could watch the staircase and the rest of the house. Moreover, she had the satisfaction of knowing that both the professor and Miss Warren were within call.

Sitting on the lowest stair – her chin cupped in her hands – she took stock of the situation. To begin with, she knew that Nurse Barker was not the maniac, since her alibi, at the time of the murder, was established. At the worst, she was an impostor who was in league with the criminal.

In that case, she must be kept under observation until they had sufficient evidence to ring up the police. Helen felt that four able-bodied persons should be able to cope with her – or him. The real difficulty would be to convince the Warrens.

It was Mrs Oates who had started the hare of Nurse Barker's true gender. Probably it was the alcohol talking, for Helen was more inclined to regard her as a harsh, jealous woman, handicapped by nature with an unfortunate appearance. The fact that she shaved could be discounted, as a stubbly lip was not an uncommon feminine affliction.

On the other hand, if Mrs Oates's suspicion was founded on fact, it opened up a range of ugly possibilities. It established a definite plot, for the genuine nurse must have been got out of the way. If the maniac had marked down Helen herself as his next victim, he would not be stopped by any obstacle from reaching his objective. But his choice of Helen was as inexplicable as the history of his crimes.

With scores of girls in the town on whom to wreak his mania, he had undertaken a perilous climb in order to reach the governess's bedroom. In the cases of the countryside murders, he seemed to have attacked the girls when the itch to kill had suddenly come upon him, but this was different. It was the more horrible, because it was a patient, cold-blooded pursuit. She imagined him making enquiries, finding out her address, tracking her down.

What appalled Helen most was the way in which his path was being smoothed. No one could have foreseen such a chapter of accidents. Although he could not have planned them, they could not be co-incidence, since each event had happened in its logical sequence.

'Why should he pick on me? I'm nobody. I don't look like a film star.'

As she cast the net of her thoughts over the past, she captured a memory. On her journey to The Summit she had remained at the railway station for about an hour while she waited for Oates's arrival with the ancient car. As her head ached from her journey down from London she took off her hat.

The bench on which she sat was under a lamp, which shone down on her bright mane of hair – the colour of pale flame. She remembered that a man had turned to stare at her, but his cap was pulled down over his eyes, so that she could not see his face.

'It was my hair,' she thought. 'But I'm an idiot. It's only Nurse Barker's idea. He's not after me. She's trying to frighten me.'

It all boiled down to the old question – who was Nurse Barker? Closing her eyes, she rocked to and fro. It was long past her bedtime, and she had passed through a strenuous day. Worn out with strain, she felt herself growing drowsy. She began to glide over the surface of a tranquil river, shallow and crystal clear. Suddenly it ended in a drop over a bottomless hole. Her heart gave a leap, and she opened her eyes with a violent start. To her surprise she was not alone. While she dozed the professor had come out of his study, and was bending over her.

'Sleeping on the stairs, Miss Capel?' he asked: 'Why don't you go to bed?'

His formal voice and appearance restored her confidence.

Crimes don't happen in well-conducted houses, where gentlemen dress for dinner.

'Very unwise,' he remarked, when she confided her proposed vigil. He passed her, and went up the stairs, holding on to the rail for support. She called after him.

'Professor, may I say something?'

He waited while she ran up to the landing.

'Mrs Oates wants to know more about that new nurse,' she said. 'I mean – she wants to know if she really comes from the Home.'

'Then why not find out?' enquired the professor. 'There is the telephone.'

In spite of his aloofness, the professor did not affect Helen with the hopeless feeling of impotence. She remembered that when she had been stunned by the thunderclap of the murder, he alone had remained unshaken.

Stimulated by contact with him, she did not want to cut the wires.

'Are you going up to bed?' she asked boldly.

'Yes,' he replied. 'It is nearly eleven.'

'Then, I hope you'll get some sleep. But, if something crops up – something I can't cope with – may I knock you up?'

'Not unless it is urgent,'

Cheered by the grudging permission, Helen ran down to the hall and consulted the telephone directory. Her habit of listening to scraps of conversation had yielded the address of the Nursing Home, which was fortunate, since there appeared to be a good crop of them. Presently, the exchange put her through to the secretary.

'Will you please tell me if Nurse Barker is there tonight?' asked Helen.

'No,' replied the secretary. 'Who's speaking?'

'The Summit.'

'But she's at The Summit.'

'I know. Will you please describe her?'

There was silence, as though the secretary wondered whether she was talking to an idiot.

'I don't understand,' she said. 'She's tall and dark, and one of our best nurses. Have you any complaint to make?'

'No. Has she a very refined voice?'

'Naturally. All our nurses are ladies,'

'Yes, yes. Did you see her get into the car from The Summit?'

'No,' replied the secretary, after a pause. 'It was late, so she waited in the hall. When she heard a hoot, she went outside, carrying her bag.'

Helen rang off with the feeling that on the whole the interview had been satisfactory.

'I'd better check up now on Mrs Oates,' she decided.

Mrs Oates had sunk lower in her basket-chair. She looked the picture of misery as she stared at the bottle of brandy on top of the dresser. 'You gave me the works,' she said reproachfully. 'You and your cawfee. I've not even got merry.'

'Tomorrow,' promised Helen. 'I've been ringing up the Nursing Home. Nurse Barker seems an awful brute, but otherwise I think she's all right.'

Mrs Oates would not give up her original idea.

'All wrong to me,' she grunted. 'I've a tin with a lid what 'as tightened up. Oates can't shift it. I'll ask her to open it, and see if she falls into my trap.'

'It would only prove she has strong fingers,' said Helen. 'She need not be a man. What's the time?' She glanced at the inaccurate clock. 'Five to eleven. That's near enough. When will your husband be back?'

Mrs Oates worked out the sum on her fingers.

'Say, one and a half hours to go, and two to get back. The old car's bound to take a rest up some of them hills. And Oates will play about, doing his business. Say five hours, at the outside, and maybe sooner.'

Helen felt a rush of new hope.

'He left about eight-thirty,' she said. 'So we've only another two hours, or so, to wait. I shall sleep like a top, once I know he's back. Will you bring your sheets down to the spare room, so that I shall know you're on the other side of the wall?'

'I don't mind,' promised Mrs Oates. 'It'll be safer there, than on top, with all the chimbleys.'

Suddenly Helen groaned.

'I'd forgotten. The professor said we were not to let your husband in.'

'That's all right,' said Mrs Oates. 'The master gave his orders for you to obey. But he wasn't giving them to himself. Didn't he pack off Mr Newton after his missus? Of course, he means to let Oates in.'

Helen was astonished by the woman's shrewdness.

'You mean it was a pose – to show he was master of the house?' she asked. 'If he was so keen to get the oxygen, he wouldn't let it sit in the garage all night. Directly we hear a knock I'll rush up and tell the professor.'

'Oates will be inside the door by then,' prophesied Mrs Oates. 'D' you think I'd let my old man wait outside on a mat with Welcome on it?'

Helen sprang to her feet, her face eager.

'I'll soon be back,' she said. 'I want to change into my dressing-gown. Then we'll make tea and be comfortable.'

When she was outside in the basement hall, she paused in indecision. It was quicker to use the back way. But as she gazed up the dimly lit spiral of narrow stairs, she shrank back, feeling that nothing would induce her to go up them. There were too many twists on the way – too many corners. Anything – or anyone – might be lurking around the next bend – waiting to spring out upon her.

Although she knew her fear was absurd, she went up the front staircase. On the first landing she paused, arrested by a glimpse of the professor's bedroom, through his partially opened door. He had not begun to undress, but was sitting in a low chair before his fireless grate.

As she lingered, she started at the sound of a muffled cry from the blue room. She waited for it to be repeated, but heard nothing.

'I wish I knew what to do,' she thought.

There was something about the noise which alarmed her – a smothered note, as though a heavy hand were placed over someone's lips.

Presently she decided that she was the victim of her imagination. Lady Warren had called out in a nightmare, or else the nurse was trying to check her snores.

But as she climbed the next flight of stairs she discovered to her dismay that she dreaded reaching the second floor. All the bedrooms, with the exception of her own, were now empty. There were too many hiding-places for anyone who might have crept up the back stairs as she mounted the front.

When she tried to open her door she thought, at first, that somebody was inside, shutting her out, so strong was the pressure of the draught. But as she snapped on the light, she saw only the rise and fall of the carpet, like the swell of the sea.

She looked around the overcrowded room, at the painted mirror, the wall-bracket to hold a duster, the photograph of Lady Warren the First, the numerous tiny shelves of the toilet-table, each with its lace mat. 'I suppose that governess-girl's room looked very much like mine,' she thought.

There seemed to be some septic aura hanging around Nurse Barker which had the property of arousing fear. She had stood for only a few minutes outside the blue room, yet her serenity had fled. It was of no use reminding herself that Oates was probably on his homeward journey; he might be as near as the front gate, and still be too late.

Up on the second floor, the full force of the gale was evident. A crack on the window made Helen look round nervously. It sounded as though someone were forcing his way inside.

Although she knew that it was impossible, she crossed to the casement and drew aside the curtain. Instantly, the black shape which had terrified her before swung across, apparently touching the glass.

It was an unpleasant illusion, as though the tree was animated by some persistent purpose. Helen redrew the curtain and sprang to the middle of the room, where she stared around her, in momentary panic. She felt that she was on the point of being attacked – like the other girl. At any moment, a window might burst open or a curtain bulge.

Although she did not know it, somewhere on the floor below a door was opened stealthily. A head swivelled around the landing – its eyes slanting to right and left. Someone stole across to the stairs leading up to the second floor.

Suddenly Helen's glance fell upon the cross which hung over her bed. In spite of the derision with which it had been assailed during dinner, the sight of it immediately calmed her terror. She reminded herself that its power was too enduring to be a fable or a myth. It would not fail her in her need.

Without a thought of the ill-fated governess, she drew her green dress over her head. Shaking it out, she braved the menace of the wardrobe. No one was hiding behind the hanging garments.

She felt more comfortable when she had put on her short blue woollen dressing-gown and heelless slippers, which made her appear smaller than ever. Stealing noiselessly down the stairs, she stopped, to listen again at the door of the blue room.

Suddenly the silence was broken by the whimper of an old woman. 'Nurse. Don't.'

Helen could not recognise the coarse voice which shouted back.

'Shut up – or I'll give you what for.'

Helen's fingers clenched into fists and her face grew red with rage. Lady Warren might be the scourge of the household, but she was old – and she was in the power of an ill-tempered woman.

But she had learned the penalty of personal interference. This time she determined that she would appeal to the professor.

The door of his room was still ajar, while he sat in his original posture. His head was turned away from her, but she could see his hand upon the arm of his chair. It struck her that it was rather curious that he should not have moved during her absence.

'If he's dropped off,' she wondered, 'ought I to wake him up?'

She crossed the carpet noiselessly, but when she came closer to the chair she was gripped by a terrible dread. The professor's face looked like a mask of yellowed wax, and his lids were clay-hued over his closed eyes. On the table, by his side, was a small bottle and an empty glass.

Seized with panic, she shook his arm. 'Professor,' she cried. 'Professor.'

She was no longer afraid of disturbing him. What she dreaded was not being able to awaken him.

22

Accident

Although Helen called him again and again, the professor did not stir. Driven to boldness, she gripped his shoulders and shook him violently. But he only fell back limply against the side of his chair, like a corpse galvanised to momentary life.

Stricken with panic, Helen dashed out of the room and rushed downstairs into the study. As she burst in, Miss Warren raised her eyes from her book.

'The professor,' gasped Helen. 'Come up to him. Quick. I think he's – dead.'

Her speech had the effect of rousing Miss Warren. She led the way, covering the stairs in long strides. When Helen panted after her into the bedroom, she was bending over the inanimate figure in the chair.

'Really, Miss Capel.' Her voice conveyed annoyance. 'I wish you would think twice before you frighten me unnecessarily.'

'But isn't he terribly ill?' asked Helen, looking fearfully at the corpse-like figure.

'Of course not. He has merely taken rather too much of a sleeping-draught.'

She picked up the bottle of quadronex and studied it.

'I do not credit my brother with the folly of taking too stiff a dose. He would not make such a brainless mistake. Probably he may not have calculated its effect on his own devitalised condition.'

She felt his pulse, and then turned away.

'He is all tight,' she said. 'We can do nothing but leave him in perfect quiet,'

Helen stayed, as though rooted to the carpet, staring down at the motionless figure. It seemed the peak of ironic fate that the professor had slipped away from them when she was just coming to appreciate his help.

Miss Warren crossed to the bed, picked up an eiderdown and laid it across her brother's knees.

'Come, Miss Capel,' she said.

'No,' said Helen. 'I – I'm afraid.'

'Afraid of what?'

'I don't know. But our very last man is gone,'

Miss Warren appeared struck by the remark.

'There has been a curiously thorough clearance,' she said. 'But I cannot see why you should be alarmed.'

'There's been a murder,' whispered Helen. 'There's a maniac somewhere. And everyone's going, one by one. I'm expecting things to happen now. It won't stop here. I may be left, all alone. Or you.'

'If you're nervous, why don't you stay with Nurse Barker?'

Helen shrank back as she recalled a recent incident.

'But I'm frightened of her, too,' she confessed. 'She's bullying Lady Warren. I heard her just now.'

Miss Warren opened her lips in indecision. It was not her habit to offer explanation, or confidence, to any employee. Some impulse, however, led her to break her rule.

'I do not usually discuss family matters with anyone outside the family,' she said stiffly, 'but I suppose you heard what happened to the last nurse?'

'Yes. Lady Warren threw something at her.'

'Exactly. It has happened before. Lady Warren is of an age and temperament when she cannot restrain her actions. Purely physical, you understand.'

Helen nodded, to show her comprehension of an evil temper allied to arrogance in a lady with a title.

'Unfortunately,' went on Miss Warren, 'the matron of the Nursing Home has told me that many of her staff are unwilling to come to The Summit. So I had to ask her to find a nurse who is used to restraining her patients. Someone kind, but *firm*.'

'I don't call her kind,' declared Helen. 'Won't you go in and see how Lady Warren is for yourself?'

'Very well. We will leave on the light here.'

As they crossed the landing to the blue room, Miss Warren frowned at an object lying on the carpet.

'What is that?' she asked, peering short-sightedly.

'A chisel,' replied Helen, brightening at the sight of it. 'I wondered where it was. I was going to try to screw up your door-handle, but I forgot.'

As she stooped to pick it up, Miss Warren took it from her and placed it on a chair inside her own room.

'It looked very untidy,' she said. 'Have you ever heard the saying:

> Sow an act, reap a habit.
> Sow a habit, reap character.
> Sow character, reap Destiny?'

Helen did not reply, for she realised that the question was only a reproof in disguise. She followed Miss Warren into the blue room. As no snores sounded from the dim white fleecy mound on the bed, Helen concluded that Lady Warren was really asleep.

'I hope she's not doped,' she thought uneasily.

The air smelt a trifle more sour, with its odours of rotten apples and rugs. It caused Miss Warren to shudder with distaste.

'A repulsive atmosphere for anyone who is not trained,' she said. 'I've had to endure it all day. It has affected my head. That is why I value Nurse Barker's services, even if you are unable to do so.'

Helen understood the hint.

'She means she'll back up the nurse, and I shall go to the wall,' she decided.

She was struck by the mildness of Miss Warren's manner when she tapped at the dressing-room door and asked, 'May we come in?'

Nurse Barker gave them permission. She was sitting, with her legs stretched across a chair, smoking a cigarette, which she laid down on the ashtray when she rose in grudging respect to her employer.

'I'm sorry to disturb you,' apologised Miss Warren. 'I only wanted to know if you'd had any trouble with Lady Warren?'

'She was rather naughty about her sedative,' replied Nurse Barker, 'but I soon persuaded her to take it.'

'Then I hope you will get a good night.'

'In this wind? What a hope. I'm staying up, like everyone else.'

'Who do you mean?' asked Miss Warren. 'I am going to bed. And the professor will certainly sleep until morning. He has taken a slight overdose of a sleeping-draught.'

Nurse Barker clicked contemptuously.

'Why didn't he ask me to measure out the right quantity?' she asked.

'The professor would hardly ask a woman to do what he could do better himself,' said Miss Warren stiffly. 'He might have been aware of what he was doing when he made sure of some sleep. He knows the importance of conserving his strength, with so many dependent on him.'

Nurse Barker was not listening to the hint of the source of her own wages. A phosphorescent gleam – half of alarm, half of satisfaction – lit up her deep-set eyes.

'Odd,' she gloated. 'It looks as if someone is clearing the way for himself.'

Helen saw panic leap into Miss Warren's eyes.

'How is that possible?' she asked. 'There is a good reason for all that has happened. Take one instance alone. Mr Rice and my nephew and his wife all left this house because I turned out that dog.'

'No, you must go back a bit further,' declared Nurse Barker. 'Did Rice know you hated dogs?'

'Yes.'

'*Ah.* Then, do you know who first told him about a dog for sale?'

Helen listened with a chill at her heart. Did the sequence of events appear harmless because she saw only the trivial links? How far back did the chain really stretch? To what dark brain did it lead?

It was a relief when Miss Warren spoke impatiently.

'Of course you could conjecture endlessly, but it is entirely futile. What sinister agency was at work when *I* forgot to screw the cap of the cylinder?'

Helen was on the point of giving the true explanation of the incident, where she remembered that she must not betray Mrs Oates's confidence. She listened, unhappily, while Nurse Barker turned the knife again.

'Now there are only three women in the house,' she said.

'Four,' corrected Helen proudly. 'I saw Mrs Oates was only confused. So I pulled her round. She's sober now.'

Miss Warren and the nurse stared at Helen.

'It seems to me,' said Miss Warren reflectively, 'that you are capable of looking after yourself.'

'I've done it all my life,' Helen assured her.

'I'm sure you're equal to an emergency, Miss Capel,' she said. 'All the same, if you do not intend to go to bed, I should feel easier in my mind if I knew you were with Mrs Oates.'

Helen, who was beginning to crumble under the combined excitement and strain, began to gulp at this unexpected sign of consideration.

She found Mrs Oates still slumped in her chair when she returned to the kitchen; but she had climbed out of her slough of depression. Some of her old jovial humour beamed from her eyes as she shook her finger at Helen.

'Stealing about on rubber heels?' she asked. 'Trying to put salt on my tail, are you. You'll find I'm too old a bird to be caught that way.'

'The plot thickens,' Helen said dramatically. 'Exit the professor.'

Mrs Oates listened to her story of the professor's comatose condition with little concern.'

'He's no loss,' she said. 'He never does anything but sit in his study, and think.'

'That's my point exactly,' explained Helen. 'Without him, we're a body without a head.'

Apparently, the same thought had occurred to Nurse Barker, for a little later she entered the kitchen with the dignity of a queen who had temporarily laid down her sceptre.

'I thought we had better have an agreement,' she said. 'In the professor's absence, who is to assume authority?'

'The mistress, of course,' replied Mrs Oates.

'She's not competent,' declared Nurse Barker. 'She is definitely a neurotic type. You must allow me to know my own subject.'

'I shall continue to take my orders from her,' said Helen. 'She engaged me, and she pays my salary.'

'Hear, hear,' Mrs Oates clapped her hands. 'Listen to the doctor's young lady, telling you off.'

'I didn't know you were engaged to Dr Parry,' said Nurse Barker.

Her lips were sucked together in a thin line while her sunken eyes gleamed with jealousy.

'I'm not,' said Helen hastily.

Although the subject was obviously no business of hers Nurse Barker seemed unable to discard it.

'I suppose it's your size,' she said. 'Rum how men always choose short women. It's a sign of their own mental inferiority. They know that your brain corresponds with your size, and they feel unable to cope with their intellectual equals.'

The speech made Helen see red, for she was sensitive on the score of her defective education.

'Perhaps they find us more attractive,' she said.

Nurse Barker lit a cigarette with fingers which shook with passion.

'You mean to insult me deliberately,' she said huskily. 'Isn't that rather unwise? Very soon you'll be left alone with me.'

'Mrs Oates will be here, too,' Helen reminded her.

'Will she?' Nurse Barker gave a meaning laugh. 'If I were you I wouldn't bank upon that.' Puffing fiercely at her cigarette, she tramped out into the hall.

'What did she mean?' asked Helen uneasily.

'Bilge,' commented Mrs Oates. 'All the same,' she added gloomily, 'we didn't ought to do it. She came down here for a crack and we turned her sour. I began it and you finished it.'

'She shouldn't leave poor old Lady Warren so much,' said Helen defensively.

'Now, don't go and be sorry for her,' advised Mrs Oates. 'She can take care of herself. Locking up them two is like shutting in a lion with a tiger. You wonder which will walk out in the morning.'

'I wish I could be sure that Lady Warren can defend herself,' Helen said. 'I've got a real fear of that nurse.'

'Don't let her know it,' advised Mrs Oates.

'No.' Helen glanced at the clock. 'I wish I knew exactly whereabouts on the road Mr Oates is at this minute,' she sighed. 'The time seems to crawl. If only I can last out till he comes.'

'Why shouldn't you?'

'I've a terror of one thing,' confessed Helen.

'Don't tell me,' urged Mrs Oates. 'You never know who may be listening to you.'

Helen opened the kitchen door and looked into the deserted basement hall.

'This is what I'm scared of,' she said. 'Supposing I heard a child crying outside. I believe I should have to go out. Just in case, you know.'

'Now, don't you go and be a fool,' implored Mrs Oates. 'In all the time I've been here there's never been a baby parked on the doorstep. Miss Warren's not the sort to come home with a bundle in her arms.'

Helen laughed as she sprang to her feet.

'I feel so guilty,' she said. 'She'll be wanting to go to bed soon, and the handle of her door is not screwed up.'

Grateful for a job, she ran upstairs, to the first floor. Everything seemed especially safe and normal as she passed through the hall. When she reached the first-floor landing she noticed that the light was shining through the transom above Miss Warren's bedroom door.

'I hope she's not going to bed,' she thought, as she tapped at the door.

'Yes,' called Miss Warren's voice.

'Oh, Miss Warren,' said Helen. 'I'm terribly sorry to disturb you, but could you hand me out the tools you put on your chair?'

'Certainly, Miss Capel, only don't leave them outside again.'

Helen heard Miss Warren's step crossing the polished boards and then saw the handle revolved in an impotent whirl.

She watched it, in slight surprise.

'Can't you open the door?' she asked.

'No,' was the reply. 'The handle keeps turning round in my hand.'

22

What Shall We Do with the Drunken Sailor?

Although vaguely disturbed, Helen felt mistress of the situation.

'It's all right,' she called. 'I'll open it, this side.'

Full of confidence; she gripped the handle, only to feel it slip round in her fingers, as though it were oiled.

'It seems to have gone completely,' she cried. 'You have the tools. Do you think you could manage to put it right?'

'No, the screw is missing,' was the reply. 'It doesn't matter. Oates will repair it early tomorrow.'

'But, Miss Warren,' persisted Helen, 'it's not right you should be locked in. Suppose – suppose there's a fire?'

'Why should we suppose it? Please go, Miss Capel. I have important work to finish.'

'Is the key your side?' Helen asked.

'No. The lock is broken, so I had a bolt fitted instead. Now, please leave me in peace.'

Helen turned forlornly away. As she passed the blue room, Nurse Barker, who had been attracted by the noise, poked her head around the door.

'What's the matter now?' she asked.

When Helen explained the situation she gave a disagreeable laugh. 'What did I tell you? She locked herself in, on purpose.'

'I can't believe it,' declared Helen. 'Why should she do that?'

'Funk. Oh, *I've* seen it coming on . . . *And* I've seen something else, which is due before very long. Your troubles are not over yet, my girl.'

Helen was impressed by the woman's perspicacity.

'Nurse,' she cried impulsively, 'I want to apologise to you. If I've hurt your feelings, it was unintentional.'

'Rather late in the day to eat humble-pie,' sneered Nurse Barker. 'The harm's done.'

'But can't I do something to make up?'

'You can pledge yourself to obedience.'

Helen hesitated to give her promise, as her thoughts flew to Dr Parry. She knew that Nurse Barker would do everything in her power to block his interference. On the other hand, he was not likely to rush over to The Summit, while the woman was a formidable obstacle to any move on the part of the maniac; she had extraordinary physical strength and a mind like a steel trap.

She gave a military salute. 'I promise, sergeant,' she said.

'This is no joke,' frowned Nurse Barker. 'I'm not sure I can trust you. In all my experience, I've never been so grossly insulted as I have by you and Mrs Oates – an intoxicated char and a raw, untrained girl.'

'Oh, nurse,' she said, '*I* never said anything to insult you.'

Nurse Barker harked back to the conversation she had overheard.

'Yes, she said it,' she agreed. 'But you were lapping up her words.'

'No, I had to humour her, because she was a trifle cockeyed. I never thought what she did.'

'*What* did she think?'

Helen was reminded of the alleged hypnotic power of a serpent, as Nurse Barker held her with a glittering eye.

'She thought you were a man,' she admitted.

Nurse Barker swallowed convulsively.

'She'll pay for that,' she muttered, as she turned back to the blue room.

Helen reviewed as much of the past as she could remember on her way downstairs. She wished that her conscience was entirely clear on the score of Nurse Barker, as she hated to feel a hypocrite.

On the whole, she felt tolerably comfortable. She had discounted the razor incident, and had mentioned it to no one. When Mrs Oates had boasted of her conquests, she had disclaimed them. Her dislike of the nurse was her own affair.

The sight of the telephone reminded her of the latest casualties, which she had almost forgotten. One fear had again driven out another; for the present, she stood chiefly in dread of Nurse Barker.

'I think I'll ring up Dr Parry,' she thought, 'and tell him what's happened.'

It was a long time before she got through to him, and when, at last, she heard Dr Parry's voice, it sounded gruff and sleepy.

'What's up?' he asked.

'The professor's drugged himself,' replied Helen, 'and Miss Warren's locked in her bedroom.'

As Dr Parry made no comment, Helen hastened to excuse her action.

'I suppose I shouldn't have bothered you. But it does seem queer the way they're all disappearing, one by one. What do you think?'

'Blowed if I know,' was the reply. 'It's hard to advise. I think Miss Warren is the wisest. Why don't you follow her good example?'

'Because – you won't believe me, after all the fuss I made about sleeping in her room – but I don't like to leave old Lady Warren alone with that nurse.'

'D'you think the nurse rough-handles her?'

'I don't know. But I do know she has a horrible temper.'

'Then I'll give you a tip. If it should come to a scrap between those two, put your shirt on the old one.'

Although Mrs Oates had voiced the same opinion, Helen was not convinced.

'Thank you for your advice,' she said. 'I'm sorry I bothered you, but you encouraged me to be a nuisance.'

'Here – don't ring off,' urged the doctor. 'I'm wondering what to do about the professor. Ought I to come over?'

'He looks awful,' declared Helen, making the most of her chance.

'He would. What did Miss Warren do?'

'Felt his pulse, and covered him up.'

'Good.' Helen could hear his sigh of relief. 'That sounds all right. She's a clever woman. Now, we'll leave it at this. If I should change my mind regarding the situation I'll bike over at once. In fact, you've only to say one word, and I'll start now.'

'You'd come for me?' asked Helen.

'For you, only.'

In spite of her exhaustion and loneliness – in spite of the menace of the night – Helen became suddenly surcharged with glorious life.

'Now I know that,' she said, 'I don't want you to come. I feel gorgeous. I – '

She rang off at the sound of a footstep on the landing. Nurse Barker was leaning over the balustrade, looking down at her.

'Who was that?' she asked.

'The doctor,' replied Helen. 'I rang him up, to tell him about the professor, but he decided that it was not necessary for him to come over.'

'He would prefer to take us by surprise,' prophesied Nurse Barker. 'I don't trust that young man . . . And hadn't you better go to your alcoholic patient? You're giving her more rope than I should.'

Filled with sudden misgiving, Helen hurried across the hall. As she opened the door leading to the basement, she kicked in front of her some hard object, which bumped from step to step with an appalling clatter. Running downstairs after it, she picked up, from the mat at the bottom, a small pint milk-can.

'Mrs Oates,' she cried, as she entered the kitchen, 'who put this at the top of the stairs?'

'I don't know,' replied Mrs Oates.

In sudden suspicion, Helen looked up at the dresser. To her relief, the bottle was still on the top and apparently untouched.

In spite of this proof of her innocence, Helen fancied she detected a deterioration in Mrs Oates. The maudlin grin, which robbed her face of its underhung tenacity, hovered around her lips, imparting a muddled expression. As Helen watched her, the lines of a sea-shanty swam into her head. 'What shall we do with the drunken sailor?'

'After tonight, I could write a book on the subject,' she thought, with the glib assurance of one who only wrote a letter as a penance.

It was evident that Mrs Oates was making stupendous efforts to concentrate on Helen's tale of Miss Warren's door-handle, for she kept repeating every point, in the form of a question.

'Oates will want some supper,' was her only comment. Helen took the hint, and picked up a tray.

'I'll help you get it,' she said. 'Get up.'

Placing her hands under Mrs Oates's armpits, she gave a strong hoist. But the woman only slipped back again.

'You must let me take it easy for a bit longer,' she advised. 'Remember, I've a half-bottle inside me. I'll soon be all right.'

'All right,' said Helen. 'I'll carry on, alone.'

It struck her that it might be a valuable test of her own willpower, to go alone into the larder. As she opened the scullery door and snapped on the switch, every corner of its clean bareness was revealed by the yellow glow. Outside, in the passage, she could hear the loose window banging against its shutter.

The sound was distinctly nerve-racking, for it gave the impression that someone was determined to force an entry. The passage, too, looked a gloomy tunnel, in the dim light. Around the bend, stretched the dark labyrinth of Murder Lane.

Helen knew that she must keep her imagination strictly controlled. She must not think of the horror which had actually taken place within these walls, or wonder if the girl still lingered somewhere in the atmosphere, the dust or the stones.

Reminding herself that she had policed this stretch herself, and searched thoroughly every potential hiding-place, she entered the larder.

Besides a side of bacon and string of onions, its shelves held so many tins and bottles that Helen's curiosity took charge of the situation. The Summit laid in a varied store of preserved provisions, so that it was difficult to make a choice. Her eye was greedier than her stomach, as she piled her tray with tongue, sardines, dainties in aspic and pots of savoury paste.

Balancing the tray on her hip, she switched off the light at the same time as she kicked open the scullery door. Instantly, there was a loud rattle, as a tin tray crashed down on the stone flags.

Helen frowned thoughtfully, for she did not like the repetition of the trick. Suddenly she was rent with a suspicion which was vaguely alarming. Mrs Oates could not hear her when she walked soundlessly in bedroom slippers, so she had placed these tins in order to have some warning of her approach.

If it were true, she had something to hide. She was not playing the game. In spite of her load, Helen crashed recklessly into the kitchen.

Mrs Oates was still in her chair, her back turned towards Helen, while Nurse Barker stood over her, with folded arms.

'Where have you been?' she asked.

'Larder,' explained Helen. 'Getting some supper for Mr Oates. We thought we could all do with a snack, just to pass the time. Could you?'

Nurse Barker nodded, while a peculiar smile flickered round her lips, causing Helen to rush into nervous explanations.

'I thought Mrs Oates and I would have ours down here and I'd carry up yours into your dressing-room. Will that suit you? And what kind of sandwiches would you like?'

'Ask Mrs Oates which she would prefer,' said Nurse Barker. 'I thought you undertook responsibility for her.'

Filled with foreboding, Helen slammed down her tray and rushed around to Mrs Oates. But, before she could reach her, the woman stretched her arms upon the table, and laid her head on them.

'What's the matter?' cried Helen. 'Are you ill?'

Mrs Oates opened one eye, with difficulty. 'I'm that sleepy,' she said, 'I – I –'

As her voice died away, Helen shook her shoulder.

'Wake up,' she cried. 'Don't leave me. You promised.'

A gleam of smothered recollection fought with the guilt in Mrs Oates's eyes, and then died out.

'Someone's – got – me,' she said. 'I'm doped.'

Dropping her head again on her arms, she closed her lids and began to breathe heavily.

With a horrible sense of helplessness, Helen watched her sink into stupefied slumber. Nurse Barker stood by, licking her lips, as though savouring the humour of the situation. Presently Helen broke the silence.

'Can we do anything?'

'Why not offer her a drink?' asked Nurse Barker derisively. 'A stimulant might revive her.'

Helen recognised the advice for a jeer. There was no doubt in her mind as to the cause of the catastrophe. Just as burglars drug a watchdog, as prelude to robbery, someone had taken advantage of her absence to tamper with Mrs Oates.

Afraid to tax Nurse Barker with the offence – even while she was sure of her guilt – she tried to keep her suspicion from her face and voice.

'What's the matter with her?'

Nurse Barker gave a scornful bark.

'Don't be a fool,' she said. 'It's obvious. She's drunk as a lord.'

23

A Supper Party

In spite of her shock, Nurse Barker's words were almost a relief to Helen. Like an explosion inside her head, they shot away the foul cobwebs of suspicion.

No treachery had been at work – just frailty, a landslide of Mrs Oates's good intentions before the pressure of temptation.

'How could she get at the brandy?' she asked. 'I'm sure she was not in a condition to climb on the dresser.'

Nurse Barker kicked forward a substantial footstool, mounted it, stretched out her arm, and removed the bottle from the top shelf.

'You forget everyone is not a midget like yourself,' she said. 'Mrs Oates is not so tall as I am, but she has the reach of a gorilla.'

Helen bit her lip as she realised how easily she had been duped.

'You must think me a gull,' she said. 'But I counted on her promise. All the same, she's not touched the brandy. The bottle's still half full.'

Sniffing scornfully, Nurse Barker uncorked the bottle, smelt the cork, and then shook out a few drops on the back of her hand.

'Water,' she remarked.

Helen looked reproachfully down at Mrs Oates, sunken deep in hot and steamy sleep.

'What shall we do with her?' she asked helplessly.

'Leave her where she is.'

'But can't I put a bandage soaked in vinegar and water round her head?' persisted Helen. 'She seems so hot and uncomfortable.'

'You'll do nothing of the sort,' snapped Nurse Barker. 'She has let us down, and we've no time for her. She's nothing but lumber. Get supper. I've had no dinner, and I'm sinking. Bring the tray up to my room. We'll have it there.'

Although the words promised a new partnership, Helen felt like a fag to a new bully.

'What would you like?' she asked eagerly.

'Cold meat, potatoes, pickles, cheese. Don't stop to cut sandwiches. Make a strong pot of tea. Remember, we've got to keep awake.'

'You don't really think there's any danger?' asked Helen apprehensively.

Nurse Barker looked at her fixedly.

'I'm in luck to be saddled with you. You're a fool and a fool is twice as dangerous as a knave. Can you do elementary arithmetic?'

'Of course.'

'Well, then, there were nine persons in the house at dinner-time. Now there are only two. How many have gone?'

'Seven,' gasped Helen, horrified by the shrinkage.

Nurse Barker licked her lips with gloomy relish.

'And do you realise what it means?' she asked. 'It means he's getting very close to you.'

Although Helen was sure that Nurse Barker was playing on her fear, her heart sank as the woman went out of the room. In spite of her malevolent nature, she was some sort of company. One catastrophe after another had so weakened her resistance that she felt terrified at being alone in the basement. Every bang on the passage window was duplicated by a knock at her heart. Although, down below, the roar of the storm was muted, the garden was nearer. She remembered how the bushes had writhed, like knotted fingers tapping the glass, and how the tentacles of the undergrowth had swayed in mimicry of subaqueous life.

'It's trying to get in,' she thought. 'Suppose there is some secret entrance I overlooked. Anyone could hide between the two staircases and in all the empty rooms.'

Her one wish was to get upstairs as soon as possible. Although she had time to gather the food while she waited for the kettle to boil, her appetite for dainties had deserted her. She hastily prepared the supper-tray, and then returned to her sitting-room to watch the kettle. As she did so, her thoughts jerked disconnectedly, like the limping music of an old barrel-organ.

'I believe Miss Warren was grateful to be locked in. But the accident couldn't have happened if I hadn't been so careless. She quoted that bit about actions and character, just to tell me it was my fault. So, between us, we're responsible for that part of it . . . And no one else.'

Although she was comforted by her logic, she shied at the question it raised. Was there some unseen link in the chain which had precipitated – or influenced – this interplay of character?

She, with her impulsive carelessness – Miss Warren, with her selfishness – and Mrs Oates, with her craving – had each acted as an independent agent – true to its own type. Yet the board was rearranged as though they had been pawns, used in someone's game; whatever the impulse of their moves, they were now placed to suit the unseen player.

The kettle coughed out a gust of steam and the lid rose, with a spill of water. Helen made the tea hurriedly and crabbed up the stairs, shooting nervous glances over her shoulder. At the top she kicked the door closed behind her.

There were no snores from the bed when she passed through the dim blue room, doing her utmost to subdue the rattle of the china. Inside the dressing-room Nurse Barker was lighting a new cigarette from her old stub. She broke into a complaint as Helen put down the tray.

'I've nearly broken my fingers trying to turn that key.' She nodded towards the second door. 'Disgusting, putting me in a room next to a man's bedroom, with a connecting-door.'

'It used to be a dressing-room,' explained Helen. 'Besides, the professor is not like that. He won't pay you a visit tonight.'

She turned away to hide her grin. Besides amusing her, the incident had raised her spirits, for it had laid Mrs Oates's hare as dead as stone. The last vestige of her suspicion faded, as she realised that Nurse Barker's fingers lacked the requisite strength of a thug.

'Shall we open the door, so that you can hear Lady Warren call you?' she asked.

'She won't,' grunted Nurse Barker. 'I've fixed her.'

'D' you mean you've sedated her, like – like babies?'

'Well, why not? That's all she is – an old baby.'

'But – it seems rather drastic.'

Nurse Barker merely grunted, as she poured out a cup of tea, to which she added several drops of brandy. Helen watched her, in astonishment, as she piled her plate with cold potatoes and thick slices of cold meat, smothered with pickles.

'Enough for a man,' she thought, as she followed the clearance of the meal with wide-eyed interest.

The spirit improved Nurse Barker's temper for she held out the bottle, in invitation. 'Like a drop in your tea?'

'No, thank you.'

'You'll need it before you're much older. That guy has tasted blood. You saw how Mrs Oates couldn't keep off the bottle after she'd started it. She had to finish. He's the same – only he's a famished tiger, with dripping chops.'

Helen put down the bit of cheese she was nibbling.

'Nurse,' she asked, 'why do you dislike me?'

'Because you remind me of someone I hate,' replied Nurse Barker. 'She was the spit of you – a little skinny thing, all legs and giggles, with frizzed-out hair, like a doll. Only, she was a blonde.'

'Why did you hate the horrid little blonde?' Helen asked, with a spurt of her native curiosity.

'Because of a man,' Nurse Barker replied. 'It was when I was a probationer. He was a doctor, and very clever. But he was so small, I could have lain him across my knee and spanked him.'

'That's the attraction of contrast,' said Helen. 'Were you engaged?'

Her interest was not assumed, because Nurse Barker's strange confidence had stirred up the sweetness of her own romance. 'Odd,' she thought, with a flicker of her submerged sense of drama. 'Here we are – the long and the short of it – coming together over a cup of tea, because we are both in love.'

'Not engaged,' replied Nurse Barker. 'Just leading up. It would have happened. But the blonde took him away from me, curse her.'

'What a shame,' said Helen, with real sympathy.

'Shame?' Nurse Barker laughed bitterly. 'It was my life. That was my only man. There's never been another – never will be.'

'Were they married?' asked Helen.

'No, she threw him over. She only wanted to take him from me. But there was only the husk of him left. Nothing for me. That's why I hate women like her. If a man wanted to twist their throats, I'd say good luck to him.'

As Nurse Barker glared at Helen the girl shrank into her shell. Her desire to talk about her own hope faded; she only sought for some way to avert the penalty of an unlucky resemblance.

'Do you know,' she said, 'you and I have a lot in common. We're in the same boat. Men have always ignored me – because I am *small*.'

The greedy glitter in Nurse Barker's eyes told her that she had swallowed the bait.

'Isn't the doctor your fancy-man?' she asked.

'Of course not. That was only Mrs Oates's fairy tale. I've never had a real affair. I've always had to earn my own living, and I've never had money to buy clothes.'

'Are you speaking the truth?' insisted Nurse. Barker.

Helen nodded, as she remembered the humiliation and neglect which had marked her girlhood. And Nurse Barker believed her, in spite of her likeness to the blonde, as she stared at her with penetrating eyes.

At that moment Helen appeared to her an ill-developed scrap – superfluous, unskilled labour – nobody's woman. If she were murdered, she would not be missed, or mourned, and one more job would be released.

But, although she felt only contempt for the weakling, she no longer bore her a grudge.

As she took up the bottle of brandy Helen gave a cry of protest.

'Please don't.'

'D' you think I'm going to pass out on a drop of brandy?' sneered Nurse Barker.

'It's not that. But after what's happened, I'm terrified. Suppose that brandy is doped.'

'If it is, you'll be left all alone. I'll risk it.' She raised the cup to her lips and drained it. 'It might be the best thing that could happen to me,' she continued. 'When he comes, he'll go for you. If I interfere, he'll turn on me, too.'

'But I'd stick to you,' cried Helen. 'There's only two of us left. If anything happened to you, I think I should go mad with terror.'

'It all depends on you,' said Nurse Barker spitefully. 'You are the weak spot. You'd double-cross me to save your own skin.'

It seemed useless to argue further. Unable to eat, Helen sat and watched Nurse Barker finish her supper. It was a protracted process, for she smoked between mouthfuls.

The small room was hazed with smoke, so that Nurse Barker's gigantic white figure loomed through a fog. Sometimes Helen's vision played her a trick and she appeared to spread out like a cloud. The atmosphere, too, was close and torrid as a jungle.

'I must keep awake,' she thought desperately. 'If I take my eyes off her, she will disappear.'

Yet, even as she strove to concentrate on her surroundings, at the back of her mind was a desperate conviction that she was trying to grip something, which, even then, was slipping through her fingers. Mrs Oates had failed her, and Nurse Barker would fail her too. But, at least, the night was passing. Apparently the same thought struck Nurse Barker, for she glanced at her little travelling-clock upon the mantelpiece.

'We may expect him now, any minute,' she said. 'I wonder what his first move will be.'

Helen checked her shudder as she realised that the bully was merely tormenting the new fag, in order to make her squeak. With a flicker of her old spirit, she made a sudden counter-attack.

'Don't forget this,' she said. 'No one seems to trouble much about me, alive – but I'd be mighty important if I was dead. If anything happened to me, here, tonight, there'd be an inquiry, and lots of publicity, And they'd hold *you* responsible,'

Nurse Barker's eyes narrowed, for she had overlooked this contingency. She had to depend on her profession for a living, and her reputation might be damaged if she had to undergo a gruelling examination at an inquest and could not disprove a charge of cowardice.

'Don't be a fool,' she said. 'We hang together – What is that noise?'

Helen heard it, too – a low, muffled thud, from somewhere downstairs.

'It sounds like knocking,' she said.

'Don't go to find out,' Nurse Barker warned her. 'It may be a trick.'

'But I *must*. It might be Oates.'

Before Nurse Barker could stop her, she had opened the door, and was running noiselessly through the blue room. When she reached the landing, the sound was clear and imperative – a loud tattoo on the front door, followed by the pealing of the bell.

Helen stopped dead and gripped the balustrade – her brain paralysed by the poison of Nurse Barker's warning. The person who waited outside *might* be Oates, who had returned – sooner than she had dared to hope. Yet – for that very reason – she dared not stir.

Suddenly a new idea possessed her. Instinctively she knew that Dr Parry was knocking at the door. In spite of his reassuring words, he had not been satisfied with the situation at The Summit.

Her eyes shining with welcome, she dashed down the stairs, just as Nurse Barker reached the landing.

'Stop,' she shouted. 'Don't open the door.'

'I must,' panted Helen, calling over her shoulder. 'It's the doctor. He promised to come. I *must*.'

She heard Nurse Barker's heavy footsteps thudding in pursuit, and she tried to run faster. In spite of her efforts, however, just as she reached the swing doors leading to the lobby, she felt herself held in strong arms.

'Hush, you little fool,' whispered Nurse Barker hoarsely, as she laid her hand over Helen's lips. 'He's outside.'

25

The Watcher

In spite of the conviction in Nurse Barker's voice, Helen continued to struggle. She was positive that Dr Parry was outside the door. It was torture to feel he was so near to her and yet she could not break through to him.

From the first she knew she was beaten, for Nurse Barker had her pinioned inside one arm, while she pressed her hand heavily over her face. The strength of her grip was amazing and Helen could only kick – feebly, but frantically – with soft felt soles.

The knocking and ringing seemed to go on for an eternity. When it ceased, Nurse Barker did not relax her grasp, but waited, until she heard a distant hammering from another part of the house.

'He's gone round to the back door,' she said grimly. 'He's persistent. And so am I.'

Helen could only writhe weakly, for her sufferings had become physical as well as mental. She felt on the point of suffocation, from the iron pressure around her ribs and over her mouth. When, after a second pause, the assault was renewed on the front door, she had reached the limit of endurance.

'Go away, dear. It's no good. For my sake. Go away. It's no good.'

As though he actually heard her voiceless entreaties, which raced in a circle round her brain, the knocking was succeeded by so prolonged a silence that Nurse Barker released her.

'Oh,' gasped Helen, stroking her neck tenderly. 'You've nearly choked me.'

Nurse Barker gave a short, grating laugh.

'So that's the thanks I get. Pity I didn't let him in. He'd have cured you of sore throats for a long time to come. You are not worth the saving.'

'You didn't save me,' Helen said. 'That was Dr Parry.'

'How do you know?'

'Because he promised he would come to me.'

Nurse Barker drew her bushy brows together. 'You told me he was not your lover.'

Helen felt too low-spirited to protest.

'What does it matter – now?' she asked wearily. 'You've sent him away.'

'Only this. It means you lied to me, just now. You tried to trade on my sympathy. And all the time you were laughing at me, up your sleeve.'

As Helen looked at the inflamed face, she remembered Stephen Rice's remark that her personal safety depended largely on the character of her companions. She could tell by the congestion of Nurse Barker's colour that she had plunged herself into a hell of jealousy. Suddenly she felt so sorry for the vindictive, unattractive woman that she lost her dislike.

'I told you the truth,' she said gently. 'It only happened tonight.'

'*What* happened?'

'Nothing.' Helen gave a little low laugh. 'But – it's everything, all the same. There's something in him that draws out something in me. So, he must feel the same, or he couldn't call to me. You understand, don't you? It happened to you, too.'

In her eagerness to forge a link between them, she caught Nurse Barker's hand. But the woman pushed her away with such force that she fell on her knees.

'Yes,' she said, 'I know exactly how it begins. I know the end, too. A hollow cheat, with frizzy hair, like yours.'

'But it's not fair to punish me for someone else's transgression,' protested Helen. 'I've done you no harm.'

'And you've done me no good. You've been pert and insolent about my personal appearance. Because I'm tall, and my face shows character, you dared to compare me to a man.'

'I never did. Oh, do be friendly, if only for tonight. We oughtn't to be fighting like this.'

'Oh, yes, I get your angle. Men find small women more attractive, don't they? But small women need protection. You'll miss me when I'm gone, and you are left alone.'

The words struck a chill to Helen's heart.

'If that happened,' she said, 'I think I should die of fear. But I won't.'

'It may.' The woman looked down her nose, while a fugitive smile flitted across her lips. 'We have assumed that the professor is drugged, and the cook is drunk. But how do we know that they've not been doped?'

It was a horrible possibility, which appalled Helen as she remembered Mrs Oates's mumbled excuse.

'Who could dope them?' she cried.

'Someone might have crept in by the basement,' suggested Nurse Barker. 'Things have been most peculiar all the night, just as if someone was at work on the inside.' She added, with sinister meaning, 'We shall know, if I pass out. I took brandy in my tea. I wonder if that's why I feel so dizzy?'

As she spoke, she staggered slightly, and passed her hand over her brow. Helen stared at her, speechless with horror. In spite of the woman's venom, she clung to her as desperately as a drowning person clings to his rescuer.

Although her common sense reminded her that Nurse Barker was using this alarmist policy in order to terrify her, events over which she had no control seemed to indicate some subterranean direction of the general withdrawal.

One after another her companions had left her. They slept, while she remained, to watch. In the end, she would be alone.

Determined that Nurse Barker should not have the satisfaction of knowing that she had drawn blood, she kept her head high and her lips steady. But Nurse Barker looked at her eyes and noticed how the pupils had swamped the iris.

Helen saw her smile, and was suddenly driven to hit back.

'I can't understand why you should grudge me my first chance of happiness,' she said. 'It's mean. When I was hungry, it didn't help me to know others were hungry, too. In fact, it was worse, for I always had bread, and could guess what it meant to those who had nothing at all.'

'Oh? So you've starved?' asked Nurse Barker.

'Not exactly. But I've gone very short, in between jobs.'

'That only proves you're of no use. There's a glut of unskilled labour. You'd never be missed.'

Again Helen glimpsed the blue star of daylight shining at the end of the tunnel.

'I wish it was tomorrow,' she sighed. 'Oh, nurse, help me to come safely through the night.'

'Why? You wouldn't put yourself out for me.'

'I do wish I could prove that I would,' Helen said eagerly. 'I was a horrible little beast. But you've grown on me. I think I understand, now, how your doctor felt.'

Nurse Barker listened in silence, her expression enigmatic. In the pause the telephone-bell rang, with startling shrillness. The sound was music to Helen's ears, and she felt a wave of relief that the wires had not been cut in true Hollywood tradition.

She rushed across the hall, her pale face suddenly vivid with a radiant glow. 'You were right, as usual,' she panted. 'Dr Parry wasn't outside, for he's ringing me now.'

She was so sure of hearing his voice when she took up the receiver that her disappointment was acute at the sound of mincing feminine accents.

'Is thet The Summit?'

'Summit speaking,' replied Helen dully. The next minute, she spoke to Nurse Barker. 'The call's for you.'

Nurse Barker arose with an air of importance.

'Who is ringing me?' she asked.

'I don't know.'

Unconscious of impending disaster, Helen watched Nurse Barker with none of her usual interest.

'Nurse Barker speaking. Who is it? . . . Oh, is it you, dear?'

The secretary of the Nursing Home replied warmly. 'How nice to hear your voice, dear. I'm still on duty. We've a rush op, and I'm trying to get Blake. He's on holiday, and I'm chasing him all over England. So, while I'm waiting I thought I'd ring you up, just in case you hadn't gone to bed.'

'Not much chance of that,' said Nurse Barker.

'That doesn't sound too bright. Isn't the case comfortable?'

'Most *un*comfortable. In fact, it's all most unpleasant and very peculiar.'

'I'm not surprised, dear. I think you ought to know that someone rang me up and asked me the most extraordinary questions about *you*.'

'About me?'

Helen caught the inflection of Nurse Barker's voice. With a sinking heart, she listened to her half of the dialogue.

'Please repeat that . . . Indeed. Anything else? . . . *What*? The insolence . . . *Who* rang you up? . . . You are sure it was a girl's voice? . . . When? Please try to remember, because I mean to trace this back to its source . . . Are you sure that was the time? . . . Then I know which girl it was, for the other had left the house . . . Not at all. You are quite right to let me know. Goodbye.'

Nurse Barker rang off, and looked at Helen.

'You wanted to prove yourself?' she asked. 'Well, you've done it. Completely. You're a liar and a sneak. If I could save your neck by lifting my little finger, I wouldn't do it.'

Helen opened her lips dumbly, in an effort to try to explain. But her mind felt as incapable of coagulation as a lightly boiled egg. She could only realise that she had alienated the defence, and that a man was prowling outside in the streaming darkness.

The man was still there, circling the house. Lashed by the gale, twigs flogged his face like wire whips as he stooped over the sodden ground to examine each small basement window.

Once he thought he had found a vulnerable spot, for a casement shook before his pressure. Inserting his penknife inside the frame, he hacked away a makeshift fastening of a peg and some string, but only to meet the resistance of an inner shutter.

The house was armed to its teeth. It was blind and impregnable as an armoured car.

Dr Parry should have been pleased by this evidence of obedience to his orders. He had advised the most stringent precautions. Yet, as he looked upwards at the blank walls, seeking in vain a gleam of light from some upper window, he felt a chill.

He had always disliked the tree-muffled isolation of The Summit, although he was a lover of solitude.

Endowed with swift intuitions – swayed by violent likes and dislikes, he recognised – and fought – a streak of superstition in his nature. At that moment he distrusted the exterior of the Victorian house, whose tall chimneys seemed to pierce the ragged clouds.

Suddenly he thought of a simple way of getting into communication with Helen. Snapping on his lighter, he searched in his pockets to find a scrap of paper. When he had discovered an old envelope, he managed, with difficulty, to scrawl a message upon it. Then he slipped it into the letter-box and gave the postman's traditional double-knock.

'That'll bring her down, quicker than a stick of dynamite,' he thought, as he withdrew to a position on the gravel drive which commanded a view of the house.

As the minutes passed, however, and no signal-light gleamed from any of the upper windows, he grew apprehensive. The lack of response was not typical of Helen's curious nature. With a memory of her sensational scampers up the stairs, he knew that it would not take her long to reach the second floor, even if she had followed his advice to sleep in the basement.

Presently he grew tired of standing in the rain, as though he were planted with the trees. It was evident that The Summit – adopting the character of a respectable widow – was not at home to stray knocks, after dark.

He was on the point of turning away, when a light glowed in a bedroom on the second floor. The window was closed, but not shuttered, and screened by a light curtain of turquoise-blue.

At the sight his face lit up with welcome. Not until he was on the point of hearing her voice again, did he realise the strength of his feeling for Helen. The glow in his heart rose to his lips and flamed into a smile. His lover's rapture made the subsequent disappointment the keener. With a shock of positive horror, he saw – thrown upon the light screen of the curtain – a furtive, crouching shadow.

It was the head and shoulders of a man.

26

Sailor's Sense

Outside The Summit was elemental fury; inside, the clash of human passions. Terrified by Nurse Barker's dark, swollen face, Helen grew almost frantic in her efforts to conciliate her.

'Oh, can't you understand?' she implored. 'It was after the murder. We were all worked up and jumpy. Honestly, I thought it would clear the air if I made certain we'd got the right nurse. You see, Mrs Oates was sure you were an impostor.'

Her explanation only fed Nurse Barker's anger. Encased in the frame of a giantess was a dwarfed nature, which made her morbidly sensitive about the impression she created on strangers.

'You tried to worm yourself into my confidence,' she declared vehemently. 'You led me on to talk of – sacred things. And then, directly after, you rang up the Home. A dirty trick.'

'No,' protested Helen. 'All this happened before our talk. I've been loyal to you, ever since my promise.'

'That's a lie. I caught you at the telephone.'

'I know. But I was ringing up Dr Parry.'

Nurse Barker only sucked her lips together in a crooked line. She knew that silence was the best punishment she could administer, since it kept the girl on the prongs of suspense.

As Helen waited, fearfully expectant of the next attack, she started at the sound of a low thud.

Her thoughts flew to the professor. In her ignorance of the effects of drugs, she still clung to the hope that he would become conscious in time to control the situation. But Nurse Barker shattered her illusion as she broke her silence to bark out a command.

'See if the old woman's fallen out of bed.'

Glad to be of service, Helen obeyed – rushing up the staircase. When she reached the landing, she checked her headlong flight and stole cautiously into the blue room.

Lady Warren lay huddled up in the big bed, fast asleep. Her mouth was open and her snores were of genuine origin.

Helen looked around her, noticing that the fire was burning low. As she carefully piled on some of the snowball coals, she was too engrossed to hear Dr Parry's double-knock on the front-door.

Nurse Barker, however, started up at the sound. Peering suspiciously to right and left, she pushed open the swing door and went into the lobby.

Her first glance showed her a white object, gleaming through the glass of the letter box. Pulling it out, she examined the note with contracted eyes. It was scrawled on the back of an envelope, which was addressed to Dr Parry, and was signed with the initials 'D. P.'.

Her heart was wrung with a spasm of jealousy at this proof that Helen's instincts had been true. While they struggled together, Dr Parry had actually been outside the door, insistent and eager.

'She knew,' she muttered. 'How?'

The girl's familiarity with the windings of love's labyrinth was a mystery to the thwarted woman, who, all her life, had hungered for a thread to help her find her way through. Only once had she ventured a little way into the maze, but had never reached its heart.

But Helen knew how to draw the heart out of a man, and how to call to him so that – at the end of a hard day – he lost his sleep, for her sake.

Nurse Barker could appreciate the extent of the sacrifice on the part of a general practitioner. Her eyes were like flints as she read the note, which was obviously meant for Helen.

Have biked over to see how things are for myself. Been knocking like mad, but no luck. When you get this, open your bedroom window, and I'll shout up to you, so that you'll know it's not some trick. But, for heaven's sake, let me in. I'll explain everything to the professor, afterwards.

From the moment she had first set eyes on Helen, Nurse Barker had been frantically envious of her. She was just the type which she herself would have chosen to be – quick as a needle and smart as paint. Although well able to look after herself, she was of fairy fragility, a quality which appealed to the protective instincts of men.

She swallowed convulsively, as she tore the paper into tiny fragments and dropped them inside the drainpipe umbrella-stand.

'Dead Letter Office,' she murmured grimly.

Meanwhile, Helen was busy in the blue room, unconscious of the destruction of her vital mail. She straightened disarranged furniture, shook up cushions, and put away articles of clothing; presently she came out on the landing laden with a big basin of soapy water and an armful of crumpled towels.

As she did so, she was vaguely aware of some stir in the atmosphere, as though someone had come that way a few seconds before her. The door leading to the back stairs quivered faintly, as though it would swing open at a touch.

Her small white face swam up in the dim depths of the mirror in the old familiar way; but, as she drew nearer, she noticed something which was both mysterious and disturbing. A faint mist blurred the glass, about the height of a man's mouth.

'Someone stood here, a few seconds ago,' she thought fearfully, as she watched the patch become bright again. Gripping her basin with stiff fingers, she stared at the closed doors. She was afraid to take her eyes off them, lest one should open – afraid to move, lest she precipitated the attack.

Suddenly her nerve crashed. Putting her basin down on the carpet, she turned, and hurled herself down the stairs.

Nurse Barker watched her as she sank down, panting, on the lowest step.

'Well?' she asked with cool unconcern.

Ashamed of her unfounded terror, Helen rapidly became composed.

'Lady Warren is asleep,' she said. 'We didn't hear *her*.'

'Then where have you been all this time?'

'Tidying the room.'

'You've not been up in your own room?' Nurse Barker asked.

'No.'

'Well, I wouldn't go there, if I were you. It's a long way up – especially if you were to meet someone.'

Again the dull thud banged in the distance.

'There it is again,' said Nurse Barker. 'I wish it would stop. It gets on my nerves.'

As she listened, Helen suddenly located the sound.

'It's down in the basement. It must be the window I tied up. It's blown open again.'

She hastened to add quickly, 'It's all right. There's a shutter up, so no one can get in.'

'It's criminal carelessness, all the same,' declared Nurse Barker, with an elaborate yawn.

'Are you sleepy?' asked Helen sharply.

'My eyes are just dropping,' declared Nurse Barker, with another yawn. 'It's all I can do to keep them open. I came straight off night-duty I ought to have had a night in bed between my cases.'

With a chill at her heart, Helen recognised the too familiar signals of extreme fatigue. While she had been afraid of Nurse Barker succumbing to some treacherously administered drug, she was, in reality, nearly overpowered by natural sleep.

As she watched her, Helen realised that her failure to stay awake was inevitable. Nurse Barker was due for a good night's rest. She had made a journey in an open car. Since then she had eaten and smoked heavily, and had taken a fair quantity of brandy. The air of the shuttered house, too, was unhelpfully close.

There seemed no connection between this latest example of cause and effect and the mysterious conspiracy which threatened Helen's safety; yet her fear of being left alone to watch was real, because the incident was timed with such horrible accuracy.

Suddenly, Nurse Barker's head dropped forward with a jerk, which awakened her. She staggered as she rose slowly to her feet.

'Where are you going?' asked Helen anxiously.

'Bed.'

'Where?'

'Patient's room.'

'But you can't do that. You can't leave me here, alone.'

'The house is locked up,' Nurse Barker said. 'You're safe, as long as you remember not to open the door. If you forget again it's your own funeral.'

'But it's worse than that,' wailed Helen. 'I didn't tell you before, because I wasn't sure.'

'Sure of *what*?' repeated Nurse Barker.

'I've a terrible fear that someone is in the house, locked in with us.'

Nurse Barker listened sceptically to the story of the rustle on the back stairs and the blur of breath on the mirror.

'Wind,' she said. 'Or mice. I'm going to bed. You can come up too, if you're going to throw a fit.'

Helen hesitated, swayed by temptation to accept the offer. If they locked the professor's door, as well as the blue room, they would be secured in an inner citadel, together with the vulnerable members of the household.

But Mrs Oates would be left outside, in the trenches. In spite of the special providence which was supposedly detailed to guard her, Helen felt she could not risk leaving her there.

'Could we possibly get Mrs Oates up to the blue room?' she asked.

'Drag a drunken log up two flights of stairs?' Nurse Barker shook her head. 'I'm not up for that.'

'But we can't leave her there. Remember, we should be held responsible, tomorrow morning.'

Fortunately Helen struck the right note, for Nurse Barker was caught by the argument.

'Oh, well, I'll have to make do with a sofa in the drawing-room.'

Helen followed her into the big tasteless room, which still blazed with electric light. It held traces of its last tenants – the careless, bored youngsters – whose pose of modern indifference had been so fatally shattered by the intrusion of passion.

Coffee-cups, with sodden cigarette-ends inside, were scattered about, together with stray sheets of newspapers, open magazines, choked ashtrays. Nurse Barker collected a couple of satin cushions, which lay on the carpet; tucking them under her head, she stretched herself out on the vast blue settee. Closing her eyes, she fell, almost instantly, into a deep sleep.

'Now, I'm alone,' thought Helen. 'But I can wake her up, if anything happens.'

As she kept vigil, she looked around her with strained eyes, dilated to black pools. There was no danger of her being soothed, irresistibly, to unconsciousness by the rhythm of Nurse Barker's heavy regular breathing. Her brain was a positive vortex of jumbled impressions.

But, through the chaos and confusion, she knew that she was chasing a memory. Suddenly it came to her. The basement window. It had been left open, for minutes on end, while the bar of its shutter lay uselessly on the kitchen table and she and Stephen Rice lapped up Mrs Oates's talk of the family's past.

Her heart gave a leap, but she tried to reason herself out of her panic. It was the hundredth chance that the criminal, with acres of lonely countryside for shelter, would rush towards a house filled with people – the thousandth chance, that he would find the one point of entry.

'But, if he *did*,' thought Helen, 'he could hide in any of the dark cellars. And then, when the coast was clear, he could make a dash through the scullery and kitchen to the back stairs.'

There was only one way of safeguarding Mrs Oates. She would have to make a thorough search of the basement. When she had satisfied herself that it was empty, she must lock the kitchen door, and take away the key.

Nurse Barker did not hear her as she went out of the room. The woman was sleeping too heavily even to be aware of the noise of the gale, which shook the long windows with its fury.

Presently she awoke with a start, and sat up rubbing her eyes. Refreshed and alert, she looked around for Helen, who had kept vigil, by her side.

But the girl had disappeared.

Dr Parry, too, no longer stood, like a sentinel, in the garden. Almost directly after the head and shoulders had been shadowed on the curtain, the light in Helen's bedroom went out.

As he waited for something else to happen, he did his best to master his uneasiness. Although he knew that because of her bush of hair Helen could not have presented the clear silhouette of a man, Miss Warren or the nurse out of uniform might have passed across the blind.

Presently he turned away. Conscious that he had let his personal feelings for a girl work him up into an unreasonable panic, he was anxious to get a second opinion on the situation. Cutting across the plantation, he soon reached Captain Bean's whitewashed cottage.

The blind was undrawn, so that he could see into the lamplit sitting-room. Captain Bean, in his shirt-sleeves, sat at a paper-strewn table – a teapot beside him. It was evident that he was sitting up late writing one of his articles on travel.

In spite of the interruption to his work, he came, at once, to the door at the sound of Dr Parry's knock. His clean-shaven face was a muddle of small indeterminate features and his original blond colouring had been scorched by tropic suns.

'You'll wonder why I'm knocking you up at this time of the night,' said Dr Parry. 'But I'm a bit puzzled about things up at The Summit.'

'Come in,' invited Captain Bean.

Dr Parry was rather astonished by the gravity with which he listened to his story.

'The fact is,' he concluded, 'there's a girl in that house that I'm not quite easy about. She's such a scrap. And she's very frightened.'

'She's reason to be,' snapped the captain, 'after that girl I found in my garden this evening.'

Dr Parry, who wanted the reassurance of scepticism, stared at him with anxious eyes. He looked haggard and unkempt, while the stubble of his chin smudged his face, as though with grime.

However, the captain gave a comforting hint of personal bias in his next sentence.

'I never cottoned on to that house. And I never warmed to the family. I'll walk over with you and have a look round.'

'No damn good,' said Dr Parry hopelessly. 'The place is like a fortress. And you can ring till you pull the wire out.'

'Police?'

'I've thought of them. But I don't know what grounds I can give them for forcing an entry. It's all in order. And I'm chiefly to blame for that – curse it.' Dr Parry got up from his chair, to pace the room excitedly.

'It's that shadow that gets me,' he said. 'In her room. It didn't look like the shape of any woman.'

'Still, there are young men about the house,' remarked the captain.

'No, they've all left. There's only the professor – assuming he's shaken off the effect of the quadronex.'

Captain Bean grunted as he rammed fresh tobacco into his pipe.

'I want the entire log,' he said. 'I've knocked about all over the globe and seen all the ugliest sights. But that girl's body, in my own garden, gave me a turn. Since then, I've been thinking of all sorts of things.'

He listened, with close attention, to the story, but made no comment. When it was finished, he rose and drew on his Wellington boots.

'Where are you going?' asked Dr Parry.

'Bull. To phone the police-station.'

'Why?'

'There's some things can't be said. You've got to prove them, by compass . . . But I never like it when the rats leave the ship.'

'Hell. Stop hinting, man. Say what you mean.'

The captain shook his head.

'You can't call a spade, a spade, when it might turn out to be a ruddy fork,' he said. 'I'll only tell you this. I wouldn't risk a daughter of mine in that house tonight for a million pounds.'

27

'Security is Mortals' Chiefest Enemy'

At first, Nurse Barker could not credit the fact that Helen was gone. She looked around her, searching, in vain, for a small blue figure amid the crowded confusion of settees and chairs. Only the ginger cat – disturbed by her noisy movements – jumped off an old-fashioned Prince of Wales divan and stalked from the room.

Thoroughly put out, she followed him into the hall, where she raised her voice in a shout. 'Miss *Ca-pel*.'

There was no reply – no soft scurry of felt shoes. She drew her brows together in displeasure, while her eyes glowed green with jealousy.

She had no fear of misfortune to Helen. In her opinion The Summit was impregnable. She had been playing on the girl's fear from a double motive – to urge her to super caution, and in revenge for fancied insult.

She told herself that Dr Parry had managed to get in touch with Helen in spite of her interception of his note.

'She's let him in.' she thought. 'Well, it's none of my business.'

With professional caution, she always avoided contact with scandal. If there was suspicion of irregular conduct in any house where she nursed, she knew nothing about it. When, on the following morning, the professor or Miss Warren questioned her about Dr Parry's presence at The Summit, she would be able to assure them that she had kept to her proper place – the patient's room.

With a twisted virtuous smile, she went upstairs to the blue room. As she entered, Lady Warren stirred in bed.

'Girl,' she called.

'Now, that's not the way to speak to your nurse,' objected Nurse Barker.

Lady Warren struggled to a sitting posture.

'Go away,' she said. 'I want the girl.'

'Shut your eyes and go to sleep. It's very late.'

Lady Warren, however, looked wakeful as an owl as she stared at Nurse Barker.

'It's very quiet,' she said. 'Where's everybody?'

'Everybody's in bed, and asleep.'

'Tell the professor I want him. You can go through the dressing-room.'

The remark reminded Nurse Barker of a grievance.

'Do you know the connecting-door won't lock?' she asked.

'You needn't worry.' The old woman chuckled. 'He won't come in after you. Your day's over.'

Nurse Barker disdained to notice the insult. She had no warning of the peril which actually would steal through that door, or the shock of unseen attack – the grip of choking fingers around her throat – the roar of the sea in her ears – the rush of darkness.

In her security, all she wanted was to settle down for the night. She was growing sleepy again. As she had no intention of explaining the sleeping-draught fiasco to Lady Warren, she made a pretence of awakening the professor. Passing through the dressing-room, she entered his bedroom.

His chair was placed directly under the high light, so that a pool of shadow was thrown over his face, which looked unnatural, as though composed of yellow wax. To increase the resemblance, his seated figure had the rigid fixity of a mechanical chess-player.

'Is the professor coming?' asked Lady Warren eagerly, as Nurse Barker returned to the blue room.

'No, he's fast asleep.'

Lady Warren watched her as she crossed the room and locked the door.

'That'll keep her out,' she thought with a smile of grim satisfaction.

'Why did you do that?' asked Lady Warren.

'I always lock my door in a strange house,' replied Nurse Barker.

'I always kept mine open, so that I could get out quicker. When you lock out, you never know what you're locking in.'

'Now, I don't want to hear anything more from you,' said Nurse Barker, kicking off her shoes. 'I'm going to lie down.'

But before she dropped down upon the small bed, she crossed to the other door, which led into his dressing-room, and turned the key, as though for extra security. In spite of the precaution, she did not go to sleep. Her thoughts circled enviously around Helen and her lover.

She wondered where they were – what they did.

At that moment, Dr Parry was suffering solitary torment, while Helen endured her self-imposed ordeal – alone. Down in the basement, a flickering candle in her hand, she groped amid the mice, the spiders and the shadows.

These shadows held possession of the passage – tenants of the night. They shifted before her, sliding along the pale washed wall, as though to lead the way. Whenever she entered an office, they crouched on the other side of the door, waiting for her.

She was nerved up to meet an attack which did not come, but which lurked just around the corner. It was perpetual postponement, which drew her on, deeper and deeper, into the labyrinth.

Footsteps dogged her all the way; they stopped when she stopped, with the perfect mimicry of an echo. Whenever she slanted a startled glance behind her, she could see no one; yet she could not be assured that she was alone.

Just as she turned round the bend of the passage and entered the pitchy alley of Murder Lane, someone blew out her candle.

She was left in the darkness, trapped between the window and the place where a girl had met with death. In that moment of horror, she heard the window burst open and the pelt of leaping footsteps.

Suddenly, fingers stole around her throat and tightened to a grip. A heavy breathing gasped through the air, like a broken pump. She felt the frantic hammering of her heart as she was swept away on a tidal-wave of horror.

Presently, the pressure on her neck lessened, as her petrified muscles relaxed to elastic tissue. In sudden realisation of her own involuntary action, she released her throat from the clutch of her hand.

The draught which had blown out her candle, still beat on her cheek and neck. Yet, even while she knew that she was the victim of imagination, her nerve had crashed completely. Breaking free from the spell which paralysed her legs, she rushed along the passage, through the kitchen, where Mrs Oates snored in her chair, up the stairs and back to the drawing-room.

The ginger cat occupied Nurse Barker's vacant place on the settee, his head resting upon the satin cushion. As she stared at him, he jumped down and followed her up to the first landing.

Still quivering with panic, Helen turned the handle of the door desperately. When she realised that Nurse Barker had locked her out of the blue room, she was filled with a healing gush of indignation.

Nurse Barker took no notice of her knocks until they grew so frantic that she was forced to get off her bed.

'Go away,' she called. 'You're disturbing the patient.'

'Let me in,' cried Helen.

Nurse Barker unlocked the door, but did not open it.

'Go back to your doctor,' she said.

'My – what? I'm alone.'

'Alone, now, maybe. But you've been talking to Dr Parry.'

'I don't know what you mean.'

When Nurse Barker suddenly threw open the door, Helen had a shock of wonder at her altered appearance. She had removed her cap, as well as her shoes. Instead of the cropped head of Helen's imagination, her masculine features were crowned with permanently waved hair.

'Where have you been?' she asked.

'Down in the basement,' Helen gulped guiltily. 'I – I remembered that I'd left a window open. So I went down to see if anyone had got in.'

The girl looked so confused that Nurse Barker realised that her suspicions had been baseless. She turned back to the blue room.

'I'm going to rest,' she said, 'even if I can't sleep.'

'May I come in with you?' pleaded Helen.

'No. Go to bed, or lie down in the drawing-room.'

Her advice seemed sound, yet Helen still clung to company.

'But I ought to stay with you,' she said, using Nurse Barker's own argument. 'You see, if anyone's after me, he'll have to dispose of you, first.'

'Who's after you?' asked Nurse Barker scornfully, whirling round, like a weathercock in a gale.

'The maniac, according to you.'

'Don't be a fool. How could he get in, through locked doors?'

Helen felt as though she were standing on solid ground, after struggling for a foothold in quicksand.

'Then why have you been frightening me?' she asked reproachfully. 'It's cruel.'

'For your own good. I've had pros like you, their heads filled with nothing but men, men, men. I had to teach you not to open the door to the first Dick, Tom or Harry. Now, I'm going to bed, and you are not to disturb me again. Understand?'

She was turning away, when Helen caught her sleeve.

'Wait. Why did you think I was with Dr Parry?' she asked.

'Because he was outside, just now. But he's gone, for good.'

In spite of the triumphant gleam in her eyes, as she slammed the door, Helen felt suddenly revived. For the first time for many hours, she was free from fear. After the creepy gloom of the basement, the landing, glowing in the midst of lighted rooms, seemed the hub of any civilised family mansion in an auctioneer's catalogue. She realised that she had just received a valuable object-lesson in the destructive power of uncurbed imagination.

'Everything that happened was my own doing,' she thought. 'It's like frightening yourself by making faces in the glass, when you're a child.'

She called to the ginger cat, who was playing around the door which led to the back stairs. But, although he preserved his character for civility, by purring and arching his back, he explained that he wished to go down to the kitchen.

Helen dutifully opened the door, whereupon he changed his mind. Instead of descending to the basement, he pounced on a small object on the coconut-matting strip at the foot of the upward flight.

Helen left him to his game of pretending he had found a mouse. Had she had the curiosity to examine what he was throwing in the air, her new-born confidence would have been shattered.

It was a small tassel of larch from the plantation. Someone had brought it into the house, stuck on to the sole of a muddy shoe, and had thoughtlessly scraped it off on the mat.

She was the only one – on the day's official register – who had passed through the plantation. And she had reached her bedroom by way of the front stairs.

Happily unconscious that the ginger cat had turned detective and discovered a valuable clue, she went down to the drawing-room, The divan invited her to rest, but she was too excited to follow Nurse Barker's advice. She forgot her anger over the woman's interference in happiness at the knowledge that Dr Parry had made a second journey through the storm, for her sake.

'I've got a lover, at last,' she thought triumphantly, as she crossed to the piano. She could only play by ear, but she managed to pick out a fairly accurate rendition of the Wedding March. Up in the blue room Lady Warren sat up in bed.

'Who's playing the Wedding March?' she asked.

'No one,' said Nurse Barker, not opening her eyes. 'Shut up.'

'No,' muttered the old woman maliciously, 'you didn't hear it. And you never will.'

She listened again, but the music had ceased. Helen had realised that her performance might disturb the remnant of the household. She closed the piano and opened a novel, only to discover that she could not concentrate on what she read. She found that she was listening to the noises of the night, as though she expected to hear some unfamiliar sound.

Presently she got up and turned on the wireless, in the vain hope of hearing the announcer's voice. But the London stations had closed down, and all she got, from the air, was an explosion of atmospherics. They reminded her of amateur stage effects, and the only time she had ever appeared in a dramatic performance. It had been a modest business, at the prize-giving of the Belgian convent where she had received most of her brief education.

The English pupils had played the witches' scene from *Macbeth*, and she had been unhappily cast as Hecate. Not only was she inaudible, through stage-fright, but she forgot the end of her speech, and rushed from the stage. The lines swam back, now, to her memory, as an unpleasant and ill-timed warning.

> 'And you all know, security
> Is mortals' chiefest enemy.'

Helen started, as though the great voice in the chimney were actually roaring the words. She looked at the old-fashioned comfort of the room – the white skin rug, the pleated pink-silk lampshade – mute witnesses against the violence of murder.

'Of course, I feel safe,' she thought. 'I'm not left alone. Nurse Barker is my ally, even if she's got a temper. I haven't got to sleep in the blue room. Oates will soon be back. And – nothing's happened.'

Yet, in spite of the reassurance of her review, she realised that she was keyed up to a pitch of unnatural expectancy. She was listening so intently that she believed she could almost catch the high squeak of a bat.

Something had twanged on her ear, like the vibration of a drawn wire. She heard it again – slightly louder, faint and wailing as the mew of a seagull.

It was a cry in the night.

28

The Lion – or the Tiger?

Helen raised her head to listen – a great fear at her heart. What she most dreaded had actually happened – and she needed to make a perilous decision.

Yet, the very fact that it had occurred aroused her suspicions. Someone with a knowledge of her character was playing a trick on her in order to draw her away from the security of the house.

This theatrical element made her tighten her lips in resolution. She had spoken, in pity, of a child crying out in the darkness and storm. And here was the child – delivered, right on schedule.

As the thin cry was repeated, Helen's lips parted in suspense. Although it was difficult to locate the sound, because of the shrieking of the wind, it seemed to come from somewhere within the house. A new dread knocking at her heart, she slowly mounted the stairs.

As she did so, the crying grew more distinct; it sounded like the weak sobbing of someone very young, or very old.

And it came from the direction of the blue room. Once again the natural element was shaping the drama – yet the result would be the same. She was being tempted to abandon her last line of defence.

Nurse Barker was the only person left to keep her company. Helen clung to that belief, as a child, terrified of the dark, will hang on to a bad-tempered nurse. She had aroused her antagonism too often to risk another quarrel.

Next time, Nurse Barker might carry out her threat to leave her alone. Helen grew cold at the mere thought of desertion. She had been used to plenty of company; too much of it, in fact, so that she sometimes craved solitude.

At this crisis, her early training left her especially susceptible to the menace of loneliness and her own imagination. She knew that she would experience all the heralds of a nervous crash; shadows would flicker over the wall – footsteps creak up the stairs.

'I must keep my head,' she resolved desperately.

She reminded herself that Lady Warren was not some gentle old soul at the mercy of a brute. At her best, she was a cantankerous old bully; at her worst, she might be a murderess. When she was younger, she had killed hundreds of small, defenceless creatures, merely for her own amusement.

Although Helen was careful to paint Lady Warren's portrait in the darkest hues, she was drawn, inexorably, up the staircase, until she stood outside the blue room.

Presently she heard smothered, hopeless sobbing. It was not assumed for effect, because it was so low that she could not have known anyone was crying if she had not strained her ears.

She flinched, as though she had been struck herself, at the sound of a rough voice.

'Stop that row.'

The sobbing ceased immediately. After a pause, Lady Warren spoke appealingly. 'Nurse. *Please*, come to me.'

Helen heard heavy footsteps crossing the room, and Nurse Barker's voice raised in a shout. 'If I come to you, I'll give you what for.'

Helen felt herself grow hot, as she rapped impulsively on the door. 'Is anything the matter?' she called.

'No,' replied Nurse Barker.

'But wouldn't you like me to sit with Lady Warren for a short time?' persisted Helen.

'No.'

Helen turned away, wiping her face.

'That was a near shave,' she murmured.

At the top of the stairs she was arrested by the sound of a high scream of mingled pain and rage.

Hot with indignation, she burst into the blue room.

Nurse Barker stood over the bed, shaking Lady Warren furiously. As Helen entered, she threw her away from her, so that she fell on her face, in a heaving crumpled heap.

'You great coward,' cried Helen. 'Get out of here.'

Like David threatening Goliath, Helen looked up at the towering figure.

'The old devil went for me,' said Nurse Barker.

'You're a thoroughly bad-tempered woman,' she declared. 'You are not fit to have control of anyone.'

Nurse Barker's face grew dark as a storm-cloud.

'Say that again,' she shouted, 'and I'll go out of this room – and not come back.'

'You'll certainly go, and you *won't* come back,' said Helen, carried away on a wave of power.

Nurse Barker shrugged her shoulders as she turned away. 'I wish you joy of your bargain,' she sneered. 'When you are alone with her, remember you *asked* for it.'

Helen felt the first chill of reaction as the door slammed behind the woman. There was something ominously definite about the sound.

With a rush of pity, she turned towards the bed. Instead of being a prostrate form, Lady Warren was leaning back against her pillows, a complacent smile on her lips. Helen experienced the sensation of having walked into a trap but nevertheless reacted with concern.

'You'd better lie down,' she said, anxious to justify her championship. 'Do you feel weak after that awful shaking?'

'What she gave me was nothing to what I gave her,' remarked Lady Warren.

Helen stared at her – the dawn of an incredulous horror in her eyes as the old lady ran her finger over her lower denture.

'I grudged the money for these teeth,' she said. 'But they're very good teeth. I bit her thumb almost to the bone.'

Helen gave a mirthless laugh.

'Someone told me to bet on you,' she said. 'But I didn't believe him. I wonder – are you the lion – or the tiger?'

Lady Warren stared at her as though she were an idiot.

'Cigarette,' she snapped. 'I want to get the taste of her out of my mouth. Quick. Haven't you got any?'

'No.'

'Say, "No, my lady." Go down to the library and get a box of my nephew's.'

Helen was only too glad of the excuse to leave the room. Too late, she realised that she had been tricked, and she wanted to make her peace with Nurse Barker.

As she reached the door, the familiar bass bellow recalled her.

'I feel sleepy, girl. That nurse held my nose and poured a filthy draught down my throat. Don't disturb me, if I drop off.'

When Helen reached the landing, the light shone through the transom above the bathroom door, while the sound of running water indicated that Nurse Barker was bathing her thumb.

'Nurse,' she called. 'I'm terribly sorry.'

There was no reply. Helen waited, listening to the splashing of water. After making a second attempt, with no better luck, she went downstairs to the library.

When she returned, with a box of cigarettes, the blue room was dimly revealed in the faint glow of the lamp. Lady Warren had switched off her bed-light and had composed herself to sleep.

Helen sat down wearily by the fire. It was burning low, for the stock of snowballs in the scuttle was running out. Every now and again a twig tapped the window, like a bony finger giving a signal. The clock ticked, like a leaking tap, and the wind blew down the funnel of the chimney.

'Here I am again,' she said, with a hopeless sense of finality. All the evening she had been fighting fate, but to no avail.

There was one comfort – the night was wearing away. Oates, she remembered, would be on his return journey. But the thought now brought no prospect of relief. Nurse Barker would refuse him admission, just as she had shut out Dr Parry – or whoever had knocked at the door.

For the first time, Helen realised the possible value of the precaution. Since she had been tricked by Lady Warren, she felt that she was groping amid a network of wires and snares.

With newly awakened suspicion, she glanced at the dim white form on the bed. It suddenly struck her that Lady Warren was unnaturally still. There was no sound of breathing, and not the slightest stir of movement.

She remembered that the old woman had been shaken violently and that her heart was dangerously weak. Smitten with sudden dread, she rushed over to the bed.

'She'll be the next,' she thought. 'I shall find her dead.'

Her foreboding was fulfilled in a curious manner. Lady Warren was gone, indeed, and nothing could have been less animate than the pile of pillows, covered with the fleecy bed-jacket, which occupied her place in the bed.

Helen stared at the dummy with the stupefaction of Macbeth when he beheld the forest marching against him. Mrs Oates was right, Lady Warren could walk.

As she stood, she became aware of a strong odour of drugs. Turning over one of the pillows, she noticed that it was sopping wet, and stained a yellowish-brown.

'She tricked the nurse, too,' thought Helen.

She had a mental picture of the struggling Lady Warren, turning her head between every mouthful of the sleeping-draught and letting it trickle out from the corner of her mouth. With a new respect for the old woman's cunning, she made a brief search of the room, although she was sure it was a waste of time. As the dressing-room, too, was empty, she rushed out on to the landing.

The light still shone through the bathroom transom, although the splashing of water had ceased. In her fright, Helen hammered on the door. 'Nurse,' she shouted, 'Lady Warren's gone.'

The door opened, and Nurse Barker stood looking down at her with unfriendly eyes.

'What's that to do with me?' she asked. 'I've thrown up the case.'

'You're not really going?' gasped Helen.

'Directly I've packed my case. Miss Warren will hear, in the morning, that I was dismissed by the domestic help.'

'But you can't do that,' cried Helen, in a panic. 'I'll apologise. I – I'll do anything.'

'Shut up. I'm through with *your* promises. I'm going – and I'm going now. That's my last word.'

'But – where will you go?'

'That's my business. I'll find a place for the night. It is not so late, and I'm not afraid of the dark, or a spot of rain.'

Nurse Barker paused, before she added maliciously: 'Once I'm out of this house, I'll feel *safe*.'

She was taking her revenge, as she drove home the horror which Helen had almost forgotten. The girl gazed at her with imploring eyes while she gave a parting thrust.

'Keep your weather-eye open. She's up to no good.' She glanced at her bandaged thumb. 'And while she's out of the way you had better look for her gun.'

Helen bit her lip as the bathroom door was shut in her face.

'She can't really mean to go out in this awful storm,' she decided.

Besides feeling vaguely frightened, she was utterly perplexed, and worried with a sense of her own responsibility. As it was impossible to guess what purpose had drawn Lady Warren from her bed, it seemed hopeless to try and find her. She might play hide-and-seek indefinitely in that house.

She might even be bent on committing suicide. Not only was she old, but her life held that dark unexplored corner. Remorse might drive her to kill herself.

Helen shuddered at the thought of finding her body hanging in the cellar. Not knowing where to go first, she went back to the blue room.

Her first glance at the bed told her that the dummy had acquired a more definite shape; and, when she drew nearer, she saw Lady Warren peeping at her with black slitted eyes.

'Oh, where have you been?' asked Helen.

'In the Land of Nod,' was the innocent reply. Her inscrutable stare dared the girl to disbelieve her statement. Feeling that it was hopeless to persist, Helen returned to her chair.

'Has the nurse gone?' asked Lady Warren.

'Tomorrow,' replied Helen.

'Quick work. I soon clear them out. I hate them. Forever washing your face! Don't move, girl. I want to keep my eye on you.'

Helen thought involuntarily of the hidden revolver; and, with her characteristic urge for information, she had to refer to the subject.

'Mrs Oates tells me you used to shoot a lot,' she said.

Lady Warren threw her a sharp glance before she replied.

'Yes, I used to pot game. D'you shoot?'

'No. I think it is cruel.'

'Yet you eat meat. If everyone had to kill their own meat, nine-tenths of the population would turn vegetarian within a week. I did my job properly. I didn't wound. I killed.'

'But you took life.'

'Yes, I took life. But I never gave life. Thank God. Get out of my room.'

Helen started, and then turned her head in the direction of Lady Warren's pointing finger. Nurse Barker had entered the room. Without speaking, she marched to the dressing-room, where her belongings were stored, and shut the door.

As Helen strained her ears, she could hear her moving about, opening and shutting drawers. Apparently she was making good her threat, and packing her suitcase. As she sat in the oppressive room she was the victim of a morbid suspicion, bred of the close atmosphere.

Long ago, two girls had died unnatural deaths in this house. But no one knew the actual truth about the tragedies. The matter was smothered in conjecture and the cases closed after a vague coroner's verdict.

'She's queer,' thought Helen, glancing uneasily towards the bed. 'Suppose she killed them — and her husband knew. Suppose she shot him so that he couldn't tell.'

Presently, she realised that the sounds from the adjoining room had ceased. With a rush of hope, she remembered that there was a divan in the dressing-room. The probability was that Nurse Barker had decided to put off her departure until the morning, and was going to bed.

The fact that she was so near inspired Helen with confidence. As she reviewed the events of the evening, she saw her present position as the logical result of her own folly. Nurse Barker had been specially selected, by the matron of the Nursing Home, to look after a tiresome patient, with whom she herself could not cope.

Helen felt overwhelmed with humiliation.

'If she's not asleep, I'll go in and tell her I've been a horrible little brute,' she decided. 'I'll ask her to wipe her boots on me.'

Creeping across the carpet to the dressing-room, she cautiously opened the door – now unlocked. Then she gave a little cry of dismay.

Nurse Barker had gone.

29

Alone

Helen stared around her with startled eyes. The disorder of the room pointed to a hurried departure. Drawers had been pulled out, while a suitcase and umbrella lay upon the table.

'She's not gone yet,' thought Helen.

But a moment's reflection robbed her of that hope. Nurse Barker would naturally leave her heavy luggage behind, to be forwarded to the Home. An umbrella, too, would be useless in the gale.

Feeling sick with suspense, Helen opened the wardrobe. Nurse Barker's outdoor uniform no longer hung upon the peg. A hurried search through the chest showed all the drawers to be empty. All that remained was a pile of cigarette ends and ash.

It was a planned desertion. With deliberate mental cruelty, Nurse Barker had left the girl alone – reaching the landing through the professor's room.

Helen felt almost overwhelmed by this last blow. Throughout the evening she had noticed the steady march of events towards some inevitable climax. While she dimly felt its objective was her own isolation, she had played into the hands of destiny by goading on Nurse Barker to take her revenge.

Yet, even so, she had been forced to make her moves, as if she were a puppet controlled by another's will.

'I'm all alone,' she thought fearfully.

It was true that others were still in the house; but hers was the only active brain – hers, the only quick body. The others were shackled by circumstance.

With a desperate need of company, she opened the second door, and entered the professor's room.

But there was no comfort here – only an increase in loneliness. The professor – still holding his rigid posture, as though carved in stone – was too much like a corpse awaiting burial.

She wanted to leave him, yet she dreaded returning to the blue room. The old woman lacked the human quality for which she hungered. At this crisis she would have welcomed the harshest abuse from Nurse Barker, could she have drawn her back.

The longing to hear another voice grew so acute that she went out on the landing and beat frantically upon Miss Warren's door.

'Miss Warren,' she screamed. 'Help.' But there was no response. She might have been appealing to a sealed tomb. Only the wind shrieked, as though a flock of witches sailed overhead, racing the moon, which glided through the torn clouds like a silver cannonball shot into space.

'She's cruel,' whispered Helen, turning away.

But Miss Warren was too soundly asleep to hear her cries. Contact with others always gave her the impression that her nerves were on the surface of her skin and exposed to the open air. Tonight, after all the accidents and alarms, she felt as though each fibre were actually bruised.

She had the natural craving of a recluse for her own locked study, but she had been picked out of her shell and made to endure hours of enforced companionship with an unpleasant old woman in a lethal atmosphere.

The storm, too, had played havoc with her nervous system. The accident to her door-handle which had imprisoned her, therefore, came as a welcome release from responsibility. She made no effort to free herself, but slipped her bolt and shut out the world.

With plugs of cotton-wool in her ears, and blankets piled over her head to deaden the noise of the gale, she was soon submerged in the slumber-sea of utter exhaustion.

Although Helen felt perilously near to collapse, her will still functioned, telling her that she must not yield to panic. She reminded herself that all the wires were not cut. She was still linked up with civilisation. But, as she went downstairs, she realised how hopelessly she had become entangled in the snare of fear. She could not ask anyone to come to the house because she dared not withdraw the bolts.

The professor had decreed that the door must not be opened; and the order had been dictated by a cool brain which prepared for every contingency. His policy had been framed in the interests of the general safety.

Since then, Nurse Barker had warned her against any disobedience; and Helen had learned – through bitter experience – that in the case of Lady Warren at least she had been right.

If she, herself, were the ultimate aim of some dark desire, then this steady withdrawal of defence was planned to plunge her into such panic that if she heard a knock she would rush to open the door.

Someone wanted to draw her outside the safety of The Summit.

'If I arranged a signal-knock,' she thought, 'it wouldn't be safe. Someone might be listening in. No. It's hopeless.'

Yet she knew that merely talking to another person would act as a tonic to her flabby nerves. She did not know whether Dr Parry had returned; her mind was too confused to calculate time or distance. But, if he were still absent, she could ring up someone else.

'The Nursing Home,' she decided. 'I'll tell them about Nurse Barker, and ask them to send out another nurse.'

The fact of having a definite reason to ring steadied her. Once more, she was Miss Capel, whose name was only too familiar to the Employment Bureau, and not a stranded nonentity. With a touch of her former assurance, she took off the receiver.

To her dismay, there was no responsive tinkle; no humming along the wire told her that she was linked up with the exchange; no voice enquired her number.

The telephone was dead.

She looked around the hall with frightened eyes. She knew that there was a natural explanation for the silence. The country lanes must be blocked with poles and wires, wrecked by the fury of the gale. This was no human plot – it was an Act of God.

But Helen would not accept it. This faithful accompaniment to the thrill-drama – the cut telephone-wire – had arrived with too-perfect timing.

'It's no accident,' she told herself. 'Things don't happen all together like this.'

She did not know where to feel safe, so great was her fear of the house. Yet she dared not rush into the storm, lest she should make the very move which had been planned by the anonymous player at the beginning of the game.

'I'd better go back to Lady Warren,' she thought. 'After all, I took her on. She cannot be left.'

She went through the professor's room, in a wild hope that he might yet awake from his drugged sleep. With his cool brain to take control, she felt she could face any danger. But he still lay back in his chair – with drawn face and clay-coloured lids – as rigid as a mummy in its case.

While she lingered in the dressing-room, she heard a scuffle and rapid footsteps on the other side of the wall.

'She's got out of bed again,' she thought dully.

If her suspicion were correct, Lady Warren did not lack the strength for a rapid scramble, for she lay composedly covered with her old-lady white fleece when Helen entered.

'Why did you leave me, girl?' she demanded. 'You're paid to look after me.'

Helen lacked the spirit to lie.

'I went to telephone,' she said. 'But – the line has been blown down. I couldn't get through.'

As she spoke, Helen became aware of Lady Warren's uneasy glances around the room. The fact that she had power to be an unwelcome obstacle to some plan, braced her up to come to grips with the old lady.

'Why did you get out of bed?' she asked.

'I didn't. I can't. Don't be a fool.'

'I'm certainly not such a fool as you think. Besides, there is nothing to hide. You're not officially paralysed or bedridden. People have got the impression that you are helpless – that's all. Why shouldn't you get out of bed if you want to?'

Instead of being furious, Lady Warren pondered the speech.

'Never tell the whole,' she said. 'Always keep something up your sleeve when you're old, and at the mercy of other people. I like to get about, when no one's looking.

'Of course you do,' agreed Helen. 'I'll tell no one, I promise.'

And then her deathless curiosity prompted another question.

'What were you looking for?'

'My charm. It's a lucky green elephant, with its trunk up. I wanted it, because I was afraid.'

As Helen looked at her in surprise, because she thought that age outlived the emotions, she suddenly remembered the cross which hung above her bed.

'I've something far better than any green elephant,' she said eagerly. 'I'm going to fetch it. And then nothing can hurt you – or me.'

It was not until she was outside the room that she wondered whether Lady Warren had wanted to send her away. But, even if she had played into her hands, she did not care, so strong was her wish to hold her cross.

'I needn't have been afraid,' she thought. 'While I forgot about it, all the time it was there – keeping me safe from all evil.'

Although the wind was howling in the empty rooms on the second floor, and anyone might keep step with her on the back stairs while she mounted the front, she felt raised above fear. Fighting the fierce pressure of the draught, she snapped on the light in her bedroom.

The first thing she saw was the bare wall above her bed.

The cross had disappeared.

She caught at the door for support, as the ground seemed to collapse under her feet. An enemy was inside the house. He had robbed her of the symbol of protection. Anything might happen to her. Nothing was safe or sure.

At that moment she felt she had reached the dividing line between sanity and madness. At any moment a cell might snap in her brain. She felt poised on the edge of a bottomless drop.

And then her mind suddenly cleared of its mist, and she believed she had found a solution to the mystery.

The disappearance of the cross was a trick played on her by Nurse Barker. The woman was hiding somewhere in the house.

Rushing downstairs to the lobby, she found that her intuition had played her false. The front door was still bolted, and the chain in its place.

'Unless she went out by the back door, which is most unlikely, she's still here,' thought Helen.

Although she was vaguely worried by her loss, the relief was overwhelming. What she now feared far more than danger outside was the threat of peril from within.

Back in the blue room, the disorder of the bed told her that, in her absence, Lady Warren had been engaged in her mysterious search. A drawer protruded from a chest, which stood in an alcove, showing that the old woman had been disturbed in her labours.

As she was out of sight of the bed, Helen went up to it and tried to close it – only to be prevented by some object stuffed at the back. Getting hold of one corner, she managed to pull it out. It was a white scarf.

30

The Walls Fall Down

Helen turned over the scarf, in fingers which had grown suddenly cold. It was of good-quality silk, machine-knitted, and was quite new. There was a smear of mud on one side and pine-needles were entangled in the mesh of its fabric.

Conscious of overwhelming horror in store, she shook it out – revealing a gap in the fringe, at one end – a jagged, irregular tear, as though it had been bitten.

With a strange cry, she threw it from her. This was the scarf that Ceridwen's teeth had closed over in her death-agony. It was horrible, unclean. It had encircled the throat of a murderer.

As from a rocket, shooting up through the darkness of her mind and breaking into a cluster of stars, a host of questions splashed and spattered her brain. How did the scarf get inside Lady Warren's drawer? Was she hiding it? What connection had she with the crime? Or had someone else put it there? Was the murderer actually inside the house?

At the thought, she felt already dead. Every cell seemed atrophied, every fibre withered. She stood locked in temporary paralysis, muscle-bound, with rigid spine and blasted faculties.

Yet while she could not see the room, or hear the sound of the wind, or feel the table under her fingers, she seemed to be looking inwards at a mental picture.

The Summit was breaking up. The walls had cracked in every direction. Those thin lines, like the forks in a flash of lightning, were splintering into fissures. All around her was a tearing and a rending as the gaps widened, leaving her defenceless to the night.

Suddenly she heard the sound of a sob, and realised that it was her own voice. In the glass she saw a girl's face – pinched and pallid – staring at her from dilated eyes, black with fear. By the aureole of crisping light-red hair, she knew that girl was herself.

At the sight, a memory stirred in her mind.

' "Ginger for pluck",' she whispered.

She was inert, waiting for the attack, instead of standing with her back to the wall. Nerving herself to examine the scarf, she noticed that it was only slightly damp.

'It would have been soaked, if it had been lying out in the rain,' she thought. 'It must have been brought inside directly after the murder.'

The deduction opened up fresh avenues of horror. No one knew the exact time when Ceridwen was strangled, except that it was round about twilight. As everyone – except Oates – was at The Summit, any person could have slipped outside, for a few minutes, unnoticed. From the professor downwards, all were under suspicion.

Dr Parry had warned her that the crime might have been committed by someone she knew and trusted. The professor worked at high mental pressure, while both his son and Rice were periodically moody. Even Dr Parry had the same opportunities, and he had visited the blue room.

This wholesale suspicion might even include old Lady Warren. Miss Warren had dozed in her chair that evening at twilight. How had she used her half-hour of liberty?

'I'm mad,' thought Helen. 'It can't be everybody. It's nobody here. It's someone who got in from outside.'

She shuddered, because at the back of her mind persisted that horrible memory of an open window.

'Girl,' called Lady Warren, 'what are you doing there?'

'Getting you a clean handkerchief.'

Helen was astonished by the coolness of her voice. Under the influence of fear, she seemed to be a dual personality. A self-possessed stranger had taken command and was carrying on for her, while the real Helen was staked amid the ruins of the shattered fortress – bait for a human tiger.

'Have you found anything?' asked Lady Warren.

Helen purposely misunderstood her.

'Yes, a pile,' she said, as she hurriedly replaced the scarf. With a handkerchief in her hand, she approached the bed.

Lady Warren snatched it from her, and threw it on the floor.

'Girl,' she whispered hoarsely, 'I want you to do something.'

'Yes. What is it?'

'Get under the bed.'

Helen's eyes fell on the ebony stick by the bed with a flash of understanding. The old woman was wandering again, and she wanted to play her favourite game of stalking housemaids.

'When I crawl out, will you crack me over the head?' she asked.

'You mustn't come out. You must hide.'

The new Helen, who had taken command, thought she grasped the significance of this move. It was a ruse to hold her in a position from which she could see practically nothing of the room.

'It's too dusty under the bed,' she objected, as she moved cautiously towards the door.

She had realised the importance of the scarf, as evidence. The police should have it in their possession, without delay. She could not telephone to them because of the damage – accidental or otherwise – to the line; but she could run over to Captain Bean's cottage, and ask him to take the necessary steps.

Lady Warren began to whimper, like a terrified child. 'Don't leave me, girl. The nurse will come. She's only waiting for you to go.'

Helen hesitated, although she remembered that, in their last encounter, Lady Warren had triumphed. Yet the balance of power did not remain equal, even in a jungle fight; today it might be the tiger's turn, but, tomorrow, the lion's.

She had not yet solved the mystery of Nurse Barker's disappearance. If she were actually hiding in the house, she might take her revenge.

'I wish I knew the right thing to do,' she thought.

'If you leave me,' threatened Lady Warren, 'I'll scream. And then *he'll* come.'

Like the flash of a *fer-de-lance*, Helen whipped round.

'He?' she asked. '*Who?*'

'I said, "She'll come." '

It was obvious that Lady Warren realised her slip, for she bit her lip and glowered at Helen, like an angry idol.

Helen felt as though she was trying to find the path which threaded a maze. The old woman knew something which she would not reveal.

It was curious how she remained shackled by ordinary conventions and considerations, even while one half of her was weak with elemental terror. But, throughout the evening, no single event had been abnormal, so that, unconsciously, she responded to the laws of civilised life.

The actual murder had taken place outside The Summit, which reduced it to the level of a newspaper paragraph. The maniac was a kind of clichéd figure, invented by the press. The most shocking occurrence was the fact that the housekeeper had got drunk. It was true that both Nurse Barker and Lady Warren were most unpleasant types; but, in the course of her experience, Helen had met others who were even more peculiar. She knew that her own fear was responsible for the grotesque fancies and suspicions which shifted through her mind.

Tomorrow would come. She held on to that. She reminded herself that she had a new job to hold down. If she failed, at a pinch she might find herself out of work again.

She must not let Lady Warren scream. If the professor was startled in his drugged sleep, there might be danger of shock to his brain. It would be cruel, too, to alarm Miss Warren, while she was imprisoned.

Besides – the whisper stirred, like a snake, in her brain – it might attract *someone else*.

As she lingered, Lady Warren's mind apparently wandered.

'There's a storm blowing up,' she said. 'It's growing dark.'

With a sharp pang of alarm, Helen realised that the room seemed to have become actually dimmer. She rubbed her eyes, but the illusion did not vanish. The electric-light was gleaming murkily, as through a slight fog.

Her lips grew stiff, as she wondered if this were a prelude to complete darkness.

One more feature of the thrill-drama had arrived, with the same suggestion of cumulative effect.

'It's getting nearer,' she thought fearfully.

In spite of her resolution, she shared her doubt with her companion. 'Someone's tampered with the fuses,' she whispered.

Lady Warren snorted. 'The batteries are running out, idiot,' she snapped.

Helen gratefully grasped at the commonplace explanation. Oates was responsible for the power-plant, and he was notoriously idle. In her nervous dread of being alone in the darkness, she had recklessly switched on nearly every light, without a thought of possible consequencies.

'I'd better snap off most of the lights,' she said.

'Yes,' nodded Lady Warren. 'Fetch candles, too. We can't be left in the dark.'

Helen looked around her for candles, only to realise that these were used exclusively for domestic purposes, in the basement. She remembered seeing bundles in the storeroom, which was next to the larder.

'Do you mind being left?' she asked. 'I must go now, before – '

Unable to contemplate a complete extinction, she rushed out of the room and down the stairs. The hall seemed to flicker as she passed through, as though the house were sighing. It was warning her not to delay; in a panic, lest she should have to grope her way through darkness, she leaped down the kitchen stairs, like a scared antelope.

Mrs Oates still slept in her chair, apparently peaceful as a good child. As she passed, Helen touched her cheek, and found that it was warm.

'Thank heaven there's a special providence to look after children and drunks,' she thought.

In the passage, a spiral of red wire gleamed through the pear-shaped hanging bulb, and the light was so dim that Helen held her breath. As she dashed into the storeroom, she expected, every minute, to be plunged into darkness, to match the horror of Murder Lane.

Snatching the candles, she rushed back, laying a black trail as she snapped off each light. When she reached the hall, she repeated the operation in each reception-room. But, while she knew that she was doing the only sensible thing, she vaguely felt that she was in the grip of a horrible fatalism which ordained that she should deliberately blind the house.

Even as the thought crossed her mind, the oasis of light in which she lingered was suddenly swallowed up by the surrounding shadows.

The eclipse was but momentary. With the next second, the hall flickered back again; but the work of demoralisation was done.

The house had given a signal to the night. So intense was her fear of it, that Helen felt a mad temptation to rush out into the night, and take her chance in the open.

Captain Bean would give her shelter; his cottage was only a short distance away, if she cut through the plantation. The trees no longer held any terror, while she welcomed the thought of the wind and the rain dashing in her face. The savage landscape had become sanctuary, because the real menace was inside – hidden somewhere in the house.

She was on the point of unbolting the front door, when she remembered the helpless inmates of The Summit. Lady Warren, the professor and Mrs Oates were unable to protect themselves. When the maniac found his prey had escaped, he might wreak his disappointed fury upon them.

With the feeling that she was going to her doom, she returned to the landing. After a pause, to recover her nerve, she pushed open the door of the blue room.

Nothing appeared to have happened in her absence. Lady Warren sat humped up in bed, almost swamped in ultramarine shadows.

'You've been gone a long time, girl,' she grumbled. 'Light the candles.'

There were no candlesticks, so Helen dropped melted wax upon a marble mantelshelf and fixed two candles in position before the mirror.

'They look like corpse-candles,' remarked Lady Warren. 'I want more. All of them.'

'No, we must keep some in reserve,' Helen told her.

'They'll last our time.'

Although the finality of the old woman's words sounded ominous, Helen was aware of a change in her. Her eyes were opened wider, and they gleamed with satisfaction as she held up one bony hand.

'Look,' she cried. 'It doesn't shake. Feel how strong my fingers are.'

As Helen crossed to the bed, she forgot her invitation.

'I'm going to sleep,' she said. 'Don't leave me, girl.'

She closed her lids, and very soon her chest rose and fell with the regularity of a machine, while her breathing was quiet and even. It was an extraordinary example of concentration and willpower, for Helen was sure that she had actually lost consciousness.

'I wonder if I shall see her awake again,' she thought.

She felt as though the last link of connection with the tangible world had snapped. In the course of the night, she had witnessed the temporary flight of so many spirits, each slipping away where she could not follow them.

Although her own lids seemed weighted with lead, she, alone, was awake in a sleep-bound world. She had to watch.

Suddenly she sprang to her feet, her heart leaping with terror. Some-one was moving in the dressing-room. She distinctly heard the sound of footsteps and stealthy movements.

Stealing across the carpet, she opened the door an inch, revealing a crack of light, blocked by the dark figure of a man.

Even as criminals give themselves up to justice, she knew she could bear no longer the torture of suspense. Screwed up to a pitch of desperate courage, she flung open the door.

To her joy and surprise, she saw the professor standing at the small bureau. At the sight of the familiar formal figure, everything grew safe and normal again. The house ceased to sway and gape as the walls closed together, to restore the security of a fortress.

She fought to keep back her tears, for the relief of having rational company again was almost overpowering. But the professor's glacial eye checked her hysteria.

'Oh, professor,' she cried. 'I'm so glad you're all right again.'

'I am unaware that anything was wrong.' The professor spoke coldly. 'I merely procured some necessary sleep.'

Something had annoyed him, for he frowned as he opened another empty drawer.

'Where is the nurse?' he asked.

'Gone,' replied Helen, feeling incapable of lucid explanation.

'Where has she gone?'

'I don't know. Perhaps, she's hiding in the house.'

'She – or someone else – has taken something of mine, which I am anxious to find. But it doesn't matter, for the present.'

As though struck by some recollection, he turned round and faced Helen. 'How did you get back to the house?' he enquired.

She did not understand the question.

'When?' she asked.

'When you were coming through the plantation. I heard your foot-steps. I waited . . . But you never came.'

At the words, suddenly – Helen knew.

'*You*,' she said.

31

Good Hunting

Helen *knew*.

The acid of terror cleared the scum from her mind, so that she felt a rush of mental activity. Every cell in her brain seemed to be on fire as – in a succession of film sequences, reeling through her mind – she saw the whole story in one ghastly moment of realisation.

Professor Warren had strangled those five girls, even as his father, before him, had murdered two servants. Only Lady Warren knew of the crimes and had taken the law into her own hands. After the death of the second maid, she had shot her husband.

But, since then, she had grown old, and her brain had greened, so that she babbled of trees. She believed it to be her repulsive duty to shoot the son – but she kept putting it off. After each murder, she told herself that it was the last; and, still, there had been another one.

But with the arrival of a new girl at the house she had smelt danger. Her suspicions were aroused, and she tried to protect Helen. She wanted to keep her in her room, where she would be safe.

When she had asked the professor to light her cigarette, she had looked into his eyes and seen the too-familiar glow which warned her that he had committed another crime. Yet, in spite of this, she wished to save him from the police. She had got up, secretly, and searched his room for any incriminating object.

Then – she had found the scarf.

Helen felt a rush of gratitude towards the old woman, even though nothing mattered now.

'I'm glad I took her part against the nurse,' she thought. Yet Nurse Barker, too, was revealed in a new light – as deserving of pity, rather than suspicion. The spirit of an intensely feminine woman – craving admiration – had been encased in an unattractive envelope. Her natural instincts had been thwarted, and she had soured into a bully.

Helen wondered uneasily what had become of her. At this crisis, she longed for the aid of the masculine strength and brutality from which she had shrunk.

She looked at the professor with incredulous eyes. Outwardly, she saw no change in him. He appeared grey, bleak and intellectual – a civilised product, used to dressing-gongs and finger-bowls. His formal evening-dress completed the illusion, while his voice had preserved its frigid cultured accent.

She could not fear him – as he was. What she dreaded, in every fibre and bone, was the transformation to come. She remembered how Dr Parry had told her that in between his fits of mania the criminal was normal.

She did her best to hold him in this familiar mode.

'What were you looking for?' she asked, forcing her voice to sound casual.

'A white silk scarf.'

The reply drained the blood from her heart.

'I saw it in Lady Warren's drawer,' she said quickly. 'I'll get it for you.'

For a second a mad hope flared up that she might yet make a dash into the open.

It died instantly, as the professor shook his head. 'Don't go. Where are the others?'

'Mrs Oates is drunk, and Miss Warren is locked in her room,' replied Helen.

A faint smile of satisfaction flickered around his lips.

'Good,' he said. 'At last I have you, alone.'

His voice was still so detached and self-controlled that Helen did her best to keep him interested.

'Did you plan this?' she asked.

'Yes,' replied the professor, 'and no. I merely touched the spring which set the machinery in motion. It has been rather amusing to sit still and watch others clear the way for me.'

Helen remembered the drift of the conversation at dinner. The professor had proved his theory that a clever man could direct the actions of his fellows. He had set himself up above God.

'What do you mean?' she asked, only anxious to stave off the horror which might erupt at any moment.

'This,' replied the professor, as though he were demonstrating a thesis. 'I could have got rid of – interference – by exercising my ingenuity. It presented quite a pretty mental problem. But my knowledge of human nature prompted a subtler – and simpler – method. To begin with, I tipped Rice off about a dog for sale. When he brought it home, I knew I had several members of the household tied to the same string.'

'Go on, do,' gasped Helen, thinking only of the passage of time.

'Need I explain?' The professor was impatient with her stupidity. 'You saw how it worked out, according to plan. I counted on my sister's cowardice and aversion to animals, also on each dominant passion asserting itself.'

'It sounds very clever.' Helen licked her dry lips as she strove to think of another question. 'And – and I suppose you left the key in the cellar door on purpose?'

Again the professor frowned, in irritation.

'That explains itself,' he said. 'It is obvious that Mrs Oates would find a way to get rid of her husband.'

'Yes, of course. Did you count, too, on Nurse Barker running away?'

The professor made a wry face.

'Ah, there, I confess my plan broke down,' he said. 'I calculated that you, in your impulsive folly, would clear her from the board. You let me down. I had to do my own preliminary work.'

He spoke almost like a schoolmaster rebuking an idle pupil.

Helen knew that there was one word she must not mention; yet in her anxiety to know Nurse Barker's fate, she risked its implication.

'How?' she asked. 'Did you hurt her?'

To her relief, the professor began his explanation calmly.

'Only temporarily. She is gagged and bound, under her bed. She must remain, as a witness, to testify that she was attacked from behind, by some unseen assailant, and that I was unconscious, during, during – '

His tone blurred, and his mind seemed to lose its grip. To Helen's horror, she saw that his fingers were beginning to twitch.

'Why did you turn the police away?' she asked with the desperate feeling that she was trying to feed a furnace with flimsy sheets of tissue-paper.

'Because they will pay me a visit, tomorrow.' Again the professor's fingers curled. 'Their time will be wasted. Yet no clever man underrates the intelligence of others. During two visits to the same house, they might notice some trifle which I have overlooked. But we are wasting time.'

Helen knew that the moment had come. It could be staved off no longer. The house was locked, so that she had no hope of rescue. Yet she asked another question.

'Why do you want to kill me?'

Perhaps, in some unconscious way, the professor's theory was being demonstrated in that tense interlude. Just as it was in Helen's nature to explore, his own instinct was to satisfy any wish for knowledge.

'I consider it is my duty,' he told her. 'I have a scientist's dread of an ever-increasing population and a shrinking food supply. Superfluous women should be disposed of .'

Helen did not know what she was waiting for, when the end was so certain.

'Why am I superfluous?' she asked wildly.

'Because you have neither beauty, nor brains, nor any positively useful quality to pass on to posterity. You are refuse. Unskilled labour, in an overcrowded market. One extra mouth to feed. So – I am going to kill you.'

'How?' whispered Helen. 'Like the others?'

'Yes. It won't hurt you, if you don't resist.'

'But you hurt Ceridwen.'

'Ceridwen?' He frowned at the recollection. 'I was disappointed. I was waiting for you. She gave me trouble, for I had to carry her over to Bean's. I did not want the police coming here. An unnecessary fatigue.'

Helen stood her ground as the professor advanced a pace. She had the feeling that any sudden action might touch the spring which unloosed that ghastly transformation.

He, for his part, seemed in no hurry to begin. He looked around him, with an air of satisfaction.

'We are quiet here,' he said. 'I am glad I waited. I was on the point of doing it, three times, this evening. In the plantation – when you were asleep on the stairs – and when you were alone in your room. But I remembered that there might be interference.'

He rubbed his fingers reflectively, as though massaging them.

'This is hereditary,' he explained. 'When I was a boy I saw my father cut a girl's throat, with a dinner knife. At the time I was sick, and filled with actual horror. But, years later, the seed bore fruit.'

A green light was glowing behind his eyes. His face was melting into unfamiliar lines – changing before her eyes. Yet Helen recognised it! Before her floated the seared face of evil desire.

'Besides,' he added, 'I like to *kill*.'

They stood, facing each other, only divided by a few yards. Then, frantic with terror, Helen turned and rushed into his bedroom.

He followed her, his features working and his fingers hooked into claws.

'You can't escape me,' he said. 'The door is locked.'

Filled with the panic of a creature at bay, Helen broke away from him. She did not know who she was – or where she was – or what she did. All around her, and within, was noise and confusion – a reeling red mist – a sound like the crack of a whip.

Suddenly she realised that the end had really come. She was penned in a corner, while the professor closed her in. He was so near that she could almost see her reflection in his eyes.

But, before he could touch her, his body sagged, as though some vital spring had snapped, and he crashed heavily down upon the carpet and lay still.

Looking up, Helen saw Lady Warren standing in the doorway holding a revolver in her hand. She wore the white fleecy jacket of a nice old lady, decorated with rose ribbons. One gay pink bow dangled at the end of a spike of grey hair.

As Helen reached her, she collapsed in the girl's arms. The effort of the shot had been too great. Yet she smiled with the grim satisfaction of a sportsman who has exterminated vermin, although her last words expressed a certain regret.

'I've done it . . . But – fifty years too late.'